THE GREATEST THING

THE LAST FAVORITE'S PAGE
BOOK 1

PATTI FLINN

GILDED ORANGE BOOKS

OTHER HISTORICAL NOVELS BY
PATTI FLINN

Véronique's Journey

Véronique's Moon

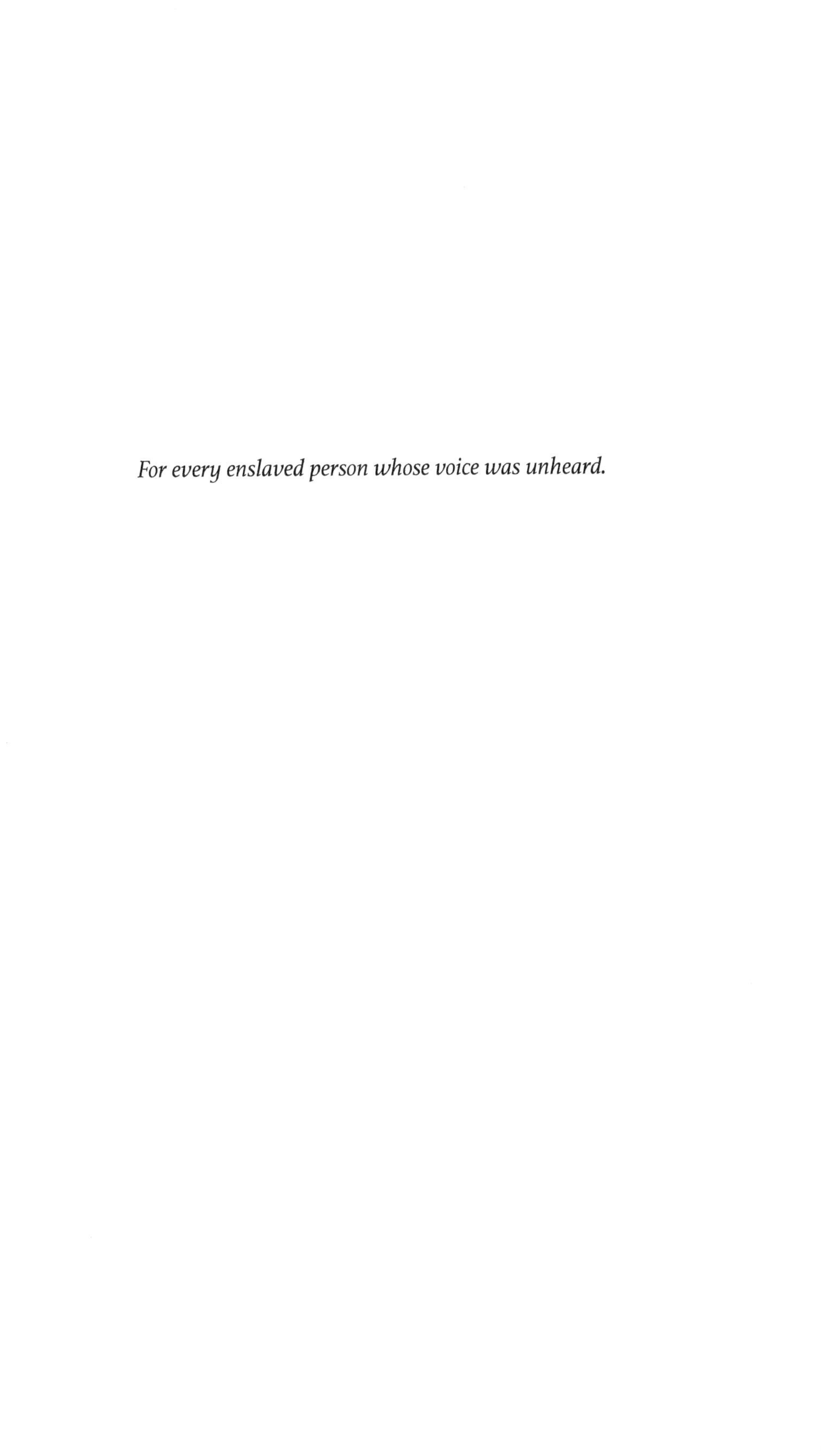

For every enslaved person whose voice was unheard.

The Greatest Thing
(The Last Favorite's Page, Book One)
Copyright @ 2023 by Patti Flinn
All rights reserved.

Ebook: ISBN: 979-8-9860600-4-0
Print ISBN: 979-8-9860600-5-7
Gilded Orange Books
P.O. Box 625
Blacklick, OH 43004, USA

PROLOGUE

September 22, 1793
Chateau du Barry,
Louveciennes, France

IN MY DREAMS the fall of the Chateau du Barry came with screams, wailing, and gnashing of teeth, but we don't always get what we want.

By the time the fall came, King Louis XVI was already dead. Of the noble class, those who hadn't yet fled were still socializing as if they couldn't see the end written in ink on expensive stationery right in front of their faces; envelopes stamped and sealed with their family crest in deep, deep red ... *wax*. It was their way to go on partying until the absolute moment the blade was just brushing the nape.

I had left the house that morning while our noble guests were enjoying breakfast. And oh, how we enjoyed breakfast at the Chateau du Barry (a.k.a. the Chateau de Louveciennes). The dining room buffet overflowed with platters of creamy scrambled eggs in butter, croissants, brioche, and baguettes to slather with more butter. Ham lardons, late autumn strawberries and cherries. Apples and pears:

sliced, spiced, and steamed. Brie and chèvre and camembert beside bowls of berries and nuts and pots of freshly whipped cream and crème fraiche. The finest steaming hot café and imported teas with little jars of sparkling sugar, shipped from our very own colonies, produced by our very own population of enslaved people they liked to call "workers." Little silver spoons sat in the sugar granules that shone like diamonds in the morning sun that streamed through the windows and glinted off all the gold accents throughout the room. *Real* gold, by the way.

It was the same bounty every single morning. The people of France were starving, but at the Chateau we still lived like we had at the Palace of Versailles—in excess to the point of obscenity.

By rights, I couldn't complain because I enjoyed the excess. Who wouldn't?

Every morning before leaving I made sure Madame had her favorite morning cup of hot chocolat which I sat upon the little table beside her bed while she was in the adjoining room being tied and strapped into her undergarments by her ladies. It had been the same routine every morning since I was ten. I could count on one hand the number of mornings I missed—the most recent being earlier this very year. The oversight had prompted Madame to do an unthinkable thing that would break us forever. But this morning she had her chocolat on time, blessed be the gods.

I walked to my favorite spot by a particular tree at the far end of the property to read. But first, as soon as I was out of sight of the Chateau, I walked into the wild area, leaned over, and unloaded my stomach into the unruly section of weeds just beyond the manicured garden. I didn't even have to force it these days—the bile came up so quickly and easily it was like I could summon it on command. It was a new skill I developed after the incident with the missed chocolat.

Officially, my name was Louis-Benoit Zamor, but they called me *the page.* They also called me all sorts of profane names, depending on the day. And, occasionally, they called me the Governor of the Chateau de Louveciennes, a title bestowed upon me by King Louis

XV, my benefactor, namesake, and the man who was "like a father" to me.

Of course, I wasn't a real noble. Nor was I kin to the dead king or his living mistress, but they had always enjoyed pretending I was, for entertainment when it suited them. It was their little joke. He was never like a father to me. People called him my benefactor, but he was really just my enslaver, even though good King Louis, the Well-Beloved, never liked to say that part out loud—his mistress no different.

I wasn't employed at this place nor at my previous home at the Palace de Versailles, though I'd always received a small allowance for snacks and an occasional café in town to pacify me. Madame had my clothes custom-made because, she said, I was a reflection of her. Appearances aside, having been sold to the King and gifted to her as a child, until I was freed, someone would forever be my "benefactor" or "benefactress."

My case wasn't rare, it was just glaringly hypocritical in a country that proudly boasted that anyone who stepped foot on its soil was considered free. My ambiguous household status was a dirty little secret Madame chose to keep hidden and a condition she'd done little to change in the twenty-two years we'd been together. Like a son to her, and all that.

It was a beautiful, crisp September morning with a sky as blue as the purest waters and the air as clean as God's first day, but I wasn't enjoying it. Beautiful days only reminded me of how dead I felt inside after the incidents of the preceding months, the worst months of my life. Since that last failed chocolat delivery. A beautiful day didn't begin to make up for the sorry state of my life at that point.

Suddenly, I heard soft, plaintive, gasping cries that caused the hairs to stand on the back of my neck. The sound of it stirred my interest. Now, it seemed, someone else was feeling a little of what I felt. and like a miserable wretched creature that longs for company, I stood up and headed back toward the Chateau, looking for the fellow wretched soul. Whatever it was must have happened while I was sitting at my tree—now, more than half an hour.

Tuning my ear, I heard several low-key voices speaking in distress. Now, this was interesting!

I kicked my stride into a gallop, finally awake and starting to feel something close to pleasure at the prospect of someone suffering. Knowing that it was wrong to enjoy the pain of others didn't stop the shiver of delight from racing up my spine.

In my own defense, this place fed upon pain and flourished under extreme instances of cruelty. I held out as long as I could, but I had become fully a part of the place. And as a spawn of evil, pain of others brought me delight.

Along the path that cut through the manicured lawn with the precision only found in the landscaping of a royal home, I saw the culprits in the group of ladies who usually bustled just beside or behind the Madame du Barry, heads held high. Today, their heads faced the ground except when they looked at each other. They appeared to be shrinking—hunched beneath heads heavy with powdered wigs atop slight bodies.

They were Madame du Barry's ladies-in-waiting, noblewomen who surrounded and doted on her. Chon, the head lady and Madame's favorite, was in the center of the group ahead of the others and moving toward me. I never noticed how the ladies' dresses took up an obscene amount of space until they attempted to walk together, their clothes conspiring to force them to fall in line according to social order. They shifted along under the silk and satin gowns as if, after a lifetime, they suddenly felt the weight of those gowns. They saw me and the group picked up speed to reach me, the one, lone, constant black man at the Chateau.

Of course, they came to me. To everyone concerned I was Madame du Barry's closest servant and confidant ... *like a son to her.* Many days most of the inhabitants and visitors barely noticed me at all and some regretted it when they did. And most days, I barely recognized the group of her ladies' maids as individuals, they so commonly moved as one mind and body. And now, it seemed they were melting into each other up top—a creature curled in on itself. Each like the leg of a spider that's been swatted, their backs bent as they cried together. And as they stepped closer, fear emanated from the mass of them and reached its tendrils toward me.

Chon wore a gown with a brilliant bodice; handsewn with a pattern of pastel-colored wildflowers. The beautiful gown paled in comparison to that spot of embroidered silk threads. The sight of it sent a lick of pain through me, hot and fast. I stared at that bodice, my lips growing parched as they always did when the embroiderer entered my mind. Memories of Véronique took my breath from me.

The motion of one of the women moving a lace cloth to wipe her eyes brought me back.

All three sets of tear-filled eyes speared me with expressions so shocked and frightened, had I been anyone else I might have been moved to care. It was the way of women like these, in a place like this, to assume I would care about them, always.

"Louis-Benoit," said the younger one on the side, picking up her heavy skirts to step toward me and looking like she wanted to pitch herself into my arms. I couldn't remember this one's name—I thought of her as *number three*. "The most horrible thing has just happened."

The entire group had reached me by now. Chon, in the center, spoke more clearly with trembling lips. "They've taken her, Louis-Benoit. They've taken the Comtesse Madame Du Barry."

My heart leapt a bit. "What do you mean? Who's taken her?"

Number three interjected: "The Committee of Public Safety! The savages came and took her away ... came into her home like they had a right, pushing us aside and forcing their way in. Madame was in her bedroom, and they didn't even stop. It was that fellow who was staying here for a while. That man with the funny eyes..."

"Yes, yes, that's where I remember him from," said *number two*. "He was staying here for a while, wasn't he? He came with these offi-cers claiming to be revolutionary servants. He said she was accused of crimes, but he wouldn't say what she's done. And they called her *Citizeness* du Barry, as if she was a common peasant! The bastards!"

"They don't need a reason!" Number three wailed in that way that children just turning adults wailed, liking the sound of the screech in their own voices. "They murdered our King for no reason at all—that good and kind man—and the Queen is sitting in a cell as we speak." She was fair and blond-haired and always seemed to be perspiring over her upper lip. I looked at it—couldn't pull my eyes away—as she spoke with pitiable desperation. "They never need a reason! The world has gone mad, when they can take good, pure, virtuous women away for … God knows what?"

I almost smiled with the irony of that question.

"But you," the youngest one went on. "Poor, sweet Louis-Benoit, what will you do? Without your Comtesse, will you just die from grief? What if she doesn't come back? What will life be for you if your dearest Madame, your reason for being, is gone?"

Number three didn't know me well. I looked up from her sweaty upper lip and into her wide blue eyes swimming with tears. I could see she was serious, which is what made it all the more preposterous.

My eyes strayed to Chon. She wasn't as young or clueless as the others. Of the three, Chon had been with Madame—and me—the longest. I was never quite sure how much Chon knew. Her eyes probed mine sharply. Maybe because I couldn't work up a tear, her lips pinched together and some tiny, infinitesimal part of her steeled a bit at my coldness, I was sure.

I needed her not to be so sharp. It would be better for me if she was too emotional to pay attention to *my* reaction, or lack thereof.

I was listening but part of me was removed—thinking, wondering, questioning, as my brain always did. It was the blessing of dissociation that had kept me sane all my life. At this moment, it appeared to the ladies as stunned disbelief. But there was a little deflection to be done.

I looked into Chon's deep brown eyes.

"But you ladies mustn't worry about me," I said, as sweetly as I could muster without losing the rest of my stomach on one of their dresses. "All worry should be held for our dear, virtuous Madame who must be suffering all manner of indignities as we stand enjoying this beautiful day. We must hold only her in our thoughts and pray she survives this like she survived the horrible imprisonment after the death of our dear Louis, the Well-Beloved. He was like a father to me, you know." It was reminding them of that difficult time and the dead king, *inappropriately* called the Well-Beloved, that finally did it.

Chon's lips trembled and her eyes welled up with water, the distance in them telling me she was, indeed, imagining Madame's last imprisonment. Her eyelids flickered in thought as she forgot about me.

Number two couldn't leave well enough alone.

"But we *can't* forget about you. You're like a son to her, also! Where will you go? You can't go back to the Palace, this time, can you? Oh, mon Dieu, poor Louis-Benoit Zamor will starve on the street just like Madame always said. I can see it now, clearly. How your life is going to change if she doesn't return. They would have been kinder to take you along with her. May God protect you."

"Oh, the poor thing," the third one said at my silence. "He's lost in grief!" Her own words brought on a fresh rush of tears, and the women huddled together, once again, wordlessly, of one mind. The spider of them moved beyond me, too preoccupied comforting each other to spend more time on Louis-Benoit Zamor.

Once I allowed them to pass with a polite nod of my head, the real fun started. Moving toward the house, I heard the frantic whinnies of horses telling me they were being harshly and quickly roused from the stables. I felt another slice of hurt knowing that my friend Henri was no longer caring for them. Having disappeared a good two months or so back, no doubt distraught by the death of his father, each day I wondered when I'd see him again. But he was yet another person gone from my life. Another person who took too much of my spirit with him.

What I didn't realize was that all the real action was *inside* the house.

I stepped inside. A chaotic noise filled the space as men and women ran, almost through me, failing to see me in their paths. They carried luggage and half-open bags spilling with clothes as if too rushed to complete packing. A nobleman bumped into me like I wasn't even there.

"Move, nègre!" he snapped, shoving me aside again with one hand. I righted myself as he moved as fast as he could to the front door.

Yes, at that moment the fog began to lift from my brain. I'd been numb for a long time until this day. First, numb with fury that settled into anxiety that settled into apathy as I was waiting, waiting, waiting...

I walked until I reached an alcove in the wall that held a particularly heavy shadow, and I slipped inside. When I stood very, very still in this particular alcove, no one noticed me at all. It was a trick I'd learned at the Palace as a child, just to stand quietly and still and it would be almost like I was invisible. Like I was a tapestry hanging on the wall.

And as something that wasn't seen, I could see all.

The clear blue sky that didn't move me at all when I was standing in it was moving me now as my nerves and emotions began to thaw like icicles under a bright, brilliant sun. Oh, there was so much fear to feast my eyes upon. Abject panic was in their faces as I was sure they were imagining the revolutionary guards would come back to take them, too. Petrified that the Englishman with the funny eyes—Grieve was his name—would come back for each and every one of them.

They tripped over their own feet and down the stairs to get out of the Chateau du Barry, partying cut short as they were, finally, feeling the blade on the nape. Madame's ladies would realize, soon enough, that they should probably leave, also. Because if the absolute monarch could be killed like a commoner, if both the Queen and her nemesis, Jeanne du Barry, could be carted away like washerwomen, it was obvious the revolutionaries weren't done. And in that case, what hope was there for any of them?

It was almost as if, until Madame was carted away, they thought they were immune. Tucked away in this special country home away from the masses, shielded from reality. Perhaps, many had been telling themselves that the King's death would satisfy the bloodlust of the new republic. That was what Madame had thought. But with her arrest today, the nightmare that had begun when the King lost his head was beginning to look like it wasn't nearly over.

If we were all doomed, at least I would go to hell happy because on this day, *she* was taken away. This day she would have to account for something. This day was a sign that I'd fulfilled my promise to myself to bring down this house and every heathen in it.

My consciousness slammed back into my brain from where it had been floating above it all as my entire being realized my work had finally come to fruition. As I watched the scene unfold, the bright beautiful day filled my soul, and my heart took flight. I was finally going to be free.

I meant to be still and disappear into the walls of the Chateau, but my body wouldn't obey. My heart galloped in my chest like a wild horse and a smile formed on this face of mine—my lips couldn't possible stay still.

I spoke softly, speaking of myself as I'd been spoken of all my life: "Poor Louis-Benoit Zamor, whatever will he do?"

PART I

VERSAILLES

1

T*wenty-seven years later*
        Paris, France, 1820

Dear Citizen of my beloved France,

These are the journals of Louis-Benoit Zamor.
Ideally, I would begin my life's account with flowery words and prose. I wish I could write for the beauty of words, but this writing is as practical as it is aspirational.

I must start by getting something off my chest: I did not kill Madame Comtesse Jeanne du Barry!

If you don't know, Du Barry was the official mistress—the Maîtresse-en-titre—of King Louis XV, grandfather of doomed King Louis XVI. (For efficiency, I might occasionally refer to them by their number, XV or XVI). As the last official Favorite—Favorite being the more informal term for the title of mistress—of the last absolute monarch of France who maintained a known mistress, she went by many names: The Comtesse Madame du Barry, or

Madame Vaubernier, or Citizeness du Barry, or Jeanne du Barry, née (born) Jeanne Bécu. Most people just called her the Favorite. *I usually just called her Madame.*

I've never denied having some involvement in bringing Madame du Barry to justice, but she lost her head because of her own actions. I never told any lie; her truths were crimes all on their own. And I wasn't the one who put the target on her back in the first place. I vigorously defend myself and my reputation against the unfair allegations levied against me.

I know many Parisians hate me today, but people hated her, too, once. Somehow, in the years since the Comtesse's execution, the rabid hatred of her has died down. Now, France loves *her! If things continue this way, she's well on her way to sainthood or martyrdom in the next decade.*

Maybe that will happen for me if I explain it all now—a cleansing of my reputation after I'm gone? Maybe in fifty or one hundred years, my name will bring a smile to someone's lips, and they'll speak of me with fondness?

I'm being ridiculously unrealistic, I know. Because no matter how many years past, she will always be considered the best of the Ancien Régime—Ancient Regime, as the English call it now— the time of kings. She'll always be considered a noble and lover of the world's greatest thing—a king of France. And I'll always be considered the worst of the Ancien Régime: a black servant who never quite learned his place.

The sorry truth is, no one would think twice about me turning her in to the Committee for Public Safety if I wasn't a black man. If we were to record all the names of all the witnesses of all the trials held by the French Revolutionary Tribunal, we'd have a book as thick as that giant encyclopedia written by the exhausted Diderot. How many of those names do you remember, I ask? How many of those individuals are still called "traitor!" on the street? My crime wasn't turning her in; it was being the black man who turned her in.

If you don't remember the before times, I remind you that Madame du Barry was the second most-hated woman in France in her time; the first being Queen Marie Antoinette. Equally despised by the kingdom and by the new republic, I feel the country projected all its anger and loathing of a poor economy and inadequate kings onto these women. I didn't hate Madame because she was a woman or her proximity to the crown; I came to hate her because of how she used both against me. And I never truly hated the Queen at all. Though, if anyone had a right to hate either woman, it was me.

Ironically, as much as France despised those two women, those two women despised each other just as much ... almost until their deaths, two months apart.

Further, I can hardly be blamed for the actions of the tribunal or the insatiable appetite of that beast, the guillotine. The beast was destined to feast on Madame whether I helped or not. Can I be blamed for not wanting to be the entrée to her main meal?

But my story isn't about the Madame, the Queen, or the men who loved them. That might be shocking to some of you who think of me only as the Favorite's page. These journals are about me—Zamor —and the systems designed to keep people like me under foot. It's about people who have nothing left to lose but a whole kingdom to gain.

I've known two kings, and they both betrayed me. They claimed leadership ran through the bloodline of the House of Bourbon, but betrayal ran even deeper. That fact matters because without their cruelty and disrespect, I might never have helped speed their demise, or I might have lifted a finger to stop it.

I know, reading this, you must be thinking: What power does a servant have to affect the life or death of a king, let alone two? *Just a servant ... none. But, as you'll soon learn, I transformed into many things during that time.*

When I arrived in France, the country was already near bankrupt, though you never would have guessed it from the lifestyle at court. The so-called wise kings had been busy sending men to fight for more territory. England, our greatest rival, was trying to claim all of the new Americas, and we weren't having it. Our monarch and the government were leaning even more heavily on the blood money earned through the buying and selling of human beings like me and my dark-skinned brethren. (Though no money was directly made off anything produced by me if you weigh the cost of me against the anticipated price of my lifetime servitude, perhaps they made a profit, after all. Don't worry, I got it back in my own way).

No one was paying attention to the ugliness of our kingdom's debt while France still led the world in the arts and education, boasting of having the most beautiful palace in existence. And very soon, we would lead the world in the proliferation of uncensored publications and literature ... but not yet. First came the transformation of thought and then came the explosion of publications.

Oh, let me take a moment to clear up a misunderstanding: Peasants didn't start the Revolution!

Everyone's blaming them for it now, especially the wealthy who have been returning to France to claim what was theirs before they fled. Some of those returning nobles have taken to hiding in alleys and attacking people in what's called the White Terror, *"white" being the color that has always represented the noble class (though you're forgiven if you mistook it to reference the predominant skin color of the nobles). After the Revolution, some of the previously helpless nobles began to attack poor people they suspected had been part of the revolutionary government. It subsided for a time, but then came back again in a second wave just a couple years before the writing of these journals.*

It's revenge, pure and simple, but it's wrong. It wasn't the poor people or "sans-culottes" who thought up the Revolution; it was educated bourgeois men with a smattering of nobles and clerics who thought up the ideas that led it. It was people like me, an educated foreigner of low birth who lived as a noble servant. But increasingly, poor people are taking the blame. It's the nature of nobles to blame all their troubles on those least able to defend themselves.

Of course, once the ball was rolling, poor people jumped into revolutionary activity with both feet because they were starving and desperate. And who could blame them? The royal house and its inhabitants were so obviously misspending the country's money and mistreating the people, forcing even the poorest to pay taxes while allowing the nobles to live tax-free. Not to mention the nobles charging peasants for the land on which they lived, charging them to rent the tools to work with, charging them to even keep a job. At one point, it was no uncommon thing to see people walking through the streets of Paris in rags, on blistered, callused, shoeless feet. And in the country, farming families starved, besieged by droughts, without seeds to plant, nor money to feed animals.

Where was our King during all this? Good question.

If you're a Christian person, you will say that no matter how corrupt the royals, it was our duty to turn the other cheek. As far as kings go, XV and XVI weren't considered brutal—they were even well-liked in their heyday—but they had plenty of people on staff to be brutal on their behalf. Still, violence isn't something the bible condones. I believe that's why the revolutionaries eventually stripped religion from France. I think the ones reveling in the violence at the height of it believed that if we weren't looking at God, He wouldn't be looking at us.

I had become a reluctant believer in God by then, and I did believe He was watching. Like most others, I started out as a nonviolent revolutionary, doing what I felt was right according to God's law. By the end ... let's just say I have much to atone for.

But many of us lay a good portion of blame for the royal demise at the feet of the royals themselves. The way the family, the House of Bourbon, ruled and their blatant disregard for the true suffering of their people fueled desperation. If you're being murdered, going on the attack against the murderer isn't a crime; it's self-defense. It may sound like justification, but when you're in the thick of it, it is reason enough.

As for those of us who weren't in danger of starving, the Revolution began innocently with a lot of talk and optimism. We weren't blinded by anger. We weren't irrational brutes. We weren't out for blood. Many of us were filled with hope for positive changes in how people were treated and taxed and clear determination on whether we were free. Some of us simply wanted citizenship in this country we loved. None of us truly anticipated what would happen or how the world would change. We never truly expected to end the monarchy. We never imagined there would be bloodshed. Not in the very beginning.

Transformations of the powerless into the powerful flourished.

Let's be frank, I was a bonafide product of the Ancien Régime, reared in an environment of opulence and excess. I hated the Régime, but I loved the excess. To the external eye, I had every reason to keep things as they were. Well-fed and educated, I wore silks and satins, precious gems around my neck and on my head, gold on my wrists, leather and lace on my feet. I had a great deal of the things a physical body needs to survive.

All those material things might seem like enough to keep a person content, but I wanted a society where I was equal to any man. A society where I could vote. A society where I could own land. A society where I could be called a citizen. A society where I could legally marry. Yes, I loved nice things, but I was willing to sacrifice it all for a society that would use my name first, and not the derisive, insulting terms blackamoor *or* nègre *as titles.*

We didn't call it a revolution until we realized it was too late to go back to how it had once been, when we'd all gone too far to even call ourselves the same people we had been at the start. And as drastic as the changes, the timeline of the movement from thought and discussion to action happened so, so fast. We hoped the best among us would rise, but we managed to open Pandora's box and once opened, all manner of things escaped that damned box—things from hell we couldn't shove back no matter how hard we tried. Beasts even more frightening than the guillotine, beasts of mind and spirit that will outlive us all. I watched as, piece by piece, the monarchy was dismantled to build a republic, and felt the pain of it.

And no matter the horrors, much good came of what we did. I speak to you as a citizen and a free man, after all. We did some good!

I'm no saint. I don't mind being honest about who I am, but I'm not the devil I'm being made out to be. I'm getting old and tired, and if I drop dead tomorrow, there are few left to speak for me in a way I would approve. So, I'm telling my story in the only voice that could ever be trusted to speak for me.

Pardon if I sound jaded.

I didn't come to the Palace of Versailles jaded; I came frightened, young, and innocent. I'll take this opportunity to use a metaphor I've often thought of: my childhood self was the most loved flower, the rose. Wild roses come out of the ground perfect all by themselves, as God made them. Men capture, re-plant, and train them. We remove their thorns to get rid of their defenses. We plant them in rows to control how they spread. We put them together in groups of colors, size, and rate of blossom. We domesticate them and take away any hope they have of growing freely. We cut and discard the unruly ones.

At the Palace of Versailles, the rose—and every living thing—was intentionally and purposefully placed; the ability to control the pattern of things was symbolic of the height of civility. Order, above all.

King Louis XV controlled those roses, the animals, all the people at court, and the entirety of France. The power of the House of Bourbon was, at times, even above the Catholic Church. So, of course, a tiny errant wild thing like me was no match for that system.

For you to understand, I must take you back. Back before the Revolution. Back before Jeanne du Barry was taken away by the Committee for Public Safety on that beautiful September day in 1793. Back to the beginning when I was first brought to France at ten years old in 1771. You will see the rose I was and how I was domesticated to fit the most civilized Ancien Régime, though we didn't call it that at the time.

I began changing the second I was kidnapped from my home. I was already broken and traumatized when I came to France, but I was still myself. True transformation came after I arrived at the Palace of Versailles and became part of the royal court. Good King Louis

XV, the Well-Beloved, in all his wisdom and glory, would soon transform me into the most perfectly twisted vicious commodity.

I was just a small example to his court of how he could be strategic in his generosity and greatness. How could he not be—he, the greatest thing in France?

Rational fellow citizen, I appeal to your sense of fair play. I'm nothing but an honest, average man with a story of transformation to share. A story that begins with good King Louis XV, the Well-Beloved.

Vive le roi. Long live the King ... and all that.

—*Zamor*

2

———————

N ear the Palace of Versailles,
France, August 26, 1771

I LOST my name somewhere on the way to France. Or it might be more accurate to say I dropped it. It didn't feel safe to say or be said, so I let it fall away to memory where it could remain safe and cherished.

My mother had created her own sweet little lullaby to put me to sleep as a baby. She used to hum it when I was sick or skinned a knee, or otherwise forgot I was a big boy and felt the need to crawl into her lap for comfort.

After I was snatched off the road while my mother shopped for food at the local market, I began to hum that song.

The errand had already been tense. For some reason, everything I said or did over the past few weeks landed on her ears in a way that grated, if her reaction to me was any indication. Lately, whenever I wanted to play, she refused. Whenever she used to smile at me, like when she was making me breakfast or helping me dress, she no longer did. And she and my father had been whispering to each other, seeming to sneak long, serious looks my way. I had hoped the trip to the market—one of our favorite things to do together—would bring back her smile. Instead, when her back was turned, I was caught up from behind with someone's hand covering my mouth and an arm like a vise around my body, carrying me away as I kicked, uselessly.

I kept humming the lullaby to myself along the journey. I tried to do it quietly, but when the kidnappers overheard, they told me to shut up. I think that's what they said. When I didn't stop, they hit me, and the shock of it—the feeling of human flesh causing pain—was so new and different it made my eyes water. At that point in my life, I'd never been spanked. The shock of being hurt shut down my music.

So, I kept my mother's lullaby inside, humming it to myself in my head, understanding the secret of captives the world over—that what is in your head is yours alone. I was put in the back of a cart with other children.

That was years ago. Still, my mother's lullaby comforted me when I was afraid. I hummed it now on the ride with this latest kidnapper.

The carriage rode over the rocky dirt road, but my backside was protected by thick padding and the brownish-pink plush material on the seat. I'd been in plenty of buggies and wagons, but I'd never seen such a fancy carriage, let alone ridden in one. I could see through the windows on the side of the carriage; the sky was brilliant blue like the azure waters in the streams by my home.

"Sit back in your seat," the man across from me said.

I had only met him that day, and I hadn't yet decided what type of a man he was. Tall, he had shoulders that were wide, rounded, and padded like a rhinoceros—as if he'd spent a lifetime shouldering his way through the world. His light brown eyes were flat, and his hair was sandy and short. He looked at me like he was already tired of seeing me.

"We'll be there soon," he said. "You've been told where we're going?"

I nodded. "They told me we're going to see the King, Monsieur?"

"You say that like it's a question. Do you think they were lying to you, blackamoor?"

I'd heard *that* word many times since being wrested from my home and passed along by a series of people with white or light skin. After seasons of being passed along in that cart while people came and went, looking us over like my mother and I used to look over produce at the market. When a stranger saw one of us they wanted, they would quietly make an exchange and then one of the children would disappear. That happened over and over for a long time as new children joined us and some of the men holding us would switch out for others. It was the same thing over many miles, through many towns, over rough road. It felt it would go on forever.

All along, since none of the white-skinned men were calling each other the words "blackamoor" or "nègre" I figured both had to do with the color of *my* skin. The sound of it from their lips made my stomach turn. They said it like it was a curse word, and this man was no different.

"What is a king?" I asked, too fearful of what was to come to keep my questions and thoughts to myself.

His face hardened. "A king is more powerful than any of your petty backwoods, heathen leaders. He's the greatest thing in the world, and that's all you need to know. He's why you're going to Versailles and not to Nantes to be shipped to the colonies with the rest. You should crawl on your knees in gratitude."

"Why are they being sent to colonies? What are colonies?"

"Mon Dieu, don't you know anything? They're sent to work in the Americas. They'll plant and harvest sugar cane, coffee, spices for us to sell—honest work to put their worthless selves to good use. You're too weak to work. Look at you, with your spindly arms and legs. You'd break to pieces after one good day of work. No, you get to go where they want someone small and harmless. A boy who looks like he will stay a boy forever, they told me. Like a living doll, that's you. Your worthlessness is an asset."

I quieted down.

~

I HAD TRAVELED with those other dark-skinned children for a long time. It felt like our caravan was simply traveling in circles, stopping in one forest or another – an endless, draining, exhausting cycle. The children would set up and break down camp, build the fires and forage for food. One young boy, just older than me, allowed me to trail him like a pestering younger brother.

"Even though there are so few of us with black skin in India, they have been finding us anyway," he told me. "Stay close to me, and I'll keep you safe."

He explained to me what was happening when the men took the little girls and some of the little boys away from the camp. We heard them screaming and crying in the night, but the boy stopped me from trying to follow when one little girl was taken, her eyes filling with tears even before the man got to her. She cowered and clutched herself and begged.

I broke away from my friend and ran to her, throwing myself on top of her.

The man didn't even break his stride. He grabbed the back of my clothes to pick me up like a sack of rotten fruit, and then I was flying through the air, landing so hard against a tree my eyes watered, and I struggled to breathe. My limbs froze with the pain. While I was pulling myself up to my hands and knees, through my watering eyes, I could see he took her away, anyway. I crawled back to my place by the fire, and the boy looked at me with eyes that said he'd seen everything.

"You only prolong the pain by fighting," he whispered to me. Once again, we listened to the sounds of the rape. I didn't understand the importance of what was happening: only that it was painful and terrible. The others were crying, and that was enough. The worst was the ones that did not cry at all, that held their grief inside. I almost wished they'd cry so we'd know they were still alive.

"My papa told me to always protect the weak," I whispered in explanation.

"You think you are stronger than any of the other ones here? Look around. You are weak. We are all weak. You can't protect anyone." A muscle twitched in his face as the muffled screams punctuated the otherwise quiet

night. "It will happen to you, soon enough. But if they don't notice you, maybe they won't take you. Maybe." He sat with his knees under his chin, clutching them as if he wanted to disappear, his eyes pointed to the ground, not at me. "No one can save them, and no one can save us. You must become harder. You are just a little boy, but they don't mind killing little children with black skin. I've seen them do it. We're nothing to them, no better than horses or cattle."

The longer we traveled, the truer his words were proven. We were all beaten for the smallest of infractions, even for asking for food or water. And he was right. One day one of the men came and took me into the woods just outside the camp. The first two times I was pulled away from camp I cried when the slaver brutalized me. Not a crier, by nature, the sound of my own loud wails surprised me, but I could no more stop the sounds than I could stop him. I wanted to claw out of my own brain, but I didn't know how. I felt like with each scream I gave up more of myself.

The third time I struggled and managed to keep silent. In the darkness, I willed myself to go numb, willed myself to imagine I was anyplace else. I willed it and, after a few minutes my body obeyed. At some point the man noticed my lack of life. He called out for another man to come over. "Make this one live again!' he called. "We haven't earned anything off him, yet!"

And then he stomped me in my back and, just like that, I was no longer numb as pain streaked up my spine and I gasped, my eyes opening wide with the shock of it.

"See, he's fine."

"He won't be fine when I finish with him, playing dead like that. I'll make you wish you were dead; you do that again."

After that I began to block time by force of will. I began to lose days, weeks, months, as they bled into each other and our little caravan of carts of kidnapped children rode through towns, making it easy for people to find us, pick over us, and buy us.

The little boy I followed whispered to me one night: "They told us it was happening, but our town leader didn't believe it until they came, and it was too late. They told us they're taking black people over the water and forcing us to work from sunup to sundown. That they keep us in shackles. That whole towns of us have been disappeared to these places over the water."

"For what?" I asked him.

"To plant and grow for them. To be like servants but without paying, and we can never leave. Ever."

"They can't do that," I said. As a child I had to believe in some authority – something had to exist to protect us.

"That's what we thought. They took ten of us kids from my town at once. I'm the only one left. Because of this."

He raised his leg. I hadn't even noticed before, but with his dusty foot in the air I now saw the thickened ridge of skin along the back of his ankle. "I tried to run. One of them chased me down and cut me with that big knife he carries. The other man yelled at him, 'fool! You can't cut him before he's sold, no one will want him now!' And I guess he was right. All my people are gone and I'm still here. I'll be riding in this wagon until I'm old, or until they can find some use for me."

"I don't understand, are they going to take us over the water, too? Why won't they just let you go home if they can't sell you?"

"I told you; I have no home. Besides, as long as I'm alive they might find something to sell me for. But it's okay, because I'm glad I'm here to help you."

I was glad, too.

Then one night at camp, a carriage arrived like a strange animal in the night. The man who stepped out looked surprisingly colorful and bright in the evening light. He was painted like the ladies in town that my mother said worked by lying on their backs. I didn't ask her what that meant at the time. Now, the thought of this man working by lying on his back floated through my head as he looked over the group. He looked over us like my mother looked over the fruit when she shopped at the street market. When his gaze settled on me, long and hard, I knew he'd chosen me as the ripest of all the fruit.

The colorful man spoke in low tones, but I heard clearly the clang of coins as he tousled them in his pocket. He pulled out a small sack and handed it to my kidnappers. And then, just like that, a different man came from behind and pulled me up by the collar, dragging me to my feet. The camp was eerily quiet, the only sound my feet scuffling on the ground as I struggled.

My friend stood up, panic on his face, but he didn't call out. He and the other children watched as I fought the hand that grasped my collar and was carried away, beyond the circle of light, and tossed into the back of another wagon. The painted man had disappeared, and I was off with yet another stranger, shoved into the back. Carried off alone, watching the little boy who stood searching the darkness for a glimpse of me.

I would later realize his panic wasn't about me, so much. His panic, the abject desperation in his eyes, was about more than the one instance of losing a boy he barely knew. It was a bigger thing. I would learn someday what that look in his eyes was, but at the time, I was simply grateful someone cared to stare after me as I was carted away into the night.

I THOUGHT about my young friend as I rode in this special carriage with the soft seats that didn't smell bad, that wasn't filled with bodies of little children curled against the elements. I had gone over the water, a long time ago. I looked at the man across from me, thinking that, with things being so different, maybe he would recognize me as a human being.

"Will the others be safe in the colonies?" I asked.

He looked at me a long time with his flat eyes. "As long as they work and earn their worth, they'll be allowed to live. Stop asking stupid questions. Hear me now. I'm Gaspard. You will call me Manager. I work for our esteemed King Louis XV. I manage many of his support staff and security. And though you will belong to the Favorite, the Comtesse Madame Du Barry—"

"—the favorite what?"

"The Favorite of the King; his mistress, the Mâitresse-en-titre. Don't interrupt me again. Though you have been purchased as a gift for the Favorite, I'm in charge of you. You'll do as I say or you will be punished severely, you understand?" He continued to stare at me. "I spoke to you, blackamoor."

"Yes," I mumbled. He then stood as best he could in the crouched quarters and, before I knew it, delivered a blow across my face that carried my head into the side of the carriage and bruised my brow. My vision blurred, and I tried to blink away the pain.

"I told you to call me *Manager*. And don't you ever speak under your breath like that to me. You answer when I speak to you."

My body still ached from a beating I took weeks ago. I no longer trusted anyone with white skin not to hurt me. I didn't think this man hit me because of what I'd called him. He looked like he just wanted to hit me. Like he hated me.

"I told you to call me Manager, didn't I?" he said again, without conviction.

"Oui, Manager."

"I am the law second only to the King. You forget it, and I will break every bone in your scrawny body."

I looked at him through slitted eyes and noticed he was still in the half-crouch stance as if he wasn't done, heaving like a panting dog. We were like that for a long moment; me hugging the side of the inside wall with an arm up to defend my head, trying not to look him in his eyes, and he over me like a beast waiting for a chance to strike.

"Manager Gaspard," came the voice of the carriage driver through the open hole in the top. "It might not be prudent to damage the King's property, as he'll be inspecting him. Besides, he's only a child, about the same age as your youngest, isn't he?"

The Manager grunted but still took a long time to sit back down. "My youngest is a boy. This is a savage."

Savage ... me? I couldn't remember ever been called that until now with this beast-like man salivating with the desire to throw me around like a doll.

"I'm *not* a savage," I said under my breath, barely to myself.

"What?"

"Nothing, Manager." I took my arm down slowly but kept my fists under my chin, shoulders hunched up to my ears just in case.

Soon, the view from the window changed. The bird's songs seemed higher, flying wider—like they were no longer confined. I looked out the window and saw we were on a lane lined by trees.

A few paces later, our carriage filled with darkness. The sudden overwhelming smell of horses confirmed that we'd entered a stable or barn. Finally, the carriage stopped, and he climbed out.

When I stepped out of the carriage, my eyes were still adjusting from the bright sunny day to the relative cave-like environment of the stables. But as my vision returned, I took in the tall, cavernous space and the candles fastened into place on the walls. Each stall was as big and grand as some houses I'd seen while traveling. We'd driven into just one of many openings in a space that seemed to go on forever, long and deep. I couldn't imagine how many horses it could hold.

"Prepare for the King!" someone yelled, the voice piercing and bouncing from the stone walls as if it came not from a person but from on high. Everyone immediately straightened, the sound of shuffling feet filling the space. Footsteps preceded the entrance of a man who walked with the assurance of one surrounded by protectors, which he was.

Two men flanked him, just a pace behind. He was pale, of average height, and portly, with a midsection that bowed out like he stuffed it nightly with rice and beans. The skin of his face looked covered in the ground meal my mother used to use to make us pounded cakes for breakfast. On top of his head was a big mane of white hair that looked like a pile of cobwebs. I wondered at this man who seemed to *want* to look like an old, decrepit thing; the color of his coat only made him look more bloodless.

All around me, the other men, from Gaspard to the man holding the broom, had bent at the waist so they could stare at the ground. They looked so silly, like the ground was suddenly so fascinating, that a burp of laughter exploded from me before I could stop it. Gaspard jabbed me hard in the side.

"Bow to the King, blackamoor!" he hissed.

I lost my smile and imitated the others. The sound of his footsteps filled my ears, and soon, instead of the ground below me, I saw the tips of the shoes of the King in my vision. They were made of what looked like the velvet I had seen women in my town wear on very special occasions, with buckles on the front. His lower legs were encased in netting.

"Look up, blackamoor, let me see you," he said, his voice grave and heavy with phlegm.

I straightened cautiously and noticed Gaspard, though he still eyed me, seemed more concerned with the King. The King motioned with his hand, one of the men beside him clapped his hands, and everyone stood straight again. He looked me up and down.

"Young, small ... good. How old are you, boy?"

"I don't know," I lied.

"They think he is seven or eight years old, your majesty," Gaspard said.

"What is your name, blackamoor?" I looked to Gaspard for permission to speak. "I am your King, not Gaspard," the man said. "Answer my question."

"I don't remember," I lied.

"No matter, the Favorite will prefer to give you a name of her own choosing soon enough. He speaks French well. This is your home now, boy. You're a very lucky young man. It is an honor to be a page in the House of Bourbon." He turned to Gaspard. "Madame will be very pleased. Send Richelieu a small gift to thank him for finding this one. And get him dressed quickly so we can present him to the Favorite at court."

I was ten, and I had a name. I thought I was being clever keeping them both to myself, but now I knew it didn't matter at all.

3

Dear Citizen,

As a small child, I wallowed in the abundance of my parents' love like any child secure in the knowledge that they are their parents' everything. They thought I was the most wonderful thing to ever happen to them. Every word I spoke, brilliant. Every silly thing I said, funny beyond belief. My smallness only highlighted the largeness of my personality. My darkness, evidence that God loved black skin because he made me.

My mother called me "the greatest thing God ever made" once, and I never forgot it. I can't recall her face when she said it, I only know my parents loved me so completely and so well, I never doubted her words. During the hard times, those words became a litany I would say to myself on a loop when I was most frightened.

I know those words are said by mothers to their children the world over. But meeting this king that the manager had called the "greatest" made me think how completely opposite I was to him. If he was the greatest, was there room for me?

*The answers would come quickly. Very soon my mother's words
would be proven a lie. Going from being a boy who remembered
love to a valueless would be a difficult, painful lesson.*

—*Zamor*

Gaspard led the way out of the stables, and I followed him
out of the darkness and into the light of day, wrapped in a
horse blanket, my face hidden on his command. From the
outside, I could see the building we'd just left was built like a giant
horseshoe made of two structures facing each other. Now, we strode
toward a massive building with two wings on the side and a middle
area that joined them with a gate.

Wrapped like a parcel in my horse dung blanket, I could only see
what wasn't blocked by lack of peripheral vision. The manager
Gaspard kept checking behind to see if I was keeping up. Each time I
met his eye but got lost in what was around me the second he turned
away.

I'd never seen real gold, but because the sheen of it on the gate
was so foreign to me, I knew I was looking at it now. Though none of
the many people who walked around us seemed impressed by it, I
stared at the giant medallion that shone where the sun struck it. In
the center, there was a face within its sun. A person in the sun.

"Hurry up, blackamoor!" Gaspard yelled.

People were dressed like nothing I'd ever seen. Women, in dresses
so big they took up the space of three bodies in lots of bright, vivid
pinks, yellows, and blues. Some carried umbrellas to shield them
from the sun. And the men wore heavy coats and robes braided with
what looked like silken thread and pants that stopped just below
their knees, with webbing on their calves like the King. Most of them
had that artificial cobweb hair on their heads. All had pale, pale faces
like the King, interrupted by lips smeared red, cheeks artificially
rosy... all like the painted man who had got me from camp. But unlike

him, they were all so busy bustling from one wing to the other or around to whatever was on the backside, they barely noticed me sweating under the horse blanket.

We entered the center building at a wing joint. The walls along the hallway were covered in fabric paneling, designed with flowers or a strange three-pronged pattern. The floors, a heavy, polished iridescent stone. And there were many rooms, each different, but each filled with accents of gold and fixtures of crystal, carved so that any bit of light reflected a thousand different ways. Bouquets of crystal light fell from the ceiling, suspended in air. It took me a moment to see the many, many candles in the bouquets, lit even in daytime. People carved from stone, in various stages of undress, sat on podiums and arrogantly looked down at us from their perch. And long swaths of material that looked too fine to be simply draping windows hung to the polished floor.

A small bark drew my eyes from the window to my other side, where a woman walked by with a tiny dog on a leash. I could clearly see at least two cats curled up in different alcoves of the long, wide hallway. A man with a box held in place by a rope looped behind his neck was calling out, obviously trying to sell some sort of street food.

I quickly picked out the servants because they wore varying shades of brown, black and gray, like me, with no powdered skin or hair. A few young ladies in modest brown shifts carefully averted their gazes from Gaspard.

I was so enraptured by everything I was seeing I barely noticed we'd gone through the building and were now leaving it to enter another one, straight into a room heavy with steam and the smell of cooking meat. It was a massive kitchen. The woman at one of the stoves, with rosy cheeks flushed from the steam, was stirring a giant vat of boiling liquid and ordering others to do the same at their stations. Then she noticed me. Her body was thin, and her dark eyes were flat, taking in my torn pants and the brown shirt that hung from me in soiled strings under the filthy horse blanket.

"Perhaps the child would like something to eat?" she said. "It looks like he's about to drop."

My mouth watered with anticipation of the large spoon she moved to grab as she began shoveling soup into a bowl for me.

"Did I ask you a question, cook?" Manager Gaspard said to her.

"Non, Manager, I meant no disrespect. It's just that the boy seems very hungry."

"He'll eat after he's presented, not a second sooner. Do you understand me? We're just passing through to the servants' quarters."

I hadn't eaten in two days, so I was staring pretty hard at that big spoon of soup when the Manager wrenched my arm, shaking me out of my trance, to pull me along. Stumbling behind him, I entered a hallway and then into a small, sparse room with a potato sack full of stuffing on the ground. There was also a small table with a candle, a stool, and a pot in the corner.

"This is where you stay. Sit down there on that bed until they come to bathe and dress you. You smell."

After he left, I sat down on the stuffed padding that barely elevated me off the stone ground. This room was little more than a cell, with walls of stone, mold growing in the corners, and cobwebs on the ceiling. The smell of moisture and mildew made me crave dryness and a good fire. I heard the soft scuffle of tiny feet and looked around for gaps in the stone wall, but there were too many gaps to count. I knew that evening I'd be fighting with the mice for warmth.

I thought about my home then. We didn't have much, but my mama had kept our home clean, free of cobwebs, dry and warm. Not like this place, where I felt the dank of underground seeping through the stones. *This must be prison*, I thought.

The door opened, and a man walked in with a water-filled bucket in one hand and rags in the other. "Take those dirty clothes off," he said. "I need to wipe you down."

I was old enough to bathe my own body, but I didn't want to get hit again today. Days of grime came off with each harsh rub against my skin, but I would have liked even more cleaning to feel right. Soon, two women came, their arms filled with material. They went to work dressing me as if they barely even saw my nakedness. The piles of fabric were slick and full, not the dress of the servants. One came at me with a fluffy white pile to go atop my head, powdering it where it sat. Once they were done, one of the women looked my way and her face lightened a bit. She pulled a piece of glass on a plate from the basket and held it up to me.

"Here, take a look at yourself, petit. You hardly look the same."

I did as she suggested, and my image came back to me. The cloth of my coat was soft in light blue. I was wearing the short pants I had seen the others wearing in the hallway and silky white webbing on my lower legs. I was thankful they didn't powder my face, but I still felt as foreign as I ever had and, to my eyes, looked ridiculous.

"Do you like it?" the woman asked.

"No, Madame, I look like the ashy things that dry out and die in the sun," I said.

She laughed and patted my jacket. "We work with what we have, petit. I think you look adorable. Like a little nobleman."

She gestured to a woman standing just beyond the door who handed her a cup. "Here, the cook says you are near starving. Drink this quickly before the Manager Gaspard returns."

I became weak in the knees at the sight of the cup but didn't hesitate. I drank the lukewarm soup down like water. She grabbed my hand around the cup to steady it, worried, I suppose, that I was going to spill it all over myself trying to get it down my throat. I didn't even notice the taste. I finished and let out a belch, causing the others to chuckle.

"Welcome to Versailles, child."

That was the last friendly welcome I would get, and I would never see that woman again. Had I known, I would have thanked her for her kindness, but at Versailles, I would find I was rarely told or alerted in advance of the important things that would affect my life. I would also learn that people were commodities, replaced or removed as easily as the wig on my head.

I FOLLOWED Gaspard through the halls again, people staring at me openly now that I wasn't hidden in a blanket. We reached a cavernous space crowded with bodies, and I let my gaze follow the columns that lifted the ceiling up, up, up... to ceilings painted with chubby, rosy-skinned babies against blue skies and puffy clouds. People draped in white floating through the sky. And it seemed blossoms of diamonds dripped from the sky, reflecting more gold, everywhere I looked.

That ceiling.

It was beautiful, but no one looked like me up there. Along my journey, at least I'd had periods of time with other children like me. Here, at this moment, I was the only one with black skin. They weren't looking at me like I was special; they were looking at me like I was the oddest thing they'd ever seen.

Finally, as if parting seas, the people in the room stood aside, and we were suddenly facing the King on a giant chair. Beside him, on an equally large chair, sat a woman with yellow hair and pale, smooth skin. She wore a lemon-yellow dress with the skirt so large it poofed out from the chair on all sides. Her neck was draped with jewelry that glistened like the things that hung from the ceiling, light all around. Her earlobes were almost lost beneath giant blue stones that caught the light every which way. My eyes were drawn up beside her where a bird sat high on a perch. Her bright blue eyes lit up when she saw me.

"A gift for the most excellent Madame Du Barry," said the King.

She sat forward, looking at me, eyes sparkling with anticipation.

"From Africa, a young page, just for you. He knows our language, my love; he has been trained just for you. He is all yours."

"Oh, my," she clapped her hands together, and the crowd responded in kind, clapping their hands together. She held her arms out to me, half rising from her seat.

Her face was sweet and friendly. Her eyes open and welcoming. But it was her arms out to me that broke through. I hadn't been hugged since my mother, so long ago I barely remembered what it felt like. And how she looked at me made me crave it.

I felt a hand push my lower back, and I stepped forward, swallowed by her embrace. I was stiff at first, but I softened in her arms.

She smelled like flowers, and I let myself give in to the embrace, feeling tears spring to my eyes. In her arms, I almost felt human again, like I was safe from everything I had been through. I closed my eyes and imagined she was my mama and hugged her back.

"Oh, how sweet," she cooed as the people made noises that suggested they were equally moved by the sight of our embrace. She pulled away and looked down into my face, her eyes probing mine with a quizzical smile as if she were looking for something within their depths. "My King, he will be like the child we never had together."

The King laughed, and she used her fingertips to brush the moisture from my cheeks, placing a small kiss on each one. And then she released my face, stepped back, cocked her head. "It's like a little African cupid, isn't it?"

I didn't understand what that meant, but I saw now the affection in her eyes had turned. Or changed. Or maybe it hadn't been real because it was gone now, as if it had been an act. She was looking at me like the people in the hallways had, like I was the oddest thing. My tears dried as I stepped back, remembering she was a stranger. She smiled widely. "Welcome, little cupid!" Applause filled the room.

"The surprise is not over," the King said, signaling to a servant who quickly moved through the crowd that gasped when they saw what he brought forward on a leash. It was a long-limbed dog with almond-shaped eyes that almost looked like a tiny horse. The servant held out the handle of the leash to the woman, whose eyes widened even further.

"Oh!" she said, leaving me as quickly as she'd grabbed me to run over to the dog and scoop it up into her arms. Everyone clapped again and smiled as she turned and looked up to the King. "What did I ever do to deserve such goodness, my King? *Two* pets! This day couldn't possibly be better."

That's the precise moment I realized all these people were insane.

What was I in this place? Not a boy. Certainly, not God's greatest *anything*.

4

———

The backside of the Palace of Versailles was studded with gardens, shimmering lakes, and a miraculous green lawn they called the *Green Carpet* that stretched before us as far as the eye could see. A massive fountain sprouted people and horses carved from stone and marble, each spewing water, endlessly.

I was told the point between the Palace and "as far as the eye can see" was called the Grand Canal. From inside, all this could be easily seen through the ceiling-high windows of a hallway flanked on one side by windows and the other by mirrors. At just the right hour when the sun shone through those windows, the rays would hit the mirrors and reflect, lighting up the space like the sun. I understood the sun on the gate now.

Two other palaces were strategically placed on the grounds out of sight of the main palace for when the King wanted to get away. But there were other special structures just paces away from the main castle that were much more interesting. The first was an enclosure they called the *menagerie*. It was a giant space blocked off by walls all around to keep in animals of all sorts and sizes. The first time I went in, I couldn't even see them until I walked down a central walkway to a central staircase, climbing what seemed like miles up, until the stairs opened onto a platform at the very top. The platform was bound by a fence to keep us from falling off the edge. But once I was up there and peered over, oh, what a sight. Slowly, I watched as animals would suddenly reveal themselves from their separated enclosures below, trees and shrubs sometimes hiding them from view.

There was an animal with a bump on its back who looked up at me with giant eyes, thick fringes for lashes, leaning over to pull some leaves from the top of a tree and stare at me some more while it chewed. And there were birds so large I almost couldn't believe they were birds. One of them was pink! And once, I saw a large cat. We had cats back at Chittagong but I'd never seen a cat like this one; black as night with muscles that rippled under its coat and eyes that looked up and followed me like it was trying to figure out just exactly what combination of steppingstones it would take for it to be able to jump up and pounce!

It was thrilling at first, I visited many times. Eventually, I would grow weary of seeing them alone and trapped in their enclosures. It made me sad for them. I felt kinship with their treatment, as every time I walked a hallway, I could almost feel these fancy people looking down on me in that same way.

So, my favorite place on the grounds became the space they called the Labyrinth; a maze of pruned and shaped trees that reached into the sky, with trails and paths studded with scenes from children's stories, fashioned from statues and fountains. The cook, Salanave, explained to me that the Sun King had created the Labyrinth to help teach his children lessons of morality. The scenes taught me very little about morality, but I enjoyed the space because fear kept the others away, and I could find peace there. It wasn't scary to *me* at all.

When the King wanted to be off the main grounds entirely, we loaded into a carriage and traveled north to a house called the Chateau de Louveciennes. The house had been built to house the builder of the Marly Machine; a huge water-wheel contraption that sat on the Seine and pumped water to the Chateau and down to the Palace. The churning of the giant wheel was a godawful noise, but grew on you so quickly you barely noticed after a couple of days. The King told me the Marly Machine was the first and only water wheel of its type, using a system of pressure to pump that water through pipes and tunnels to the chateau and down river to the Palace. It was the pressure from the wheel that brought the Palace fountains to life, spewing water, endlessly, like they were natural springs. I didn't understand how something so giant could sit on top of water without sinking. I didn't understand how anyone could pressure water so that it would move where they wanted. It was all amazing to me.

As part of my initiation to royal court life, I was taught how to behave, when to speak, how to bow my head, and how to walk behind Madame and the King. I learned how to stand in a room— with my hands crossed in front of me with my head bowed—and never to show my back to the King. So, then I had to learn how to walk out of a room backward without crashing into furniture.

I was supposed to always stand in the closest doorway behind and nearest to Madame unless explicitly told otherwise by her or the King or the Manager. I found out the Manager was also the King's head of personal security. When we were in the dining room or a salon Manager Gaspard liked to take the opposite us. I didn't see the point in that since he was too far away to protect the King if someone should attack, but he seemed to want the King to see *him*. Instead, he posted a second guard behind the King, as well.

With my position behind Madame and Gaspard's in front of her, we were always opposite each other. His spite-filled glare was on me whenever my eyes happened to swing his way. I started to wonder if he cared to look at the King at all or if his position was just an excuse to glare at me. But whenever Madame spoke to me, Gaspard's eyes flickered away, her voice a magic release from the prison of his stare.

In this place, only nobles were allowed to directly look at anyone. We servants, Gaspard included, weren't supposed to look our betters in the eye. It was the way my father had taught me never to look a fierce dog in the eyes. I told myself over and over that they were fierce dogs to keep myself from looking at them directly when they spoke.

But sometimes, Madame would take my chin in her fingers and

force my face upward, demanding I look at her when she spoke to me. As I looked into her large eyes, she would soften them and smile, and for an instant, I'd feel safe.

Everyone called her beautiful and I suppose she was if beauty was in comparison to the others around. Her skin was clear and pale and her eyes large and blue. Her hair and wig always seemed to be placed carefully and everyone seemed to blush under her smile, so I suppose she was what beautiful meant, just like the king was what greatness meant.

But sometimes, when she looked at me her gaze, still on me, would grow cold. Sometimes she pulled me down onto the ground, propping herself up by her elbows, and forced me to share her stare for long minutes. Once it was so long the King had left, changed, and returned to the room to find us on our stomachs, chins in our hands, still staring. I wondered if she was frozen in place or ill, but whenever I tried to shift my gaze away, she would reach out with both hands on my face to keep me looking at her. "You are mine," she told me. The King said nothing, but I could hear him sit and pick up a paper to read. It was like they all knew to leave her be. Like her behavior was normal.

As appreciated as Madame was among a small circle of her close friends, she seemed to be hated by most of the rest of what they called "the court," the network of nobles and their families who lived at the Palace. Some of the more important families had whole suites with living areas. Some of the nobles of lower rank simply had a room. I was told, back when the previous King had built the Palace, he'd forced the families to move there, but now, they cherished the proximity to the King and fought for the right to help him dress himself in the morning, standing in a line, hopping up and down in anticipation of being allowed to help him slide a foot into one of his delicately pointed leather, buckled shoes.

But they didn't like Madame du Barry. I could tell from the way they turned their noses up to her when she passed and giggled under their breath when she left a room. She told me the King had given her the Chateau de Louveciennes and the Petit Trianon palace as gifts, so she sometimes went there with just me and her ladies. I knew it was to get away from the people in the Palace. In her spaces, she seemed fully and completely in charge. And then, immediately upon returning to the main Palace, she would change, laughing a bit harder, showing off a bit more, keeping me near to her with something close to desperation. To my eyes, no matter how she tried to project herself larger, she shrunk a little whenever we returned to the main chateau at Versailles.

One day I was sitting by Madame Du Barry's side in the gardens of the main chateau while she stitched, surrounded by her ladies. The air was perfumed with the flowers that sprouted in ordered chaos all over the grounds, and the grass was mildly damp from the morning dew that hadn't yet burned off. Inside, the Palace was more crowded than usual with visiting generals paying homage to the King, so Madame had declared we should come outside to the gardens.

"Did you see the tall one," one of the maids said to another, speaking about the men they had been discussing for a good part of an hour. "He was a handsome one. I wouldn't mind if the King should require him to live here at Versailles."

The other smiled slyly. "How clever of you to mention that in the company of the one person with the greatest influence over our dear King."

"I would never..." she said, blushing and sneaking a look at The Favorite, who, though embroidering, was listening to everything.

"If you mean me, I have no influence over his Majesty or who he invites to stay," Madame said, cutting through the chatter. "But perhaps he would like to know my opinion. If so, what should that opinion be?"

Her maid flushed with happiness and moved eagerly to supplicate to the Madame. "That his stature and importance require that he spend more time with the King and his esteemed officers ... to strategize."

Madame winked at her. "I will see what I can do to assist the strategizing," she said, sending them all into peals of laughter that died when one of them whispered loudly.

"It's the Dauphine! Here she comes, Madame!"

I didn't know the *Dauphine* was the wife of the future King, the *Dauphin*. Or that the dauphin was the grandson of the current King Louis XV. I only knew when the woman came through the halls or walked the grounds of Versailles, everyone bowed to her with a deference not awarded to Madame Du Barry. They bowed low, like they had for the King.

Madame quickly dropped her embroidery onto the bench beside us and stood as the group of women walked by behind her. She curtsied quickly and deeply, as did we all, and looked expectantly at the woman leading the pack. It was a useless effort. The woman passed with her head high, sparing not even a glance at Madame as she kept moving. Madame flushed red, and her hands fluttered in embarrassment as she sat back down again, followed by her ladies and me.

"Who is that?" I whispered to the woman closest to me.

"Goodness, child, don't you know the wife of the future king? That's Marie Antoinette of Austria."

One of the other ladies said a little louder, "You'll always recognize her. She is the haughtiest, snootiest woman in the room. Thinks she's better than everyone. Quite audacious, considering she's not even French. At least our Madame is a true French lady. But I suppose any woman would be unpleasant whose husband still won't touch her after all these years of marriage. And being no more than a girl, she must be eaten alive with jealousy to see our Madame's beauty and full womanhood on display. It is sheer envy, for certain."

"Now, now," Madame said, still unable to meet anyone's eyes, her face red. She fumbled with her embroidery while not really doing anything, as if just needing to busy her hands. "None of that. I'm certain she simply didn't recognize it was me." The ladies didn't respond, but their awkward silence spoke volumes. Finally, when she couldn't stand it any longer, Madame put her embroidery down firmly and stood, picking up her skirts to storm off down the path to the Palace. The women looked at me, and one gestured with a jerk of her head that I was to follow.

I hardly wanted to leave—I was enjoying the fresh air—but then I saw the Manager Gaspard out of nowhere standing across the garden on the lawn, looking like he would pick me up bodily to move me along.

I followed like a shadow as we walked through the Palace. She was moving very fast, but I was young and unencumbered by that massive skirt. Despite the throngs of people, we moved up the stairs to her apartments, into her bedchamber and descended, again, through another narrow hallway. Suddenly, we were in the King's quarters. He sat at a table writing and looked up at her intrusion. His face looked like no matter what she was about to say, he'd heard it before.

"What is it, my dear?"

"She snubbed me again. That Austrian bitch!" She burst into tears, water seeming to sprout everywhere at once, her arms flailing. "Publicly! She stood no farther from me than you, and she put her nose straight up in the air and ignored me. I've done nothing to that woman! Why does she hate me?"

"My dear, don't let it bother you. She will come to love you someday."

She took the handkerchief he handed her and paced, tears drying up and eyes glazing over as she looked at nothing. "I helped arrange the most beautiful wedding of a lifetime for her, and I did it gladly. It was *my* idea to build the opera house for her wedding, and she hasn't an ounce of gratitude. She treats me like the dirt on the bottom of her shoe."

"Don't distress yourself, my love. I'd say she's the one who hasn't yet lived up to the bargain. An unconsummated marriage is not a marriage at all. I expected more from the future queen."

I watched as Madame's face transformed from soft and vulnerable to hard, the planes of her cheeks firming up as if hardening clay.

"She behaves like I'm nothing more than a scullery maid." Even her voice had changed, going deeper, moisture dried. "I'm the

Mâitresse-en-titre, the *Favorite* of the most powerful king in the world. I'm almost a queen, myself! She is nothing but a spoiled child fortunate enough to be given the chance to be in this family because of *your* graciousness! By insulting me, she shows the world that she has no respect for the choices of the King. Her behavior makes it clear she questions your judgment in choosing me as Mâitresse-en-titre. My feelings are of little concern, but she mocks *you*, my King, and that is unforgivable!"

The King's writing hand slowed as he dropped his quill into the bottle of ink. His face increasingly grew red as he turned her words over in his head.

The next day I shared Madame's conversation with Salanave, the cook. The no-nonsense woman and I had an affinity of sorts. She wasn't very old, though she moved like she was. My mother would say a woman like Salanave had an old soul, whatever that meant.

"I don't understand," I said while eating soup at her table. "Why does the future queen hate Madame?"

"Why do the other servants hate you?"

"The other servants hate me?"

"Of course, they don't think you belong here, petit. They don't like that a black-skinned child comes here and is dressed as if he's a royal. They don't understand what makes you better than them, that you get to be by the side of the King and his Favorite."

Salanave sat opposite me, sipping on a cup of tea.

"And they hate her for many reasons. There's the fact that Madame convinced the King to send away the Dauphine's Austrian friends. And the fact that the Dauphine has befriended the King's daughters, who hate the Madame and have filled the Dauphine with all sorts of scandalous stories about the woman. But the real issue between the Dauphine and Madame is much more basic. I'm going to tell you something, young man: There will never be a time in the world when a wife will willingly bow down to a mistress, even if the husband is not her own. On top of that, the rules of royal society say that a common woman isn't worthy to be an official mistress, even if the King has bought the noble title for her, as he did. Only *noble-born* prostitutes are suitable for the King. The young ladies of age to serve the King in that way, and their families, will never forgive the Comtesse for taking that esteemed position. They think Madame should have been in his group of nameless, faceless young women that he beds in his *parties*. If you tell anyone I said that I shall call you a liar to your face. Now, finish your soup, petit."

5

———————

Dear Citizen,

It was such a strange condition, sometimes even I forgot that though I was in the upper echelons of society, I wasn't a part of it. Sometimes, it amused Madame and the King to allow me to participate as if I were the child of a noble. I learned to dance like them and held Madame's hand to help her out of the carriage. They seemed thrilled every time I performed. During those times, Madame doted on me. After years of being carted around like a sack of potatoes, I'll admit, I let my fancy new clothes and the apparent adoration of the King and his Favorite to cloud my judgment.

Correction—I had no judgment at all. I thought I understood the situation. I was wrong.

I soon learned the duplicitous nature of the civilized royal court. A person could smile in your face and stab you in the back. On the first floor, they were gossiping about the third floor, and then it would switch. Words meant nothing because these people lied as easily as drinking a glass of water.

*Madame, too, often tried out faces on me. With my chin in her
hand, she would open her eyes wide and declare her love for me and
then seconds later the expression of love would drop, and she would
look at me like I was a stranger she'd never seen. I realized she was
practicing her masks on me. Just like the first time, when I was in
the shadow of her smile, I felt special. When the mask dropped, her
face was a blank page, eyes empty as if life had never lived in them.*

--Zamor

My mother used to have a way of putting things into
perspective. When things went opposite of what she
wanted or expected, she would remark to my father that
God found His humor in his children's expectations.

I expected much from these people because they were wealthy
and powerful. But then, I would see a nobleman relieving himself in
a dark corner. Or people fornicating in a salon out in the open in
front of the world—you had to know which salons to avoid after
dark. I imagined my mother's voice saying to me: *Look, these people
have everything, but they shit on the floor and rut like beasts in broad
view; the so-called pinnacle of civilization has them reverting them to
animals.*

Another thing my mother would say was that God had decided to
gift me with the odd bit of muscle strength in my arms. Even as a
toddler, I'd been able to lift things that should've been too heavy. One
time she asked me to carry a load, piece-by-piece to my father to put
on the mule. Instead of carrying it to him in bits like she expected, I
carried the entire load on one trip. My father had looked down at me,
surprise on his features, and then he and my mother laughed in
amazement and surprise.

So, though I was small for my age, with my great upper body
strength, I was able to help the adult servants now. One day I was
helping the laundress by carrying loads of bedding to the laundry

room. I wanted to do it because I didn't want to lose my one saving grace from lack of use.

The load was easily almost my own body weight. I bumped up against the large, boiling cauldron and tipped the linens into the water. I was stirring the boiling, funky brew with a giant stick when I overheard two male farmhands talking about Manager Gaspard in the hallway outside the laundry area.

"...drinks himself into a coma at night and wonders why his wife is bedding another man. He used to be well-respected. He'd still be in the royal army if he hadn't slept through a shift and helped lose us the war. You'd think he'd be grateful the King took pity on him, but he's still a miserable bastard. If it weren't for the fact that he saved the King once, he wouldn't be here now."

They went on about how the King was happy just to have one person beholden to him and that the country had soured on Louis, *the Well-Beloved*. They said the King spent so much time away from the Palace because he hated the nobles he was leading. I lost the rest of the conversation, but I remembered how the King's face had turned colors when Madame suggested people were criticizing his judgment.

One night I was sitting beside Madame at the dinner table. When one of the servers bent to load my plate, Gaspard stepped over and said softly: "He's a servant. Bring him potato mash, hot cereals with stock, or scraps like the other servants."

The servant stopped and passed me by, giving the rich meat stew to the others.

Sitting beside me, Madame didn't say anything in response even when the server returned and ladled the gruel into my bowl, but the second Gaspard looked away, she slipped some venison onto the edge of my bowl where it was next to hers.

I looked around for Gaspard.

"It'll be our secret," she whispered. "Forget Gaspard, you're a part of the family." She squeezed my shoulders in a sideways hug.

Happiness flushed through me, and I looked at her profile and her small, discreet smile. It seemed a thousand eyes watched me spear the meat with a fork and carry it to my mouth. It was like chewing cooked vegetables, it was' so tender; the flavor of meat roasted in the hot oven in its own juices was delicious beyond description. I closed my eyes in ecstasy for a second, and when I opened my eyes and my mouth to deposit more meat, I caught the eye of a man sitting further down the table. He looked a little like the King, but he had a weaker chin and rounder cheeks. He kept his eyes on me, and I looked down. I wasn't supposed to look at them.

I'd never spoken to the future king or been introduced to him. I only knew him from his resemblance to the King and where he sat beside the Dauphine.

Madame pulled over a little saucer and gave me more meat. I used my knife and fork to eat with gusto. Madame smiled and winked at me, which might have meant more if I didn't see her, in the very next moment, lean to her other side and feed a bit of venison to the little horse dog that sat on her haunches between Madame and the King.

Blood rushed to my face in embarrassment, and the meat lost its flavor. When she leaned over to talk and laugh with the King, I spit the meat out into a napkin.

"Give my accolades to the cook," the King said, waving his hand toward the empty bowl in front of him with the dregs of white cream. It was a velouté that had gone over well with their friends the last time we had it at Louveciennes. He'd already eaten but was now watching the rest of the room. "Our dear cook Salanave took a cauliflower and made this wonderful soup. And it was the lovely Madame du Barry who suggested it to her, wasn't it, my dear?"

Madame's cheeks blossomed pink, and she looked bashful. "It was only a suggestion from a modest woman."

"She's never been modest a day in her life," someone whispered loudly. Madame heard it, too, stopping for just a moment, only the slight pause in her eating and the sudden redness in her pale cheeks giving it away.

The King heard it, too, but he continued. "In honor of this

wonderful soup and this wonderful woman, any dish with cauliflower shall be called a 'du Barry.'"

"Oh, stop, Louis," she blushed again and swatted at him while people chuckled at the display.

"I demand it!"

"But isn't this peasant food, Your Majesty?" A nobleman asked with a laugh. "It seems hardly worthy of being tasted by our king."

Madame's cheeks flamed hot red, and she touched the corners of her lips lightly with her napkin. Her head swiveled to the Well-Beloved, and I saw his face from where it faced her, growing stiffer and firmer than before.

"Does someone in this room dare to tell me what to eat? Are you questioning the King's discernment?"

The room went stock still. Suddenly, the man who'd spoken was sputtering his apology.

"Never, absolutely not, Your Majesty. It-it looks like a lovely, lovely soup."

"Apologize to the Madame du Barry, and perhaps I will ignore your lapse in judgment." All eyes swung to the man, who seemed frozen. "Did you hear what I said? Apologize to the lovely Madame du Barry!"

The King's voice was loud like cannon fire, and the man practically jumped out of his seat at the sound of it. He stood and tried to rectify it quickly.

"Please forgive me, Madame, I spoke out of turn, and I was wrong. So, so wrong. Why, this soup looks more splendid than anything I've ever had in my life. It is only my ignorance of excellent food that caused me to misspeak. Please accept my sincerest apology to you and to you, our most wonderful, honorable King."

He bowed hard. When I looked at Madame's face, there was a hard little smile on tight lips that matched the hardness in her blue eyes. She gave a tiny, tiny nod, and beside her, the King's face went from angry and serious to wide, open, and happy.

"Alright!" he lifted his glass and nodded, also. "Here's to the

Velouté du Barry and every other du Barry dish to come from the kitchen of the House of Bourbon."

And just like that, the tension was broken.

I went back to my gruel.

"Young page," the King said, surprising me. "Madame says you have been a good companion to her." He spoke in the way he had, not looking at me. "That you have read with her and that you enjoy listening to music in the salon with her. The instructor, Barnier, says you are an excellent student, quick to learn even the difficult English language. He says for someone so young, you have an amazing memory and grasp of knowledge, especially for a blackamoor. I do say, you are proving to be a credit to the royal house."

Madame reached over to give me a squeeze of affection as the visitors watched our show.

"In fact," the King continued, "I would say of the many pages of all our noble friends, you are truly the best and most accomplished. A testament to the lovely Madame du Barry, who is truly the greatest hostess and benefactress in all of France. You have quickly become an integral part of our humble household. Madame has even fondly referred to you as her *son*," he chuckled.

I looked around and saw the glances of those nobles who also did not make eye contact. They looked stiff with insult. Madame blushed with pleasure and continued to eat her food daintily. He continued.

"I have spoken with Madame, and we have decided you deserve a gift. You are a prudent child, so I have no fear of allowing you to ask for whatever it is you want." A gasp went up in the room and there was a low mumble amongst the nobles about the generosity of the King. *What will he ask for?* they whispered. *Jewels? More magnificent clothes?*

"What would you like, young man? Do you want a pet? I saw a pelican in the parlor just a short while ago that looked in need of a caretaker."

A few people laughed, but I felt the seriousness of the situation in my bones. Maybe this was my chance.

"Or a sport?" the King continued. "A small horse you can use for all your own to ride with Madame? Something more to your size, about the size of that dog of hers?"

More gasps. Some people looked on with wide eyes and glared at me.

"I don't need anything…" I said softly.

The King's face split into a genuine smile, and he raised his glass in happiness. "Intelligent and humble. You delight me more each day, page."

"…but can I go back home?" I asked.

The room quieted once again. All the faces in the room seemed to swing my way and then back to the King. He cleared his throat and put his wine glass down, retaining a stiff smile.

"Whatever do you mean?" he laughed. "You *are* home."

"To my family, Your Majesty. From where I was taken."

"You weren't taken. You came to work like every other servant at the Palace. You are confused."

I was starting to *get* confused. I tried to be helpful and educate him. "Your Majesty, I was taken by the slavers from my home. You remember, the Manager brought me to you after I was taken as a slave?"

"Hush, boy. If you were taken into slavery by traders who intended to send you to work in our French colonies, then it is your captors who must free you. Whatever happened before you came to Versailles has nothing to do with this court. We have no slaves in France."

Across the room, a man in a shiny orange jacket with a thin strip of hair under his nose and a coating of powder so heavy over his face no glimpse of pink shone through looked me over and said: "Your Majesty, perhaps your new 'son' doesn't know about the Code Noir doctrine your great grandfather put into place. He will have to track down his master in the Americas and New France if he wants his freedom, isn't that correct?"

Someone immediately hissed, "Shut up, you fool. You know we lost most of New France in the war."

The King sat quietly with his eyes on the table, pretending not to hear, though it was obvious he did—the room wasn't that large. He picked up his glass and gulped his wine in large swallows.

I could feel the increasing tension in the room, but I was more conscious of the tension inside me. *This was my chance.* The King had offered me anything, and I only cared about one thing. Foolishly, I continued. "They said I was for you, Your Majesty, so doesn't that mean you have the power to free me?"

More whispers: *Is that blackamoor questioning the King's power? Is that nègre interrogating the King? Does that blackamoor dare to imply he knows more than the King?*

My head swiveled as I heard the whispers, but I couldn't tell who said what.

The King spoke calmly. "You serve me and, like my other servants, have a job to do. And I have no desire to release you."

"But I do not get paid like the servants..."

Now, the King's smile disappeared entirely, and someone snickered as he went red. I looked around the room. It was Gaspard's sneaky smile that told me I was in trouble.

"Do you have a place to lay your head, page?" the King yelled. All chatter stopped. "Food to eat? Clean water to drink? The *Favorite* of the King feeding you meat from her own plate and draping you in the finest silk, allowing you to be in her presence? Mon Dieu, you are *more* than well-paid, child. Any man in this room would give his life to be in your position, and you will do well to remember it!"

His voice was so loud by the end I could almost feel his breath ruffle my hair two seats over. Almost as soon as he stopped speaking, Madame shifted slightly—imperceptibly—away from me. I saw the future queen tilt her head and followed her gaze to three women who sat some ways on the other side of the room—the King's daughters.

I sat quietly throughout the rest of the meal, my face hot from the gaze of all around me. When I glanced at the King and Madame, neither would look my way.

"Why is he sitting at this table?" the King said to Madame. "He's a servant and has no place here with nobles. He's forgotten himself, but I'll make him remember!"

I wanted to cry, but I refused to let the tears come; these people wouldn't see me cry today, I decided. I sat stiff and angry until Madame said softly, annoyance in her voice: "Go to your room, page. You'll not be coming to dinner again until I decide you've earned your place back."

I stood and bowed quickly to the King and the Dauphin, walking backward out of the room so I could see them all as they snickered and snuck glances at me. They ate up my discomfort ... feeding on it like maggots on rotting meat.

I had thought because they called themselves civilized and educated, they were fair and reasonable people. But in this place, they were more like feral beasts, waiting for any sign of weakness to pounce.

I exited the room; the doors closed in my face. Knowing they were feral beasts erased any expectations I previously held about what these fancy people would or would not do. They would do anything. Only, they'd do it in jewels and silk.

I could almost hear God's laughter at my naïveté but knew He would be proud I was such a quick study.

6

———

I slipped out of the quarters from the back and ran around the building. Once out of the immediate sightline of the bedrooms, I relaxed a bit. People came and went from Versailles at all hours of the day and night. The royal guards were concentrated around the family sleeping quarters and not focused on the perimeter of the building, as large as it was. In the dead of night, I slipped across the way and into the giant arena of stables, disappearing into a pen full of quieted horses. I picked the one on the end because she was awake and alert. It almost seemed like she was waiting for me.

I knew how to ride horses already from my upbringing at home. I ran my hand along the horse's side to let her know who I was, as my father had taught me. One of her large eyes rolled my way, getting as good a look as she could in the darkened stable. I said to her softly, "Let's ride, my friend. Take me away from this place. Take me home." And then I quickly saddled her, led her out by the reins, mounted and led her in a gentle trot away from the Palace. It wasn't until I was a good bit away down the tree-lined road that we picked up speed.

Riding away from the Palace felt as good as the cool night air on my cheeks. My excitement rose at taking matters into my own hands.

Though I hadn't any idea of where I was going, at that point the where didn't matter as much as the leaving.

I rode until I'd left the manicured grounds and entered the real spaces again, where trees grew wild, and grasses tangled and fought with wildflowers. The position of the moon in the sky told me I was headed south.

I couldn't think of how long it might take me to get home and didn't dare imagine I was headed in the wrong direction. Now was not a time for those thoughts, I told myself. Now was a time for bold action. I would ride all the way home. I would be brave and strong, and my town would be so impressed and proud of my courage.

I gently kicked the horse to move faster. The moon illuminated a patch of white on the nose of this otherwise dark chocolate horse. It was beautiful.

"I'll call you Lightning," I said to her, my voice low but still starkly clear in the night. "Your nose is as brilliant as a strike of light in the moonlight. We're friends now, Lightning." Her ear ruffled a bit from the air of my breath as I spoke, and it made me happy. I thought perhaps she understood what I said. "Of all the horses at Versailles, you are the best."

I wasn't lying. The horse picked up on the gentlest of motions, allowed me to lead her and wasn't distracted by anything. While it felt good when I left, the evening was getting more frigid by the minute. I kept talking to her to distract from the cold.

"My family will be very impressed with you. And I know my father will be happy to pay for you. Though, to my mind, the King owes us at least a horse after the ordeal I've been through, don't you think? Even a horse as special as you." Our conversation kept me going when I heard rustlings in the woods beside the road. Talking to her kept the fear at bay.

By the time the moon had fallen to the tree line and rays of sun were rising on the other side of the sky, I had made it to a small town. Lightning's hooves sounded loudly in the very early morning of a town waking up. A man in an apron came out of his front door and turned over a sign outside his door. The sight of the horse didn't catch his attention, but when he looked up and saw me sitting atop of it, he immediately grew more alert and called out to me.

I thought about stopping, about asking where I was. He spoke French, so I was obviously still in the country. But his face didn't seem friendly, so I ignored him and kept riding, hearing him call out behind me. I was searching for something, someone, who would show themselves to be safe though I didn't know what safe would look like.

But I took too long to decide because up ahead, a group of men on horses blocked the road. As I got closer, I saw they were all stern-faced. I tried to lead the horse around them, but they moved and surrounded me.

"Come, now, son," said the one leading the pack. He had gray, stringy hair gathered in a ribbon low behind his neck. These men were not dressed like the people at Versailles. They wore plain clothes and pants that went all the way down, like the servants. No pretty colors or wigs or powder. Just tired, suspicious faces.

The houses were short and made of stone, the streets close and cobblestoned. Every sound carried, and apparently, every face was familiar, for they didn't even have to speak to each other. They moved as one body around me.

"You know you're the King's property," the man continued. "We won't let you put this town at odds with the King. Let's go, son."

I didn't know how they knew that. And though I had ridden horses since I was a young child back home, I didn't know how to move the horse to get around them. I tried to use the reins to avoid the men, but they were much more experienced with leading their mounts and blocked me. Every movement I made, one of them countered me until finally they had tightened around me, and there was nowhere to go.

"I just want to go home to my maman and papa," I finally said. One of them jerked back in surprise.

"Listen to how he speaks—proper like the King himself. Maybe he's not the new blackamoor page? Does a page speak like that? Do you have freedom papers to show? Show us your papers, and we'll leave you be."

"Papers? I-I don't have anything."

A hatchet-faced man looked at me with disgust, his face curled in anger. "He's not a noble. This is the King's blackamoor everyone is talking about. The educated slave who dines on meat and wine while my children are walking on shoes with holes in the bottoms. This is what our tax money is spent on. He's treated *better* than citizens."

"That can't be—we don't have slavery on the mainland," another one said. "That's the rule. There are no slaves in France, only free black people and servants. It's been that way for generations."

"And yet, here we stand with the King's blackamoor slave before us, telling us he wants to leave and trying to run."

"Should we help him?" one asked. He was a younger man with dark brown hair down his back and on his face. He looked at me like he was pained. All seven others looked at him.

"Are you mad?" a man said angrily. "The King's army will string us up and set fire to the entire village. No, the boy goes back. The way I see it, he's got nothing to run from. And maybe we'll earn the King's favor for returning him."

The leader jumped down and, before I knew it, had grabbed the front of my shirt and pulled me off the horse. It felt like I was swarmed by a thousand hands as they tied my arms with rope and forced me as a passenger onto the back of another horse, looped to the rider. Then we all rode back to Versailles.

I tried to speak to them. I explained I was taken from my home. I begged them to help me escape. The man who had spoken to save me hung back, but I felt his eyes on me and saw what appeared to be shame on his face. As the manicured lawns and straight trees of the Palace came into view, I quieted down. They'd stopped listening to me.

They hushed as well. I doubted they'd ever actually been this close to the Palace, the way they looked at it with something like awe, something close to fear. Once we reached the stables, I looked up to see Gaspard and several guards standing there, waiting as if he had no concern at all that I wouldn't return. Just standing there with his arms crossed over his chest. He watched while one of the townsmen pulled me off onto the ground. Immediately my mouth filled with the dust of my own impact against the dirt floor.

"We found this boy on that fine horse trying to get through our town, Monsieur. You'll tell the King that we returned his property safe and sound?" the gray-haired leader said, his head bobbing as if trying to decide whether to bow or look Gaspard in the eyes. He reached back to fumble for Lightning's reins, and the man who had ridden him—too tempted by the beauty of the King's horse to resist—jumped off, longing in his eyes as he went back to mount his abandoned horse, sad and tired in comparison. The leader handed the reins to Gaspard.

Gaspard hesitated, and at that moment, seeing the indecision in his eyes, I realized I was in great danger. He looked like he wanted to murder me then and there, and the expression on his face was thoughtful, like he was considering how to do it. I looked at the townsmen whose faces wore the same unsettled expressions I was feeling.

"Please, Monsieur," the leader said, fear in his voice. "We will cause you no problem. Long live Louis, *the Well-Beloved*," he mumbled, his trembling lips trying to smile. He dipped his head and bowed. The entire group seemed frightened now, no longer even noticing me. They all made a half-hearted effort to bow, but their eyes were on Gaspard. Some looked around, only now noticing a couple of guards standing silent in the darkened corners of the stables. How many were hidden was impossible to tell in a space this size. We might have been surrounded as far as they knew, and the fear showed on their faces.

"What is your town?" Gaspard asked, his voice smug, his expression confident.

"D-Dourdan, Monsieur."

"Dourdan, yes. I come to your town quite a bit. It would be amenable to me if I did not have to pay such high charges in the tavern I frequent. Perhaps you can arrange for the King's personal guard to be received with the graciousness befitting his station. And a bit of change when I come, to give to the King, of course."

The men looked at each other and then at one in particular, whom I assumed to be the owner of a tavern. He nodded quickly, vigorously, his eyes pained as if he wanted to cry. "Of course, Monsieur, you are most welcome at any of our local taverns. We will not accept any payment from your hand, befitting your station."

Gaspard's eyes lit with greed and satisfaction, and he looked about to continue—to ask for even more from this foolish group of men—but luck was with them that day. At that moment, the sentinel announced the King's approach, and Gaspard whispered to me: "Get up, get up, black bastard!"

As always, the sound of the shoes of the King and his entourage arrived before him, but soon Louis was there looking down at me in his white wig and bored expression, in his dressing gown and robe. The townsmen straightened and bowed as best they could on their horses as I struggled to get up with my hands still tied. He looked me up and down.

"Is it true you were running, page? You would disrespect me in that manner? No matter now, you surely have it out of your system, as there is no place in France that will harbor you. You work for the King until he releases you, and I do not. I refuse. You are a smart boy. You understand the folly of your ways?"

"Your Majesty," one of the townsmen interrupted, having taken his hat into his hands, bowing from atop his horse. With the King there to witness, he got a little courage back. "Some of our group thought the child was a noble, but as soon as I saw him, I knew he was yours. Only a page of the most honorable King Louis, *the Well-Beloved,* would be dressed so fine and speak so well. Some in our town might have easily mistaken him for a thief and harmed him. But I saw him and said we certainly must get him back to our King immediately."

The King looked at the party and then nodded. "Give them recompense for their inconvenience," he said to Gaspard, whose face was stone as he fumbled in his pocket for money, which he handed to the gray-haired leader.

"Oh, thank you, thank you, Your Majesty. You are truly the most honorable and the greatest of all kings…"

Louis XV had already left the stables. Gaspard, cranky that his opportunity had passed, told the townsmen: "What are you waiting for? You'll get no more here."

The group left with only the man who had wanted to save me looking back at where I lay on the ground. And then they were all gone.

Gaspard looked down at me, blocking the light. "Trying to escape was bad enough, but stealing one of the King's horses should've gotten you hanged. That horse is worth three of you. If you were anyone other than the Favorite's page … think of that the next time you consider doing something this stupid again. And think of this…"

He delivered a kick to my head, and everything went black.

7

———

I woke in my room. The darkness disoriented me. I had trouble remembering where I was, what day it was. I had trouble remembering who I was. I raised my arm to look at it in the dark, and slowly, my memory came back.

I lay there but didn't feel myself. I was sleepy but afraid to close my eyes. I must have fallen asleep anyway because I woke again when I heard footsteps scuffling outside my bedroom door. Seconds later, the door opened, and a servant came through with a lit candle in one arm and a pile of clothes in the other.

"What day is it?" I asked him, pulling myself up slowly. My head was pounding. I felt something on my neck and reached up, touching the something dried on my neck, with a trail up to my ear.

"Use that washbasin and rag to wipe that blood off and put these clothes on. Be quick about it." He tossed the clothes onto me and left the room. I reached down, my body moving slower than I was telling it to. I finally got my fingers to obey and picked up an edge of the material.

"Hurry up!" the boy yelled from outside the door. I pulled off my dressing gown to put on the clothes. Then, I realized I still had the stuff on my neck and used a rag to wipe it, the basin water turning pink. I was so focused on the blood I didn't pay attention to the fact that the clothes weren't day clothes, just some billowy gown-like thing.

"Monsieur, what time is it? There are no breeches."

"Get dressed in what's there and do it quickly, or I'll beat you, blackamoor."

I looked around the room for some boots to pull on and for the piles of clothes that were usually in the room. They were all gone except for a pair of boots in the corner. I didn't have stockings and the boot felt funny on my feet. While I was trying to pull on the second boot, the door crashed open, and the servant was there again, frowning. He hurried over to me to wrest the boot off my foot.

"Who told you to put these on? You do what I say!" He threw the boot across the room and just as roughly pulled the second one off.

"The floor is cold!"

He was beyond hearing, so focused was he on jerking me to my feet.

"Come on, now, we can't keep Gaspard waiting."

He took me by the arm, and with each step on the cold floor, my toes curled as he marched me out of the servants' quarters across the grounds where a coating of white lay over everything; winter giving us a taste in autumn. I didn't even remember feeling cold during my escape attempt, and I wondered how much time had passed since then. By the time we reached the main Palace, I was so grateful to be out of the cold I practically ran through the halls to keep up with him.

As we walked through the hall of mirrors, the view from the floor-to-ceiling windows looked down upon the white, glistening wonderland reflected in the mirrors. It felt like we walked through a sea of snow broken by wall sconces and golden accents. The candles almost didn't need to be lit with the reflection of white snow, the lakes, and moonlight.

I'd seen snow since being taken from my home, but it was still new enough to be wondrous to me. My steps slowed, and I drifted to the windows, enchanted by the sight of it sparkling as it came down like sprinkled sugar covering all the grass and the tops of trees, landing softly on the surface of the ponds that had not yet frozen. It covered the ground like billions of glittering diamonds, lighting up the Palace like sparkling dust. I spread my palms on the glass of the closest window, and the icy freeze almost attached my hand there. My breath froze as I breathed out a cloud. It was so pretty I wanted to stay there. I wanted to go outside and spin in a circle beneath it.

I was jerked away by the servant who hissed at me, "If I have to tell you one more time, blackamoor, you'll be sorry. Come along!"

We went through the hallway and beyond, moving through the rooms until we got to one of the larger salons. Even at the late hour, plenty of people were inside the room sitting and standing in their fancy clothes under outdoor coverings, drinking glasses of wine. I saw their hands, white with cold, swirling the wine as if the motion could generate warmth. Faces covered in white powder over skin as white from the frigid air, as if we all stood outside; the fireplace in the room not enough to heat the massive space. They parted and glanced down at me as I was jerked along to the center.

"The King promised a show," a man said after spotting me. "I guess we know what that's to be now."

I looked at the man, trying to parse out information from the expression on his face.

"I think I know what this is, and I'm not going to stay around for it," another man said to the woman beside him, who looked both worried and confused.

"What's happening?" she whispered.

"Let's go."

"But what's happening? Should we take the child with us?"

"Are you mad? He's the King's property. Let's just go."

The couple leaving seemed to spur others, who looked around and bustled out behind them. The people who remained in the room didn't look at all alarmed. One man settled himself into a chair, his eyes sparkling as he took a large swallow of wine from his glass. And then I saw Gaspard standing on the far side of the room. His look of satisfaction made me truly cold. Colder than when I'd been walking on the bare ground.

"Took you long enough," he said to the servant, who ran off quickly. The Manager took my arm and turned in a tight circle, swinging me to gain attention.

"Guests and friends, the King has called you here for a show to celebrate the first snow of the season. We promise it will be well worth leaving your warm beds! And it's starring our very own page!"

Another couple stood and hurried out, looking back.

"You'll miss the show!" Gaspard laughed after them. He was still laughing when, suddenly, he reached down and began pulling off my shift. Confused, I held it tighter to me. My efforts to keep my clothes made the crowd laugh.

"Look at how hard he fights; the blackamoor has strong arms!"

The people in the room laughed as I lost the fight and the cold set in. The doors opened, and two servant girls were ushered in. The placid expression on their faces told me they had done this before and they got busy with efficiency and purpose, one pressing against me while the other pulled off her shift and came at me with her hands.

By this time, I wasn't new to relations but I'd never been violated in public, for the world to see. I'd never been violated for entertainment. My head swam as their hands came at me and my body faster than my mind could keep up. And when I was stripped bare and the audience clapped and howled, I escaped my head.

I WAS FLOATING ABOVE, looking down, over the heads of everyone. Fear was below me in the little boy on the ground. He was staring up at me, his eyes so large and frightened I felt bad for him. I wondered why all the people gazing down at him didn't see that fear and leave him alone. But I was glad I wasn't him.

It was safe above, safe from what was going on below. But part of me felt that this might somehow be dangerous, also—to be so removed from myself.

Myself. And who was I? I was forgetting my name. I couldn't remember where I was. I was floating, and all sound, all sight ... everything that made me human was gone. It was frightening, but still, it was safer than what was happening below.

And then, the sound of a shout permeated my cloud as if someone yelled directly into my ear and I was falling, fast ... too fast ... falling back into that body below. Back to where I didn't want to be. Where Gaspard was shouting at the boy. Where he was laughing at the boy. Some people against the wall looked away like they didn't want to be there, but the rest of the room was laughing so hard they could barely catch their breaths.

Laughing at ... me.

Like a thunderstorm clap, I was immediately back in that boy's body, looking up. With the noise and the stares. The girls pulled their clothes on quickly, their lank hair falling into their faces, one of them escaping, immediately. The other hesitated only to glance at my face while the crowd clapped and laughed. The laughter.

I got to my feet, but I had trouble holding my head up. Looking at those people hurt my eyes. Hurt my spirit. I ran to the exit. Two guards barred the door, but I didn't stop, planning to bust through them both if I could, but they opened them at the last minute, and I was free.

"Run, blackamoor, run!" Gaspard yelled, laughing, behind me.

I ran like I had never run before. My tears nearly froze on my cheeks as I ran, wondering how far I needed to be before I would get to a place where people were human again. I ran past the surprised faces of stray people in the hall. I ran through the white, icy hall of mirrors that had lost its enchantment. I ran and ran.

In my room, my fingers fumbled my blanket over my shoulders, and then I sat on the stuffed sack that was my bed staring at the stone wall in front of me. The room was all shadows, lit by only one candle, and I was happy it was dark. Hugging my knees to my chest and staring at the walls, I willed my mind to forget. I willed my mind to take me out beyond the glass in the hall. Somewhere out in the snow where I could spin in a circle under the icy shards of heaven. Or up even higher, above where I'd been hiding.

I knew, instinctively, that giving in would be my death, but I'd already died. I'd died when I left my body to float above. I died when I was surrounded by wolves, helpless as a rabbit. I was dead from the second I came to this place, and I didn't mind escaping to the icy, glittering snow. Removed from it all. Safe. Safe.

Slap!

The sting across my face stunned me, and I looked up, surprised, at Salanave, who squatted on the floor beside me. Her face was flat, as always, but I saw concern in her eyes.

"There you are. I thought I'd lost you." She had a towel in a bucket of water beside her. She wrung it out and came toward me with it. But when she'd brought me out of numbness, the fear and pain came back quickly and my eyes sprouted tears. I wiped them and my leaking nose with my arm, and she took the washcloth and wiped them. "Let me help, son."

I leaned away from her, huddled into myself, and she stopped at the suspicion on my face.

"I won't hurt you, petit."

I had trusted her before, and she hadn't proven false yet. And I needed kindness. I allowed her to hold my face with one hand and wash it down even as the tears and snot kept dripping from me.

"You stay strong," she said, wiping my face with hard, rough swipes. "Don't let them break you. That's what they want. You made the King look foolish in front of his court and then defied him." As she rubbed, I stared at the stone wall beyond her. "In his eyes, he had to punish you in front of them; a king who cannot control a child is no king at all. That's what these people do, chèr; they break people. You're lucky he didn't have you beaten to within an inch of your life, too. It's not your fault, most of us servants know what to expect. You came here alone, and you don't know yet, but you will learn. You have to learn to be as small as you can. That is the only way to survive a place like this. It's not easy. It's the hardest thing in the world to shrink down into what you have to be in a place like this. Think of it like a game. A play. Do you know what a play is? You play a character, no? You play the fool, the pet, the weak, harmless one..."

Her voice sounded wet and muffled, but no tears fell from her. She was strong. I looked for something in her face that would give me insight into her strength, but it was frozen. Her brown eyes pierced mine. "You let it seem like he won, but don't give them that. You do what you need to do to make them feel powerful, but you keep all of yourself intact. Do you understand?"

"I don't have to be small at home," I needed her to know. "I have a maman and papa. You are not my maman. I don't want to be strong. I want to go home." Sitting there, I felt like less than the mice that stared at us from within the cracks in the wall. "You're not my maman."

Salanave stopped wiping my face and looked at me a long moment, then she wrapped her arms around me and held me.

"No, I'm not your maman. Your maman would be more tender with you. My tenderness is for my own children, but I like you. I will hold you for a moment, like your maman. Tell me, if your maman was here, what would she do?"

My head filled with the sweet lullaby my mama used to sing when I was sad or scared. I let it soothe my nerves. With the song came the memory of my home and the quiet, modest safety of walls that were plain but encompassing. A little green grass and the familiar sound of the few chickens we owned. The feeling of my mother's embrace like a cocoon that held me with such grace and purity and confidence, my shoulders dropped as I let myself imagine she was my kin.

"There, you don't have to tell me," Salanave said. "I can see she is comforting you even from afar. That's what mothers give; love that knows no time or distance. It is there forever. I'm not your mother, but I am your friend. And we are here in this place together, aren't we? We will look out for each other. You must forget what happened today. It meant nothing to them; let it mean nothing to you. Get strong, chèr. Keep remembering your family's love. That will sustain you. You understand?"

She pulled away to look at me again. Her eyes were just as flat on mine as ever. I appreciated her then, at that moment, and knew for the first time she truly was a friend. She was also a woman who was smart and not one to sugarcoat things. So, neither would I.

"I hate them," I told her plainly. "I wish they were dead. I hate them all."

She nodded slightly. "That's it, petit. Like I said, whatever sustains you."

8

———————

W hen I opened my eyes the next day, I blinked away the sleep to see Madame sitting in my room on a chair, her eyes on me. I got the feeling she'd been there for some time. I sat up quickly, clutching the rough blanket against me, and her eyes took in the action, widening in surprise. Then her lips curled in a smile, and she looked at me slyly.

"Aren't you the little play actor? My, my, to make such a fuss. The whole Palace is talking about how you ran naked, screaming through the halls last night as if you were back home running through the wilds of Africa. You're not in Africa anymore."

"I'm not from Africa. I'm from India."

"Your skin color says otherwise, chèr, but one of those places is no different from another. You're now in a civilized society. I've decided what your name will be. A very good friend of mine, François Voltaire, wrote a wonderful play about a wild, young heathen slave who is brave and strong and learns to be a good, Christian man. I shall call you Zamor, after that character. What do you think?"

I didn't care what they called me.

"But Madame, last night they made me ... made me...."

"'—they made me, made me'..." She put her fists up to her eyes, pantomiming like she was crying before dropping them to spear me with a look that said she was growing tired of me. "Child, any boy in France would gladly give a year of his life to be in the position you were in last night, and here you're acting like it was a punishment. If the King liked you any less, he would have punished you for real. Why, *two* girls! ... you're almost a grown boy, aren't you? But the disrespect and whining have got to stop. We've given you much leeway, but you disobeyed our King, and that reflects badly on me. No son of mine would behave that way. He gave you a public display because you were so imprudent as to publicly try to embarrass him. Now, we'll have no more of that, shall we? Shall we?"

The hurt was swelling in me and turning into something that hurt less and burned more.

"Non, Madame."

"Good," she stood and brushed her hands down the front of her gown, looking around the room and finding it wanting from the way her nose wrinkled. "It smells like mold. Don't give me a reason to have to come back down here. Now, get dressed quickly. Salanave is making a tray that I want you to take to us over to the Petit Trianon. Vite! Vite!" *Hurry, hurry!*

In the kitchen, Salanave gave me a tray of glasses half full of red wine. As it was early morning, I was confused. She shrugged at my questioning glance.

"Be careful with these," she said. "Missing or broken glasses gives Gaspard an excuse to beat someone. Even when he knows the nobles like to throw them into the fireplaces for sport."

The glasses clinked against each other as I picked up the silver tray. "All these? All the way to the Petit Trianon? But don't they have wine and glasses there already?"

She avoided my eyes. "Oui, but they want you to do this so you will. It's no big thing, really. Just walk slowly and try not to jostle them, and you'll be fine. Take them there, put each glass on the table against the wall in the foyer, and leave. Don't go poking around—God knows what you're likely to see. Leave them on that table and come back with this tray, you understand?"

"Oui, Madame," I said. I took the tray by its two handles, and the glasses began clinking. Salanave frowned and stepped forward.

"You'll never make it all that way holding them like that. Here," she picked it up, put it on my shoulder, moved one of my hands underneath to grasp it from the bottom and the other to the handle in front. "This will help you keep it steady and take some of that weight. Remember, no sudden movements, or it will all come tumbling down. It will start to feel heavier halfway there, so let the weight rest on that shoulder. Counting helps. Count your steps to take your mind off the worry—to help keep your concentration."

With that, she ushered me out the door on the path to the main Grand Canal walkway. It had never seemed so long, and I'd never had to dodge so many people. I took to the edge of the path to try to avoid them, taking small steps to avoid rattling the glasses.

The snow had melted in the morning sun, and it now felt like a true fall day, though a chill lingered. The path was pebbly and damp underfoot, and I took small, small steps. At some point, I stopped having to dodge people and realized I must be far away from the Palace. But those few glasses and the tray were starting to get heavy.

"One, two ... one, two..."

Up ahead, I saw a path veering off from the main drag and took a right to head to the little palace.

"Don't you break one of those glasses, blackamoor!"

Gaspard's voice came at me from behind so fast, loud, and close, I almost lost the tray but clutched it quickly, stopping where I stood. His footsteps came up heavy, and then he was standing in front of me. His smile was mean, and I wondered if he would just slap the glasses off the tray. His face said he wanted to.

"Oh no, I'm going to let you prove yourself. I hope you do a better job today than you did last night. Let's hope this task doesn't end in you naked and crying like a baby. Though, you did entertain the crowd, which is the most important thing."

My cheeks and eyeballs burned, and I struggled to keep my lips from trembling. "Pardonnez-moi, Manager. I must get these to the King."

He stood there a moment longer. Then, he stepped aside. "Off with you, then. Unlike you, I respect our King. Bring him what he asks and be quick about it; they don't have all day. Run, blackamoor, run!"

I didn't run. I kept going. I gripped the tray harder to keep focus and soon heard Gaspard's hard footsteps behind me, the sound receding as if he was going the other way. And then it was just me. I kept walking. "One, two ... one, two..."

By the time I reached the palace, despite the cold, the heaviness of the tray had deadened the feeling in my shoulder, and a line of sweat was coming down my face from under the heavy white wig. My legs felt like thick tree trunks, resistant to moving, but I had only to get the glasses inside. I took the front stone stairs carefully, clutching the tray more firmly so I could release one hand to open a tall glass-paneled door.

I spied a table directly in the foyer and took my small steps, careful to get to it and, blessedly, kneeled to put the tray as close to the surface as possible, then pulled the tray from my shoulder to rest on the table. The glasses jostled a bit, but they were intact. My shoulder had lost all feeling, though.

I pulled the wig off and wiped my brow with it, then unloaded the glasses quickly with the hand I could still feel fully. Remembering what Salanave said, I turned to leave when I heard the King's voice booming...

"...Is that you, page? Come say hello!" A woman's laughter followed.

I froze. Salanave had been clear, but I was afraid to anger the King again. I walked to the open door and saw the King lounging on a chair, Madame lounging on his lap. They both looked at me like they were surprised to see me.

"Oh, Zamor, we decided against socializing this morning," she said. "The King just wants to spend quiet time with me. We won't need the wine," she said innocently.

"You've chosen a name, I see. Good job, my love. Now we have something to call the impudent little shit. Why did you come all the way out here, boy? We have plenty of wine here already; I don't know why you would bring wine from the Palace. Why would he do something so silly?" The King asked her, his eyes sly and amusement lighting up his features.

She blinked as if she didn't know.

My cheeks burned. I'd been made a fool of again. "Pardonnez-moi," I said, bowing. I backed out of the room and left quickly, my eyes burning from wanting to cry. Their laughter followed me down the hall and out of the building. Without the extra weight, I left much faster than I came, throwing the ugly wig on the ground on my way out.

I should have gone back to the Palace, but I wanted to be left alone. So, I walked the short way to the Labyrinth instead. I walked in with my eyes down, letting the endless path soothe my nerves. Vaguely, I noticed when I passed the grand central statue where I usually turned back, but I kept going so I'd be left alone. Finally, I stopped and took a seat on an available bench.

A bird landed on the ground in front of me and chirped at me. At least, I imagined it was speaking to me. It took my attention for a while, and when it finally grew tired of speaking to a boy who didn't have the good sense to speak back, it picked up its wings and flew up ... up...

Until that moment, I hadn't realized how tall the trees in the Labyrinth were. Easily the height of four grown men stacked on top of each other's shoulders. It was a curious thing I'd never noticed. I curled up on the bench and lay my head down.

I was startled awake by the whipping up of the trees at the top. Slowly, I sat up and looked around. It wasn't night, but a storm began to come through, and those tall trees blocked the remaining light. The sun had gone, and I knew I'd stayed way longer than I should have. It was long past time to leave.

Taking the lane back the way I came, where there should have been an opening, I ran smack into a wall of trees. I went back and took another direction that seemed to go for a long time but then dead-ended.

My feet were starting to swell in my shoes, and I could feel the blister that would come, burning hot. *If I keep going, I'll find my way out*, I told myself. Jogging made me feel new energy, so I picked up my knees and began to sprint, figuring the faster I got dead-ended, the faster I'd eventually find the right path. Back and forth I went, moisture beading on my forehead despite the chilly air.

The gray sky was causing sharp contrasts now, and the statuary scenes I was passing were different from any I'd ever seen before this night.

"But that can't be," I mumbled, looking at a scene that looked the same as one I'd passed minutes ago. "That can't be."

I lost track of time as I walked down paths that led to nowhere and then tried again and again ... and again. Minutes or hours passed, and the dull sun fell below the tree line, abandoning this little boy who the Sun King's Labyrinth had not been made for. I was lost and now it was darkening. Truly darkening.

Madame will think I'm doing this for attention, I thought. The King would punish me again in some horrible way I couldn't imagine. And the Manager... I suddenly realized I'd left the silver platter at the Trianon when I was supposed to bring it back. Fear began crawling its way up my spine. I could see that platter in my mind's eye and hear Salanave reminding me that the Manager looked for any excuse to beat someone. I hadn't dropped a single glass, but I forgot the platter. And as badly as I didn't want a beating, it was better than the other punishment the King might order. It was the thought of the other punishment that drove me to panic, my heart pounding in my chest. The thought of the laughter of nameless, painted people looking at me like I was a creature and not a boy drew whimpers from my throat.

The statues that looked harmless in the daylight came alive in the shadows. Even the greenest trees turned into black fronds, then solid black walls, disappearing like everything around the Palace stage disappeared when the actors took the center, acting in candlelight. There were no human actors in the Labyrinth, but the stone and marble statues seemed to absorb all the existing light, glowing like pieces of the moon.

And there were so many scenes, one around every corner, sharp stone elbows poking into me when I made a wrong turn. More than once, I found myself staring into a face with blank eyes that seemed to be trying to speak. And something in that silent communication, mouths agape and bodies frozen in movement going nowhere, felt familiar. Too familiar.

Trembling took over my body, and I spurred my legs to run again. The faster I found all the dead ends, the faster I'd find the exit. That was my theory, anyway.

I heard the wash of rain seconds before a massive sheet of it dropped onto me and the ground in a splat. Then the ground trembled under the rumble of thunder. Still, those elbows kept poking me, and as the freezing cold rain soaked through my clothes instantly, like I had jumped into one of the lakes, now I couldn't see. And it was harder to breathe with the cold water pouring down.

I'm going to die. I felt it, deep inside. The boy lost to his home was now going to die lost in a Labyrinth. Forever lost.

I sank down on a bench across from one of the glowing statue scenes and a sharp crack of thunder rumbled the ground, followed by a brilliant strike of lightning that lit up the space in sudden, blinding whiteness. Even whiter was the statue in front of me.

I thought about what was waiting for me. Dying here was bad, but what I was going back to if I made it out could be worse. And if what had happened last night wasn't considered real punishment, what was?

The scene was of a fox and children interacting before me, the fox in mid-flight, water spewing from its mouth, and two children crouching with fear. In the daytime, when we went on fox hunts, they looked so helpless and scared. But the fox in front of me looked angry, like the spirit of a thousand hunted foxes filled it with wrath. While I knew it was a statue and it couldn't move, it felt alive underneath the marble. Alive and looking for me in the whiteness.

I stared at it as the rain soaked me, my bones growing cold and as still. Suddenly a memory flashed through me of last night. It was a visceral thing. When I'd been floating above it all, I hadn't felt anything, but what flashed through me jolted me like something took hold and shook me full force. Those two girls touching me in private places, putting my hands on them, too. Forcing reaction from me when I didn't want to give it while all those faces looked down, powdered and white with painted on lips, holding wine in frozen chalices and crystal and laughing at me. Laughing.

It was almost as if I was still down on that floor, the horror of it reactivated. I gasped and shook my head, trying to shake away that memory. I was fine with hovering above. I didn't want to be in it!

My head was pounding now, and I searched for something to calm me. From far off, a lullaby tried to reach me, but when I opened my lips to hum it, a crack of thunder stole the music from me and took me back to last night. And then back to that camp from so long ago, hearing little children taken to the woods. I heard the same cries, only this time they came from me. It was me feeling powerless and afraid and clutching myself. Me, being dragged off into the woods where the children cried...

My head clouded as my limbs grew stiff with cold.

I didn't want to be here. I didn't want to be on the floor of the salon. I didn't want to be in France. I didn't want to have to run from the manager. I didn't want to wear the stupid clothes. I didn't want to be in this place at all. If I could hover now like I did last night, I knew I'd be safe.

Miracle upon miracle, at the next lightning strike that washed the world in white— as that cold marble fox and I stared at each other—I let myself be lost in its frozen nothingness. Finally, I felt myself lifting, going up to that new place where I was safe, and nothing hurt. I was out of myself, somewhere above, trying to float up and out of the Labyrinth.

And I was happy there. I stayed there, blissful.

"There he is!" I heard a voice call from a distance. Down below, I saw a woman rush forward with some sort of blanket which she threw over the body of a statue frozen on a bench.

"Help me!" she called to two men who came into view carrying torches, dragging their feet.

"You help him. He was stupid enough to get himself lost, and you're stupid enough to follow. You can find your way out."

I recognized the voice. It was Gaspard.

"Manager! You can't leave us without light!" Salanave screamed.

"Give her a torch if she wants it. It'll be out soon enough, just like the others, and I don't plan to be in here when the last one goes. I suggest you get a move on, cook." His words prompted one of the men to put a torch in the torch holder, already sputtering under each drop of rain. They turned and left.

Down below, Salanave was rubbing her hands up and down the boy's arms, trying to get him to speak to her. Now she was alone, still talking to him. I heard the panic rise in her tone. Finally, I watched her raise her hand and heard the slap. Suddenly, I felt it. I was down in my body, and she was in front of me, shaking me, my cheek burning. Lightning filled the space, but instead of the white eyes of the statue, it was Salanave's brown ones.

"Oh, dear Lord, I thought you were gone for sure this time," she said, her voice coming out with what looked like steam in the rain. The softness in her eyes hardened to flint. "Why do I have to beat you to wake you up? This rain will freeze tonight, and Gaspard would have left you out here to die. If I'm the only one fighting to keep you alive, then I'm one too many. I'm not responsible for you—I won't do it again. I have my own children to worry after, and you're not mine, do you hear me? Come along. Hurry! Hold onto my cloak."

I hesitated because this angry woman wasn't a Salanave I knew. But at my hesitation, she hardened even further. "I said, grab my cloak. Do it now!"

"Yes, Madame Salanave," I said through numb lips. My mouth wouldn't stop moving, my teeth chattering beyond my control.

The torch wasn't out just yet, and she tried to shield it as she walked quickly, head down. She moved so fast and sure, very quickly the path before us opened up, and then we were out of the maze, the path to the Grand Canal visible before us.

At the Palace, she gave me dry clothes and put me in the kitchen by one of the giant ovens wrapped in blankets. While the others set out working on the food that was served all but the quietest hours of the day, Salanave brought me hot soup to eat while I shivered. The way she plopped the bowl down before me and wouldn't look at me told me she was still angry at me.

"You want to die, you do it on your own, don't do it on a task I sent you on," she mumbled.

"I'm sorry, Madame Salanave."

She rubbed her hands up and down my arms roughly and sniffled. I realized how cold she must be. I offered her the cup of soup I held, and she looked surprised but pinched her lips and shook her head curtly.

"Will they punish me again, do you think?" I asked her.

She slapped the towel she'd been using to wipe the table clean down. "Is that what this is about? Hear me well, petit: we serve at the pleasure of the King. He has the right to do what he wants with us anytime he wants and any way he wants. We are his subjects."

"Because he's ordained by God," I repeated. She turned away.

"That's right. And that means you might get used sometimes. Don't think of it as punishment, think of it as ... dues. Payment for living this charmed life."

"I don't want to live this life. They didn't ask me if I wanted it."

"And they never will."

"How did you find me, Madame Salanave?"

"You can drop the 'Madame.' Salanave is fine. I'm not your mother, I told you. If you go into the Labyrinth, take a baguette with you. I hid it from Gaspard under my cloak. As you go in, tear off pieces of it and leave them along the path. Not right where people can see it easily, but along the edges so only you can see it when you look for it. So, you can find your way out. I heard of somebody doing it in a story once, and it works. There's always a way out of any trap, mon petit," she said. "You just have to know to be prepared for anything. Because sometimes you don't know if you are walking into one. And sometimes you end up paying more than you want to get out of one."

I heeded her advice, but she didn't need to worry—I wouldn't be going into the Labyrinth again. I didn't need to because a piece of me was left inside it just like a piece of me was left in the woods on the way to France, and another piece of me would forever be left on that palace floor.

9

———

Frederick Barnier was a small, round man with full rosy cheeks that always shined like they had been buffed with cloth. He didn't seem excessively old, but the many folds and wrinkles above and underneath his eyes told a different story, as did his inability to stop his eyelids from constantly blinking as if he were always in the middle of a windstorm. His sandy-colored hair was wispy, and he never left a place without leaving behind a strand or two, of which he was aware. Constantly, he brushed the little table he used as a desk or his own coat while remarking that by the time I turned twelve, he'd be completely bald.

It was easy to like the inappropriately cheerful man. There was no earthly reason for him to be good-natured with the way most of the kids treated him, yet he was always happy. Sometimes I grew impatient with him teaching slowly like he had all the time in the world. I stayed behind for an hour or so after the other children left—noble children who spent their days harassing me—I stayed to ask him questions about the day's lessons.

Barnier worked out the lingering ragged edges of French, my second language. The English lessons were coming along so well, I wanted to start with another language, but he didn't know Spanish. I asked him to get me books so I could start learning on my own. He taught me history, mathematics, and literature, and when I stayed behind, I could ask him whatever I wanted.

The week after my escape attempt—and that other thing—as soon as the last child of the group session closed the door behind him, Barnier turned to me, his rosy cheeks ripe with concern.

"What were you thinking, Zamor? I heard you tried to escape after turning down the King's hospitality in front of his dinner guests. Mon Dieu, to speak to the King that way... to ask him that in front of all those people, and then to run. What were you thinking?"

He said nothing about the other thing the King had had done to me, so either he didn't know, or it didn't matter. I bristled at the omission. As much as I liked Salanave, her explanations had soured me, sounding suspiciously close to blaming me for what had happened. I didn't want to hear that from Barnier, so I didn't enlighten him on my punishment.

"He asked me what I wanted," I reminded him.

"You must know he didn't *really* mean it. Come now, you're not a little boy anymore; you've been around enough by now to know a bit of how the world works. He offered you a horse to impress the court, and you should have taken that. Instead, you stole one. Now he's on me asking what I'm teaching you as if I put you up to it."

"But I *was* taken by slavers. If that's the truth, then why am I wrong for saying it? If he is right for enslaving me, then why shouldn't he say so? The townspeople said it's against the law to enslave me. How can he hold me if it is against the law?"

"He can because he's the King; he can do anything. The laws belong to *him* to do with as he pleases, not for you to question. Besides, everyone knows the King is a fervent supporter of the slave trade in the colonies. It has been very lucrative for this country. And you are special. He wanted *you* because you are young and smaller than the average child of your age, and you picked up the language easily. He will always claim he hired you as a page. The Duc du Richelieu had them capturing many young boys until he found you."

"What happened to the others?"

"I don't know. I'm sure they're fine." He glanced away. "There's no point in imagining what you will never know. Somehow you made it, and that's all that's important. Don't you understand how fortunate you are? You could have easily ended up on one of the ships in Nantes to be sent to the colonies or the Americas to do hard labor. So, you mustn't make the King angry, son. Be happy at your good fortune."

"If I ride faster the next time, I might get a big start and get to my family before they can catch up. And my father, my village, will fight for me," I said, excitement rising.

"Now, now, haven't you been listening? It's time to grow up!" He looked at me like I was being ridiculous, but then his features softened along with his eyes.

"Ah, son, you cannot ride fast enough to get out of France before the royal guards find you, and there is no town that will harbor you for fear of the King's wrath. Don't you know where you are? Don't you remember how you got here? The journey?"

I thought I did. I was in that cart with the other children for what felt like years, being carted around. But after the painted man chose me, I was dragged away to another man in another cart with different children. We traveled a long time until we reached a place lively with activity on the edge of what seemed like more water than the world could hold, and I was put on a boat. I spent most of the time on the boat below the floor, sick in the bowels of the ship, losing my stomach into a bowl so often my slavers wouldn't come near me, disgusted by the smell. It seemed like I spent as much time in that boat that I had on land before it, as the days ran together. But then, finally, the incessant movement stopped and when I came up to the top, we had reached land. A different man grabbed me. A different cart. A different long journey with different children. And then, finally, one day I ended up in a wooden house-looking structure in the woods.

"SAY IT AGAIN," *the man said, from where he stood over me. Me sitting on the floor made his voice seem to come from on high. I looked down at the paper and the words there. Five hours since waking from a bucket of water in my face, I felt no more awake. The word swam in front of my face while my stomach grumbled.*

"...Mon-sure...?"

Thwack! The slap came against the side of my head. "Say it right!"

My ears rang. My lips bunched. I gripped the paper with my hands, willing my fingers to stop shaking because if I tore that paper, I'd get a beating. I took a deep breath to try again stuttering with the effort.

"...m-mon... mon..."

I felt the air move and waited for a fist to land against the side of my head when...

"Monsieur. Bonjour, Monsieur."

The girl's voice beside me had stopped a certain punch and I looked over at the little black girl. She was just a bit older than me, but she was catching on quicker than me.

"He's the one who needs to!" the man said. "I can't afford to deliver the two of you separately, it will eat into my profit. We're all three stuck here until the both of you learn, dammit, and I'm tired of being out here in the woods with the animals and you two. I'll beat it into him if..."

"I'll keep helping, Monsieur," she said, quickly and quietly. "I'll help him learn."

By this time, we'd been in that little room for almost a season, and I knew she had earned the trust of the man because, even though she was a child, she was way smarter than him and had figured out how to calm him down. This time, it was referring to him as a gentleman.

"He's young, Monsieur, it takes him longer. But I'll help and he'll get it. You'll see."

"Because the longer it takes the more impatient they get. He's been sold and his owners are expecting him!"

"Oui. But they expect him to speak French like a French person, that's what you said? I promise, we will all speak like native French people when we leave here. They will be very pleased with you. Maybe even give you a

bonus to make up for all the difficulty you have faced here having to deal with us."

The man stopped, mulling this over, the thought of extra money never having occurred to him.

"Do what you have to do to get him speaking right, fille. I have little patience."

And she did. We both spoke the same language, so I knew we came from the same, even if not the same town. After the man keeping us finished trying to drill the new language into me, he fed us bowls of gruel cooked over the fire in the wall and then retreated to a place he had created for himself in the opposite corner of the room.

She worked with me. He still slapped or punched me, and the others, when his patience wore out. But in the evenings, when he crawled into the corner of the hut and pulled the blanket he'd strung up for privacy closed, she would sit with me.

"Why are you helping me?" I whispered to her one night as we lay in on the floor under coarse blankets, the cold from outside seeping into our bones as the fire in the wall died. My lips were shaking with puffs of air letting out even more heat.

"They took my sister months before they raided our village again. When they came the second time they killed my parents and when they took me they said I would now be property of France, like all the others. She's all I have. If I'm enslaved, I can tolerate it so long as I have her. I'd never be able to get to France by myself."

"But how do you know for sure? And how will you find her? What if they take you away someplace else?"

"I don't know for sure, but I pray that I will end up with her. I pray that God will bring us together." Her voice quivered with her response, I couldn't tell if from cold or from emotion.

It seemed a fantastical notion that she could ever find her sister just by making it to France, but it seemed to make sense to her and kept her chin up and her voice strong. She taught me with patience better than the man did with violence. Long after he was snoring every night, she would still be teaching me in the light of a candle as the wind whistled through the cracks in the slats of wood, letting in frigid air.

"Monsieur... say it that second part softly, like a whisper," she instructed me. And finally, one day, when the man barked at me to say it, his hand balling into a fist prepared to punch the words out of me, I said...

"Mon-sieur." I said that second part like a whisper. His hand relaxed. After that, the lessons came faster as the girl's lessons built upon each other until the senseless sounds and letters became words of a living language...

STANDING THERE in the room with Barnier, this came back to me. But then, so did the reality that since I was taken there were whole periods of time I lost to blackness. Some from lack of consciousness. Some from simply going numb. It was like huge chunks of information had been taken from my memory like pieces of a puzzle. And the pieces I knew were all out of order. So, I didn't remember the journey in the way he was asking.

"I was born in 1762. I remember celebrating my fifth birthday. What year is it?" I asked.

"It is 1772. You've been here a year," he said as I did the numbers. Before Versailles, I had seen at least two seasons pass and snow cover the ground. Could I have been lost to the forest and the water for four years?

"Can you show me where we are and where I'm from?" I asked.

"Good idea." He turned to take a large piece of folded paper out of his bag and unfolded it on the table, along with a few coins. He took his finger and traced one of the shapes. "This paper, it's called a map."

"I know what a map is." I came closer to look. I'd never seen one this advanced, with so many lines.

"Well, look. This mass is France. And this..." He took his quill and put a spot in the upper middle section of the country. "This spot is where we are at Versailles. Do you remember when you traveled with the Madame to visit the noblewoman in Champagne last week? Remember how much time that took?"

I nodded, remembering being exhausted by the trip.

"Champagne is here," he made another spot that seemed two

fingertips away. It seemed impossible that something that seemed so close could be so far. "And where is your family, Zamor?"

"Chittagong, Bengal," I said, excited.

"Bengal, are you sure? I was told you were from Africa."

"My parents were from Africa. They were taken by the Portuguese to Chittagong but were never sold. They met and fell in love there and I was born there. Everyone in my community was black."

"Ah, I had heard rumor of African Indians but had never met any," he said. He smiled at me. "Until now."

I watched him closely, eager to see even a spot to represent my home on that paper. As his finger moved further away from the mass of France, the blood and hoped drained from my soul. It went farther and farther and farther from France. "Here is Bengal, your home. It used to be the Mughal Empire, but it's part of Britain's East India Company now. France was interested in the territory also. That explains a bit of how you ended up here."

I looked back and forth from Versailles to Champagne to Bengal while my mind did the calculations. We said nothing for a long moment, and then I rose, walked over to the window and looked out at the impossible outside, the insurmountable obstacle of getting home.

When I looked away, I saw a piece of pottery on a table. It was like a small child's piece of cooked clay, no doubt meant to cheer the space. It didn't cheer me; it was an affront to the despair of the moment. I picked it up and then threw it down against the floor with all my strength. The sight and sound of the shattered clay stopped my despair, and I immediately felt better.

10

—————

Dear Citizen,

You are probably thinking you're reading the diary of the most pathetic creature you've ever had the misfortune of coming across, but I assure you things would soon change for me.

I won't recount how bad it was for me sometimes. I can't bring myself to write down all the ways they humiliated me; I don't have it in my spirit to lay myself bare in that way. What made it all worse was that, secretly, I was struggling to remember my parents' faces. Truth be known, I was struggling to remember any little bit of me I'd been before the kidnapping. And by 1772, I no longer remembered my true full name.

I was forgetting me and, coincidentally, in this place, everyone— from the King to the nobles to their children—all set out to remind me that I was the smallest. Whenever I poked my head up, I was knocked down again, literally and figuratively. Their treatment of me stripped away the layers of who I used to be.

Before you judge me, I implore you to remember I was a child. I'd never had a chance to develop anything of character—no chance to truly learn what I should be as a person before they began stripping away the little bit of me that thought I was something. So, I fell easily to hating myself.

But then, numbness began to give way to anger. Because while I was forgetting my parents' faces, a tiny part of me remembered what it felt like to be loved, and I missed it. Oh, how I missed it. An echo of that feeling lived deep inside, and it chafed with every insult and bristled with every slight. A thousand tiny cuts in my confidence were hard to keep healing over and over.

This isn't a fairy tale. No godmother waved a wand to turn me into a crown prince. But very shortly after my episode in the Labyrinth, I grew tired of being set upon.

In my ten-year-old wisdom, I was about to find my own ways to protect myself. Desperation became my motivation, and it would bring out the worst in me.

But to be fair, the worst parts of me were the parts that kept me alive.

—Zamor

11

"**G**ood evening, Madame," a noble boy around my age said to her as I trailed behind her through the dining room for dinner. He was so hospitable to her I should have suspected something—the noble-born were never that nice to her by choice.

He was one of two boys standing to the side of the room against the wall. One of them wore a very light blue satin coat and breeches, his dark brown hair gathered in a matching blue ribbon that hung low on his neck. Light reflected off him like he was a bright new present.

We walked the narrow space between the wall and the polished wooden table. Madame's dress barely allowed space on either side of her, so I was forced to walk about two feet behind due to her train. She passed them, and as soon as her face cleared, the boy in blue looked at me, his face twitching in a smirk as he elbowed the shorter blond child beside him. They both watched me like vultures watching a wounded animal.

As soon as I passed, the brown-haired one stuck out his foot. The room whirled, and I fell hard and headlong into the shiny wooden table. My mouth took the blow on the way down, causing my teeth to split the lip inside.

The room exploded with laughter. I was stunned for a moment but then pulled myself up, touching my fingers to my face. I saw Madame laughing quietly behind the palm of one gloved hand. Snickering, delicately and ladylike.

I pulled a lace square from the pocket of my embroidered satin jacket and pressed it to my busted lip. It was immediately saturated red, but she had already turned to keep walking, and I kept going behind her to my place at her side.

Madame snapped her fingers to a servant who ran off and came back soon with a sturdier cloth for me to hold to my lip, switching out my handkerchief until the bleeding slowed. Across the table the brats watched me, smiling. Very pleased with themselves.

The King gave a brief hello and started his meal while everyone waited. He chewed without lifting his eyes, as if he dined alone. Finally, after some minutes, when he was on his third course, he lifted his hand and gave a little wave, and then the room relaxed, and everyone began the ceremony of eating.

Madame motioned me to lean down and whispered in my ear: "Don't sulk. The parents of those children are very important to the King. I have to keep these people happy, Zamor. It's a difficult thing. I love you so much and hate to see you hurt."

I wasn't stupid, but I was still a child. She spoke so sincerely it was easy to believe her.

I spooned some broth-flavored meal into my mouth and looked over at Madame's plate and the plates of the other diners. They were eating meat. Maybe it was venison. It smelled good. I reached over and took some from the platter with one of my bare hands, earning gasps and whispers as the other diners noticed. When my hand came way it was with a chunk of the most greasy and delicious piece of meat I'd ever seen. I began to eat.

"That's right, page, you take what you want in this place!" The King called out, leading to laughter as everyone went back to what they were doing.

"Alright then," Madame said. "You may have it."

I already did. I was chewing when a servant came up beside me. It was a boy about my age with red hair. He held a bottle of wine over my glass, uncertainly, until the King noticed him and swirled his finger. The boy poured me glass of red wine, eyes large. Then, just before he stepped away, he whispered:

"You're very brave. Want to play later?"

I looked at him and his face held no deceit. I nodded, eagerly, and wiped my mouth with my sleeve, whispering back, "I'll bring you some of this." He watched as I took some of my meat, looked to make sure no one was watching, and wrapped it in a napkin. His eyes were steady on the package like it was gold instead of a bit of meat.

"See you later!" he said, moving on to serve more wine.

They called him Leroux—*the red-haired one*—and he was the son of one of the gardeners.

"But I can't garden," he said over a mouthful of venison meat as we sat together on a bench along a path in one of the garden groves. It was late but most of our work was done and, frankly, no one was looking for us. Madame had gone to bed early with the King and I was happy to have finally met a friend. He continued to talk as if no one ever listened to him and he finally had someone's ear. "I kill everything I try to grow. My papa says he will kill me if I kill another one of his plants. He says my hands are like giant bricks and don't do anything but kill."

"I never tried to grow anything," I told him. "Is it hard?"

"It's impossible. What's your name?" He looked at me, still chewing.

"Zamor."

"Thank you for the meat. If I took it back to my room my papa would take it from me, or he'd accuse me of stealing it. That was something, seeing you just reach over and take it like that. Aren't you afraid of the King? He could have cut your hand off for stealing!"

"Madame gives me meat, anyway. I knew he wouldn't cut my hand off. How long have you been here?"

"Mon Dieu, what a silly question. *All my life*, of course. All of us kid servants have. We grow into our roles. Don't you know how things work? I come from four generations of gardeners."

"But you can't grow anything,"

"Still, all my kinfolk worked for the House of Bourbon, we're very proud of that. My maman worked in the kitchen. She died so now it's just me and papa. He doesn't like it being just us two, much. I'm trying to make it so I'm not a burden to him. So, he'll love me."

"But if you can't be a gardener, what will you be?"

"What I am. A servant. And when I grow up my kids will be servants here, too. It's an honor to be a servant in the House of Bourbon."

Our first conversation was the most serious conversation Leroux and I ever had. Most of the time we played a game where one of us tapped the other on the shoulder and the one that got tapped would chase the other. Of course, I made the rule that we could never take the game into the Labyrinth for obvious reasons. Or we played with stones. Or we posed in funny positions next to the statues of stone people.

Madame called Leroux a "lowly" servant, but I didn't care, and neither did he. He was my friend and I needed friends.

One day, I was walking in the botanical gardens and drifted from the main area into a hidden, weeded section behind a shrub. Hidden from sight, it was an area that wasn't as well-kept because it didn't need to be. I noticed a strange-looking plant with a flower that protruded with a berry in the center. It didn't look like a raspberry or any fruit I knew. I reached over to pick it.

"Stop! Don't touch that!" said a man who came over to me, fast. "What are you doing over here messing around with the devil's berries. They don't bother you, don't bother them."

"What's a devil's berry?"

"It's that fruit right there you were about to pick!" He came over and swatted me away, getting me to step back. "Touch that with your hands and it will kill you, boy."

"Then why don't you pull it out if it's so dangerous?"

He straightened and looked at me. "You're that new page my boy's been hanging out with, aren't you?"

It was Leroux's father. There were around a hundred gardeners so the chance I found Leroux's father was a surprise.

"Yes, Monsieur. If it's dangerous, why's it here?"

"Gaspard send you?" His face twisted with anger. "You tell that son of a bastard that I come from four generations of gardeners, and we have been loyal to the House of Bourbon. They caught the man who poisoned all those people. Anybody else gets poisoned, it's got nothing to do with me."

"The Manager didn't send me..."

"I've been loyal to these royals! Always! A garden full of belladonna..."

"What's belladonna?"

"I just told you, devil's berries! How many times do I have to say it! How should I know why it's still here. After all those poisonings in the house you would have thought the King would want it gone, but who knows... maybe he didn't like the people that got killed. I don't know. It's not my business. It was planted by the Sun King. It's still here because the Well-Beloved hasn't told us to pull it and that's all I know. And, in case anyone's asking, I've worked in this garden full of belladonna all my life and never once have I ever even considered slipping a devil's berry into *anyone*'s food." He swiped his arms to stress the point. "And I could have. I've had plenty of chances. But I love the House of Bourbon and I love my King and I would die for him. You go back and tell that to Gaspard, the asshole."

He marched away like he'd ended an argument I never knew we were having. Later, I told Leroux.

"Don't pay him any mind. He talks like that when he's mad. The Manager Gaspard comes around to needle him sometimes and it gets to him. He likes to scare the gardeners. But it just makes my papa suspicious of everybody. He wasn't even the head gardener when all those poisonings happened. But he's always worried he'll be blamed."

I was watching Leroux talk but my mind was stuck.

There was poison in the garden? Easily accessible poison? Until the moment the gardener had spoken, I hadn't even considered the fact that there were means to poison something, if someone were so inclined.

Unfortunately, my friendship with Leroux ended almost as quickly as it started when an accusation from a nobleman that my friend had spilled a full chamber pot all over the man's three-hundred-year-old hand-carved wooden bed post and the contents had sunk into the wood and warped it. Leroux denied it, of course, but he and his father had to stand before Gaspard who took the side of the nobles and fired Leroux and his father on the spot.

I was out in the hallway when the nobles left the room looking smug and the Manager Gaspard came out, glanced at me, and kept going. When I poked my head inside, Leroux was pleading his case.

"I swear, papa, I didn't do it. It wasn't me! I—"

The gardener back-handed Leroux so hard the boy staggered. I winced.

"You've been nothing but a nuisance since you were born and now you've lost me my identity in the esteemed House of Bourbon. You gave that bastard just the reason he wanted to get rid of me. I wish you'd died with that red-headed bitch of a mother of yours."

Leroux held his reddened cheek, eyes welling with tears and his father pushed past me out the door. I came inside.

"I'll talk to the King and tell him," I told Leroux.

"No, don't do that. My papa wanted to believe them. You weren't in here. The first thing he did was offer to send me away, almost before they got the lie out of their mouths. Didn't matter if I did it or not. No matter what I do, he hates me. I'll go live with my aunt, she's nice."

And just like that, my one friend was gone.

12

———

I was walking down a hallway on my way back to the servants' quarters when, suddenly, I was flanked on both sides and behind by three different boys. "Hello, Mr. Goose," one of them said to me. I barely had a chance to look at him before they wrestled me into a hallway. The lead boy, smelling of escargot and privilege, pinned me to the wall with one hand against my chest while the other two held my arms.

Now, I knew whatever was coming was inevitable. I was outnumbered, and there was no way to wriggle free. So, when I saw somebody hand the leader a little pot with a spoon sticking out of it, I knew what was next.

"The goose wants to be fed," he said, his face wearing a furious smirk. He was sweating as if the sheer thought of attacking me was making him overheat. I pinched my lips shut and tried to turn my head one way or the other to get away from what was coming, but there are only so many ways you can move your head when you're trapped. Finally, in my twisting with him trying to catch up, we converged in the same spot at the same time, and I felt the jarring clang of silver against bone as the spoon hit its mark.

He shoved a pudding into my mouth, clanging the spoon against my teeth while his friends tried, unsuccessfully, to hide their laughter. His brow was red and fevered from this hurried assault as he proceeded to spoon faster than I could absorb or swallow, the yellow, gelatinous porridge spilling out over my lips and chin. As I struggled to keep from choking, through my watering eyes, I saw Madame standing not ten feet away. My benefactress kept her face pointed away from me, so I only saw her profile. I tried to call out, was stifled by another spoonful, and then fell silent. I let my eyes glaze over and choked my way through the process while she chatted and sipped eau-de-vie from a tiny glass.

I couldn't lie to myself anymore. After almost a year, I'd be a fool not to see she was just as bad as the rest of them, armed with a unique talent for ignoring what she didn't want to see.

The physical attacks weren't the extent of it. It became the Palace pastime for those nobles to find new ways to insult and degrade me with endless jokes.

Look at how ugly it is.

How can you bear to be near it all the time?

The little heathen might learn something from being around good Christian people.

It's like a little monkey, only monkeys are cute.

It. The term "it" was worse than the insults or the names. ... their laughter rang in my ears long after I heard it. It bounced off the walls and plagued my dreams.

When it got very bad, I would stand up and storm out of a room, only to be followed by their laughter, with Madame's voice one of the loudest.

"Don't take it personally," Salanave told me. "When they're torturing you, they're not torturing her, and she'll take that respite at anyone's expense."

I had laid my head on the table, exhausted. It felt like I couldn't lift my head; my eyes always found the ground, like those men in the stables the first day I arrived. It was safer to keep your eyes on the ground in this place.

"Hey, there," she said, her voice buoyant like she was trying to infuse excitement into it. "On to more important things. I have a project for you, petit. I need you to take care of my levain."

I lifted my head. "What's that?"

She walked across the kitchen and took hold of a jar sitting on a counter close to one of the stone ovens that was always stoked. "There are jars of levain all over this kitchen, but this one, I brought with me when I earned head cook after the last one died. I brought it from home. This levain is seventy-five years old, give or take a year. She's a beauty, isn't she?"

I looked into the jar at what looked like ugly wet dough. "You lie."

"I'm not! This levain was passed down from my grand-mere. She requires regular food and water to stay alive, and I provide it faithfully."

"Alive? It's just nasty-looking dough, Salanave."

"Nasty? Is my bread nasty? It doesn't look nasty when you're slathering it with butter and shoving it into your face, Monsieur. Dough comes to life if you feed it. We keep it alive so we can continue to take pieces from it to make new bread, just like you've seen the gardeners take clippings to make new plants. Instead of food through the soil, we feed the levain more of what made it to keep it alive. Don't believe me, watch and see." She proceeded to walk over to a bowl, grab a handful of wheat flour, and toss it in. She followed with water and stirred with a wooden spoon. "You saw what I did. That's your job from now on—keep it alive, like your very own pet."

At my look, she rolled her eyes. "Fine. Come back in a couple of hours and you'll see." She covered it with a cloth, and I left while she was putting the jar back on the counter next to the warm oven, annoyed that she was treating me like a stupid, gullible child. After doing my chores, I returned to the kitchen, really only to find something good to snack on, and remembered my pet. I walked over and snatched the cloth off the jar to find the mass was double the size, puffy, and wobbly, smelling like the fermented wheat drink I'd smelled some people drinking on game night.

"You see?" She had come in quietly and her voice over my

shoulder was warm. "Like I said, it comes to life when you feed it. You can't see them, but the dough itself turns into lots of little eaters. It's going to be your job to feed her every couple of days when she looks low."

And so, I did.

I was fascinated by the way the mass of nothing would sit in that jar quiet and still until I fed it, and then it would billow up to double its size while Salanave took some out every day to make baguettes or rolls or thick loaves of bread. I started speeding through my chores so I could run to the kitchen to check on my project.

Then, one day, Salanave fed the dough, stirred and covered it, and handed it to me. "Take it over to that far corner over there and leave it on the table."

"But it's cold over there. The eaters will die."

"Do what I say. We'll leave it there for a couple of days. Don't feed it until I tell you to."

I was confused. First, she told me taking care of it was my responsibility, and then she told me to leave it to freeze next to a window.

Every day when I looked at the jar, it seemed like the dough was sinking in on itself, becoming a mass of nothing. But just like that first day, it was taking every bit of my attention. I was thinking about *her* when I worked, and whenever Salanave's back was turned, I would slip the cloth off to look at my ward, only to have the cook yell at me to cover it back. Every day it looked worse.

Four days later, I ran in from doing my chores, pulled off the cloth, and felt a sinking in the pit of my stomach when I looked down at it. There was a layer of black liquid on top. She had lost her life's blood.

"Zamor! Cover that up!" Salanave yelled at me.

But looking down into that jar made me feel like the world was ending. My eyes filled. "You're killing *her*, Salanave! The eaters are dead!"

"Calm down," she said, coming over, looking down.

The jar was ice cold in my hands, cold as winter. Cold as frozen marble and stone. "The eaters are dead, Salanave; you killed them! Everything dies in this place. I hate it here!"

She must have finally realized I was on the verge of a full-blown fit because she stopped teasing.

"Shush. Calm down. No one's killing anything, petit. You think I would kill my own levain passed down three generations for a joke? Look, let's bring it over next to the fire again." When she prodded it with a spoon and I saw the dough was gray underneath the black liquid, finally the tears spilled over onto my cheeks.

"It's dead underneath the dough blood!"

"Dough blood? What in the world? What an imagination on you! No, it's not blood; it's just bile. You know—how you feel when you're very hungry, and something is rumbling in your stomach even though there's no food in it? All the liquid down there churning, wanting something to eat, trying to come up your throat? That's what this is. Wipe your eyes, petit; you are simply too sensitive. You go from crying to completely numb. There's no middle ground with you. Look, let's feed her."

She didn't bother making a game of it, letting me do it—she looked like she'd do anything to stop my blubbering. I wiped an arm across my cheeks, watching her finally give it flour and water and a good stir. I looked at her serious face, thinking Salanave was no better than the rest, torturing a living thing the way she was. I had thought she was a good person, but I was wrong.

"See, it's fed. It's fed! Now go. I'll leave it here by the fire to get nice and toasty. Now, go pull yourself together; I don't need Madame down here asking me what's wrong with you. Come back tonight after dinner, not a minute before."

After dinner, I would come and find my project dead, I knew. I didn't want to see a dead thing. I took my time, and it was the longest day ever, but after the meal was over, I dragged myself into the kitchen to wait for her to tell me it was dead after all. Salanave was over by the table, slicing thin, thin pieces of ham and looked up when I came it. Then she went back to slicing.

"Go ahead," she mumbled. The jar was on the counter, almost dwarfed by a cloud of puffy, bubbling dough rising up and spilling over the edges of the jar, still clinging to the main mass by strands. It was like it was holding on to itself with arms. I ran over to it and looked it over from all sides, my insides brightening and a stupid smile spreading over my face.

"You see? It's fine," she said, her voice defensive.

"No thanks to you," I told her, feeling renewed protectiveness. "You might have killed her."

"*Many* thanks to me! How do you think it stays healthy? Anything can grow in the best conditions. Of course, it was happy over by the fire being fed regularly and stuffed like a spoiled little pig. So, I shocked it out of complacency. I took away its comfortable home and readily available food, and the other little eaters woke right up."

"What other eaters?"

"The *warrior* eaters that wake up when the dough is uncomfortable. The ones that know how to eat just enough to survive and curl up tightly to save energy and heat. Just like people curl up in a ball when we're scared or cold or trying to hide—that's what the levain does to protect itself while those warrior eaters go into survival mode. Even cold and hungry, the warriors get stronger. They figure out how to survive on next to nothing. They get mad, and that generates heat. They steadily churn along making that, what'd you call it...? Dough blood? It's just a side effect telling you they're still alive. So, when the dough finally gets a little warmer—and they get some food and feel out of danger—the soft-bellied ones wake up again, and all of them come out to celebrate. Back to life but something new. Healthier and stronger. And better tasting—more personality and flavor. That's how she's still alive after seventy-five years. And if we keep doing it right, she'll live long after I'm gone. But she'd never have survived this long if all she had it was easy. She'd be too weak to weather the storms if she never had to fight."

I was captivated by her story and the dough. I didn't know if Salanave meant the story to touch me so deeply, or if she was just really fascinated by her own levain, but I thought about it for days afterward, thinking that if a plant and bread dough had little eaters in them to help them survive, maybe I did, too. Maybe my eaters were what sent me up above when I was scared. Maybe the eaters were where my greatness lived.

One day I was in Madame's apartments with her ladies when one of them carried Madame's chamber pot to the window, dumped it, and then pulled back in mock concern, proclaiming loudly out the window, "I'm so sorry, Madame la Dauphine!" Then, to the room, she said, slyly: "The Dauphine practically walked *right under* the chamber pot."

Madame's ladies dissolved into peals of laughter, and though Madame didn't join them, I saw her eyes glisten with delight as she powdered her cheeks. So much for feeling kindly toward the future queen she expected to be great friends with. Nothing like a bowl of steaming hot piss and shit raining down upon your head to inspire friendship.

The look on Madame's face—the barely noticeable little look of satisfaction—made her chin come up and put a gleam in her eye. That's when I realized the secret.

The little warrior eaters in me kept me alive, took me out of my body and sent me up above when I felt like I was dying, but I never truly fed them afterward. Or maybe I did. I fed them with my own pain. And the more I gave it, the more I felt.

But the people at court grew in popularity, in happiness, in stature, and in reputation in direct proportion to the devilment they did to others. Madame and all these people fed on the pain and discomfort of each other and of me. They became *stronger* because of it. With every tear I shed, the person who caused it stood a little bit taller, looked a little more satisfied.

As Madame sat powdering her cheeks, flushed with pleasure, I could almost see her warrior eaters feeding and billowing up in satisfaction at the insult meted out to the Dauphine on her behalf. I could feel the power floating off her in waves, her cheeks blossoming pink with pleasure over the Dauphine's humiliation.

I saw it clearly, now. My previous mistake had been feeding on *my own* pain, eating myself up from the inside. No more of that—not when I could sustain myself on the pain of others and grow my strength by doing more of it. By directing the pain outside of myself, I would save myself and become something new. Something great.

13

———————

One morning, I woke early, padding softly to get to the kitchen before anyone else. The room was empty, pots and pans gleaming from the faint burgeoning sun like a twinkle of light in the sky. I had a candle in my hand, but the room tossed shadows around that made the room seem more like a dungeon than the kitchen that would be alive with wonderful smells and warmth soon enough.

But I would start the good smells myself. I took a small saucepan down from a hook and then opened the front of the stove. A pile of wood lay against a wall, so I grabbed some sticks to shove into the oven. Then I used Salanave's flint to start a fire and closed the front. I poured water from a pitcher into the pan and added a thick spatula of brown paste from a pot she kept close by. Then I took an egg from the counter, beat it in a small bowl, and after the chocolat water came to a simmer, pulled it off the heat and mixed in the beaten egg.

I set two bowls onto the wooden worktable and poured the heated chocolat into each bowl. Now, for the real reason I was here.

I walked through the room and into the storeroom beyond. Shelves of food supplies, more pots and pans and dishes, cutlery, and next to the kitchen, boxes and buckets filled the space. I raised my candle, looking around, then thought to look lowest to the ground under the bottom shelf. I crouched, tilted the candle, and was rewarded with the thing I came looking for, grabbing it in my hand.

"What are you doing, petit?"

Salanave's voice surprised me, and I looked over my shoulder quickly, forgetting to shield what was in my hand. Her sharp gaze lit upon it as I shoved it back out of sight.

"Nothing," I lied. "Only looking for sugar."

"The sugar is in the kitchen where it always is. And why are there two bowls of chocolat on the table?"

I stood and headed into the kitchen, trying to look innocent.

"No important reason, Madame Salanave, I'm just bringing chocolat to Madame and the King.

"Taking chocolat to them both? You've never done that before. When did that start?"

"Today," I said. "The King and I had a nice conversation yesterday, and I wanted to show him how much I appreciate him." I settled the two bowls on the tray, willing her to leave so I could finish what I'd started. I forced my face to be still, but unlike Madame, I had trouble looking her in the eye when I lied.

She slipped quickly into the storeroom, and I knew she was double-checking what she had seen me shove back into place. When she came out her normally expressionless face was stiff with anger. She glared at me hard, and I fought to keep my eyes from shifting away from hers.

"You must have had a nice conversation with the King yesterday to make you want to do such a kindness for him today. I didn't know you even knew how to make chocolat."

"I watch you."

"Yes, you watch a lot of things, don't you? You and the King, both a pair of watchers, aren't you? Well, Madame thinks *I* make the chocolat each morning." She walked over and took the two bowls of chocolat. I watched, dismayed, as she dumped one into the sink. "I'll not have her telling the guards I suddenly decided to bring the King chocolat he didn't ask for, and I'll not be questioned as to why her morning drink tastes off. As long as they believe I'm responsible for their food and drink, nothing that is not made by my hands, or the hands of the other cooks will come out of this kitchen." She dumped the other and turned back angry.

"*Hers* wouldn't have tasted off," I said. "Only his, and he doesn't take chocolat often enough to notice." Under her stare, I withered a bit.

"I should turn you in myself, right now. The last man who tried to harm the King had his entrails spread across half the countryside after the horses finished pulling him apart. If anyone finds out that I didn't..." She didn't finish the sentence but punctuated her anger by banging the pot back onto the fire, filling it with more water and the waxy-looking brown paste. "The next time, I might not be here to save you from yourself. Hundreds of people are in and out of this kitchen all day; it might have been any one of them and not me."

"I didn't need you to save me. It would have worked."

"Thank God I stopped you, then. You are old enough to understand that if anything were to happen to anyone in this place, you are the first person who would be suspected."

"Me, why me?"

"If you don't know that by now, then you are truly still a child and not smart enough to get away with what you were about to try." She came over to me and took my shoulders in her hands firmly, looking into my face. "You'll never try that again, and we'll never speak of it again. Because if anything happens to him, I will turn you in myself and claim to be as clueless as everyone else as to how you could do such a thing. You say otherwise, and I'll call you a liar to your face. You will be out there alone, and you will hang."

14

"**C**ome in, Zamor."

I'd been summoned by the King. Though we had dinners together and sometimes played board games together, I never forgot what he'd had done to me. He was standing in front of a window, staring at something in his hand when I stepped inside.

"Come here." He turned to me and handed me the thing in his hand. I looked down and was immediately intrigued. It was a tiny clock. I'd seen many clocks in the Palace, but none this miniature. It was small enough to fit in my palm and ticked softly. I put my ear to it, and I couldn't help but smile at the sound of the tiny machine chugging along.

It was only then that I noticed there were many little clocks in this room, on the desk, hidden behind glass, sat on tables...

"I like the mechanics of things," he said. "Machines and science. Astronomy and the stars. Science intrigues me. It's amazing what men make when inspired, like this thing they're calling *electricity*. The scope of what they say it can do is mind-boggling. They take power from the heavens and capture it to make machines run."

My mind started working. "How can they take power from heaven?"

"I don't know, but they say they can use it to light up rooms, so we'll never need candles at night. Fake light that we can turn on at will. There is an American named Benjamin Franklin. He came here last week. He wanted to discuss his theory of taking energy from the sky, from a lightning bolt."

I thought about the lightning bolts the night I was trapped in the maze. This Franklin person was right, I believed. The lightning was a living thing.

"You're a clever child, Zamor, with a smart tongue. You beat me at chess, and I don't even let you. Instructor Barnier tells me you're a strong learner. Despite your previous poor behavior, he thinks you're worth keeping."

"Instructor Barnier is wrong," I mumbled, my head down. I was taking my life in my hands, I knew, but I couldn't help myself. "I'm not worth keeping. You should send me home immediately. I promise the longer I stay, the smarter my tongue will get."

"No, you will stay here and learn to curb your temper. I've noticed it. Many people have. It's sharp, fast, and cutting. You'll need to dull it as we all must do it. Even me. I can't always say what I want. I sometimes fight my own tongue to stay still in my mouth, but I do it because to use it to cut down the people I need most will cause me more harm than any pleasure speaking can provide. We express ourselves in other ways when we can't with our tongues. As you've been demonstrating."

I bit my lip and handed his watch back to him. I stepped away from him, clasping my hands behind my back and staring at a wall like I had seen the other servants do. He continued.

"Monsieur Franklin will be back here again next week. You'll meet him when he comes. Ask him all the questions you want. My children and the Dauphin, none of them believe in electricity, but something told me you would."

I didn't respond. I wanted to meet Benjamin Franklin, but I still hated the King.

"I don't want you to be a wooden doll; I want you to speak, Zamor!" he said testily. "This is no place for whining or holding a grudge. If you can't move beyond petty grievances, you will have a hard time surviving at Versailles. This is a den of thieves, cowards, and whores, any one of them with enough money to fund a small country. If you don't stand firm, they will tear you apart."

"They already do, and you let them. Madame lets them. You punished me for speaking honestly to you, and now you tell me you want me to speak honestly. Why can't I go home?"

"Because Madame looks for you every morning and breathes a sigh of relief when she sees you. The Favorite loves you very much. She has few friends in this place, as you know. You're not here to wear fancy clothes or to walk like a shadow behind her; you're here to be her support. You're here to be one person she never has to worry about, something she can call her own. Besides," he gave me a quick sideways glance. "Your parents don't want you anymore; otherwise, they wouldn't have sold you to those slavers."

My blood gelled in my veins. "That's not true. They love me."

"That may be, son, but they also can't afford you. They felt it was kinder to sell you to people who could keep you fed than to watch you slowly starve. But you don't have to believe me. You tell me, did your parents have the money to keep you?"

My parents didn't have any money. We ate fish sometimes but mostly grains and vegetables from the garden. My mother worked at home and did cleaning work in the village. My father worked the docks and always came home tired, and still, we never had money for what we needed.

"Cardinal Richelieu didn't take you from your home, did he? He picked you from a group of children that had already been sold into slavery. He *saved* you from a difficult fate." A flash of memory of the painted man coming into our camp at night and picking me out made me wonder, a tiny sliver of wonder, if he was telling the truth. "You made such a fuss a short while ago I sent a messenger to your home."

My lips grew numb with trembling and hope. "They went to my home?"

"Yes, we explained to your parents that we have you and you are safe and well-fed, but that you missed them, and we could easily send you back if they wanted. They expressed their deep love for you but asked us to keep you here. They understand that you have a much better life in this household than anything they could provide. And they mentioned that with age, you'd been increasingly more difficult to deal with. Different from the sweet boy you used to be. They thought perhaps a firmer hand would shape you into a decent young man and thanked us. So, you see, there is no need to feel sad at all. *They* want you to be here."

I remembered how distant my parents had been to me before I was taken. I remembered the sneaky glances and the whispering. I remembered how my mother stopped wanting to play with me and stopped smiling. Was it true? Was it me?

Pinpricks on the inside of my eyelids made me blink. He took a handkerchief from his coat to push into my hand as he walked from the window to a sideboard lined with decanters of varying shades of amber liquid.

"*You are home*, Zamor. After that first uncomfortable bit, you've been doing an excellent job becoming a part of this household. You've learned your lesson. The Favorite would be heartbroken if you were to leave, so you will not leave, and that's that. And now that your parents know where you are, I'm sure if their circumstances should change, they'll come for you. Now, let's not discuss this again." He had looked back and forth among the decanters as if the decision of which to choose was of the utmost importance. He settled on the tall one and removed the cap, proceeding to pour the reddish drink into two glasses. Capping the bottle, he moved back to his desk, handing one drink to me on the way while motioning me to sit in the chair opposite his desk. I sat, numb. It was hard to focus my eyes.

"Drink, Zamor. It will help."

I moved the glass to my lips, took a drink, and coughed with the burning down my throat. But I liked the way it burned, even with the bitterness. I felt the warmth streak down the inside of my body and liked that my mouth was now the center of my attention. I took another drink.

"That's it. Good cognac can fix many things. Fine things can make even the most difficult of situations palatable. I've given you license to use your voice, and I haven't punished you for saying what you want to the nobles, have I? I've let you at them, and I've been kind to you, haven't I?"

It didn't seem a question he wanted an answer to since he immediately sipped his drink and leaned back in the chair that groaned in protest, his coat trailing on the ground and exposing his portly torso and small breech-covered legs.

"Now tell me, what else have you learned from your instructor?"

I took more of the cognac and clutched at the chance to think of something else—anything else—other than my parents selling me to slavers.

"I've learned more from watching people," I mumbled, still smarting. "People around here praise you a thousand times a day, which is curious. I think, surely a man who is so powerful doesn't need so many people telling him that he's powerful. Just as I don't need to be told I'm clever." His quick look at me made me follow up. "But I'm just a lowly page, it doesn't matter what I think," I said. Small. I was trying.

He smiled wryly. "No, please, continue. Here in private quarters is the proper place to express yourself, and I really must know what's on your mind. Come, tell me."

"There are too many people here. Sometimes I just want to go where there aren't so many people."

"That's why I built the Petit Trianon so long ago for my last Favorite, for when it is too difficult at court. It's like the Favorite's own little palace. When we are at Louveciennes or the Petit Trianon, she almost feels as if she's Queen."

"Why can't she be Queen if you love her? Why not marry her?"

"That's not the way things work. The church barely tolerates her as my mistress; they would excommunicate me entirely if I went so far as to try to marry her, even if she would never be Queen. They would declare me insane and force me from the throne, and no woman is worth that. I offer her what I can."

"But you're the King. The greatest and most powerful."

He looked out the window, but his face settled into a sardonic expression as if he knew I was trying to dig into his open wound. "I am great, but the royal court is a universe. Even though I'm at the center, I need the support of the stars. The *Sun King* needed to be with lots of people. He was a brilliant man, but he needed constant attention. He was at his best in this environment. He would put on plays and act in them. He liked to dress up and dance for the court—he loved the applause. Like a planet in the solar system, he needed that system. But he would tell me, 'Keep them busy, Louis. Keep them gossiping and spying on each other and trying to outdress each other and learning how to put a million forks down for dinner service. Keep them busy with all that so you can be busy running the country without interruption.' It made sense to him, but I'm different. I would have built a smaller palace..." he trailed off as if remembering.

"Is that his face on the gate?"

"Yes! He was a good man, great grandfather. He had to watch as many of his family, including my parents and older brother, died within days of each other. Soon after that, his own wife died of sorrow. I was too young to know what was happening; I was only two when I lost them all. He told me a couple years later how horrible it was to watch his son and heir die of smallpox. For the rest, it was measles. Only by the grace of God I was spared due to a kind nurse insisting I not be bled. It was the bleeding that killed my older brother, she thought. I daresay she was right because here I am. Though I had many nightmares of what they must have gone through, watching their life's blood be drained from them. The agony. I still think on it sometimes."

He gazed outside the window as if he was watching his history play out before him. His powdered face had a bluish tint where his dark stubble covered his chin. It looked strange against the white wig.

"Great-grandfather tried to tell me everything he knew about how to be a king. Nights, I would fall asleep in his arms as he drilled instruction into me, but I was too young to retain most of it. He had me greet visiting dignitaries; leaders of foreign lands were bowing to me when I was four years old. I think he knew his time was up and was desperate to prepare me. I became King a year later and was happy to be whisked away to the Tuileries Palace in Paris for a while, but they brought me back here when I was seven, and I've lived here ever since. You tell me, Zamor, does this palace seem like a proper place for a child? Being on display constantly? I quite enjoy the dark places and tunnels because they are quiet and still, when you're fortunate enough not to run into people in them. So, I will go to the Trianons when I want, curse anyone who has anything to say about it. But there are some things I like very much, like my gardens. And you, you seemed to enjoy the Labyrinth before that incident, didn't you? That was a lesson to you. Now you know beautiful things can be a trap, too. In some ways, you have had a much easier, simpler life than mine, Zamor. You had a decent childhood, and now you are a proper young man. Not a child anymore. You have had the best of both worlds." He drained his glass. "People don't consider how difficult it is to be a king. Maybe the next time you complain about being here, you will remember that some of us have never known a real home, and you will be more considerate of our feelings."

I was turning over his logic in my mind as he proceeded to shame me.

"And don't be so quick to complain, young man. You will have me believe you only care to serve yourself when it is the Madame Du Barry you must impress. I like you. Keep my love happy and you'll be rewarded. I have written it in my will that upon my death, you shall have the freedom you seek. Freedom to go back home and find out firsthand that you weren't wanted, just as I said. Though, I shouldn't have told you; now you'll be wishing for my death in earnest."

He didn't even realize I was already wishing for his death in earnest. But if I killed him now, Salanave would tell on me.

No matter, at least I knew no matter how he'd die I'd be free. I just had to keep him thinking we were friends until he did. My dream of freedom had been competing with my dream of watching him die and I realized I could have both.

With just a little patience.

15

———

I was vibrating with excitement as the small group of us friends and family sat in the King's private dining area watching him eat. The skin of the pheasant leg he bit into was brown, crispy and glistening from having been basted in butter and roasted in Salanave's oven. Judging from the way his cheeks were smeared with fat and grease, her gamble paid off. He washed it down, guzzling his wine like water.

The room full of people fidgeted. It was always difficult watching the King take his time to eat when you were hungry. We would wait like we always did. But today, I fidgeted for an entirely different reason.

"Madame," I leaned over to speak with her. "I have to relieve myself."

Of course, I was back by her side for dinners. I think she was bored without me there to poke fun at when she needed to generate a laugh.

"Go on, but hurry back," she told me. I left the room and walked down the hall to a cupboard where just this morning I stashed something special away. I found the jar I had placed in a satin knapsack and carried it like a present back into the room. The King had finished, and the others were eating—my timing was perfect—and I walked straight over to the brown-haired boy who'd tripped me. He felt me beside him and looked up, his eyes tight with suspicion and his cheeks smeared with fowl fat. "What do you want?" he barked through a mouth filled with food.

I tipped the opened jar onto his plate so quickly he didn't even know what was happening until the black bugs had covered it and were scurrying all over his plate, his clothes, and across the table.

Oh, the racket made with nobles jumping up from their seats, yelling, and brushing bugs from their fancy clothes. Pleasure spread through me like a blossom in spring as I watched them run. It was fantastic!

I walked over to the wall next to the King and Madame and waited for whatever was to come. It didn't matter what they did; I was enjoying this moment so much, I knew I'd replay it in my head forever.

I held my jar, waiting for the King to explode with anger, but instead, when I snuck a glance in his direction, he was smiling as the nobles he secretly detested ran from the room. I believe he felt his own release of resentment towards these people.

"Page," he said, as in acknowledgment, giving me a nod.

It was almost as if he thought I did it for him. I hated him as much as I hated the brown-haired boy and all the nobles, but somehow, he was smiling as if my action was one of contrition and not a sign of disgust of for him and his court both.

"Don't encourage him, chèr, he'll become a terror," Madame said. She had risen and was looking at me suspiciously, holding her skirt up and dodging the insects. Funny, she didn't have any trouble seeing me now.

Someone had judiciously ushered in the child servants and children of adult servants, rightly assuming they wouldn't have a problem gathering the bugs. They ran around trying to catch them, the smallest ones giggling over the feeling of the little legs running over their hands and chasing after them like it was a game.

"The page will stay and help them gather the vermin," the King said, standing to take Madame's hand. "Come, my love. We will dine in your apartments. Page, have Salanave send something up for the Madame to eat. And wine. Lots of wine." Salanave was livid I had ruined her meal, but the revenge was worth even the threat of her wrath.

It was my first and one of my very few public acts.

My next attack was the boy who force-fed me. I went outside searching for him and while I didn't have a plan other than threatening him—I was newly brave—for some reason, the minute he saw me, he took off running. Maybe because he was alone and vulnerable. Maybe he was so used to doing dirt, he knew if anyone got him alone, he'd be in trouble.

I chased him down off the main drag of the gardens into a secluded area, caught up to him and pushed him so he fell into a puddle of muddy rainwater, the splash loud and messy.

He was larger than me, but he went down surprisingly easily. He didn't put up a fight at all. I knelt to grab a handful of squishy mud, pushing it into the front of his collar as he tried to stand. His leather-buckled shoes kept slipping from under him when he tried to gain traction, landing him back on his ass. His face twisted as he jarred himself.

I grabbed another handful of mud, this one for that mouth of his that loved to laugh at me. I held it in front of his face.

"Listen here, goose, you're going to eat this."

"Get away from me. I'm going to tell my father…"

"…you're not going to do anything, boy, but eat this dirt!"

"I won't! You're going to be in so much trouble."

"From who, the King? He likes me, boy! I'm the one who eats dinner with him every night. You only get to do it every now and again when he can't find anyone better. Where are you and your family? Eating in the other dining room. You're practically a servant, only not an important one, like me. The King won't believe you over me."

"My father will!"

"So what? Your father means *nothing* here. You mean *nothing*.

You're going to eat this pudding just like the goose you called me. All of it." He tried to stand, and I kicked his leg out from under him—there were advantages to being close to the ground. He might have been hurt at that point because he winced and tried to roll to one side away from me. I grabbed the back of his collar to hold him steady.

"Eat this pudding, goose. Eat it!"

Yes, I shoved that handful of mud right into his face, slapped it against his mouth, and he must have taken a lot in on an inhale because he began to sputter and retch. Peals of laughter exploded from me as I looked at his mud-smeared face and watering eyes. It was funny, seeing it happen to someone else for once. It felt great being on the other end. And now, he knew what it felt like to be laughed at.

I let go of his collar, and he spared me a sideways glance before quickly crawling away on all fours, clearly humiliated. I realized if I decided to tell the court this boy was taken down by me—a little black boy half his age and size—I might get into trouble, but he might be disgraced.

He scurried as fast as he could, ruining his stockings. I thought about chasing him but, as he finally got his feet under him, decided he'd had enough.

I watched him disappear down the path. It had been easy. It was like he wasn't even used to fighting. Like, just the feeling that he was under attack took away all his defenses. I mean, he was one of the meanest bullies in the house but couldn't take a fraction of what he'd given me. It told me that if I could get one of the noble brats alone in a hallway or in a tunnel or any place we couldn't be seen, I might be able to beat them handily and quickly.

Belatedly, it occurred to me that one of these kids might be able to get me into serious trouble. So, I started carrying a burlap sack hidden somewhere on my body that I could whip out and put over their heads, slap them several times, and then disappear while they were getting their bearings, ideally without them ever seeing it was me. Whenever the mood struck me. It became a game. Though on occasion, I didn't use the sack because I wanted them to know it was me whipped their asses.

Of course, they complained to their parents, even the ones who couldn't confirm I was their attacker. The parents went to the King. I know this because I overheard one or two telling him that an unknown culprit was targeting the boys. Listening through the doors of the tunnels, I had to hold in my laughter hearing them whine.

And then, the King would call me to stand before him. The parents would glare at me with or without the offended child next to them and demand explanation. I would make myself small, small, small and speak to the King with the look of a simpleton on my face.

"Your Majesty, I don't know what he's talking about," I lied each time, my face innocent and frightened. I was eleven, but I still looked a tiny eight.

One time, Madame was there. She kneeled and took my chin in her hand. "Zamor, did you do what they are saying?" she asked, staring into my eyes. I believed she was trying to scope out my dishonesty. But she was the one who taught me to lie with a straight face.

I looked her back, widened my eyes and stared right into hers while telling a bald-faced lie. "No, Madame, I would *never*..." I put a little quiver in my voice. I shivered. My performance was so convincing that whether he believed me or not, the King could pretend he did.

"Your child must have walked into a wall in his sleep," he would wave a hand dismissively. "Now, stop making a fuss."

The last boy I beat in a corridor burst into tears at the King denying his account. His father had to drag him from the room.

"Really, Marquis," the King called to him on his way out. "Your son may have to fight for his King someday and his tears will not win any battles on the field."

The nobleman turned red but bowed and followed his child from the room. The King smiled brightly at me. "Pour us a café, Zamor, and come sit."

Of course, my turn from victim to perpetrator wasn't always

smooth. The adults came after me stealthily, like I went after their brats, and so I had to put them in their places.

There was an incident with a nobleman who caught me and beat me with his belt in revenge for a private beating I'd given his brat in the dark. The next night he woke to the smell of smoke, only to find his prize wig on fire. I didn't quite expect the fire would burn the wooden head the wig sat on *and* the dresser of drawers. It took his piss pot and that of his neighbors on either side to put it out. If they hadn't put it out, the whole Palace might have gone up in flames.

As it was, when called in front of the King the next day, he insisted I started the fire. As fate would have it, another nobleman whispered to the King that prior to the fire, the man had been bragging to anyone who would listen that his wig was at least as attractive as the King's.

His boasting saved me. Instead of being punished as the starter of the fire, I earned the King's respect as someone who would go to any lengths to defend *him*. It worked in my favor because it just so happened that the nobles with the biggest egos—and most prone to annoy the King—were also the ones who usually came after me. Win-win.

But I learned to put a little distance of time or location between me and the results of my work. I started bribing other servants to do my bidding with treats from Salanave's kitchen or charmed them to want to. I used stolen slices of Tarte Tatin—*the upside-down apple tart* —to buy alone-time in the nobles' rooms from the cleaning staff. After all, it only took five minutes to rub the itching ivy from the King's botanical gardens all over the sheets of a nobleperson, and the reward was tenfold. I even got some to stand guard while I hid behind the panels of walls in the tunnels to listen to private conversations. There was no love lost between servants and nobles.

Noble kids and their parents started to avoid me and stopped poking fun at me, at least to my face. Word got around that I was mean and sneaky. They said I was devious and cunning. What they didn't say was that I was smart. Being smart about being mean was more than anyone at court had ever expected from this particular page, nor knew how to deal with.

Salanave was right: making myself small was working well for me.

Where deed didn't apply, I used words, my dry, sarcastic wit cutting them down to my smallness. I complimented one man on the pet he kept on his head. Another person earned my praise on the color of his artificially rosy cheeks and the way they made him look like the cherry-colored shells of the fancy crustaceans. I revealed embarrassing family secrets at the dinner table and used noble children and servant children to spread gossip. I became the court jester, and if the disloyal nobles were the targets, the King never stopped me.

Part of me worried my actions would encourage the King and others to think me the very things they called me, but it felt too good to stop, and I needed to feel good about *something*. My hatred for them all was my greedy levain.

It was a well-fed pet.

16

Dear Citizen,

So, you see, I became what I did out of necessity.

I'd like to make something clear: I never targeted the innocent! The people I went after came for me first! I was acting in retribution, not simply for the sake of it. And I tell you, it felt good to start feeding the people at court something other than my pain. And just like Salanave's levain, I developed into a new, different thing with each incident.

I didn't know how to get to my safe place at will, but I no longer needed to. I had found the middle ground Salanave had spoken of; it was life changing.

—Zamor

The King was spending more time with me these days. From going with him on his hunts--even sometimes without Madame--to strolling his botanical gardens as he explained botany and the science of plants and their healing properties. I thought he should be more concerned with botany's killing properties as they had already been put to use in this place. But, I was trying to stay on his good side so he would make good on his promise to free me after he died.

He seemed to like my conversation, but that was hit or miss. Other times he forgot about me for days at a time. I asked Madame for advice on how to earn his favor. She was thrilled with the chance to talk about herself to someone who appeared to care.

"When he invited me to the Palace all those years ago, I was in the parlor—just being myself—and he was in the tunnels, watching me through the crack of one of the openings," Madame continued as she stitched. "He fell in love with me exactly as I am. He could have any noblewoman, but he wanted *me*." She said in a way that seemed like she was trying to convince somebody. "And that's why he likes you, Zamor. You're like me. Young. Guileless. He treasures that. Everyone's afraid of the King, but if you show no fear—while still respecting him —he'll love you for it."

It was the only lead I had, so I took what she said to heart. I watched how she was with him and copied her. I spoke to him as comfortably as if he was an average man on the street. I continued to beat him at card games and chess. I was sarcastic when he asked me to get him a drink. I poked fun at his powdered wigs, his wide girth and his aging skin. He took it all as good-natured jest, sometimes laughing boisterously.

As long as I appeared to be laughing *with* the King and not *at* him, and as long as I meted out even worse treatment to the nobles he hated, I stayed in his good graces. He grew to like me more and more. Our relationship became so close so soon, it aroused suspicion even among the King's staff.

Back before I got lost in the Labyrinth, Salanave had told me to deliver that wine to the Petit Trianon, and to come straight back without stopping, no matter what I heard. I had no idea, at the time, she'd been trying to protect me from walking into an orgy. I didn't even know what an orgy was until one day when I managed to walk, wide-eyed, into one of the King's private salons that never seemed much use for anything. The second I walked through the door I found myself staring at the king, butt naked, in the midst of eight or ten equally naked women, all climbing over him and giggling at his attempts to grab one here or to snatch one there ...

They weren't even all women, some looked like girls. Watching me take in this scene straight from hell seemed to please him. He was all smiles as he told me to replace the empty wine bottles on the sideboard. Leaving the room, I asked one of the other servants what the word was for what they were doing, and voilà. Orgy.

"Stay, Zamor!" the King yelled to me another time when I'd been summoned to bring wine, bread, and camembert to his bed chamber only to find he and Madame were in the midst of a game where he chased her around the room, and she laughed and giggled. Not unlike when Leroux and I were playing except Madame and the King were both naked, his jewels flapping freely like he hadn't a care if anyone saw him that way.

Another time they were in the midst of relations. I wouldn't dare call it love-making. It was like watching some horrible tragedy—the death of a deer or a someone breaking a limb—to see those two people go at each other like wild animals. And once, she was busy doing creative things with her tongue while he forced me to stand there and hold an entire conversation with him (if you call nodding and saying "yes, Your Majesty" a conversation) about how much he loved the smell of the anise that was growing in the garden and how —if he were not the King—he would be a gardener or an astronomist, both professions of the mind.

"It's the height of civilization, my boy. To explore all aspects of science and the stars. The stars affect everything, even the plants we grow," he said, chewing on a chicken leg. "My great grandfather knew this. They didn't call him the Sun King for nothing. Science is the future. It's every—" he stopped mid-sentence, eyes rolling back into his head. When the chicken leg fell from his hand onto his chest I looked away, but not quickly enough to avoid seeing the expression of ecstasy cross his features. I stared at the wall, willing the strange noise coming from him to stop until, finally, it did. And when a few seconds had passed without sound, I glanced over to find them both looking at me. Their laughter filled the room at my open discomfort.

"You may leave now, my boy," the King said, with a wave of his hand toward the door, while Madame cuddled up against his chest like a satisfied cat.

Later, on one of our walks he asked if I wanted to join one of his parties and told me that I could have one of the many, many girls who serviced him.

"You're shy, like the Dauphin", he said, speaking of the young man who would someday be king. "You have to come out of your shell. Let the people know you are brave and courageous. Let them see you being bold, and they will respect you."

I didn't believe that. I'd seen him bold many times now and I only respected him even less. I had no taste for that kind of public spectacle. Frankly, the fact he would even bring it up as if I could enjoy it after happened to me on the floor of that salon was foul, all things considered.

But still, if the goal was to become his friend, to outside observers, I was one of his favorite people. Never more so than the day he called me into his study, a look on his face like a mischievous child. Always happy to find him with his clothes on, I stepped inside.

"Come, come," he waved me in. "You," he called to the guard. "Close the door behind you. Hurry up over here, Zamor, come see what I have."

I thought maybe it'd be another tiny clock, so I came over to him behind his desk and looked down at a drawing in his hands. It was some sort of design with tassels, bows and little balls.

"What is that? A lace collar?"

"That, my boy, is not lace. Those little balls are where the diamonds will go. Diamonds are precious gems from Africa, each mined, cut and polished. Each will be worth thousands of *livres*."—dollars— "It's a necklace, see? A gift for the excellent Madame du Barry. Isn't it magnificent?"

I tried to count the number of diamonds but kept losing my place. "All those little balls, diamonds, each worth thousands? That would make this very expensive."

"It's the most expensive necklace ever made in all the world for the woman I love more than anything else in the world. Her beautiful neck deserves to be adorned with it. The Church and society say I can't make her my Queen, but she is more important than a queen to me. She will look like it."

He went on about something called "carats." I didn't know what any of that meant. All I could think was that when he sent his emissary to my parents, their answer might have been different if he'd given them just one tiny, tiny little ball from that necklace.

He continued to blather about the whiteness of his lover's neck and how the necklace would look against it, how he wanted to follow it up with matching bracelets and rings to adorn her delicate fingers. After swearing me to secrecy, he dismissed me.

I was still smarting and running over what I could do with one of those little balls when I stepped outside the door into the hall beyond the guards to find Gaspard standing there, arms crossed over his chest. His eyes had that look he always had when they settled on me: a combination of disgust and hatred. I turned to avoid him, heading down the hall. His footsteps sounded on the floor, following behind me.

"You think you're special, don't you, blackamoor nègre?"

I kept walking. "No, Manager," I mumbled.

"Oh yes, you do. I see it in the way you strut around. You didn't strut when you first got here, did you? You ran. You ran like a little coward."

I flushed with the memory of that night and stopped, turned and looked at him. He was smiling, remembering my humiliation. He stopped, too, expectation and excitement on his face like he was waiting.

"You have something to say?"

"Why do you hate me, Manager? I've never done anything to you."

His smile melted. "I don't trust you, blackamoor. I look at you and see one of the animals from the menagerie, got loose and thinks it's people. You, you talk like a person, but you think like an animal. You think I don't see those wheels in that brain of yours turning and planning, trying to figure things out? Trying to manipulate our King? You're a snake, but instead of slithering around in the grass on your belly, you walk on two legs. You think because you've fooled the King, you've fooled me? The King has never met something like you. He doesn't know."

I would have befriended the devil himself to earn my freedom, but that didn't mean I liked it. That didn't mean he had a right to try to make me feel bad about it.

"I haven't done anything!" I yelled.

Instant fury blossomed red in his face, and he reached out quickly, punching me across my jaw. With his size and the force of it, I was propelled across the hall, catching the edge of a wooden table. Stars clouded my vision, and tears welled with the brunt of the impact to my torso, dropping me like a sack onto the ground. Through my watering eyes, I saw curious onlookers at one end of the hall. The guards who were still outside the King's study were at the other end, looking like they didn't know if they should do anything. They wouldn't; they reported to Gaspard. He got away with whatever he wanted.

The Manager shrugged as if shrugging off his fury like a coat. He straightened, walked over and looked down on me like he couldn't imagine how I got down there. I used my hand to test if my jaw still moved from side to side.

"Get up and stop making a scene. I trust you'll remember this the next time you raise your voice to me. But I'm patient, I'll teach you the lesson as many times as you need."

He stepped over me and walked away.

Fury helped me pick myself up off the ground. I wondered if I could take care of him with the belladonna, too. Brushing myself off, I was hit with an epiphany: The manager was angry that the King liked me! That meant my plan was working. And maybe the King's fondness toward me could help me even further.

That evening when I went to Madame's apartments to join her on the walk to dinner, my bruise and swollen chin were on full display. She was chatting with her ladies but stopped instantly the second my face popped up over her shoulder in her mirror. She swiveled as quickly as she could in the melon-orange gown, the large skirt hampering her speed. She took my chin and turned it so she could see it clearly.

"Who did this to you?"

I could blurt it out. That would be easy. But I kind of wanted to try something that I'd seen other people around here doing. I wanted to kill him with kindness.

"I would never want to get him into trouble," I looked down like I couldn't bear to look her in the eyes and keep something from her. "... we all rely on him so much, and I know he didn't mean to hurt me so badly..." It was enough.

"I see. Go to your room, you're not to join me at court or for meals until these bruises have healed. Tell the cook to make sure to give you meat for dinner. And some madeleines and chocolat. I'll take care of this."

She picked up her skirts and left her apartment, followed by bustling servants and her ladies. She headed down the hallway that led to the King's bedchamber. I walked the opposite direction, through the halls and out of the main palace to the kitchen, struggling to keep the smile off my lips.

I was happy anyone was championing me. I was tired of the constant humiliation. It wasn't the pain of a beating I couldn't take; it was the fact that I had to take the beating at all. The fact that I was supposed to take it and take it and take it...

"I'm to be fed like a noble tonight," I told Salanave, loading a basket with a plate of the pulled meat, bread, cheese, roasted potatoes in garlic with crème fraiche and leeks cooked with strips of lardon. I lay a napkin over it and then layered sugared grapes and currants, more cheese, and a pile of madeleines—the sweet, buttery cookies Salanave had learned to bake after the King had brought them back from a visit to Lorraine. I used my other hand to reach for a bottle of wine ... hesitated.

Salanave said: "Oh, by all means, use that battered face of yours for all it's worth. If I know what I think I know, you'll end up paying for all this one way or another, so you might as well enjoy it tonight. And should I bring Armagnac to finish your meal, Monsieur?"

I'd never had Armagnac brandy, but there was no time like the present.

"Yes, please have it sent to me," I said in my haughtiest faux-noble voice, my nose impudently in the air as I turned on my heel and carried my bounty to my room. I was practicing being a noble and doing a great job at it if I did say so myself.

But when I settled in my room, as I used the corkscrew on the wine, I thought maybe the cook was right. I might have put Madame on Gaspard's tail, but he would get me back for it, somehow. The thought of *how* ruined what would've otherwise been a perfect evening.

I started drinking straight from the bottle to stop the worry about what was going to happen to me at Gaspard's hands. I'd had a taste of wine here and there, but never a bottle to myself. Soon, I was enjoying the floating feeling that made me even hungrier. Now I understood why the King always kept his cups full.

I feasted, lay down for thirty minutes and feasted more by the light of the small candle, the feast holding down the bile of my suppressed rage. I couldn't even touch the brandy after the bottle of wine, but I stored it away. Sleep came so quickly! One moment I was on my bed shoving cookies in my mouth, and the next, I woke up staring at the ceiling. My stomach roiled, and I made it to my chamber pot just in time to empty the entire meal. But once my stomach stopped twitching, I went back to finish the rest of the salty pulled pork and leeks since they would be the first to go bad. I stayed up all night eating that food.

The next day, when I stepped out of my room, head pounding, I overheard two guards talking.

"He practically shredded the man," one was saying. "Demanded to know how the Madame was supposed to enjoy her page by her side with purple bruises that clashed so horribly with the orange silk she had planned them both to wear at court? *'Are you trying to make the Favorite a laughingstock?'* he said. Oh, how we wanted to laugh out loud. You should have seen his face, beet red with embarrassment. He starts stuttering and bowing, begging for forgiveness and vowing never to upset her again. I never saw him look as low as that." They laughed, disappearing down the hall.

Even with my pounding head, I knew to steer clear of the manager. I didn't join Madame at court until the bruises had faded. I tried my best to lie low, but one night, Gaspard opened my bedroom door.

"Time to go back to court, blackamoor. Madame needs you to carry her train. Hurry up."

I looked at him dubiously, then hesitantly walked toward him. I slowed when I got right up to him, and he put his arm out, gesturing for me to move ahead. Just when I took a step, he punched me in the side. I fell over and crashed into the wall—again—and onto the floor, trying to catch my breath.

"What do you know," he said. "Not a bruise to be seen. Hurry up and get yourself to court. You don't want to keep Madame waiting."

I never reported him to Madame again. Instead, with every blow I took, the great house of King Louis XV lost another lovely porcelain plate, figurine, or piece of art, the broken fragments of my fury buried in the dirt outside the servants' quarters.

And then I graduated to stealing, which was much safer and more discreet than breaking things. Thousands of people lived in

Versailles, and it was impossible to trace where things had gone. If I was smart and not too greedy, no one would ever notice a missing silver spoon or a hairpin or a small bracelet or silk handkerchief. And perhaps, one day, when my parents changed their minds and came to take me home, we could sell those things for money. If my family came, that is.

17

1⁷⁷⁴

Dear Citizen,

Today, there are some people who still believe the royal family is ordained by God to rule—that it's in their bloodline.

When I was taken from my home, I didn't yet have a strong religion. But at this time in the world, most of France believed in a Christian God and the Catholic Church—likely due to the religious persecution perpetrated by Louis XIV before my time. For most of the population, anything done by the King was done so with divine permission.

The Church was at the disposal of the King, so when he ordered it shut down for the purpose of ceremony, it was. That was what he did when the two of them took me to Notre Dame at Versailles, where a bishop baptized me in the name of the Father, the Son, and the Holy Ghost. The King became my godfather, and thus, they named me after him because—as Madame explained—Zamor wasn't a decent Christian name. She said I needed a full name so that God would love and accept me.

They named me Louis-Benoit Zamor.

The King and Madame seemed enthused by the whole thing, but I was caught up in our surroundings. Something about the church being so still and silent captivated me. I'd been inside the place before, but it was different on this occasion. The quiet woke up my spirit like it never had.

The peace I felt in the church took away a bit of the sting of the ceremony. As I explained to you, I had a name before I arrived in France, but it seemed I had put it away for safekeeping so well I had lost it for good. Instead, I would forever be called by the name of a man I hated.

And at the same time, the King informed me he was giving me a title: the Governor of the Chateau of Louveciennes, his little hunting lodge home in the country some fifteen minutes north. He said the title with a flourish of his arm, as if he was bowing to me. It made the two of them laugh hysterically. I'll never forget that day, walking back to the main palace with the trees swaying in the breeze as the sun was setting, the two of them giggling in front of me, and Gaspard snorting behind me—it was all very undignified and hurtful, as you might imagine.

The fact that the King was already drunk at the time made the whole scene pathetic. He was, generally, an affable drunk unless angered. In a drunken state, he commonly thought anything that made him laugh was hysterical. With Madame sneaking glances behind them, looking at my face, and then whispering to him—

clutching his arm while they laughed at me—they looked a perfectly happy couple.

Even though the title was a joke, it stuck. Everyone began calling me Governor, with a flourish, followed by much laughter. Even today, walk into any Paris establishment and even if the barkeep is unfamiliar with me as Louis-Benoit, tell him I am the Governor of Louveciennes, and he will reply: "Oh, you mean Zamor, the traitorous nègre page!"

I wondered if God knew about the false idol who called himself the King of France. I wondered if God had seen how this king was doing unholy things and claiming they were allowed and endorsed by God Himself. He was the Almighty, so of course He must.

I felt a tiny morsel of guilt about trying to poison the King, but not for his sake. My guilt was for what my mother might think of me for actively setting out to take a human life, even of someone who courted death. I asked God in my evening prayers to make it so if my mother ever found out that she would understand.

At the cathedral, I had felt true closeness to God. Since then, I learned that according to Christian faith, God could be with us anywhere—that His son Jésus Christ made it so. If that was the case, I truly appreciated Jésus Christ because I could speak to God alone, in the little dungeon of a room, and He could hear me. Of course, I said the same prayer every night:

Please God, *I prayed.* Strike down the King and make me free.

Looking back, I feel that God, knowing that this particular twelve-year-old had no real idea of what he was doing, took the situation out of my hands. He didn't answer my entire prayer, but He settled part of it.

His plan was far better than anything I could have planned myself, even if I did help a little.

—Zamor

$$18$$

"Come, Louis-Benoit," said the King one day in April as I was brushing Lightning's coat in the stables. "Come with me to the Trianon."

Madame had already walked over with her maids, and the King didn't feel up to walking. I loaded some of his luggage into the carriage and now climbed in to sit across from the King. We would go to the small palace for days, maybe a week or two, given the number of items he was bringing.

Skirting the Palace grounds to take a quiet road along the perimeter, we saw a lone figure up ahead on the side of the road. As we came closer, his dress made it obvious he was a nobleman. He had a slightly confused, quizzical look on his face as if considering some internal conundrum. As we pulled up beside him, and the King banged on the roof to tell the driver to stop, I noticed the man's cheeks and forehead were covered in a slight sheen, the sun glinting off them.

It wasn't hot enough for the sun to make him sweat, but if he'd come from far away, which it looked like he had, he might have worked up a sweat from the walk.

But it was his eyes that struck me. They were red and darting a bit.

I'd seen that look long ago in Chittagong. It had been the first indication of a sickness that had swept through town. This sickness had kept my family and many others shut up in our houses for long spells because it was contagious. Whenever my parents had to go into town, they'd wrap themselves up to avoid contact. An episode with one person had wiped out two families; afterward, the rest of town had been extra careful to recognize the signs. It came and fortunately it went.

Because I'd seen the sickness and recognized it, I shrank away to the opposite side of the carriage as the King leaned out of the window. It was obvious the King had never seen anything of its sort. Or, at least, he'd been too young to recognize it when it struck his own family. This ignorance made him vulnerable now. My senses sharpened to full alert.

"Hey, you, are you lost?" asked the King.

"I-I am come to visit the Palace of Versailles," the man said as if he hadn't heard the question.

"Yes, yes, are you lost, I said?" And then the King did the thing that would prove serendipitous to me. Perhaps it was because the man was obviously a noble, with jewels around his neck and heavy gold rings on his fingers. Perhaps it was because he was of similar age to the King, who felt sorry for a fellow man. Whatever the reason, the King opened the carriage door and got out to speak to the man.

I instinctively wanted to call him back, one human being to another, but something in me stopped me. My inner voice said, *don't you dare stop this.*

"Are you lost?" the King asked as he stood before him. The man seemed at that moment to recognize to whom he was speaking—apparently, the carriage with the royal fleur-de-lys hadn't been enough—and dropped down to one knee, bowing.

"Your Majesty, sire, yes, I became turned around on the grounds, I do believe."

"Well, we are headed away from the Palace, but you are just there.

Just cut through those trees and you'll be in the gardens. Please, stand."

The man stood up. His eyes were now fevered and watering, though I couldn't tell if it was from sickness or fear.

"Don't despair, man," the King said, growing impatient. "You will be home in no time."

At this, the man's eyes truly filled with tears. "Oh, to be home. I so want to be home."

Oh, to be home. I so want to be home.

It was those words that made me sit up straight. Those words that spoke to me viscerally and told me that God was here, sending me a sign that He had heard my prayers.

His words were nonsense to the King, who was so used to ignoring people, he might as well have already left the scene. I'm certain he was thinking ahead to Madame. So, I took a gamble.

"Sir," I yelled to the man, leaning partway out of the carriage. "Do you not want to give the King a kiss of gratitude for his help before we go?"

The King looked slightly confused, but being so used to being kissed, he leaned forward, and, in the coup-de-grace, the man grabbed his hands and pressed both royal palms to his mouth in gratitude.

"Thank you, Your Majesty." The man then cupped his own cheek with one of the king's hands and held it there. The King, finally uncomfortable, pulled his hands away, nodded and headed back into the carriage.

I had already climbed out the other side. "I will ride with the driver, Your Majesty," I said. "I want to tell him about a dip in the road up ahead, so we aren't jostled too much."

"Very well, then."

I climbed onto the upper seat, praying to God the King would take his sickness-laden hands to his own face. Maybe take a big, deep breath. Maybe rub his eyes. Or put his fist to his mouth in pensive thought as he sometimes did when he was riding and looking out the window. I wasn't sure just how the contagion spread, but I knew closeness was paramount—the closer, the better (or worse, as it may be).

The ride was smooth. I'm sure the King thought it was because I was being helpful to the driver in avoiding the ruts in the road. I did feel some guilt; I didn't need anyone else to get sick, after all, and we were all headed to the hunting lodge. But what was I to do about it without explaining the danger—and my part in helping it along?

At the Petit Trianon, I helped unload the King's bags, giving him a wide berth. And when later he went on a hunt, I stayed behind. I was told he came in from the hunt looking ill and complaining of a headache. Madame went to nurse him, thinking he'd had a bad meal. By the next day, it was apparent it was more than just rancid meat. A day after, the doctor came, and Gaspard gathered the King to head back to Versailles. With the King looking so bad, he rode alone in the carriage. Our entire party headed back as well.

I requested to walk home for the fresh air.

As I walked back, the breeze brushed my skin, and I breathed the sweet, clean air deeply. I watched as the carriage slumbered on the road to the Palace. The clap of the horses' hooves made me think of that night when I'd tried to escape.

From here, there was nothing but trees. I could walk for days and not run into anyone. The sound of birds was so pleasant I took longer than I needed to return, but when I got back, I went up to Madame's chambers. She wasn't there, but the door to the hallway was open. My curiosity was too strong to keep me there.

I ducked into the passageway and, at the end, cracked open the door. Usually filled with a row of people waiting to dress or feed or kneel before the King, his chamber was emptier than usual. There was a doctor and a nurse, and I could see Gaspard at the far end of the room looking on, nervously. The King lay in the bed that dwarfed him, like a tiny child being swallowed by blankets.

From my little crack, I could only see a sliver of his face. It was deepening red and glistening with sweat, but I could clearly see two blisters on his forehead. Two blisters that looked just like the blisters I'd seen on the person in my village. It worked! I shut the door quickly and backed away. I turned and ran through the passageway. When I burst into Madame's bedchamber, she was just coming into the room, and I stopped short at being caught. But she was too preoccupied to be angry.

"What did you find out? They wouldn't let me into the room. I should have gone through the hallway like you did. How is he?"

Her face was panicked, but I told the truth. "There're blisters on his face and he's sweating like he's burning up." The blood drained from her face. She knew. She crossed herself quickly and sat heavily on the bed. "I'll have some tea sent for you, Madame," I said.

"Yes, thank you."

I left her room but looked up and down the hall. Instead of heading to the kitchen, I turned and headed through the hallways on the legitimate route to the King's quarters. The closer I came, the more people were bustling in the hallway outside, whispering and sighing. Two guards blocked the door, which opened at that moment; a woman with a scarf wrapped around her lower face came out, along with a man in medical robes with a scarf wrapped around his mouth in the same way. It was the doctor and nurse I'd seen inside who, apparently, had finally deduced the King's sickness was contagious. She carried a bowl filled with pink-tinged water, forceps of some sort, and a rag partially submerged. Gaspard was at the far end of the hall, speaking to some of his guards. By the time the doctor and nurse moved to pass me, I spoke softly but firmly so my tone cut through to them.

"You are tending to the King, Doctor?" I asked. They stopped and looked at me.

"Yes, what of it?"

"I'm the King's page," I said. "He talks to me a great deal. You are aware his parents and brother died of illness?"

The doctor perked up at this. "Yes, I know his family died of sickness. His father and his brother." I'd always wondered what the people who lived beyond Versailles knew about the goings-on of the royal family. Now, I knew, not much.

"His grandfather, father, mother and brother all died of illness," I said, leaving out any details that would impede my effort. "The good King has told me how difficult it was to lose his family to illness. He told me that if only the rest of his family had been bled like he was, they might have lived. Have you bled him yet, Doctor?"

The man looked doubtful and afraid he had done something wrong.

"I haven't. I thought that maybe I wouldn't."

"What?" The horror on my face was sufficient to induce panic on both the faces of the doctor and the nurse. "Are you trying to kill the King, Doctor? Why do you intentionally ignore his wishes?"

"The K-King hasn't asked to be bled," he stuttered. "He's not even conscious to give any instruction."

"I see," I said, understanding and concern filling my words with sincerity. "In that case, you wouldn't have known from his lips, but surely you have studied the family medical history?" His silence told me what I needed to know. "Well, Doctor, no one needs to know how ill-prepared you are; it's only important that you do what is expected. If you start now, you could simply say the advanced nature of his illness has led you to determine he should be bled. As his page, I assure you those are his wishes. But, of course, you must do what your medical education tells you is most prudent. Please, sir, save our King. We are lost without him."

I plastered a look of fear and desperation on my face and then turned away to walk slowly down the hall. I overheard the panicked whispers between the doctor and the nurse. I stepped back when I saw Gaspard come into the hall and overheard the whispered questions. I didn't know how close the king and Gaspard truly were. If the doctor told him what I'd said and Gaspard knew it to be a lie, I was going to be beaten within an inch of my life.

I waited for the Manager to storm down the hall looking for me. I waited, heart galloping in my chest. Then, I heard the doctor call to a servant to "gather all the small glasses available; the King is to be bled." And smiled.

Over the next few days, I wondered if I should feel guilty for my part, albeit small, in the King's illness. But he'd brought it on himself with his cruelty and hypocrisy. And God, I was sure, played the most important part. The word was out that he'd contracted smallpox, though no one knew how he'd gotten it. His quarters were restricted to only his doctors, Madame and his daughters, who alternated schedules to keep from him from being alone. I, conveniently, was nowhere around in his time of need. I stayed in the garden mostly because there was no telling how far the illness would spread.

The other residents of the Palace never saw the King, never saw how smallpox was ravaging his body. His face slowly became so encrusted with pustules and boils, it hardened into a mask. Madame's passageway was closed and locked so no one could access his room, but I'd long since lost interest. I knew he had the illness that spreads, and I had no intention of joining him in death.

Servants said he woke up occasionally and every time would wail, "Why am I being bled? Oh, sweet Lord Jésus-Christ, help me!" before he would pass out again. Rumor had it that at the last, he screamed he was being punished by God.

But I knew the truth. His death wasn't punishment. His death was necessary. God had simply, mercifully, granted the earnest prayer of a new believer and recently baptized little boy.

And finally, one day, the sentinel cried out: "The King is dead! Long live the King!

Alléluia. Hallelujah.

19

———————

Dear Citizen,

Someday I would look back and remember how it felt seeing that man on the empty road, the harbinger of the King's impending death, standing there as if sent to fulfill a mission. It would teach me something about prayer and how God worked.

It would teach me that far from the broad gestures that fill bibles, God can work in gestures so intimate that a single person in this whole wide world might be the only one to get His message.

In all, twenty-nine people at Versailles died, no doubt some infected by the King, the others by the nobleman who had followed directions back to the Palace as instructed. A gruesome, ugly death. Mostly servants, of course.

I felt bad for the servants, but I didn't feel it was my fault. Who knew how many people the nobleman had infected before he ran into the King on the road? No one ever attributed the King's death to

*the stranger, and the driver hadn't seen evidence of illness on him,
so no one would ever link it back to the King. Or me.*

*The nobles at the Palace fled to their chateaux in the country to
wait for notification of safe return.*

—Zamor

It wasn't safe for the new King and Queen to live in a home besieged by smallpox, so shortly after the Well-Beloved's death, we gathered out front to watch the couple and their luggage bundled up into two carriages outside the gates. XVI's face was hard and firm; his eyelids were red. Beside him, Marie Antoinette seemed more alert, nodding at people who bowed as she passed with her head up and her back straight.

The Queen was ready to take to her new position, I thought, while her husband darted quick looks at her. They were helped into the royal carriage, her tall wig barely clearing the opening. Off to the Tuileries Palace in the heart of Paris, where they would stay while the Palace of Versailles was fumigated of the contagion. Then, they would prepare for the Dauphin's coronation at Reims.

As soon as their carriage pulled away, I immediately went to my room to choose the items I would take with me, realizing I didn't have a big enough bag. I'd have to borrow one from Madame. I planned to take Barnier's map to guide me and sell my stolen goods to eat along the way. How long would it take? Months? Maybe I would hire a carriage. Maybe a ship! I was giddy with excitement and plans, imagining my mother's and father's astonishment at their son returned, dressed in silks, with an education and some money still in his pocket, but the royal couple didn't return until the summer of 1775. On that cloudless day, their entrance was greeted with cheers and applause. The nobles were already back, and the house was fully staffed; everyone was well-rested and prepared to suck up to this brand-new King, including me.

I only needed wait to be summoned. But as the days passed with no word, I began to get antsy. I waited until I couldn't wait any longer. I found the new manager, straightened my jacket, and ran a hand over my hair that I had shaped in what I hoped was a comely fashion. I was thirteen, and things like that were starting to matter to me.

"Monsieur," I said after the others had fallen away. He had watery eyes that made him look like he'd been up all night. "I'm the page of our deceased King Louis XV."

"Yes ... and...?"

It seemed too important to rush, but he looked ready to shuffle off at any moment. "The deceased King promised me my freedom upon his death. That he would set it in his will. I'd like to discuss my terms of release."

His eyes crinkled as he burst into laughter. I didn't think there was anything funny about it. I looked around at the people staring at us as he laughed and laughed. I hated being laughed at. My face flushed with blood.

"I'm serious, Monsieur," I said, though my pride was stung.

He straightened and gathered his composure. Now that my humiliation was complete, his face settled into impassive indifference. "You are right to come to me with this nonsense because others wouldn't be so kind with you. The Well-Beloved left nothing of the sort in his will. You're a child, so I'll excuse your ignorance—to think a king would care enough to put the fate of his servant in his will? Now, doesn't that sound ridiculous when you hear me say it out loud?"

It didn't. My chin came up. "I was more than just his servant; I was his godchild. He and the Madame du Barry baptized me under his own name. I was the child they never had, as everybody knows." I almost bit my tongue saying the next part, but whatever it took... "the Governor of Louveciennes, and all that."

"Well, now that you tell me that, I'll let the new King know that he has some competition for the crown." I didn't appreciate his poor humor. "Truly, boy, that is the worst argument you could have made. Anything to do with the Madame and her influence over our poor, deceased King, God rest his soul, will get you no advantage here. Get back to work. Our Queen has no need for a blackamoor page, but the Palace still needs servants."

I stood silent for a long moment.

"Will I be a free citizen servant?"

"You'll be what you were before without trailing around a woman holding her skirt, though I can't imagine your use beyond that. Be happy for a place to lay your head. The second you are no longer useful, you can be easily dispatched. There are actual French citizens who would gladly give up that citizenship to be in your shoes. Don't make a nuisance of yourself."

I watched him walk off. My hands kept bunching. It couldn't end like this!

I turned and headed to the King's quarters. Two guards blocked my way, but fortunately, the doors were open, and Louis XVI sat at his writing desk, a quill in his hand.

He wasn't a handsome man. His face was too pudgy and round, his dark, thick eyebrows the most notable thing on his face. His skin was pale, and his jaw had surrendered itself to a smooth slope that began under his bottom lip and kind of melted downward. His brow was furrowed like he was in the midst of something unpleasant.

He looked up and, surprisingly, said, "Let him in."

As soon as they stepped aside, I made my way into the room, walked up to him and bowed. "Your Majesty. I am—"

He lifted a hand. "...what do you need, Zamor?"

"Your father..."

"Grandfather. My father's been dead almost ten years. I'm missing him keenly now. He was a good father. Kind. He should have been King; he would know what to do. I haven't even started yet, and I get this," he swatted at the papers on the desk before him, with many lines looking to be awaiting a signature from his quill pen. "Grandfather has left us in debt, and I'm supposed to find a way to dig us out. I wish I could wake up, that all this was a dream, and grandfather was still alive running things. But I'm trapped."

"Why don't you leave, then?" I asked him. It occurred to me as the most reasonable solution because that was what I planned to do the second I could.

"What do you mean?"

"I mean you're free. You can go anywhere you want anytime you want, can't you, your Majesty? You could sneak out. I bet most people don't even know what you look like. You could disguise yourself and leave the country, and no one would even know. That's what you can do when you're free."

He scowled and looked down. "But I'm not free, I'm the King. Besides, I would shame the House of Bourbon if I abandoned my people. I owe it to Grandfather to make our ancestors proud. We are ordained by God to lead France and that is what I will do." He said it without passion, like it was a statement he'd heard a thousand times and never questioned. Without passion or soul. "What is it you need, Zamor?"

I'd never paid much attention before, but this new king wasn't all that much older than me. Not yet twenty years to my thirteen. And for someone who was now King, he looked scared. He looked at me sideways from under hooded lids, like he was afraid someone would slap him. But I noticed he looked at everyone like that now. Sideways, full of suspicion.

"King Louis XV said he would write my freedom into his will for when he passed."

He looked at me a long time and said, "Anyone could see he liked you very much. He allowed you to get away with a great deal. And you spoke to him like Madame du Barry, as if he wasn't the King. She took great pleasure from ordering him around like he was *her* servant —a prostitute off the streets, not even of noble blood. They say some women can drive men to madness, and he was a prime example. He took her abuse and seemed to enjoy it. I found it disrespectful."

"I'm sorry, Your Majesty, I meant no disrespect."

"You were only doing what Madame du Barry taught you. Loose

women are especially good at bringing out the worst in people. And though my grandfather didn't mind, I could tell that you meant to insult him sometimes. I understand it; I know what he did to you, forcing you to perform in front of all those people. He wasn't in the room, but he was watching, just like he always watched. I imagine you resented him for that. And for the way they treated you."

I didn't respond because my blood was hot with the memory and the anger that came with it.

"I will never allow a woman to drive me to distraction like that," the young King continued. "But that would never be a problem with my wife. She respects me. But to your question, I'm afraid he lied to you. The will has been read, his confessions made, and all requests honored. He is happily ensconced in heaven, and he didn't arrange for your freedom. He didn't mention you at all, of course. He was the King; he wouldn't have involved himself in such matters."

"But he told me..." panic was rising, and my blood was heating up with fever. "He promised."

"I'm sure he did. He promised me I would be allowed to have some say in who I married, and then when I was fifteen, one day he says, 'Let's take a ride into the country,' and there I met my future wife for the first time and was married to her days later. It was easier for him to tell me what I wanted to hear to pacify me, you see, like what he did with you. Sometimes a lie is just easier. But I don't care enough to pacify you. You cannot be free or a citizen."

My mind worked furiously. "I understand that he didn't arrange it, but *you* can do it..."

"I can, but I won't. Louis XV believed strongly in the value of slave holdings. While we don't have slavery on the mainland, the practice of it is a good thing for France. That is what you represent; you, who were enslaved and are now a strapping, intelligent, educated page. You're a shining example of Christianity—a black person able to be educated, molded, and still stay true to his master--though we discourage education for regular slaves. You are part of the royal house, which is the only reason you've been educated, of course."

"But it's a contradiction, Your Majesty, for me to be a slave when there's not supposed to be slavery on the mainland."

"It is, indeed, but look at the alternative. If I allowed you to leave, it would be seen as a criticism of my grandfather, and it would reinforce all the worst fears of the people who already think there are too many free blacks in France. It would encourage those annoying abolitionists, and they would never stop pestering me, thinking if I free one, I should free others. I'm not getting into that mess. For greater reasons than anything going on here, there can be no question that I support all my grandfather's decisions. If I'm to break with him on something, it won't be a thing as insignificant as whether his whore's servant can go on his merry way. You will stay as our servant. If it makes you feel better, no one but us two needs know you're a slave. You can pretend as you have been."

Pretend? I hadn't been pretending anything. My lips went numb, and the world felt like it was moving though I stood stone still.

I was a fool. All that praying for the last king to die. The aborted poisoning, the smallpox, the bleeding … all for nothing. I was in the same position as before. The King's death had delivered me nothing except his death.

King Louis, the Well-Beloved: sour saliva filled my mouth at the thought of him. The moniker twisted in my soul. 'The Well-Beloved' was a lie, and the creature who'd died without setting me free wasn't a man at all. He was a beast, as were all these people, this new King no better.

He looked at my face. "Now, then, don't look so upset. Because my grandfather was so fond of you, you still have a home at Versailles. You can stay and serve here even after the Madame is gone."

"What do you mean? Where is Madame going?"

"You should speak to her," he said. "But hurry, she's leaving soon." I still stood, stunned. He picked up his hand and gave it an odd little wave. "You are dismissed. Oh, and no more dinners at the King's table. Eat what you want, but you'll take your dinner with the other servants from here on out. Now, leave me."

"Yes, Your Maj—" I didn't need to finish the word; he'd already forgotten I was there. I backed out and left the room.

I passed the guards and made my way through the hallways, instead of the tunnels, to Madame's chambers to find her maids folding and stuffing things into her traveling trunks. Their faces were blotchy, and they looked ready to cry. Two guards were in the room watching over Madame, equally flushed and red.

"Where are you going?" I asked abruptly.

She looked at me sternly. "I'll forgive your tone because I love you, but my nerves are stretched as tightly as a drum. My heart is broken. It's pain on top of pain on top of pain. What is that expression on your face; why do you look angry?"

I couldn't keep the resentment out of my voice. "The King made promises to me that he didn't keep. He promised my freedom at his death. I only asked for one thing, and he lied."

That sweet-faced, so-called kind lady stepped forward and slapped me hard across the face. I heard one of her maids snicker, and I burned with anger.

"How dare you?" she hissed. "The King was a saint. I hope he, in heaven, forgives you." She shook her head and went back to packing, looking away from me. "Don't make me hurt you, Louis-Benoit. I am in deep grief and won't tolerate even the suggestion of wrongdoing on the part of the King. He loved you. He allowed me to name you after him just as if you were his own son. Any promises he made you I'm sure he meant to keep. Now he's gone, and they are throwing me out."

I don't know what I'd been thinking. That she would care that I was hurt and betrayed? That I was upset and sad? No. My feelings were nothing to her. She'd put all her strength into that slap like it was her job. It was the first time she ever hit me with her own bare hands.

"Where are you going?" I asked stiffly, giving her the side eye.

"My Louis is not even cold in the grave, and his grandson is sending the woman his grandfather loved more than life away from her home. But he's only doing *her* bidding. Marie Antoinette, the bitch, will finally drive me away from Versailles, as she always wanted," she said. "But it will be fine, I'm sure I won't be gone for long. They'll tire of their petty revenge soon enough."

"That's all," one of the guards said to one of the maids who had pulled out a second trunk for all Madame's extravagant dresses and personal toiletries. She reversed course and went to the bureau toward some jewelry that was laid out.

"No, no jewelry!" the guard snapped. "What you've got packed there is enough. She won't be attending any more parties."

Madame and the three ladies looked at the guard in horror.

"But that's not even a quarter of Madame's things," one of the ladies said.

"She won't need them at the convent. She likely won't even wear what you've already packed."

"Which convent is it?" Madame asked, one hand fumbling behind her for the hand of one of her maids, who grasped it firmly, water in her eyes and her chin wobbling.

"The Abbey du Pont-aux-Dame."

The women wailed and burst into tears. To her credit, though her face grew red, the tears didn't fall from Madame's eyes.

"Alright. Don't cry, my dear ladies. I am certain I shall meet many kind souls in that place, though none as dear to me as you. You must pray for me that they shall see my humility and take pity upon me."

"It's time," the guard said, speaking to another. "Tell the coach that Jeanne Bécu is on her way down." He motioned to servants to take her trunk. One of the maids whispered to the other, "Why is he calling her that, like she's a commoner and not a noble?" only to be shushed by the other. Madame straightened and came to me.

"My sweet Louis-Benoit," she grabbed me in a hug. "What is to become of you? You will surely starve on the streets from grief."

I was still stunned by how she had turned on me and knew at that moment what would hurt her more than anything. "Oh no, Madame. The King has asked me to stay. As a valued member of the family."

She pulled away quickly, looking into my face to see if I was lying. She saw the truth in my nonchalant stare. Her eyes flashed with something sharp and primal for a millisecond ... until she gained her composure. "Aren't you the clever boy. That's wonderful. Do not forget me. Pray for your Madame as I will pray for you."

20

———

Dear Citizen,

So it was that Jeanne du Barry was banished to a prison-like convent for a year, and the second part of my prayer was answered in that I was freed of her, *physically. During that time, she would find ways to stay in my life and keep herself in the minds of the court.*

The first letter I received from her was scribbled on hard, scratchy paper. Her message: "Please send my lovely stationery." It was delivered directly by Gaspard, who stood around, stone-faced, while I went to one of the storage rooms where her belongings had been shoved. I found some of her nice paper and a quill with a small bottle of ink. I gathered some linens and some undergarments. Then I bundled it all up in twine, with a sprig of lavender on top. He shoved it into a bag, gave me a "Gaspard" look that said he hated me and left with the package.

I didn't realize when he took the bundle that I wouldn't see him again for a very long time. Instead, one of the guards who had been a second to him would come by for deliveries for Madame. He would also continue to deliver her letters to me and to other friends in the court. She refused to be forgotten.

While I wasn't allowed off the grounds without a chaperone, I was about to experience a level of freedom within the court that I had never known since coming to France. My job as a servant kept me busy, but beyond that. I was mostly left alone to do as I pleased.

This new freedom happened to coincide with the time of my life when I was becoming a man. My voice was changing, I was grow- ing, and I was beginning to have thoughts and desires I never had before. Having been set upon as I was as a child en route to France and at the Palace as its welcome gift, until this time the act of sexual relations repulsed me. I could only remember the humiliation and fear and helplessness and pain of it. But now, my body was stirring in ways I never expected.

--Zamor

After the King's death and Madame's exile, everything changed.

It was almost like the universe had delayed my transi- tion into manhood until it was safe, and I could do it in private like God intended. Once they were gone and I realized I was staying and had no one to ride my tail, manhood came in hot and fast. Suddenly the women fascinated me. Or, rather, they fascinated the bits of my body that had only ever been abused. Exploring myself became one of my favorite pastimes; and allowing myself to be explored by women of my choosing--in private--taught me how pleasurable rela- tions could be. I practiced every chance I could get, most especially with a servant girl named Hannah. We practiced together a lot.

Then the noblewomen came knocking. It happened out of the blue. One of them called me to her room to show me something that needed attention and before you could blink, she had coerced me—

and my greedy body—into doing what I normally did with Hannah. She charmed me with praise for the body I never thought was charming, going on about how I'd grown into a fine-looking young man. This was a surprise to me because during the previous two years I'd been called everything from a devil monkey to a hideous troll. But I *was* a little taller, I told myself that was what did it and not the fact that I was making myself readily available to trysts however and how often they came.

As for those nobles, they got on differently with each other, likely to do with all the boundaries required in social order. The chaste couples, the older adults, and people with anything to lose behaved themselves. That's not to say they weren't dallying on the side, but they kept it quiet and did their business in the privacy of their quarters. But Versailles was full of young adults with a lot of money, resentful at being stuck in the Palace with their parents. And full of the indecent.

All one had to do at the Palace was wait for nightfall. After the decent folk went to bed everyone else came out to play. When the halls, rooms, and salons were dark and lit with only a few flickering candles or the occasional small fire in a fireplace, the public copulating began. Not every room, but enough. Because us servants were being called all hours of the day or night for wine or water, we never knew if we would walk into a room with a group of people listening to someone quietly playing a piano or into a room with a group of naked people writhing, en masse, on a floor strewn with rugs, circa the deceased Well-Beloved.

Hannah and I shared stories and laughed at those nobles as a prelude to taking off each other's clothes and doing the same things, but in private like God intended. She didn't want any more from me than I wanted from her, which made her a joy to be around.

"You have to be careful," she told me once, after we'd finished and were straightening up in the loft of the cow barn, trying to keep the straw out of our clothes. "If you get someone with child there's no way to deny it with your skin color. Husbands can demand you be punished by the King, and that could go badly for you. If you were a gentleman, they could demand you to a duel but as a servant," she shrugged. "I don't know what would happen to you if you shamed a noblewoman. Shouldn't want to find out, I'd think."

Until she said it I hadn't even considered I could get someone with child.

"Have you worried about that?"

"Oh no, I've got ways to stop that happening. Besides, nobody cares who a servant girl gets pregnant by." She leaned over and gave me a quick kiss on the cheek before she climbed down the ladder and disappeared from sight.

At fourteen, those kinds of thoughts don't come into your head, but once she said it, I decided to cut back on regular relations. I started being creative with orifices that didn't lead to baby-making like I'd seen Madame and the Well-Beloved do. Hannah showed me a few things and a few of the noblewomen showed me others. I found that the more creative I was, the more the women loved it, so much so, one of them began sneaking into the lower bowels of the Palace searching for me in the servant's quarters. She caught me one day when I was walking up the narrow stairwell from the servant's quarters to the main floor, the space cramped and dark, as always.

"Ah, why hello, Louis-Benoit. Fancy seeing you here. I was just ... just ..." she reached over and grabbed a torch from the wall sconce. "...just looking for a little light. Fancy seeing you here."

"Madame," I quickly dipped my head and stared at her flushed face. "What a pleasant surprise. I certainly never expected to see you here. I'd invite you to my room but it's no place for a woman of your esteem. You look like you could use some air. Might I accompany you on a gentle stroll of the gardens? Because it is getting late, you see, and a lovely woman such as yourself shouldn't be out all alone. Perhaps you should send word to your husband that you are being chaperoned by a servant of the court, to put his mind at ease for the next hour. Or so."

Her quick smile of glee transformed her face. She nodded. "I shall send word to him, immediately, so he doesn't worry, and meet you in the Orange Grove. Don't take too long!"

And then she put the torch back and picked up her skirts to run up the stairs.

I didn't mind the woman. She was nice as far as noblewomen went. That is, until she became attached to me. She started showing up wherever I was, giving teasing smiles to me. But, eventually, she grew reckless, coming to find me when she couldn't see me and giving dirty looks to whatever woman I happened to be talking to.

One day as I picked up glasses in an empty salon, I felt her body pressing into mine from behind and felt the point of something sharp press into my back.

"If I see you with the Marquise again, I will slice you open with this dagger, bâtard!"—*bastard!*. The hissed threat told me she was becoming too taken with me. I never expected this. I wasn't particularly handsome—didn't have money, title or esteem—nor had I used an excessive amount of charisma on her. And yet here was a woman from the upper echelons of society obsessed with me. I didn't understand it.

I set the glasses down and turned slowly. I was learning to be a smooth talker and practicing more every day. But she had a weapon so my heart beat in my chest.

"Madame, be reasonable. I can't be seen only with you. I'm only trying to protect you and your reputation."

"I don't care. My husband beds whoever he wants, and I'm supposed to sit quietly while he makes a fool of me? Well, I can't do anything about him but I can stop you. No one would even care if I killed *you*."

Truer words were never spoken.

"Wha—Madame, why would you say such a thing? You know have eyes only for you." I reached down and took the knife and tossed it across the room. "There, that's better. There should only be passion between the two of us." I said the words. Even to me they sounded like fake drivel from some useless book, but her shoulders drooped, dramatically, and she pitched herself against me, lips fastening on mine and arms around me, as I looked to see if anyone was passing by. Finally, I saw the edge of a coat and pushed her away, calling out to the passing man.

"Bonjour, Monsieur!"

She swiveled to look at the confused face of the man who barely missed seeing our kiss. Almost being caught was enough to bring her senses back. She straightened herself, looked at his passing figure, and turned back to me the second he passed.

"It's not that my husband would ever believe anyone if they told him you and I are together. He thinks you're an ugly, idiot nègre, that's what he calls you when we're alone."

She walked away and my smile died as I watched her to leave. *And what have you been calling me, Madame?* I wondered.

The whole thing soured me. I realized the woman wasn't obsessed with me as much as toying with me out of boredom.

I took a trip through the tunnels to their room, pocketing some small trinkets and leaving a mark, should anyone be paying attention. And then I managed to avoid that noblewoman because being with her was no longer any fun. But it wasn't soon enough.

One day I was summoned by the King. I stood inside his office, the room now with far fewer clocks and watches taking up space on the shelves and tables. The noblewoman's husband was already there, looking peeved, arms crossed over his chest and foot tapping, impatiently, when I arrived.

"Louis-Benoit," XVI said like he was already tired of the conversation. His manager stood to the side. "This good man says his wife has been spending time away from him. He said some time ago he witnessed you and she walking the grounds and he's annoyed that a servant of the King's court would encourage her neglect of her husband by making himself readily available to escort her over the many miles of the grounds of the Palace."

I breathed a sigh of relief as the husband began whining.

"It seems logical, Your Majesty, that if a woman only wants to walk day-in and day-out that there is something wrong with her in the head." I bit down on a laugh that came out like a hiccup, earning me a look from the husband. "What I'm saying is that your page should refrain from being so helpful. Frankly, I think he is besotted with her. I mean, look at him. To be in the presence of one such as elevated and lovely as my wife gains him a lot of attention. It is almost like he is attempting to replace the Madame du Barry with my lovely wife. I simply suggest your page is missing the leadership of a woman of elevated class, Your Majesty. Perhaps you can help him find someone else's skirts to follow after."

"Very well," XVI said. "Zamor, leave this man's wife alone, she will have to find another escort to endlessly walk back and forth with her for miles on end without complaint. And you, Monsieur," he turned to the husband. "... don't ever come to me with this nonsense again. What happens between you and your wife is between the two of you. Or, if you continue to prove your inability to deal with the royal court, I can send you and your wife to your country home and give your spot to another worthy family. You understand?"

The husband nodded "Thank you, Your Majesty," and we both began backward walking towards the door.

At the door, I gestured him to go ahead of me with a little nod. He, smugly, straightened his coat and exited, with me following. The second I heard the door shut I stepped up beside him. Of course, I should have left well enough along but I was still annoyed by him and his wife. And I was certain he would cut off his left foot rather than to face the King again.

I turned to him with a little smile, my feeders kicking in, glanced at his head and leaned in to whisper. "I pissed on that wig on your head, and I bedded your wife many, many—many—times. Run and tell the King if you choose, and I will tell the world before punishment can catch me." I nodded, briefly. "Bonjour, Monsieur." It was a gamble that I was young and cocky enough to take. He turned red as I sauntered away, pleased with myself.

He never said a word. They left the Palace soon after.

21

Dear Citizen,

In hindsight, I can clearly see my mind should have been on figuring out how to make the moves that would benefit my future. I could have worked hard to befriend the new King. I could have worked to find someone else to champion my freedom. I could have focused on learning a trade that would allow me to earn a living outside of court. I might have done any number of things.

But I was fourteen and still angry and not thinking strategically.

I went in a different direction. I soaked up the education Barnier provided, and I focused on how to make the new King miserable. I told myself I would find the King's weakness to use to my advantage, somehow. I convinced myself it was a strategic decision. And perhaps that was part of it, but in retrospect, I can admit that my next moves were driven more by something less noble than strategy.

I wanted out of Versailles but wanted revenge more. I wasn't a

*master manipulator ... but I was a burgeoning one. In the years
that followed, I would hone my craft and suffer its consequences.*

—Zamor

"My maid told me you are very close to the King. She says you are like a member of the family," said the young noblewoman who had joined me without invitation, strolling by my side along the path.

I was filling a basket with imperfect flowers the groundskeeper had just finished pruning from the perfect gardens. The guard would be by in an hour or so to pick them up, wrap them in wet fibrous material and then carry them four hours to Madame. Hear her tell it, no other flowers in the world were as nice as even Versailles' castoffs.

I stopped in my tracks at her comment. A stupider statement I'd never heard. Family? Family? Family didn't treat family the way the King had treated me, forcing me to stay when I so obviously wanted to leave. It caused a bubble of anger in me that I wanted to release, but I stopped myself.

I was making an effort not to lash out since I already had a reputation for having a short temper. I taught myself to find the value in any information that came my way, and I was curious about what I could do with this. So, I straightened my back and gave a most gracious smile.

"That is true," I lied, picking through to find a peony that was almost perfect but for a tiny brown spot on the edge of one of its ruffled edges. Just like these people to throw away a perfectly good flower for nothing. "As the godchild of our deceased Louis the Well-Beloved, it is almost like our King is my very own brother."

Her cheeks lit pink with thrill over that statement, and her hands fidgeted.

"I wondered if you might know—if you might have an idea—of how best to gain the King's attention. I have spoken with other noblewomen, and they preach patience. They tell me to be myself and he is sure to notice my beauty and humility. But…" she wrung her hands. "I have been beautiful and humble for months now. I worry that he does not even notice me. I heard that the Madame du Barry wasn't quite as humble. And that our esteemed Queen is not … has not…"

Ah, there it was. Well, for all her faults, there was much about Madame to be admired. For a working woman to charm the most powerful man in the country, the world even, was no small thing. As Salanave had said, in no uncertain terms, Madame had skills. And because I understood how lust could drive a person this woman was playing right into my hands. I decided to take advantage of the opportunity presented to me.

Bending down, I picked another pruned flower and did what I'd seen Louis XV do time and again—took my time responding. It made her anxious as she strolled beside me, awaiting my guidance. Finally, I spoke.

"Kind lady, I would never want to steer you wrong. I am but a lowly servant."

"Like a brother to the King…?"

"A lowly brother to the King, yes. I would never presume to tell you the manner in which a young woman of your station should behave. But I will tell you that the Madame du Barry caught the eye of our deceased King through her guileless, bold nature. She disregarded social mores and presented herself to him in all her glory. Perhaps King Louis is like his grandfather and prefers the bold over the proper. He strolls the grounds every day at noon and then retires to his chambers to nap. An enterprising woman might decide to … surprise him and take matters into her own hands."

She turned the idea over in her head. "Oh no, I could never…"

"Then you absolutely shouldn't," I backpedaled. "It was merely a thought of what a bold woman might do. You are not that sort. You are a proper lady. I regret I have no advice to offer, Mademoiselle; I only know the behavior of a very improper former Favorite. Good day."

I turned and walked the other way immediately, leaving her

standing there in doubt and confusion. I resisted the urge to turn around and see if she was still watching me.

I didn't care if the King got laid. I wanted to know if the King was susceptible to temptation. I wanted to know how to manipulate him. I wanted to find out if he was amenable or if the very thought of having a tryst would repulse or embarrass him beyond measure. And it was fun to try out my new talents.

I was so focused on what was going on behind me I almost barreled right into the Queen herself, who was now directly before me.

I tried to avoid direct contact with both the King and Queen. In fact, I'd specifically come to the grove because I'd been told the Queen was in her hamlet. The hamlet had been built on top of what had previously been the Labyrinth. The day I walked the grounds and saw the tall trees of the Labyrinth being cut down, I felt both sad and relieved. I had loved the place once. Sometimes I could still pull up my last experience inside it with shocking clarity.

They removed the statues, leveled the ground, and created a tiny, fake English farm with an idyllic scene around it, complete with a little barn for a cow and chickens and a windmill. Everyone in the hamlet dressed in costume as if they were living on an actual farm and the milkmaids really did, sometimes, take milk from the cow. The Queen particularly liked sitting on a stool outside, as if she was a common farm girl. She'd bring her friends to join her. A royal pretending to be an average peasant— it was the height of entertainment.

But apparently, she'd tired of her hamlet today because here she was before me. I stopped and bowed my head.

"Your Majesty," I stepped to the side to allow her to pass, but instead she looked me up and down, along with the ladies that surrounded her, taking in everything.

"What is that you have there, Zamor? You've developed an affinity for trash? Or has the Madame du Barry rubbish taught you that?"

The ladies snickered. My ears burned.

"Your Majesty. It is just that..." I could have lied, but why?

"Madame requests that if there are flowers the Palace does not want that perhaps we can send them to brighten up the Abbey."

Her eyes sharpened, and she took in the scene with new eyes. "I see. What else has been going to her at the Abbey?"

"Not much," I said. "Just some of her old linens, some writing paper, a small bottle of scent…"

"And how do these things get to her? Who's transporting items and messages?"

I was hesitant to say; I had no ill will toward the guard and didn't want to get him into trouble. "I don't know his name, Your Majesty. I only know he was ordered to do it by the former manager, Gaspard."

"Gaspard," she sneered. "We lost two of the most insufferable individuals in Jeanne du Barry and her creature, Gaspard. Good riddance, I say. I will have a talk with this young guard. He's not been given permission to be her deliverer. And I will tell you—nothing of the Palace of Versailles is ever to go to her again. Not linen, not dead flowers, not a pile of shit. Do you understand me?"

I bowed. "Yes, Your Majesty." I waited for her to pass, and she soon walked away, followed by her flock.

The second she passed, I tipped my basket over to dump the pile back onto the grass.

22

———————

I headed back to the kitchen to see what Salanave had as lunch leftovers. She didn't disappoint. The kitchen tables were covered with the dregs of the roasted pheasant lunch with roasted pheasant bones in a pot. The tender meat had already been served to the court, but the bones made a fine stock for soup with carrots and mushroom, celery and wine. My mouth watered immediately.

Salanave's eyes found my empty basket, and like the wise woman she was, she figured it out immediately.

"No more flowers for Madame, I see. I'm surprised it took this long for the Queen to catch wind."

"It makes no difference to me." I took a knob of bread from the table and began to eat.

"Why would it; you've got your hands full," she said, turning back to stir the soup. "You think I don't know it was you caused that boy to go streaking through the plaza butt-naked just when the King came out for his daily walk? It won't matter what his tastes are if he finds out it's you who's provoking him. One of these nobles is going to tell him, and then where will you be?"

Salanave had quickly figured out my plan to find the King's triggers.

My first thought had been that maybe the King was a slave to the drink, like his grandfather. So, I made myself available at dinner to top off his glass whenever it got low. I tripped over myself to fill goblets to the brim with wine. I made countless trips to the wine cellar to restock. I would offer him wine and follow up with brandy. I would offer him rum and follow up with champagne. Finally, I determined this particular Frenchman had a tolerance level too high for my plan.

Then I thought maybe it was a bad temper that would weaken him. I sauntered through one of the salons where nobles milled about talking about nothing and my eyes found a particular young man. I'd seen the man beat other players at table games many times. He looked twenty or so and appeared bored. I stood next to him, my hands clasped behind my back and staring ahead in the fashion of the servant I was.

"Bonjour, Monsieur. Fine day," I said.

"Yes, I suppose it is. I would rather be anywhere else. But I have to be here. Family obligation, oui?"

"Ah, I know only too well," I said in support. "I know what would liven things up. The King happens to love to play chess. Perhaps you should offer him a game, for fun."

He perked up. "You think he would?"

"Chess is one of his favorite games," I nodded toward a sideboard where a board and the pieces sat. "But so few people here know how to play he never gets to enjoy it. Imagine, your family obligation would be more than fulfilled were you to put a smile on his face."

He perked up fully. "I do thank you, young man. I think I will do just that." I smiled as if the idea was nothing and walked away to another part of the room. Far, but close enough to watch.

See, one could never be sure if a plan would work out, but I felt by that time I understood the King enough to know what would prick his pride. One thing I knew about his grandfather—that man enjoyed a game and didn't mind losing, even to me. His grandson, not so much.

The young noble went to pick up the game and its pieces that sat in a little basket beside and took them to a table where he laid them out properly. Then he walked over to where the King was speaking with a group of elders, bowed, and gestured toward the table. He smiled as his lips moved, and the King nodded and then followed him to the table. Once he sat and they began to play, the conversation in the room quieted as we all watched.

As I knew he would, the King rapidly began losing. And the noble he played against grew more excited at every passing second as winning came nearer. His smile grew larger, he talked more, he made gestures, and somehow, failed to notice his own father looking on from the side, his face a mask of worry.

If there was one good thing I could say about the deceased Well-Beloved it was that he could laugh at himself, within reason. He was relatively confident, as far as aristocrats went, so he wasn't threatened by something as silly as a game. All reasons why he never minded me beating him. But this was XVI, a different king.

Finally, the noble knocked over the King's king, and XVI's face flushed red.

"I did it!" The young man jumped up from the seat, too happy to notice the quiet. He was so excited and celebrating so loudly his father had to call out across the room: "Assez!" Enough!

The boy stopped and finally felt the mood of the room. Fear flowed over his face.

"Your Majesty, my son is too foolish and full of himself to notice what we all see clearly—that you allowed him to win to save his dignity. You are truly a magnanimous and selfless King."

The man bowed deeply. His son looked around, now scared, and did the same.

Louis stood and spoke. "No, no, this young man beat me fair and square. What kind of a king would I be if I dashed the confidence of one so young? You should be proud, young Duc, that you were not immediately trounced by your King." He stood, and the court bowed as he left the room with the Queen following. Once he was gone, I had a hard time suppressing my smile and immediately left also. I slipped into a tunnel to weave my way up to the wall just outside his quarters, where I heard him tell the Queen to kick the boy and his family out of the Palace and strip him of his status.

"Your Majesty," she said in the patient tone she used on him. "You showed yourself to be magnanimous. What would it look like for you to now punish the family? The court believes you to be fair."

And just as quickly, he calmed down. "I thought I had him. This won't make me seem weak? If I let it pass?"

"Not at all, my King. How can you be weak who are the most magnificent?"

I WAS DISAPPOINTED the King hadn't completely melted down, but I got another chance soon when a group of teenage noble sons gathered on the plaza and, when I passed, took to mocking me.

"There he is," said the leader of the pack. "The strange little servant who thinks he is as good as the nobles. The one who struts around like he has gold up his backside."

He was new, this one. The others in the group watched. They might hate me, but they knew action against me would come back to them in unpleasant ways. One or two looked like they wanted to laugh but would save it until I wasn't there to see them. This new one hadn't been schooled.

The chess player had been for fun and curiosity—I had no malice against that boy, and so I was happy he wasn't seriously punished for bruising the King's ego. But this new one was asking for what he was about to get.

We stood by Apollo's Fountain—a massive central gathering place. From the middle of the water rose sculptures of the Sun King's symbolic namesake with his horses. It's at this fountain that the boy had been tossing little pebbles.

"You mock me," I said. "But *you're* the one throwing stones into the wrong side of the King's fountain."

"What do you mean?"

"I mean, any simpleton knows you toss pebbles into the north end of the fountain for good luck and to honor our deceased Sun King. Throwing into any other quadrant is an insult to the House of Bourbon."

"Is that true?" He looked quickly to his friends, who stared back at him blankly. They didn't know any more than he did. But it was high noon, and the King had just made his way on his daily walk to survey the plaza from the balcony above. The newcomer wanted to make a good impression.

He hurried quickly to the north end of the fountain, bent down, picked up a handful of rocks, and began to throw them into the water. Then he double-checked that the King was looking and picked up a particularly large stone, smiled at the splash it made, and looked up to the King for approval.

Of course, *I* knew the act of tossing stones into any quadrant of the Sun King's fountain was an insult to the House of Bourbon, so while Louis XVI and his guards were glaring at the offender, I stepped back out of the limelight with an expression on my face that showed I was just as horrified as everyone else.

Young people don't always know the rules, but you'd think their parents would teach them some things before they came to live in a house with the King. You'd think they'd learn before they decided to mock and deride an established member of the household, like the former King's page.

Unlike the chess player, the rock thrower and his family *were* kicked out of Versailles, and the father stripped of his noble status. What a shame. I felt good. Actually, I felt great.

Some three weeks later, out of the blue, I was summoned to speak to the Queen. I walked into her salon and bowed as she finished writing a letter.

"Hello, Zamor. How are you feeling?"

"Feeling, Your Majesty?"

"Yes, you must be terribly tired. You've been so busy lately annoying his Majesty. I know it's you behind the foolish antics of some of our families. You are highly persuasive, but your mistake is in assuming the pawns you move around on the board are too embarrassed to admit they've been moved by you. You are wrong. Each has been eager to explain how they'd gotten advice from the nègre servant who is like the King's very own brother. That alone should get you flogged."

I flushed. I hadn't expected them all to talk. Did no one have an ounce of pride?

"I only said I was the godson of the Well-Beloved, Your Majesty. They assumed the rest on their own."

"Your second mistake was planting a whore in my husband's bed. Now we have a crew boarding up the tunnel that your mistress used to crawl her way to the King's quarters like an animal in the night. All else might have been forgiven, but not that girl being coached on how to throw herself at my husband." I'd heard through the grapevine when they'd pulled the naked woman from his bed, she had called out that someone had to be *"bold enough to give the King what he needed!"*

"I had nothing to do with her disrespectful words, Your Majesty. I can't imagine what would've possessed her to—"

"—stop. I have no interest in your denials, and I couldn't care less about that idiot girl. The King will not take a Mâitresse-en-titre. There will be no repeat of dear Louis, the Well-Beloved's, folly, with his whore disguising herself as a lady and a bevy of young girls picking up the slack. It's no wonder he was always tired. It wasn't his fault; the poor man lost his wife, the Queen, and was very lonely when your Madame preyed upon him. My Louis has a wife who loves him and no loneliness to fill with local street trash."

I wondered how many tunnels they would brick up. How would I listen and spy if the tunnels were blocked?

"You're an enterprising young man, Zamor. You absorb how things work. You learn the politics. When you first arrived at the Palace all those years ago, I didn't think you would last six months, you were such a tiny scared little thing, and they were abusing you so badly. I thought you would climb into your own head until Madame tired of you or could no longer tolerate you and sent you away. You still had that little accent and that constant look of shock and desperation. I felt bad for you, but there was nothing I could do. And then you changed and surprised us all. Less than three years later and you speak as though you were born in France. It reminds me of something my mother used to say. Whenever she saw a child with something unpleasant—a large forehead or nose or gangly arms and legs—she would say the boy or girl would grow into it, that one day no one would even notice the offensive part. She used to tell me, 'Don't worry, 'Toinette, you'll grow into those manly hands of yours'." She smiled wryly. "It was insulting, to say the least, but she wasn't wrong."

"Your Majesty?" I was confused. She continued.

"Sometimes we rise to meet our greatest challenges. You seemed a sweet boy when you arrived. The ugliest thing about you was this place into which you were delivered. The royal court has chewed up and spit out the best people. They tried to do it to me, but I have survived, and so have you. But you didn't just grow to meet this challenge—you've surpassed it in all the worst ways." She gestured with her hand up and down my length. "Everything wrong about this place is standing before me in one slim, nondescript, misplaced young black man. Being tricky and conniving, putting people up to do stupid things for fun, sneaking through the tunnels, manipulating other children, *having relations with noblewomen* as though you don't know better, when you do. It's not your fault. Still, it's just a surprise. I can't say that I don't like you, Zamor. You understand that sometimes things must happen for a reason other than the obvious. So, with that in mind, the King and I feel it's time for you to move on."

My heart began to gallop in excitement. All the years I had hoped! Finally, I thought. I'll get my freedom!

"It's clear now where your loyalty lies, and it's obviously still with your mistress, who would surely approve of your crass behavior."

My galloping heart slowed as confusion clouded my brain. Would they send me to the Abbey? When I spoke, my voice came out as weak as I felt. "But Your Majesty—"

"—I told the King how the Madame was pilfering royal property and having it sent to her hovel. I was hoping she would be further punished, but the King is softer of heart than I am when it comes to her. He never hated her quite as much as his sisters, and he has grown tired of dealing with her and being asked about her. We've both decided the Madame has been chastened enough. She'll be released and returned to you. The King has graciously given her the Chateau de Louveciennes because it was such a special place for her and his grandfather. She will also have all the gifts from the Well-Beloved returned to her, including you. Right now, she's staying at a temporary location until Louveciennes is fully stocked for her return. You, Salanave, some of the ladies of this court who love her so much, and some of her most loyal guards will go with her to Louveciennes. And, per your Madame's request, we are working hard to find her faithful Gaspard to manage her new home. Won't that be nice?"

My stomach turned. This wasn't what I wanted at all. I could see in the Queen's eyes that she knew exactly what she was doing. She knew how Gaspard hated me. She knew this was the last thing I wanted. I had toyed with Palace politics, and she was showing me how small a player I was.

Who was I fooling? I wasn't even a player at all. I was a child who thought he was getting over when all I'd done was play myself right back to where I'd started. Now I knew it wasn't a game when one side had all the power and the other only had things to lose.

"I tried to convince the King to write up your freedom papers, but he felt it would further damage his predecessor's reputation, already almost destroyed by the whore. And he felt it would be wrong to reward you for bad behavior. But we are still fond of you, so you're welcome to visit anytime you want. But I should think you'd be happy at the chateau. Didn't our dear departed King proclaim you to be the Governor of the Chateau of Louveciennes? Such an important role. You'll look so handsome lording over your own household. And please, take that old horse you love so much, the black one with the white stripe? It seems it has become increasingly difficult to get along with."

23

Dear Citizen,

*In 1777, after being released from exile and spending time in the
country, three years after the King's death, Madame moved back
into the Chateau du Louveciennes. She would never again be
allowed to step foot onto the grounds of the Palace of Versailles, and
she no longer held the illustrious title Mâitresse-en-titre. But like
wearing a new pair of gloves, she slid into her title of* Comtesse*,
emphasizing her status as a wife of a nobleman, even if in name
only.*

And Gaspard returned like a hound straight from hell.

*I arrived at Louveciennes at fifteen years old. Though most of my
innocence was gone, I still held the hope that sprouts undeterred in
youth. I no longer took anyone at their word. I no longer believed
anyone in the world around me cared if I lived or died, was free or
enslaved.*

And I wasn't alone in my disenchantment.

—Zamor

"A bitch, that one," Salanave said one morning while stirring hot cereal in our new home, her sadness finally morphed into anger. For two weeks, she came to the new kitchen each morning with eyes the shade of radishes. I couldn't tell which one she was calling names.

We servants, maids, stable hands, and guards had moved into the Chateau de Louveciennes first, to prepare the place for Madame. While I'd been there before, some of the others hadn't. Salanave had trained people who worked at Louveciennes and occasionally sent food over, but she'd never worked the kitchen herself. When she walked in the first time, her eyes had gone up and around, surveying the confines of her new space. Likely comparing the small room to the massive kitchen at the Palace. She hadn't said anything then, but over the next few weeks, her stoicism broke down as reality set in. Today, she couldn't look me in the eye while she stirred.

"She knows I have a family, and she knows Madame pays less. 'Oh, but Salanave,' she says to me. 'I thought you'd be happy with the change. In the two years since the death of the Well-Beloved, you've never roused yourself to make a dish in honor of your new Queen, so it was obvious to me where your loyalties lie.'" She said it with a sneering impersonation of the Queen, her sarcasm dulled by the sadness underneath it. Mystery solved on which bitch she was speaking of.

After Madame's exile, Marie Antoinette banned cauliflower from the kitchen of the Palace, calling it a gutter vegetable as tasteless as the woman who loved it. General consensus among the servants was that the Queen couldn't stand the thought of du Barry's name on anything coming out of the Palace kitchen. By that time, all of France was making "du Barry" cauliflower dishes, but the royal family no longer was.

I believe if the cauliflower soup had tasted of the gutter as the

Queen claimed, Salanave would still have a job at the Palace. But she'd messed up by creating a delicious soup for the Comtesse. I could imagine the Queen waiting breathlessly for what Salanave would make in *her* honor. She could have asked the cook to create something, but that would have been beneath her station. The King could have easily ordered Salanave to do something special that he could fawn over and name, but he didn't have his grandfather's flair for the dramatic. And for some reason, Salanave had never even thought of it. And it was that issue that sealed Salanave's fate.

"Only one cook in this house and less money," she groused. "I'll never see my kids. Curse these people to hell." She shoveled more meal into the hot water and stirred with a viciousness to stave off tears.

"You can teach me, Salanave," I told her. "Let me know when you want to leave, and I'll cook. No one will even notice you're gone."

She stopped and turned to me, straight-faced. "You must think I'm crazy. To give you control over this kitchen ... looking for sugar in a bag of rat poison."

I couldn't fault her logic. "And still," I shrugged. "You *would have* more time with your family."

Her lips wiggled. "You are a sick, sick little bastard. But I appreciate the horrors you're willing to unleash on my behalf. Don't worry, I'll train one of the servants to be my backup whether Madame wants me to or not. Now get out of my kitchen and let me learn this tiny, tiny place. It's like *I've* been exiled."

With the Queen overseeing the new cook at the Palace, new pastries began coming from the kitchens. The "croissant" was particularly loved, but it was just one of a crop of new hybrid pastries, unlike the sweet desserts and familiar breads served in most patisseries of large cities. And though Marie Antoinette's name wasn't stamped on the new pastries, soon they became known as *viennoiseries,* with corresponding storefronts popping up in the cities, all named after the Queen's beloved city of Vienna. The fact that France loved these pastries inspired by arch-enemy Austria only made them hate the Queen more, that she could bring something to France too delectable to be resisted.

Madame climbed out of the carriage. She was still what people would consider beautiful, but I saw the tiny lines at the corners of her eyes and the light layer of padding, where before she had been slim. She glanced my way, and I could see in her eyes that something about me must have seemed different to her, also. All of us servants stood in a receiving line to greet her, and once on solid ground, she flashed one of her characteristic angelic smiles.

"It's so wonderful to see you all at my glorious home. Don't you all look so proud and well-put-together? I expect you to keep that up. This house shall be as well-respected as the Palace of Versailles. We shall host the best and most elite in all of France, and you must always look the part. We'll be the envy of noble houses throughout France."

She was lecturing us while walking the line, straightening collars and fluffing lace fronts as she passed. Just in the few minutes since she'd stepped from the carriage, I saw some of the servants melting under her attention. The ones who had never met her were instantly in love. The ones who knew her were already softening as she paid special attention to each. Now she stood before me, looking directly into my face instead of down. She looked at me, her expression both guarded and cautious. The last time we saw each other, I was showing her my ass, figuratively. Now, she didn't know whether I was friend or foe.

Neither did I. But I pasted on a light smile to put her at ease.

"You've grown, Louis-Benoit. You are like a real man now. I do hope our time apart has made you appreciate the love and kindness I've always shown you. Now, be a dear and get me a cup of chocolat."

She picked up her skirts and headed toward the house. Gaspard, who had been following behind her, looked at me warily. He, too, had aged in the two years' absence, losing the thickness of hair on top of his head and, apparently, losing a razor to shave the hair from his scruffy face. His eyelids were puffy, and there was a layer of fat where a sharp jawline used to be.

He was still broad-shouldered and built like an ox. He looked me over as if measuring an opponent. I wasn't a tall man by any means, but I wasn't the tiny child anymore. I could see him sizing me up to determine if I was still as easy to beat. Maybe wondering if I was still of a mind to take it without fighting back.

I was smart enough to know that physically challenging him wouldn't end well for me, and it wasn't on my mind. There were other ways to best people like Gaspard. I hadn't considered how things might change with my place in the household now that I was older until Gaspard stared me straight in the face.

I didn't look down or away. I wasn't afraid of him. The worst he could do was hit me. It had been a long time since I'd been hit, but there wasn't anything new about it.

His jaw flexed a bit, and when he turned to walk away, he made a point of shouldering me as he passed. My shoulder and arm moved with the impact, but I didn't fall, and it seemed ridiculous to me that a grown man would still be trying to intimidate someone a fraction of his age and size, after all these years. I couldn't hold in the quick laugh that escaped me.

Gaspard's steps stopped. I straightened my face, waiting for him to come back and punch me in the side. Or the jaw. Or, knowing him, my back. But, finally realizing a blow wasn't coming, I looked behind me to see he was standing, facing the house, with his back straight and his hands clenching and unclenching. Clenching and unclenching, like he wanted to do someone bodily harm, but something was stopping him. And in one of his hands, just the tiniest of tremble.

Oh, how things change. He was weaker of body but smarter than to show it to me. Or, more likely, smarter than to show it to Madame.

I was smarter, too. I'd done myself a disservice by getting ousted from the Palace without a plan. I now understood freedom wasn't about jumping on Lightning's back and riding away, hoping I could convince people to help me. My parents never came for me, and I accepted that the King might have told the truth about them. So, France was my home. I wanted freedom to honestly proclaim myself a French citizen. Freedom to live my life without fear or worry or limitation or intimidation. Freedom to stand up to a man like Gaspard and have the right to have him arrested for hitting me. Freedom, even, to leave this country if I wanted to. When I left the Chateau de Louveciennes, it would be for *that* kind of freedom.

With the exception of my upper body strength, my size had always been the weakness Gaspard knew, but now, whatever caused that tremble in his hand was his.

Ten minutes later, I brought Madame her chocolat, placing it on the dressing table in front of her as she sat, looking in the mirror. One of her ladies stood behind her, brushing her hair. She glanced at my reflection.

"It's like I never left," she said. "Everything is exactly the same."

Her shifting eyes told me otherwise.

Almost immediately, she started having visitors. The first round wasn't the kind she wanted. They came to see how far she'd fallen, came with their eyes pinned to every movement, every hesitation, every sign that she was a diminished fallen woman. They insisted to her face that she'd managed it well and looked the same as when she went into the convent. But the second she stepped out of the room, they whispered under their breaths about her.

She wasn't stupid; she knew. But she kept her head held high, and I admired her a bit for that. Until the last guest from the first round of guests left. Then she turned on me.

After dusting, I was in the kitchen watching Salanave train two servants. The boy was just a little younger than me and seemed to be hanging on my every word. I was showing him how to dry the plates so they wouldn't spot when Madame came into the kitchen, color high and eyes hard.

"Louis-Benoit, where are the clothes I bought for you? And what is," she was clutching something in one of her hands. "What is this, Louis?"

I didn't understand the question. The others stopped what they were doing, unaccustomed to the frantic tone in the voice of their new benefactress. I handed the plate to the boy and stepped towards her to see. I noticed the gold quilted braiding with matching gold buttons. It was my navy-blue velvet coat.

"Answer me!"

"It's my coat," I said the obvious.

"What happened to the clothes I had made for you? The clothes that match me? Where are they?"

"I outgrew them. They had new ones made for me."

"They? You mean *her,* don't you? That wonderful woman who kept you even after shoving me out like trash. I thought they loved you there, Louis. I thought you were the new golden child, but I see I was wrong because they kicked you out. I should have known it was she who would pick out something so ugly, but I would have thought you were smarter than to let them make you a navy coat ... knowing I would never wear navy!" She threw the coat at me.

It had been a while. We were new to each other again, but I wasn't sure how to deal with her the way she was.

"I'm sorry, Madame, navy is a color I like, so…"

"*You* like? Who gives a damn what *you* like? You're here to complement me, like a pair of shoes or a scarf! No wonder all our guests were laughing at me, with you dressed in ridiculous clothes, looking like an idiot! I didn't see a single turban back there. This is what I come home to? Your blatant disrespect? You listen here, child…" She strode at me fast, right up in my face. "I don't care that you've grown an inch or two or have a little fuzz over your lip; you belong to me. Do you hear me? From start to finish, I made you. There would be no Louis-Benoit Zamor if there wasn't the benevolent Comtesse Madame Jeanne du Barry, esteemed mistress of the Well-Beloved, once the most powerful man in France!" She was heaving breath through her nose, her eyes focused on my face. I tried to look away. "Look at me, Louis-Benoit."

I looked her in her eyes. I saw her attempt to soften her face, to lower her voice. To calm herself and smile. Once our eyes were locked, she tried the old way.

"I love you so, so much, Louis; you're like my very own son. Don't make me angry; you know how much it hurts me. I've made a pile outside your room of the clothes that clash with me, and I expect you to dispose of them. I'll get you new clothes. The best clothes. But first ... get rid of that ugly navy. You'll get rid of the navy for me, oui?"

She was now soft and sweet again, imploring me. She put her hands up to cup my face. "The Chateau du Barry will be the rival of any home in the kingdom, and that includes the Palace. You will help me, won't you? Because you love me, don't you? Say it."

It was one thing when I was a child, but I was almost a man now. Old enough to be embarrassed by being forced to perform like this. I was also old enough to know there was no place for me to go. She held my fate in her hands, and she would make me pay for our years apart, for how she felt when she was forced to leave while I was allowed to stay.

"Say it," she repeated, her eyes boring into me, one hand stroking my face like I was the most precious thing.

"Of course, Madame."

"Of course?" She laughed prettily, but her eyes were hard. "You say 'of course' if I ask if you want butter with your toast. What do you say to *me*, Louis-Benoit?"

Stroking up and down my cheek. Eyes boring into me, but no warmth in them. I wanted to bite my tongue. I wanted to cover my head. I couldn't even work up a fake smile.

Maybe part of me had expected being shut away would have done her some good. Maybe I had forgotten all of who she was. No matter, I was here, and she was stroking my face. I was captured in her death stare.

I said... "I love you, Madame."

Her face lit up. "What a sweet, sweet boy. Mon chèr, how I missed you. Get rid of the navy, oui?" She kissed me on one cheek, then the other, released my face and walked out of the room. For a long moment, I stared at the ground. Then, I heard Salanave's whisper.

"Mon Dieu, do you think she lost her mind in the Abbey?" Back at the Palace, the cook really hadn't spent that much time watching Madame and me together, stuck in the kitchen as she was.

No, Jeanne du Barry hadn't lost her mind. I had, to think there wouldn't be repercussions. She was simply reasserting her dominance over me. I had felt a taste of freedom, and she was reminding me what I was in front of all these people who thought I was a servant, like them.

I looked up and found three sets of eyes on me, including the boy who had looked up to me minutes ago. Humiliation had taken over now, and I relapsed to what I'd been so long ago.

"What are you looking at?" I snapped at him. His face was instantly awash in hurt, which I ignored. I walked over, snatched up the navy coat, stalked out the door and outside.

I loved that coat. It was the first piece made for me with no one else in mind, in a color I chose. The first thing I had for myself and myself alone since arriving in this godforsaken country. Tears filled my eyes, but I blinked them back, taking a torch from the wall to set it on fire.

I wiped my face brusquely as I watched the coat burn. My survival feeders sprung back to life.

24

———————

Dear Citizen,

*Our re-orientation to each other was awkward, at best, but it
wouldn't stop at her stomping on my briefly held confidence. No, she
had to humiliate me in all ways to make sure I was back in line.
Humiliation or punishment ... they're both really the same thing.
She was always good at both.*

--Zamor

I carried a tray with small pot of hot water, two cups and saucers and little pots of sugar crystals, cream, and loose tea leaves up the stairs. One of the other servants had told me one of the noblewomen wanted tea so here I was, carrying it to her room instead of her coming down, which made much more sense. I slowed when I saw Gaspard standing outside her door, then proceeded. He and I felt no need to speak to each other unless necessary or unless he was barking orders. His eyes watched me as I leaned close to the wood since I had no free hand to knock.

"Duchesse," I called through the door. "I'm here with your tea."

I heard soft conversation on the other side of the door that grew louder with the speaker arriving, the door opening on Madame, herself. She smiled at my surprise.

"There you are, right on time. You can put the tray right over there on the bureau, please, chèr." I walked over. "The Duchesse and I were discussing our time at the Palace. You might not remember, she lived there with her husband for about a year. Now he's off doing business in Spain or Portugal or wherever."

"Italy," the woman said. She was sitting on a small two-seat sofa situated just below the window so she could look out. It was a cloudy day, but the window was open, the soft white sheers billowing in. She had dark hair that contrasted with the whiteness of her skin and her face was plain except for what appeared to be a flush working up her neck as she gazed out as if to avoid looking at me. I didn't remember her and probably wouldn't have. She muttered, "This time it's Italy. The next, who knows."

I nodded in acknowledgment of her, giving a quick bow, prepared to leave. Instead, Madame had quietly moved into the space between me and the door.

"It's criminal how these men treat us, isn't it, chère?" she said to the woman and then looked back at me. "Louis, the Duchesse and I were thinking of tea but then we changed our mind. Or, rather, I changed *her* mind. Why sit alone in a room drinking tea stewing over a man off doing God knows what."

"I love my husband!" The pale woman looked at us when she said that, as if making an argument.

"Of course, chère, I have no doubt. Still, he's not here and you have needs." They looked at each other and began giggling like schoolgirls, at which point I turned to pick up the tray again.

"No matter, it's no bother for me to take it away."

"Put it down, Louis-Benoit, you can take it with you after."

"After what, Madame?"

"Louis," she smiled slyly, "I don't know if you realize you made quite a name for yourself these past few years at the Palace as the wildly wicked and sharp-tonged young page. I hear you can lift a woman up and pleasure her in the air; *surprisingly* strong! they say. Now, to me you're just my sweet baby boy, and always will be, but boys grow up. I almost blush over what I've heard of your exploits with many of the ladies at the Palace."

Now I was stopped still. I glanced over at the Duchesse who was looking down but fanning herself with her hand as that flush moved up over her jaw.

"I told our dear guest you'd be happy to satisfy whatever needs she has in her husband's absence. You'll do that for me, won't you?"

The blood began moving up my neck now. She couldn't be saying what I thought she was? I stepped toward her and spoke under my breath and Madame did the same, her face a mask of sweetness as our heads bent towards each other.

"No, I don't want to," I said.

"Oh, now, don't be contrary. You did it all the time at the Palace."

"I wanted to do it, then. I don't want to now."

"Let me be clear, Louis-Benoit, I know I made it sound like a question, but it wasn't. You spread yourself freely at the Palace you can damn sure do it here for my guests. For my sake. This woman is important, Louis-Benoit, she has important friends all over the world. She's only asked for one thing and if I can give it to her, I'll be in her good graces. *I need this.* The Chateau du Barry is going to be the most popular home in all of French nobility and we will get that way be being the most hospitable." She said it like she was a teacher, schooling me under her breath like she was beginning to lose patience. "The Chateau du Barry will be known for sending people away happy and if that means someone has to put in extra effort then that's what will happen. Think of it this way: we all must contribute where we can. Consider it a personal favor."

"But I'm not a—"

"—you're not a what?" Her eyes cut hard at me, staring at me like she was daring me to say it. We were the same height so, eye-to-eye she glared at me, waiting. A strand of hair fell into her face, blowing with each breath that tickled the skin of my face. Her voice became even softer and sweeter, as if she was speaking to a child. "You think you're better than me, don't you? You think you're smarter? You're neither. Mon Dieu, you've been doing giving it away this entire time! Just do what you're used to doing and add a little finesse. You've seen me at it, you know how it's done," she said, smiling softly. "She's so anxious to be with you I doubt it will take you more than a quarter hour. Or ..." she pulled away slightly and widened her eyes like a thought had just occurred to her. "... oh, did they invite you back to stay at the Palace again? Should I pack your bags for you? You've got someplace else to lay your head, do you?"

Her sarcasm cut like a blade. My eyelids kept blinking and I couldn't look her in her face, anymore. My voice had lost any bit of tenor it had. I felt like I wouldn't be able to do it even if I tried. I felt like a boy again.

"Is everything alright, Madame?" The pale woman called out, firmly. "You said he would. You promised I could have what I want."

She promised. She promised me like I was a hairbrush to pass around.

"Madame, I-I-I... I can't. Please don't ask me to. Don't make me..."

"Oh, chèr, you *can*. We all can." She splayed her hands in an expression that said there was nothing on earth any human being couldn't do. "We are all exactly what we need to be when we need to be it." She put a hand up to grasp the back of my head and pressed her forehead to mine as I struggled to keep my composure. "I know you thought you were special. It's never been you, my love. The greatest king that ever walked this earth, *he* made you special through *his* greatness. And *I* make you special. *I'm* the reason anyone even knows who you are. Now, don't make this more difficult than it needs to be, my heart," she raised her fingers and swiped away a bit of water that had escaped one eye, pressing a kiss against my cheek, gently. "Gaspard will be just outside the door to make sure everything goes as it should. Now, be a dear... make me proud."

She swept out of the room, closing the door behind her, resolutely. I stood, frozen, for a long moment until the woman broke my spell.

"Well, what should we do now, young man?"

I looked over and found her chin raised in challenge, eyes reflecting some sort of coquette look as if she was a pure, virginal damsel and I was a handsome rake in a romance novel thirsting for her.

Madame was right. I could do it, even though I had to summon the image of my old friend Hannah to get through it. Even though I had to close my eyes and close my ears to the sound of her. If romance was what she was looking for, she didn't get it. She got it fast and rough and angry, before my brain had time to catch up. I did the work, the whole time with the litany—I am not a whore, I am not a whore—running through my head.

Of course, saying it didn't make it so.

Afterwards, I buttoned my trousers and straightened my clothes. Then I walked over to where the tray sat on the bureau, grabbing it to carry it away. Gaspard was outside, I knew. He had probably listened to the whole thing. My humiliation was his favorite thing.

The teacups jostled against each other as I used an elbow to turn the doorknob. By that time, the Duchesse was breathing hard in exhaustion and when the door swung inward, Gaspard was standing there. He glanced inside the room at the woman still sprawled on the bed and looked back at me.

"You're very good at performing now, aren't you?" he smirked. *"Run, blackamoor."* He whispered, his words bringing forth a wave of memory and pain. They did their damage as my face heated.

"Go to hell," I said, making my way down the hall, eyes burning.

Later, after a bang on my bedroom door I opened it to find one of the servant children carrying a platter covered by a cloth napkin.

"Bonsoir, Monsieur Zamor. Madame says I'm to give you this for a well-done job."

I pulled the napkin off to find a plate with a large cut of seared beef. One of the best cuts, I could tell. These days I pretty much ate what I wanted, but still, the best cuts of meat were left for Madame and the guests. This one was perfect, just shy of cooked, sliced so the pink flesh shone juicy and tender, and surrounded by asparagus and carrots with a little pot of beurre blanc to pour over it all. It smelled delicious. My stomach turned.

The boy's stomach grumbled as he tried not to stare at my plate.

"Your mother works in the laundry, doesn't she? And your sister gathers the eggs?"

The boy nodded. His little sister was also always dropping the eggs, if I recalled. But his mother was one of the good people at the Chateau. Whenever I helped her with laundry, she thanked me. She took more than her fair share of abuse from the other staff members because her two children were there underfoot. But she was one of the best workers at the Chateau, raising her children to work hard, also.

I covered the plate with the napkin again.

"Listen here. You take this back to your room and share it with your mother and sister. And don't let anyone know you have it, or they'll take it from you. You hear?"

His eyes widened and nodded. "Oui, Monsieur. Merci, Monsieur Zamor!"

He was a ghost as he rushed away with the food. I was able to keep my bile down for another few minutes until it caught up to me and I wretched into my chamber pot.

25

———————

I dreamt I was in the Labyrinth being chased by hounds. Every time I ran into a dead end, I was petrified turning back would lead me into the path of the hunters. I couldn't see them, but I knew who would be on those horses: the Well-Beloved, Madame, and Gaspard would lead with all of the royal court behind them. I ran into another dead-end wall of trees but this time, when I turned back to try a different route, the dogs were there in front of me, blocking my path. I walked backwards, holding my hands out in supplication so they wouldn't attack, hearing the celebratory voices of my hunters laughing as my back hit the wall of trees.

And then the hounds lunged forward!

When I raised my hand to ward them off, a flash of white caught my eye. I looked at my arm and it was cold white marble. I looked down at my body and, instead saw the stone body of a fox. The hounds stopped and whined with confusion, pacing together in front of me like lost puppies. And when the group of hunters came into view before me, the Well-Beloved stepped forward to scold his dogs.

"Silly dogs," he said in his jovial way. "There's nothing here but this fox statue. Don't you know the difference between stone and living animal?" he laughed. He laughed. He laughed. I sat up in bed breathing fast, my dressing gown plastered with sweat as I struggled to right my breathing and slow my heart.

The dream didn't leave me, nor did the feelings it unearthed. Madame was trying to destroy my soul. I could let her, or I could fight. I could turn into that stone statue, or I could face her with the fire of my humanity.

Three days later when the guests were leaving the dining room after dinner, Madame leaned over to me.

"The woman who sat at the end of the table, the Marquise, she will need your assistance tonight. You can go on up now."

Invisible fire streaked up from the pit of me as if it had been waiting for the strike of flint to set it off. That strike was set by Madame's request; my face suddenly hot with the force of it.

For three days I hated myself. Three days I'd castigated and criticized and couldn't bear to look at myself in a mirror for what I'd become, and she was asking me to do it again. Three days of feeling like I had barely escaped the death of my spirit. My heartbeat sounded in my ears.

"No, I won't," I said, albeit weakly.

"Come now, let's not go through this again," she sighed, as though fatigued.

"I won't do it again," I said, louder and more firmly. "Not now, not ever."

She stopped to say goodnight to one of the guests and when it was only she, Gaspard, and me left in the room she stepped over to the door and shut it. She turned back, spearing me with an irritated look. Then she walked over to the place on the buffet that held all the bottles of alcohol. It reminded me of when the Well-Beloved poured me my first cognac, when I learned my parents had sold me. Now, as she poured herself one in a crystal-cut glass, the amber liquid twinkling in the firelight, it seemed the cognac would accompany another important conversation.

Taking a deep swallow, Madame turned back to me.

"I don't know what you're thinking to speak to me like that, but as I said, you will do as I say." She said it, dismissively, like I was an idiot.

But I was about done with being treated like one. I took a deep breath and my next words came without a tremble.

"I will not, you evil bitch."

A moment of stunned silence. Then, suddenly, Gaspard's footsteps as he ran across the room, flinging a tray table aside, to grab my coat in his hands. The table crashed to the floor as he pulled me up to stare into his face, nostrils spewing snot, and veins popping in his forehead skin.

"Gaspard! Let him go!"

"You filthy piece of trash," he snarled at me, covering my face in saliva. "I should tear you to pieces. I should—"

"—Put him down, now!"

He breathed like the snorting bull he was, but then my feet landed on the ground as he released me.

"Why are you always defending him?" the manager whined, eyes on Madame.

"Violence doesn't solve everything, Gaspard, he's a child trying to prove he's a man. Louis-Benoit, if you're going to try to insult me make it something I *haven't* heard before. It's almost like if I were to call you a worthless nègre. See, how it doesn't even sting you've heard it so many times? Now, I understand that young boys want to display some sort of misguided pride..."

"I'm not a boy."

"Oh, but you're acting like one. You, obviously, still need guidance. I'm *guiding* you, Louis-Benoit, to think with your head and not your pride. Let me guide you to become the best you can be."

"I'm not doing it and I'm not saying it again. Him," I jerked my chin his way, "listening at the door like a pervert. Kick me out if you want, I'll sleep on the streets."

"You, on the streets?" she laughed. "You've lived a charmed life, so I think I need to remind you the streets are not, in fact, lined with silk and gold. Only a person who's actually lived on the streets is qualified to say something as asinine as that. It just proves what a child you are. How would you even survive?"

"I don't know, maybe I'll do what you're trying to make me do.

Apparently, I'm good at it. I can do it for myself as easily as I can do it for you."

Her smile fell. "Except for the fact that you belong to me."

"I'm not doing it."

"Oh, for Dieu's sake!" Gaspard said, his now-red face showing him about to blow. "You'll do what she says and without that mouth of yours."

"Or what, you'll hit me? Go ahead, there's nothing new about that. You still can't make me."

"This is what happens," he said, turning to Madame and gesturing toward the length of me with his hand. "Look at what the two of you have done."

"What are you talking about?" she asked.

"You let him get away with murder! Now he stands there telling you what he's going to do like he has a right."

"You're blaming me?" Her face was incredulous. "Maybe if every solution for you didn't involve a fist, he'd be more inclined to do the perfectly reasonable things I ask. But he doesn't trust me because of you!"

"I've only tried to enforce the rules! But I can't enforce rules that you don't set. He walks around like he's the king, himself. I knew the second he arrived he'd be trouble, spoiled little..."

"I've raised him the best way I know now!" She bent at the waist to scream at him, hair flopping into her face. "No one will ever know the difficulty of being a mother! No one ever appreciates us! He holds my heart hostage and he knows it!"

If it wasn't real, it would be hilarious. If it wasn't my life, I could sit back and find it all entertaining, that these were the people I was left with. That this was my life,

My face screwed up on its own. "You're not my mother! You're not any kind of mother! You're just a woman trying to pimp me out, but I'm not doing it!"

"You'll do what I say! Gaspard will watch you do it, if that's what it takes..."

"...that's sick!" I screamed. "You're both sick!"

"Sick or not, you will do it, chèr, because I say so!"

"Finally," Gaspard said, sarcastically. "Maybe five years too late, but at least she puts her foot down."

"Don't you think you can speak to me like that," she said to him, her eyes sharp. "You're no better than he is, overstepping your bounds. He will do what he's told, and you will stay in your place."

I couldn't have Gaspard watching me again. I would die. Not figuratively, I would literally die if I went into the cold place again, and I'd never find my way back. Nothing I was saying was moving her. In fact, they seemed to be coming together in their plan to force me. My mind scoped my options as an invisible band of stress tightened around my head.

"I'll tell the Queen what you're making me do," I said. They both quieted down, looking at me. Madame's face grew blank of emotion and Gaspard looked surprised. I'd hit my mark. "Yeah, that's right, I'll tell her you're trying to raise the status of the Chateau du Barry at *my* expense. Maybe she'll take me back then, so I can tell the world how low you're willing to sink. She'll make you into a laughingstock, having to buy respectability by selling the talents of the page gifted to you by the deceased King. That you can't draw interest on your own and need to sell me to convince people to come? It will shame the court *and* the King. Forget being banished from the Palace, they'll banish you from France, *entirely*."

I pulled it all out of my ass in desperation, but it was plausible enough to make wipe the mask from her face. Her eyes went glassy as the ramifications rolled through her head. Because though she'd felt free to be as promiscuous as she wanted with the King, that was her official sanctioned role. Without that role, her reputation was always at risk. There was no doubt the Queen would finish that reputation off if she knew about me and used me against her.

In the midst of their stunned silence the door opened behind us, and we turned to find the Marquise Madame had spoken of stepping inside the room, to the dismay of a servant who followed quickly, face fearful at having failed to stop the woman.

"Madame, is everything quite alright? I could hear your voices all the way down the hall. Why was there so much arguing? And how long must I wait for my entertainment?" She looked at me like she had looked at dessert at dinner. My eyes sped to my benefactress who looked at me for a long moment. Then, her shoulders dropped in resignation and frustration.

"Fine," she hissed to me under her breath as she walked past, presenting her smiling mask to the guest. "I'm so sorry for the noise, my dear Marquise, we are a family here and as such we, occasionally, have our spats. I was mistaken, my Louis is feeling out of sorts this evening and can't possibly do you justice."

The band of stress around my head loosened—the dogs fell back —and I could breathe, again. But the woman wanted what she wanted. The Marquise's annoyed look gave way when her eyes settled on the Manager.

"Alright then, I'll take that one," she gestured toward Gaspard. His face melted in one of his smirks, showing how clearly ridiculous he found that idea. But as one... two... *three* beats passed without word, he swung his head to spear Madame with a look of incredulity. She raised her hands as if helpless, one hand fluttering behind her head and settling on her hair as she shut her eyes briefly.

"Okay, no, I'm sorry, my head of security is not available, either, but I have an even better idea. We just took in a new apprentice; strapping young man heads taller than these two and shoulders as wide as the door. Beautiful man who came to us all the way from the mountains. Dumb as a rock but a national treasure, all the same. It's a pure sin for such a work of art to have been hidden away in the Alps all his life, but he's here now. Young man," she called out to the servant still standing inside the door. "Go get the new apprentice, tell him I have a job for him."

I breathed in relief. I was sorry for the new apprentice, but I was happy for me. The Marquise left, pacified, and Madame gave me a side-ways glance. Her face was wiped clean of emotion, telling me there was much emotion going on in her now.

"Feeling very proud of yourself, I'm sure. Don't make too much of this, young man, I still run this place. You threaten me again and you'll be sorry." She said the words, but not with conviction. I heard the doubt in her voice, and I was sure Gaspard did, as well. His eyes were glued to her, fists clenching and unclenching, uselessly.

I gave a brief head bob. "Bonsoir, Madame," I said, leaving the room.

Walking down the hall my heart slowed the pace of its beating. The band around my head relaxed entirely. And now I was trembling, this time with the amazement of having won this battle.

I passed the young apprentice coming the opposite way. He was, indeed, heads taller than me, with broad shoulders, and innocent excitement to impress Madame on his handsome face. He dipped his head at me, briefly—he hadn't quite figured out if I was a fellow servant or a low-level noble—and kept on to the dining room. I didn't know how he'd feel about what he was about to be ordered to do, but I couldn't worry about everyone else. *Every fox has to survive its own hunt*, I thought.

PART II
———
(THE ROAD TO PARIS)

—————

26

1 *785, Eight years later*

Dear Citizen,

I grew into manhood among the pristine lawns and meticulous gardens of the Chateau du Barry. Just north of the Palace, guests of the Chateau were treated to a lifestyle befitting royalty and included people who secretly resented the formality and haughty snobbery of the Palace. Low-level nobles without the rank to request audience with the King loved to visit the Chateau where they were doted on, and their bruised egos soothed.

By the age of twenty-three, I had stopped asking Madame to free me because she took such extreme pleasure at turning me down. She always found an excuse—her hard-boiled egg was perfect— who would get it for her if I wasn't there? It was raining; who would hold the umbrella over her head if I wasn't there? And the always constant—who would get her morning chocolat if not Zamor? She always delivered these excuses with a pretty smile and color high in her cheeks that told me her feeders were being well-nourished on the pain she caused me with each denial.

I needed a plan to survive once I figured out how to get free. Right now, my resources came down to my brain, cunning, and proximity to the seat of power. And a never-ending supply of nobles to steal from. I'd be a fool not to use those resources.

And, yes, I was still allowed at the Palace! After my initial humiliation at being kicked out, I now took any and every opportunity to visit Versailles because I wanted to know what the servants knew. To be welcome, I did my best to soften my rough edges. I stopped making enemies for the fun of it. I moved with purpose while making it look like I had no purpose but to serve. Soon, they didn't even notice me; one more page walking through busy halls was nothing to them. Information became my currency and discretion my protection.

Though the King and Queen recognized me, unlike before, I didn't dare draw too much attention to myself. If anything, once I was no longer immediately underfoot, the Queen used me to her advantage, speaking whenever I was within earshot about certain things going on in her court. What new dress the Queen was having made and how much it cost. What new musician would be playing in the Queen's salon. How extravagant the Queen's hair would be for the next ball. I quickly figured out the Queen was using me to annoy her nemesis, who soon began to do the same, dropping tidbits in my ear about nobles who came to the Chateau du Barry to get away from the craziness of the Palace.

But I kept some bits to myself, especially when I thought sharing the information might blow back on me. For example, the time when Madame pointedly said to me, "I do hope the Queen stops putting that dot on her face. Everyone thinks it looks ridiculous. I would hate for her to be embarrassed." I wasn't fool enough to pass along the insult.

Access to the Palace came with other advantages. On one visit, I heard the most beautiful music coming from the salon, and when I reached the doorway, I was surprised to see a tall black man holding the violin. I'd never heard a musician of his caliber, let alone a black one.

Barnier told me his name was Joseph Bologne, the Chevalier de St. Georges. He was so handsome the women in the salon were paying more attention to him than to the music, including the Queen. His visits to the Palace became regular when he began teaching the Queen piano. But it was the string music that struck me. I begged Barnier to get me a violin so I could learn how to play. Once it was in my hands, my love for the violin would last a lifetime.

--Zamor

27

I strode through the halls of Versailles to the servants' quarters and looked up to see a short, stocky man striding just as force-fully in the opposite direction. Immediately, I turned to follow him.

He took the hallways like a maze he'd memorized, and once he'd gotten down to the dank back room of the servants' quarters, he stopped dead. I took that opportunity to hook an arm around his neck from behind, pulling him down backward. But he was strong. He used an elbow to knock the wind from me, loosening my grip for just a moment. In that brief second, he slipped from under my arm, turned and grabbed me under one leg, using it to flip me over and the other arm to cut off my air. I struggled, but his massive bulk was impossible to escape.

"Same thing every time," he ground in my ear. "If you can't learn, there's nothing I can do to teach you." My eyes watered and felt like they would pop out of my head, so I slapped the dirty cobbled floor in surrender. "Giving up so soon?"

I would have surrendered if I could talk. He released me. I sucked in air and turned over, giving him a dirty look and clearing my throat.

"I'm starting to think these lessons of yours, Fabian, are just excuses for you to get out your aggression," I coughed.

"Of course, they are. I put up with the shit these royals are shoveling all day, I have to find something to knock around, and you'll do," he smiled.

Fabian had an irregular smile born of years of fighting other men in his home province for money. His nose lay on his face like a twisting worm trying to escape the skin, also the result of too many breaks. He was short but abnormally strong, and it suited him in the roughest areas of town. I met him because one day I overheard him complaining that working the grounds at Versailles was making him soft. It occurred to me it might be worth a little bit of my small allowance to get some lessons from him on how to defend myself. So far, all I had learned was how to continue to take a beating.

"How did you get the upper hand again?" I asked, picking myself off the floor.

"How? Pain, Zamor, pain makes you weak." He clasped one hand behind my neck. "You have to understand pain is inevitable. Once you know that, once you know *it will come no matter what you do*, then you can hold strong when it happens. Remember your goal. It will be bad until it's not. Do you want to look back and realize you could have withstood it if you only held on a little longer? Withstand as long as you can for that day when you can beat the bastard's ass."

All the servants at the Palace and Louveciennes knew about how Gaspard hated me. Occasionally, he would attack just to remind himself he still could, but not often these days. "I'm not concerned; he's a dying fossil. I just know that someday I'll be out in the world, and I need to know how to take care of myself."

"Pipe dreams, my friend. Madame will never give you your freedom papers. There's a running bet in the servant's quarters that you will be by her side in that chateau until the very end. I have two livres says she will never let you go. And when the time comes, and she passes from this earth, I'm sure only the wails of the Marly Machine will drown out your cries of grief."

It was a familiar sentiment that Madame and I were that close. No matter what I said or did, people were convinced they understood our relationship. I had long stopped trying to disabuse them of the notion; they would think what they wanted. For some people being close to Madame was some special—like she said—and they would defer to me differently than they would if I was a regular servant. So, if it helped me, I would keep my lips sealed and allow the rumors to reproduce as rumors do.

But Fabien's words made me shudder. I couldn't think of anything worse than to die by the side of that woman. That would mean I failed at everything I ever hoped to accomplish—first and foremost, freedom from her. "You're wrong," I said.

Fabien smiled and punched me on the shoulder. "You'll do better next time. Now get the hell out of this palace and back home; you know they hate you here."

On my way out, I stopped by the massive kitchen and filled a bag full of pastries, some to eat and some to give to Salanave, who liked to keep up with the royal pastries out of professional competitiveness. It was important to her since she had been transferred from Versailles to Louveciennes—a demotion, really—that she keep up her baking skills. While she'd grown to prefer the smaller kitchen, it still wasn't the Royal Palace.

I walked from the building across to the arena and the stables. I climbed on Lightning, giving her a nudge, and we galloped out of the stables, picking up speed as we left. The wind against my face felt cool and pleasant. Always, that short ride to and from the Chateau was one of the best things about my present situation.

Salanave's eyes lit up a bit later when I opened my bag to reveal the pastries and baked goods I'd wrapped in paper to keep safe. She wiped her hands on her apron and came at the bag with her hands and sparkling eyes, pulling out our favorites. Salanave and I had come to love croissants.

"Who's coming tonight?" I asked her.

"I don't know," she garbled over a mouthful of pastry. "But if you find out, let me know."

I didn't like not knowing what was happening in the house or who was on the premises. I had bad memories of some popular nobles from childhood and did my best to avoid them for both our sakes. Sometimes we hosted first-time guests who had never known Madame as the King's mistress and didn't know about me at all. But more often, guests came having heard of me, arriving to stare me down until I would be forced to say something abrasive enough to shock them out of their bad manners. Knowing who was coming helped me decide how my evening would go.

I left the kitchen in the direction of Madame's study, passing aristocrats along the way, tipping my head to them as I passed. They barely looked my way. It was the gift of the servant to be unnoticeable. Insulting, for sure, but it had its advantages. Even I, unique as I was to the rest of the staff by virtue of my skin color, had grown to become part of the scenery in this place. Until I opened my mouth, I was as insignificant as a potted plant.

Compared to the Palace, the Chateau at Louveciennes seemed a tiny home. There were no tunnels to sneak through or hidden panels in walls to hide behind. I learned to be more careful and strategic about my research.

On this day, I popped the rest of the croissant in my mouth and looked around the empty hallway. An unlit candle sat in a sconce on the wall. I grabbed it and walked to her study, where the door was cracked open. Through the sliver, I could just see the side of Gaspard from where he stood against the wall inside and heard Madame's voice.

"...Vandenmyer will finish up the paperwork," she was saying. "He's very discreet."

"It shouldn't be long," a man's voice said. "I only need to turn over some property, and that will go quickly. I'll then be able to pay you immediately. I can't thank you enough, kind Madame..."

At the sound of shuffling papers and a scooting chair, I pounced away from the door just as it opened. Quickly, I pulled open the drawer of the closest hallway table and was peering inside when Madame noticed me.

"Oh, Louis-Benoit..."

"Madame," I looked up as if surprised. "This hallway is so dark I was looking for … ah, here it is." I pulled a candle from the drawer and held it up. "I will light it to ease your way."

"Thank you, Louis. Sometimes he is very thoughtful," she joked with her guest. "I already have a candle here, but light that one and leave it, then help my maid prepare my bath. I have a fancy for a soak after dinner."

"Of course, Madame," I said.

The thin, sandy-haired man's face was all lines and stress. He looked past as he passed by, shuffling behind her. Gaspard came last, watching me light my candle against an existing flame. He wanted to catch me in a lie so badly I could feel it. I smiled at him and went about securing the candle in its wall sconce.

The Manager hadn't been able to catch me in a lie since I was young, that's how good I was. Disappointment clouded his features, but he followed Madame, and once they rounded the corner, I slipped into her office to see what the meeting had been about.

Heading over to her desk, I looked down at a page that lay on top. It looked like a report of property value. After moving it aside, I saw her open ledger underneath. The neat, elegant writing listed $5500 livres, a little more than the amount of the property value, and the man's name beside it. The ink had smudged slightly where she'd laid his document on top.

It was obvious she was buying his property or using evidence of his property to give him a loan. I wondered how many of the other nobles who visited the Chateau were doing the same? Though she was making a bit of money, likely as a fee for the transaction, she wasn't a lending institution. What reason could there be for her to engage in the inconvenience?

I added it to the list of things the Comtesse did to keep herself ingratiated with society. She was no longer connected to the royal family by title, so I assumed she was eager for any way to stay involved in the lives of the highest society.

I went back to the kitchen, grabbed an apple from a bowl on the counter, and took a chair at the wooden table upon which Salanave was slapping down bread dough with vigor. She was still using the same levain, and I could smell the fermented yeast in the air.

"There's a ledger on Madame's desk that looks like she's making a loan to one of our guests."

Salanave and had something of an understanding. I wouldn't reveal what she told me, and she wouldn't tell anyone I'd planned to kill the last King. Confidence on both our parts was prudent.

"It is the life, I tell you." *Slap!* went the dough. It was a poorly kept secret that the cook in any kitchen was both highly adept in matters of finance and well aware of the affairs of a household. "Still getting an allowance from France, earning interest on the money and the property Louis XVI gave back to her. And helping the aristocrats to earn their allegiance, which is even more valuable. She's still competing with the Queen, petit. I hope it doesn't come back to bite her."

28

———————

S tuck at the Chateau, it was hard to get a break from people. But with limited choices on where I could go—and a childhood memory that didn't endear the neighboring towns to me—I was relegated to finding a safe place as far away from the house as possible, while still on the property. That meant the stretch of lawn, bordering thicket of trees, and the grounds of the pavilion beyond. I took Lightning and we found our spot along the side of the huge expanse of grass leading to the outdoor fountain and amphitheater on the way to the pavilion. I sat down under a tree while the horse enjoyed the breeze for a pleasant hour. Then we were interrupted.

"There you are." I looked up. A young man, whose brown hair looked like it was cut in his mother's kitchen, came striding towards me. He seemed to me a big child, face spotted with tiny freckles and tight in annoyance. He came at me purposefully with great strides and stomped past me to Lightning, who was grazing on wildflowers in an unkempt section of lawn.

Lightning was about twenty-four by now, and she acted like it. Aside from simply refusing to move when she didn't want to, she had taken to being mean to riders, so she was in the stables most of the time, except for the trainers and me taking her out to exercise. I still loved her as much as when she and I had made our escape together.

The young man had a curious way about him. Even as he stomped angrily my way, he tapped his big thumb against his thigh, pausing after every four or so taps. I was hypnotized by this oddness when it suddenly ended with his grabbing Lightning's reins and looking up at me to give me what I was sure was meant to be a dirty look. "We've been looking for her for an hour. Duchesse Mirabelle wanted a ride, and I wanted her to have the oldest, gentlest horse. You might have told someone you were taking her. Move out of the way."

He was obviously new because though Lightning was many things, gentle wasn't one of them. In fact, being taken away from me abruptly might introduce him quickly to her ill temper.

"You're taking away my ride," I said. "*You* move out of *my* way. I don't need permission to take that horse."

"Yeah, why not? Everyone else needs permission. That's right— according to the other servants here, you think you're better than everyone ... I forgot."

"Better than you, for sure," I said. "Best not forget next time."

He glared at me, his errant thumb with the life of its own tapping against Lightning's saddle where his hands rested. "Why does she keep you around? Everybody talks about what a pain you are." I could see one of Lightning's big eyes roll to look at him, getting more agitated with every moment.

"That tapping is annoying her. I suggest you stop."

"No one would tolerate you other than Madame, you know. I've heard all the rumors. She must be s saint. I never listen to gossip but if you're going to make my life difficult, then..." his words were cut short as Lightning—having had enough—took off.

"Told you," I mumbled, putting a placeholder in my book.

Fortunately for the boy, he wasn't strapped to Lightning, but her quick exit jerked the reins from him, and as I was getting up, he was falling backward. He fell so hard that for a moment he was silent. I stepped over, looking down at his freckled face as his eyelids fluttered, fighting unconsciousness.

"Hey, boy," I said down to him. "Can you speak?"

"Of course, I can," he sat up and then immediately fell back down, losing the fight.

"Great," I mumbled, pushing my book into my waistband. "Not only don't I have a ride, now I have you."

A little while later, l had dragged him by his legs back to the stables, my folded shirt strapped to the back of his head with the rope he used as a belt to keep his hard skull from taking any more abuse. The blacksmith came out to see what was causing the strange dragging sound.

"Ah, Henri tripped again, did he? He is clumsy, that boy. With all that counting he does, you'd think he'd count his steps so he could stay on his own two feet." He bent down to look at Henri's head and called for somebody who knew how to patch people. That was my cue to leave.

I cleaned up for dinner and later that evening stood quietly in the room listening to Madame try to impress a new dinner guest, some Duc from the south. The Duc was husband to Duchesse Mirabelle, who was complaining of a terrible ride with an unruly horse that kept trying to buck her.

"It's a miracle I'm alive," she said between bites.

"...so sorry, my dear. We'll get you a more pleasant horse next time," Madame said.

"No harm done," the Duc said as if it was his backside. His wife gave him a dirty look. "It's hard to control horses. Speaking of which, have you had a chance to see the Queen's new horse? Lovely, majestic beast with red-brown hair and a mane that shines in the sun. Fitting for our beautiful Queen."

Madame's lips grew tight with annoyance. I knew the look.

"Our Queen is truly most beautiful and intelligent," she said, spooning a bit of crème brulée into her mouth as she looked down demurely. "And resembles so closely her brother, the Honorable Holy Roman Emperor. It's amazing how his handsome face looks both the same and different on her." Her innocent tone and demure expression did nothing to take away from the viciousness of the insult. The two of them focused intently on her as the promise of gossip hung in the air.

Annoyance sliced through me. She was reckless. She didn't know these people. They could easily leave here and go straight to the Queen to report what Madame was saying. Normally I didn't interrupt when she was bad-mouthing the Queen, but I could see the color brewing on her face. Stepping close to her, I leaned down with my wine decanter to interrupt her thought process.

"Wine, Madame?"

She glanced up at me, a quick frown flashing and disappearing. "My glass is still half full—of course not." She waved me away and continued speaking. "Though honestly, I don't imagine one would ever deny they are closely related; it is almost like she is a muted, very muted version. Something about the bone structure that suits him well, but her...?" She raised her eyebrows in question, and the visitors laughed.

"Madame," I said. She looked at me sharply. "Wine?"

"Mon Dieu, my dear Madame," the Duc said. "Take some more wine so this man may relax. He seems determined to give it."

"He doesn't care about the wine," she smiled at them slyly. "Louis-Benoit is trying to censor me. Sometimes he forgets I'm the parent and he's the child."

"I'm twenty-three."

"One's children never grow up in one's eyes. Please, Louis, stop this and then step back and allow me to finish my conversation."

"By all means." I started pouring, and pouring, and pouring to nervous snickers around the room. I filled it to the very top, close to overflowing. "Is that enough? Now at least you can say the wine made your lips so loose."

The room exploded in laughter, and she smiled, feigning shock.

It wasn't unusual for us to snipe at each other. Mostly I just stayed to myself, but we had an odd relationship. She was forty-two, but we behaved more like siblings, especially when we got on each other's nerves.

"Mind your business, page," Gaspard said from across the room.

That annoyed me even more. Of all people, he should know better. But I stepped back.

"Yes, I heard the Emperor came here incognito a few years back," the Duc said as the memory came to him. His wife's cheeks grew ruddy with the scent of juicy scandal. "If I do say, it was very bold of you, Madame, to invite the Queen's brother to Louveciennes."

"Invite?" Madame scoffed. "I didn't invite him; he came of his own volition. What woman on earth would turn the Holy Roman Emperor down if he showed up on her doorstep, rakishly handsome and requesting only a little to eat and a quick view of the Marly Machine? Though he loves his sister like any brother would, he refused to stay at Versailles. The stress there. He needed to be where he could think clearly. I don't know if you're aware that he came to France on a mission," she leaned forward in a fake whisper. "An *emergency* mission to ... entice the King into performing his duties. To teach him how to get in the mood. The dear Emperor told me it was truly difficult to see his sister so heartbroken that her own husband couldn't rouse himself to touch her. It's a blow to any woman's ego."

"Oh, that would truly be mortifying," the Duchess said, eyes sparkling with the salaciousness of the conversation.

"But as I told him, she could hardly be blamed. She was merely fourteen years old when they married; what could she have known of how to please a king? It takes a grown woman to know that. Or at least a skilled one, which she wasn't either. Of course, it was not my place to give this advice, but I did demonstrate the little I know of men with the kind Emperor, who was a willing and rapt student. After his visit with me, the Emperor had his visit with the King, and miracle-upon-miracles, a short time later the Queen was with their first child. Voilà ... I saved the monarchy."

The Duc and Duchess dissolved into laughter and applause at Madame's wit, thrilled at the morsel of information. Across the room, Gaspard smiled at her audacity, his face shining in a way that it never did for anyone else.

It was no secret that Emperor Joseph II had visited Madame du Barry upon her return to Louveciennes, a visit that coincided with a period when the entire country was seven years waiting for the King and Queen to consummate their marriage. Nobody really knew if it was lack of desire, a medical condition, or just an aversion to having relations while the entire court stood outside the bedroom door waiting to hear the sounds of the coupling (I could certainly understand that). It seemed XVI lacked his grandfather's proclivities towards watching and being watched.

By the time the Holy Roman Emperor came to visit his sister at the demand of his mother, Empress Maria Theresa, news had spread through all of Europe that it was the Queen's fault France didn't have an heir to the throne. At the time, there was rampant speculation about his true motivation for visiting his sister's arch nemesis, but no one had dared suggest anything untoward had happened. Until now, that is ... the story from the Madame's own lips would spread like wildfire.

"That reckless *coquine*"—*hussy*—"is going to get us all hanged," Salanave said when I told her later. "This could come back on all of us if the Queen is in a mood. If Madame is exiled again, we'll all be out on the street!"

"...And he stood there smiling like it was funny," I said of Gaspard. "I thought his job was to protect her. He's smiling like an idiot while she puts a target on her back."

I'd learned my lesson about screwing around with people of power just for the hell of it. I wasn't planning to do it again without a purpose and a real shot at succeeding.

Salanave frowned. "I give it three days before the news gets back to the Palace, tops."

For a rumor that vicious, we might find out while burning in our beds that the Queen had sent guards to burn the house down.

29

And then... retribution.

"It's a lie!"

Madame's shriek rang through the house on her return from visiting a noblewoman in town. Her three ladies ran behind her, trying to keep up with her aimless, erratic steps. It looked like she was leading them in some strange dance in fits and starts over the foyer floor. She stopped suddenly and turned around, bending at the waist and yelling at them: "Leave me alone!" The ladies stopped and reared back, but Gaspard stepped forward authoritatively, only to get two hands against his chest, pushing him away with all her might. "I don't want you! Leave me alone, all of you! Where is Louis-Benoit? I want Louis-Benoit!"

I was standing right there in the doorway of the foyer, but it wasn't until I took a step forward and the movement swung her red-rimmed eyes my way that I realized she was drunk. Gaspard kept wine in the carriage to help her relax during long trips. The day trip wasn't that long, but apparently, something had driven her to hit the bottle to make her this drunk.

When her eyes finally focused on me, she staggered across the marble floor, hands grabbing my silk vest and the lace cravat in a death grip. "Louis-Benoit, they lie! They're all lying to me! And I know who started it. We all know who started it!"

I didn't have an idea what lie it was, but I knew exactly who she meant, and she was probably right. I was just relieved we were no longer living in suspense. The Queen had a network of noblewomen at her disposal, and apparently, had decided rumors were retribution enough. It was through one of those women that she spilled her most potent secrets.

Gaspard came over and hissed at me. "Get her upstairs, you fool, do you want the whole household to see her like this?"

"I'm the fool? I'm not the one who unscrewed the cork, but don't worry, I'll clean up this mess for you, as always," I snapped back, annoyed. "Come, Madame, let's go upstairs."

Indeed, a man on the second landing was standing in his doorway, and I heard another door crack open just wide enough to peer out without being seen, searching for the source of the ruckus. As we went up the stairs, heads poked back inside their rooms when I glanced their way.

It was a pitiful sight. She was trying to melt into me as I hooked an arm around her waist while she talked to the side of my face and stumbled over her own feet. Heads of nosy guests poked out of their rooms and quickly darted back in when I looked their way. I draped one of her arms around my neck to help support her weight.

"They are spreading lies all through Paris ... all through France," she said, her eyes large in her flushed face.

"No matter, Madame."

"They're saying my Louis offered me up. That he told the bishop he was sorry and damned me to hell as a succubus."

"...I'm sure all lies, like you said."

"But there was a whole roomful of ladies, and they all got quiet when the one said it. They looked away from me like they do. You know how they do! When those rich bitches look away from you and down at their tea. They're all saying it, all the noble-born women. Mon Dieu, they've all been saying it all along!"

"...Gossip. Just gossip."

She tripped, and I had to haul her up the last few steps while she prattled on. Her hair had long escaped its pins and looked a mess all over her head.

"You don't understand. They're saying my Louis never even waited for them to ask … that he was *eager* to deny me. That he couldn't wait! She said he referred to me as a … a common …. And then the one looked at me and said, 'Oh, I'm sorry, dear, I thought you knew. Even the most wonderful men can be cruel sometimes,' she said in that smarmy, fake sweet way. And then they all got quiet, like they do. You know how they do!" Her face scrunched up all at once and she let out a wail so loud another door opened.

"Madame, is all well?" said a man visiting for a couple of weeks with his mistress. He looked at me like I was the perpetrator of some crime against the woman in my arms. "Madame, if this blackamoor is…"

"Get yourself into your room, Monsieur," I snapped at him. "Before you go calling names don't forget *you're* the guest here. Don't forget your place."

"Did you hear that?" he whined, answered by a following— useless—Gaspard assuring him that "the blackamoor" was her most trusted servant. I bristled at the term, which was exactly why he said it. Bastard.

By the time I got her to her room, she was clutching onto me like she'd fall to the floor without me to hold onto. I pulled her along, her skirts seeming to want to pull her to the ground, and finally deposited her onto her bed.

"Get some sleep, Madame; you'll feel better in the morning. I'll send in your ladies."

"No!" she said when I moved to leave, grabbing me again and pulling me down beside her. She held my arm, her fingers digging into me.

"He wouldn't have done that, he wouldn't have done that," she continued like we were still in the midst of a conversation, her head shaking back and forth like it was me she had to convince. Gaspard came in and his eyes hardened immediately at the scene.

"Madame, this isn't proper," he whispered. "They will gossip even more than they already do because of this one in your bedroom."

First, I was a *blackamoor*; now I was a *this one*. It was ridiculous to me because I'd been in her bedroom since I was ten, but suddenly it was improper to him; *now* he cared about what was improper? Gaspard stepped forward to try to physically remove her hands from me.

"Don't you touch me!" she screamed so loudly he jerked back in surprise.

"But Madame, I was only—"

"Comtesse! I am Comtesse to you, you snake! All those years I was locked up and you were out in the world. What did you do to protect my good name? What did you do for me? You were always only *his* protector; you were never mine. He wanted to fire you time and time again, and I stopped him. Me! But your allegiance was never to me, was it? At least Louis-Benoit never forgot me, sending me lovely packages. Even as angry as he was with me, he still treated me as befits my station. Where were you?"

Ah, that was it. This wasn't about her sudden trust of me; it was about her sudden distrust of *him*.

"I did all I could, Mad—Comtesse, but you know the Queen had me removed from the premises. Just like you. But I was the one who arranged for my second-in-demand to send those packages. Tell her, blackamoor."

Now, I might have corroborated his story if he hadn't followed his plea by calling me a name. I sat silently and let that indict him. He looked like he wanted to throttle me.

"You liar!" Madame seethed. "You're a liar just like all of them. At least I can trust Louis-Benoit. I don't always like him, but at least I can trust *him*. I want you out of this house."

His face fell like she'd taken his favorite toy. "You don't mean that."

"Don't tell me what I don't mean," she fairly spit at him. "Get out!"

Gaspard speared me with a look of pure hatred, turned stiffly, and left the room. Almost as soon as he was gone, her eyes took on a focused, fevered look.

"Oh Louis, Louis, my King, you couldn't have… you couldn't have done what they said." She turned to me, grabbing my lapels, her eyes wide like saucers.

"How could he have called me those things? How could he have given that to her? How could he hand me over to the woman who hated me the most when I only ever loved him with all my heart and soul?!" Her words became louder and more garbled by the second.

"I sat by his side," she wailed, eyes sprouting fresh tears and her hands jerking my clothes on each point. "When he was covered with boils, and no one could bear the smell of his rotting flesh, I stayed with him. None of the other girls were there. His precious daughters weren't there. That piece of nothing that calls herself the Queen, she was as far away from that room as she could get! I didn't see his sickness, Louis-Benoit, I only saw him, the King I loved and would give my life for. I held his hand until they pulled me away and forced me to leave, and now, I hear from strangers that he begrudged me even that. That he blamed me for leaving him alone. They made me leave! I would have stayed by his side, forever!"

I noticed her talk had morphed from disbelief to acceptance. I could almost see the truth flooding through her.

"How could he? How could he?" she asked through dry, cracked lips.

Very easily, I wanted to say. Loyalty was a fool's trait and not one of kings. My lips twitched with eagerness to deliver that truth, but my façade was in place for a reason. I'd learned that truth was rarely valued by this particular woman in times of stress.

These wealthy people, I thought. *So callous and uncaring when you cried, but let something hurt their feelings and they expected the world to cry tears for them.*

It wasn't even new news. So many years old, the word had traveled all through the country and probably outside of France several times over. The only one who hadn't heard it was she. Years of these women smiling in her face and laughing behind her back. And, finally, the Queen had been provoked enough to remind Madame what the nobles *truly* thought of her. Now she looked like a fool, stripped of every ounce of dignity.

I could have told her the *Well-Beloved* only loved himself. I tried once, but she slapped me across the face and called me ungrateful, so it was hard to feel too much pity.

At this moment, I could cut her to the quick if I chose. But I saw in her blotchy face and sagging shoulders the kindred spirit of a lowly person allowed to feel greatness for a moment, only to have it snatched away. I gave in to a white lie, giving more compassion than was deserved to this woman I'd once hoped would be a mother figure.

"Dying people will say anything," I said to her softly. "Faced with a lifetime of sins and the possibility of everlasting damnation, I'm sure he would have asked forgiveness for any one of his life's choices if he thought it would ease his way into heaven. It was obvious to everyone that he loved you. It doesn't matter what anyone says. It only matters how he treated you and what you know. How you felt when you were with him. How he loved you."

Tears welled in her eyes, and she nodded hard, lips pinched together with resolution. "Yes. Yes. You're right." Water fell down her cheeks, and she lay her head against my chest, tears wetting my clothes.

We hadn't hugged since I was very young, back when I was innocent and scared and wanted to believe that she truly cared about me. These days, sometimes she would take my arm as we walked, or I'd help her out of the carriage. But it was always formal between us, until now.

"I came from nothing, you know," she muttered, raising her head. "I was a bastard, and no one ever let me forget, not even my own mother. When I was a girl, they used me like a dishrag, passed from one adult to another. When I grew up, *I* decided to make something of myself. Why bed a thousand peasants for pennies when I could bed one king and live like a queen? The man who controlled me, he thought it was his idea to get me in front of the Well-Beloved, but I put that thought into *his* head. I let him think it was his idea because men are threatened by women who think. I let him think it was his idea, so he'd be my ally and not my enemy. And he was. I made him believe he was smarter than us all. That's what men like, to feel like they're great. I know men. So, then, he was working for me even though he didn't know it.

"The first time Louis stood in front of me, I knew he was mine. I knew he would love me more than any queen or even the mistress before me. I knew my life would change if I could be what he needed. He was depressed and sad, and he needed joy, so I brought it to him. And because I didn't shame him for who he was, he loved me. No common peasant woman has ever held the title of Mâitresse-en-titre. I vowed to be the last Favorite he would ever have, and I was. No one will ever take that from me." Then she spoke more softly, her face losing its desperation. "He and I couldn't have a traditional family. I refused to bring a child into this world for them to shut away in a convent or shun like an embarrassment—like his other illegitimate children. So, he brought me you. We were a family. We were our own little family unit, the three of us. We were happy."

I didn't respond, but she had already looked away and released me, yawning.

Chon was already waiting outside the door when I left, wringing her hands, obviously listening. I stood aside as she walked in, followed by lady two and lady three (I could never remember their names), who immediately swarmed Madame with hugs and kisses and words of comfort.

Downstairs, Salanave was pouring steaming liquid from a little pot into two cups like she'd been waiting for me to enter the doorway. I sat down and reached for my cup.

"She brought it on herself, always poking at the Queen," she said through tight lips. "All that going on and making a spectacle was pure theatrics. It's a curious affliction of these noblewomen that the moment they hear something they don't like, they lose the ability to stand on their own two feet and have to find a man to lean on. Sloppy drunk just from a bottle of wine ... nonsense. I've seen that woman down two bottles of wine like water, as clear-eyed and clear-headed as you or me standing here."

"What do you mean, Salanave? Why would she fake being so upset?"

"I'm not saying she faked it. I'm saying she knows how to compose herself when she wants to. Lived at the Palace all those years being openly snubbed and knew enough to keep that sweet little smile on her face until she could get the King alone to complain. Never made a spectacle like this one."

Of course, I knew Madame was a manipulator, so I didn't dismiss her words out of hand.

"It was going to be you or Gaspard she stumbled to; it *always* is. She likes to keep you two sniping at each other, begging to be supplicants. She doesn't have a receiving line like the Queen, but she's got the two of you lining up to be her favorite."

I felt a lick of irritation. "I don't beg to be a supplicant, Salanave..."

"...she should be treading lightly after that whole necklace situation."

The *necklace situation* was the most recent sordid scandal, involving a prostitute impersonating the Queen, a nobleman foolish enough to think the Queen wanted him, and that most expensive necklace in the world, the one fashioned from the drawing the Well-Beloved showed me all those years ago. The one with all the little balls. It was now missing, and the country believed Marie Antoinette had heisted it to fund the Austrian army while simultaneously cuckolding Louis XVI by having an affair with the nobleman.

France blamed the Queen. The Queen blamed Madame, around whose neck the piece was intended to have been placed. Salanave continued...

"Half the reason some of these nobles come here at all is because of all the rumors about her relationship with you. Instead of denying it, she puts on a show like tonight. Making people think there's something going on. She should be ashamed of herself."

I blinked in surprise at that. "Nobody seriously thinks we have anything going on," I scoffed.

"*Everybody* thinks it, petit. Why do you think they come and, first thing, focus on you? You watch, those guests of hers will leave here spreading the word that you carried her to her bedroom, and she clutched you like a lover, no thanks to her. As long as she has someone in this household they think is more depraved than her, there's always a scapegoat for her bad behavior. They say your African blood infected the Palace—that your exotic nature influenced our dear, deceased King to be as depraved as he was. And she's not helping to change that story, not a little bit."

I felt Salanave's gaze on me, and when next she spoke, her voice was lower and calmer, seeming to catch onto my discomfort.

"I can see from your face you're in a decent place with Madame at this moment. Maybe you're feeling a little sorry for her even. But as you've said a thousand times, it doesn't matter what they say, it matters how they treat you. Rest assured; she'll give you another reason to slip rat poison into her chocolat."

"You know," I took a sip of the fragrant tea and gave a mirthless smile at the impassive look on her face. "For someone who warned me never to speak on a certain thing again, you keep bringing it up, Salanave. There's a bright spot, though. At least Gaspard is finally gone," I mumbled. "*That's* a good thing."

"He'll be back tomorrow."

30

———————

He was back "tomorrow." When I saw Gaspard and Madame speaking in low tones as they walked by in the hallway outside the dining room while I was setting the table, my ears were instantly on fire with anger. I didn't like being made a fool either.

I finished dusting and headed back to my room, where the stable hand who had hated me just two days earlier was waiting for me. His face blossomed red upon seeing me.

"They told me you brought me back to the house from the pavilion the other day and even protected my head," he said.

"I might as well have; you'd already disturbed my peace. What about it?" I waited for him to complain about it being my fault for taking Lightning in the first place. Anything I did in relation to the other servants was commonly met with suspicion.

"I just wanted to say thank you. For my head and getting me back. And after I was rude and all."

I was confused. "I only brought you back. It wasn't anything."

"Two weeks ago, I fell off a horse—"

"—You've been here two weeks?"

"I've been here two *months,* but two weeks ago, I was out running errands with Gaspard and was snagged by a low-hanging branch. He left me there and told me if I couldn't stay on a horse, I deserved to walk. I walked half a day to get back to the Chateau on a sore ankle."

"Ah well ... *Gaspard...*" I said, and he nodded, his face brightening in a knowing expression that bordered on a smile. He wiped his hand on his pants and held it out to me.

"I'm Henri, from Paris."

So unaccustomed to be offered a hand, I looked at it and him for a long moment in suspicion. Then responded in kind. "I'm Zamor."

"I thought you were Louis-Benoit."

"My friends call me Zamor."

"You have friends?" he asked sincerely.

"I don't know. Do I?"

He smiled fully this time. "Want to help me with the horses, Zamor?"

"My horses?" I asked. "Sure, I'll let you tend them. Just be sure to do a good job. Take special care of Lightning; she's sensitive."

Henri and I became the oddest of friends. He was a bit younger than me and held a strange combination of sensitivity to life's injustices with an age-old weariness born of poverty. He was a good soul trapped in a cruel world. Just the type of friend I needed.

BUT I COULDN'T SHAKE Salanave's words about how the world saw me. I couldn't shake thoughts of what it might be like outside of our cocoon, and frankly, I was going batty being at the Chateau and feeling like I wasn't making an ounce of progress. What was going to Versailles worth if I didn't have anyone who cared about what I might learn? The only time I was away from the Chateau or Palace was when I joined Madame on her visits to other nobles or dressmakers throughout the country, and I hadn't met a trustworthy noble in my life. My brain was full of ideas and questions with no one to share them with, no one to guide or challenge me. Salanave had my back, but she wasn't interested in ideas or much beyond the scope of her daily life. Henri and Fabian were friendly but not my intellectual equals.

Barnier looked up when I entered the little schoolroom at Versailles the next day, accustomed to seeing me after the children left. My formal education ended long ago, but I still visited Barnier just to speak with someone who had a life beyond the royal sphere. A teacher at heart, he couldn't resist conversations with someone who wanted to learn. I was a sponge, and I still craved knowledge like water.

"I brought more books, Louis. These novels are popular," he said, digging through his bag to pull them out. I felt that flush of excitement every time I got my hands on a new book. My eyes caught on one of them.

"What's that? *The Social Contract.* Another novel about arranged marriage?"

"Ah, good guess, but no. This is by Jean Jacques Rousseau, one of the Enlightenment philosophers. He was very popular for a while, along with Voltaire. You remember Voltaire and the King were friends?"

"How could I forget him, being the creator of my namesake. Zamor, the errant slave come to find God and all that. I almost wanted to avoid the bible just to spite him and that story." I looked over the front and back of the book.

"But you haven't read his Enlightenment works—which is what he's most well-known for—and I don't think I've ever brought Rousseau. They became terrible enemies at the end."

"In that case, I would be happy to read this Rousseau."

"Very dry material, if you ask me, but he had his followers. With the Enlightenment now gaining popularity again, all across Europe this time, you might want to take a look to keep up."

I put it into my leather satchel. "Is there anything in that book about the abolition of slavery and the Americas? Or any news elsewhere?"

"I don't get into town as often as I used to and am behind in sorting through all those publications. I read that now that the Americans are free from the British crown, they have no intention of paying back France for all the money we loaned them to win their freedom. There would be no America if we didn't bankroll all those weapons to fight Britain. Now that they're independent, they've kissed and made up with Britain, and the two of them only want to do business with each other. The King is not happy."

That explained some of the tension that pervaded the Palace these days. The King seemed stressed every time I saw him. In the few conversations I overheard in the tunnels, he was begging the nobles to let him tax them. They might as well have sat him down in a corner and told him to shut up. If the Americans weren't paying us back, it was no wonder he was stressed.

"But what about the black people?"

"No new news there. The Americans, the French, and the British —none of them seems much interested in the freedom of black people. Though there are pockets of people in the American territory developing a distaste of slavery. I hear some slaves are attempting to get to New France ... or, what *used to be* New France."

Before we lost it. France had lost the area just above the new colonies to the Brits in the Seven Years' War, just before the new country fought its own battle for independence.

"How many wars can we lose and still be called the most powerful country in the civilized world?" I asked, but my mind was on what he'd said about black people escaping to freedom. "Do you have your map?" Barnier dug into his pack and pulled out the map, unfolding it onto the table. I found Louveciennes quickly. "Tell me. There must be places outside of France where a black man might go and be welcomed."

Barnier looked annoyed at my trick question.

"A black *free* person of France may go anywhere and be welcomed, within reason, as you know. There is *no* place a black man who's not free can hope to escape and be certain of his safety. You know this, Zamor; why do you make me say it over and over? All anyone has to do is take you to the docks in Nantes and sell you to one of the slave ships. Anyone can sell you if you're not free, if they are that sort. The only thing that protects you is the thing you hate most—the fact that you are already claimed by the royal family and Madame. Besides, there is no place in this country you will live as well as you do now. The rest of France is starving, son. Here, no one bats an eye when you spread caviar on your toast and down champagne like water. Even Gaspard has given up monitoring your food because he'd be punishing you constantly, and he doesn't have the energy. You can't tell me you don't like all those advantages."

"Well, of course I like the advantages, Barnier, who wouldn't? But one thing doesn't have anything to do with the other. I enjoy fine things, but I know I won't live like this when I leave. I still want to leave. Even if I never go back to India. Do you really think I'd stay just for the caviar? That I'd choose fine food over freedom?"

I could see from his eyes he did. He was being sincere, but I'd realized long ago that no matter how well-meaning, Barnier would never understand. He was a kind man, but he wasn't brave and had his citizenship.

"Can you get me a map I can have for my own?"

"No. I won't help you get yourself into trouble."

"With whom? Gaspard would kiss your feet if you found me a way out of here."

"I couldn't bear Madame's tears," he said. "She'd be lost without you."

His face said he was serious. Even after all these years of friendship, his loyalty still belonged to the "Madames" of the world; her tears were enough to justify his complicity in keeping me tethered to her. Another thing he would never understand was that as long as he was loyal to her, he could never lecture me on what I should be satisfied with.

"Alright, fine," I said, flipping through the pages of the Rousseau book. "I'm going crazy in this place. I want to go to town, read the current news. I hear that printing presses are sprouting up like wild mushrooms. People bring papers here to the Chateau, and it seems no two people ever have the same one."

"Like I've never seen in my life. And I hear many people are having discussions in coffeehouses and bars about how society should change and what the government is doing with our money. *Common* people and peasants. It's amazing, really."

That was it. I'd never find a way to survive from within the royal circles.

"I'm going to Paris," I told him.

"Paris? On your own?"

"My life is slipping away while I'm holed up in this house fetching chocolat. There's a world out there I want to see. I might not be able to leave France, but I can leave this chateau and find people who aren't beholden to my benefactors."

I wondered if he'd try to talk me out of it or convince me there was no point in it. I could see the battle on his face. He hesitated but then said: "You'd be surprised, Zamor, at the conversations that would have found people rounded up and tossed in prison not too long ago. In any given bar in the center of town, people are talking."

I was pleased that he didn't let me down this time. "I'll find a way. Paris, it is."

31

Dear Citizen,

Once I had the idea to go to Paris, nothing was going to stop me.

Amazingly, I convinced Madame to let me to go out into the world to spread the good news about how much dead King Louis XV loved her. She was thrilled but knew better than to send me alone. She made Barnier and a member of her security team come with me in the beginning, which was fine. Anyone but Gaspard.

Eventually, as I consistently returned without incident, Madame allowed me to go alone by horse or carriage. So long as I was back in the morning to serve her chocolat and by her side when she wanted me, she didn't care what I did with my evenings.

She probably should have.

--Zamor

To fit in, I spent some of my hard-earned money to buy the rough full-length pants and plain muted-toned tops the common men—the sans-culottes—wore. I always took a seat in the back of the room or at the bar, ordered cheap wine or beer, and watched. Watching was what I was good at, after all.

Every single establishment had a back door, a back hole, or a back cut-out where people would quietly sneak in and out, looking around to make sure they weren't being noticed, but *I* noticed. Just like in the Palace, deals were made behind doors and in spaces like that.

As an outsider, I made a concentrated effort to befriend the barkeeps and servers. One server, whose good graces I'd earned by alerting her to a patron stealing her tips, caught me staring at the back doorway one evening.

"I can see what you're thinking but don't do it, chèr," she said. "I wouldn't want to see you hurt." She was beside me, unloading empty glasses one by one from a tray onto the bar, where the bartender pushed them off to one side instead of loading them into the wash basin. "You have to be *invited* into back rooms; you can't just go in. They'll think you're a member of the secret police. Especially dressed like that."

I looked down at my carefully bought clothes. "I'm just a common man who happens to serve nobles. How do I get invited, Mademoiselle? And what's wrong with my clothes?"

She put down her tray and leaned towards me, speaking under her breath. "They look custom-tailored to fit you. We common folk wear what we can find or make, and they rarely fit as well as yours do to you. You look like a wealthy man pretending to be a commoner."

I looked around. "Well, technically, I'm a sans-culotte, too."

"If I were you, I'd start at the smaller cafés. That's where you'll find common men seeking out fresh minds and new perspectives. But you can't seem *too* eager. You can't seem like you *want* to be in the room. Don't ask and don't press. They'll watch you and size you up, and if you're approved, they'll come looking for *you* without you having to ask. Once you're trusted, all the back doors to Paris will open to you. Voilà."

She winked at me and walked off across the bar to continue her work.

I was thankful for her advice even though it seemed like I was already doing exactly what she said. I went home and ripped out some seams in my clothes to make them look less new—though it seemed a waste of good tailoring—and began frequenting the smaller bars.

In the meantime, back home I finally opened the book Barnier gave me one day, and read:

"...Man was born free, and he is everywhere in chains. Those who think themselves the masters of others are indeed greater slaves than they."

--The Social Contract, Jean Jacques Rousseau

THE HAIRS on the back of my neck stood up as I looked down at the words on that page. I was in my bedclothes in bed, but now, though it was late, and I was tired, something in me woke up as if a bucket of cold water had been thrown upon me. I knew I'd be up all night.

I became greedy for Rousseau's thoughts, staying up nights reading the book by candlelight, eyes watering with excitement. It felt like every word had been written with me in mind.

I found kinship with my soul-deep belief that government can only thrive when it is not just representative of its people, but actually is its people. The notion that a society that enslaves its people against their will is a society that fights itself and is not a true sovereign political body. I was enrapt.

"Man's first law is to watch over his own preservation; his first care he owes to himself; and as soon as he reaches the age of reason, he becomes

the only judge of the best means to preserve himself; he becomes his own master."

—Jean Jacques Rousseau

IT WASN'T that every piece of the work resonated, but the ones that did stuck with me so strongly that I forgave the work its problems. I started carrying the book around, reading when I was sitting with Madame, riding in the carriage, or taking my lunch outside. Reading and re-reading, studying the words and sentiments.

"To renounce freedom is to renounce one's humanity, one's rights as a man and equally one's duties. There is no possible quid pro quo for one who renounces everything; indeed such renunciation is contrary to man's very nature; for if you take away all freedom of the will, you strip a man's actions of all moral significance. Finally, any covenant which stipulated absolute dominion for one party and absolute obedience for the other would be illogical and nugatory. Is it not evident that he who is entitled to demand everything owes nothing? And does not the single fact of there being no reciprocity, no mutual obligation, nullify the act? For what right can my slave have against me? If everything he has belongs to me, his right is my right, and it would be nonsense to speak of my having a right against myself."

--Jean Jacques Rousseau

THE RECOGNITION of a moral covenant between slavers and the enslaved spoke to my basic humanity in a way I'd never read. In his way of thinking, slavery would be less a question of might and force and more an agreement with expectation on both sides. He obviously spoke of a type of slavery that existed in years past where people could voluntarily, and temporarily, exchange their freedom to pay off a debt or to atone for a crime.

Slavery as it existed now was of such imbalance it perverted nature. It broke every law of humanity.

Though much of the work was theoretical, I found his examples of the government personified as an entity—the thought that any future iteration of government would son to the father (the original government)—compelling. That, just as when a child grows up, they are supposed to become their own individual, an iteration of an existing government in its space, time, and circumstance is right. That the option to accept or reject the ways of its father fully within its rights ... brilliant. That a government could be different based on changing times and circumstances. And I immediately connected the idea of the "father" government to the system of royal life 'd lived under since arriving in France.

Reading his words was more than enlightening; it gave me hope.

Every night, sitting on a stool in my bedchamber beside the small evening fire that soothed my bones, I felt warmth take root within me. His words weren't just new; they were *mine* in belief and spirit. If I could put to words my feelings and thoughts about my position in the world, they would be the words of this man. The fact that there was someone else in the world, not even of my skin color, who sought to make an intellectual argument for the modification of our way of life was almost more hopeful than I could bear.

I tried to explain Rousseau to Henri when he interrupted my reading by sitting himself down next to me by my favorite tree.

"I don't know any of that you're talking about, Zamor; you know I can't read well. I only know numbers."

"That's why I'm telling you what it says, Henri. It explains... what is that?"

He reached over and handed me a card showing his winnings in recent card games, smiling smugly.

"I don't know words, but I know numbers. I told you I'm the best player in town. I won enough in that game to buy oil for one month's fire at home. Don't have to read to win at cards; you just need instinct."

I shook my head. "No, you just need luck. You can also be unlucky and lose everything. I saw plenty of nobles at the Palace wager the last of their family inheritances playing cards in the King's parlor. Come now, Henri, they'll let you win just to hook you and keep you playing for a bigger payoff. Don't fall for it."

He shifted and avoided my eyes, stiff with annoyance. I already knew he didn't want to hear what I had to say. "Easy for you to say. You only have to look after yourself. I have my family to support."

He, his mother and sister worked their fingers to the bone just to survive. His father was too ill to work. Sometimes, even with the three of them working hard, there was not enough money to feed them each day. But with Henri working at Louveciennes, occasionally Salanave would slip him a loaf of bread or some soon-to-rot vegetables that he would hide until he could smuggle the food home. And he wasn't the only one she was slipping food to. I knew he didn't get paid much tending horses; he could ill afford to wager his pay.

Henri took his card back, now looking grouchy at my lack of appropriate wonder at his prowess and eager to change the subject. "You've set off the visiting duchess. She says you are insolent and rude, and that Madame would be smart to be rid of you."

"She's right," I admitted. "Hopefully, one day, Madame will come to that same conclusion. The nuisance of having papers drawn on me has to be less trouble than having me around."

"You criticize my gambling, but you're doing worse, hoping to annoy your way to freedom. It already cost you the Palace. The price to you is high if they decide to cut their losses. But if anyone can accomplish escape by irritation, it's you," Henri said in that happy, harmless way of his. Because it was Henri, I didn't take it as insult.

"I wouldn't recommend you do anything to get yourself barred from dinner again," he continued. "Who knows, we might have another hero like the Marquis de LaFayette, fresh off his success in defeating Cornwallis in the Americas. I never expected him to be so young. And you spoke to him, didn't you?"

"If you call asking him if he wanted more coffee speaking to him, then yes. We had a wonderful conversation about how he takes his drink. Cream and no sugar."

Gilbert de Motier, the Marquis de LaFayette was considered a French hero, and I desperately wanted to ask him about the Americas, where he'd been fighting alongside their President Washington in the American Revolution. At thirty-one, he was young to have such a stellar reputation, but according to Barnier, he returned to France an abolitionist in nobleman's clothes.

As much as I wanted to speak to him, the night he came, I had no opportunity to get him alone to ask about the black people in the Americas. But now he was a hero favored by XVI and the Queen. One had to be careful when speaking to a friend of the King. Out of prudence, I let the opportunity to speak to LaFayette pass, but I was disappointed.

"My sister and I don't think my papa will last the season," Henri admitted matter-of-factly, though he wouldn't meet my eye when I glanced at him and picked at a fingernail, telling me he was trying not to break down. "Every bit I make, I'm saving to feed us. I'm saving for his burial. He's petrified of getting a beggar's burial."

"I'm sorry, Henri. I'll give what I can if it helps."

"He worked all his life. I'm guaranteed to work until I wear out like he is. Meanwhile, these people who come to this place, they drape their pets in jewels. And they've never worked a day in their lives. I know it's right. I know the royals are appointed by God to rule us. We all have our place in life. But Madame and the other ones who are just rich without being royal, it hardly seems fair. It's a reality I accept, but it is bitter. I come here and have moments like this when I can sit under this tree and see the green grass and the river—it's beyond beautiful. And for this one moment, I'll feel guilty all night because my family doesn't have this to look at. My father will die never having seen any place like this."

His thoughts on his place in the world soured me. He was one of those who believed the royals were great. I couldn't help but add my two cents.

"I don't care what they say about the royals being ordained by God. You and your family deserve happiness just like they do."

"And yours," he said, finally looking at me.

I shrugged. "For a long time, I remembered my parents' faces, but I can't any longer. I just remember they loved me once. I keep telling myself so I don't forget entirely. Sometimes I feel like I never existed before I came here. I don't remember India and I wouldn't recognize it if I was standing in the middle of it. Were it not for you and Salanave, I'd disappear."

"No, not you. You would never disappear. Especially not now that you are making friends in Paris."

"You should come with me," I said, brightening. "Maybe both of us can make friends with people who aren't so bound by social order."

"There's no such thing," he said.

Activity at the door of the servants' quarters caught our attention as a group of servants walked a little way and shook out the blankets in their arms, stale from having traveled in the carriages. It meant there were new guests.

Sometimes nobles would send their servants and pages to Louveciennes to be instructed in royal etiquette and proper servant behavior by someone of Madame's station. It appeared we had a new crop.

One or two black servants had been to the Chateau briefly before, but this day drew our attention. She shook out blankets with arms that were thin but strong, judging by how she jerked the heavy cloths to and fro in the wind. Her skin was the color of new red earth when the sun shone upon it. Her hair was hidden, caught up in a hair wrap.

"She came in yesterday with the latest group from the east."

I remembered that I'd seen the women when Madame and I returned from a trip into town a few days ago. The three were lined up in front of the house, being drilled by Gaspard.

"They never stop coming, the nobles and their staff," he continued. "All for a chance to say they've been entertained by the Madame.

She is more popular now than when the old King was alive. More popular than the Queen. Do you think the Queen knows?"

"I'm sure she knows and doesn't care," I said. "There can be only one Queen. She's not threatened by anything happening here." I couldn't imagine there was much about the goings-on of nobility that the King and Queen didn't know. It was the goings-on of regular people I was certain she was clueless about.

The blankets didn't stand a chance as the woman whipped them out, determination on her face and lips pinched closed to keep from inhaling the staleness of the linens. Something about that look on her face made it difficult to look away. Her clothes were no more colorful than any other servant's—drab and, I daresay, ugly—though they fit her well. But that look on her face, so determined. So purposeful. My staring caught Henri's eye.

"You want to meet her? It can be easily arranged."

"What, no. Why would I want to meet her?" I said, looking away, growing hot from having been caught. I'd always thought it silly the way others mooned at each other and fell for the slightest bit of attention. I didn't plan to become a person like that.

But over the next few days, I couldn't stop searching for a glimpse of her. And it wasn't long before a letter came in the post from Burgundy addressed to Véronique Clair. I already knew the curly-haired woman was Chloe—though we barely knew much more of each other beyond that—so Véronique had to be the dark-skinned, serious-faced woman or the giggling one with the long, brown hair.

In either case, it was a curious thing for any servant to read or write. I asked one of the children where the room of Véronique was, and they directed me to a door. It didn't solve the mystery, but I waited for the child to leave and discreetly slipped the letter under the door. Reading wasn't something servants wanted to be known for, as it led to suspicions that they saw themselves as above their station. I knew first-hand.

32

L *ate 1788*

THE SOUND of my urine stream seemed excessively loud next to the alley wall outside of the tavern. *Too much beer this time,* I thought. But what else was there to do? It'd been weeks, and I was no farther along than when I first started coming to Paris. One more cup and I'd head back to the Chateau.

I was visiting smaller drinking spots and making a conscious effort to stop openly staring at the doorways to those back rooms. I shifted my gaze, pretending not to notice anything while I was noticing everything.

I walked back into the tavern. The space looked lonely, with a table of three against a far wall and a man looking like he'd fallen asleep in a corner. As I walked back to my vacated spot, I saw a sheet of paper lying on the worn wooden counter. I looked around to see if I'd missed anyone leaving quickly, but maybe the bartender that left it. I pulled the page over and read it.

"WHAT'S THIS?" I asked Barnier the next day, putting it on the table in front of him. "I thought the bartender left it, but he said he didn't know where it came from. It was sitting on the bar when I came back in from taking a piss."

"Hhm? Let me see," he held the edge of his glasses, pulling the paper up to his face. "Oh, that's a decree of freedom. Occasionally, enslaved people will petition for their freedom. Or at least, they used to. You know, because of the maxim."

"What maxim?"

"The one that any person who comes to France is free upon stepping foot on French mainland soil. But as you know, it's not like it sounds."

I heard him, but his voice was getting twisted in my head as I watched his lips move. Because he couldn't possibly have been saying what I heard. "It's a maxim? I thought it was only a rumor. There's a process for people to petition for freedom on the basis of that? A legal process? Are you telling me I can petition for my freedom? Why am I just hearing about this?"

"It's not as simple as all that. It wasn't really a law, and it's not active. First you would have to find an avocat"—*attorney*— "to help you petition the court and parliament."

He'd taught me years ago that even though the king was the absolute monarch, Parlement was the mechanism that ran the government; very important things went through both bodies. But he never mentioned this.

"Why am I only now hearing about this, Barnier?" I couldn't get over that fact. "All these years ... all the times I tried to get away from Versailles, and I could have gone?"

"No, you couldn't have gone, son; you were a child. Where would you have gone? And once you'd grown up, it hardly seemed worth mentioning. No good could come of all that. Your life has been so fruitful, and you're too volatile a person. Telling you would only have led you down a path to nowhere. Best to leave something like that alone."

I'd always liked Barnier, but at that moment I wanted to hit him. I badly wanted to. He must have sensed it because he looked at me out of the corner of his eye as though he thought he might need to take a step away.

"It's just that it's not that simple, Zamor. You have to have representation to petition, and then they have to petition the King for his permission. You see the problem?"

I looked down at the decree and the name there.

"Do other people actually win their freedom this way?"

"I don't know. I really don't. I wasn't trying to keep it from you; I just didn't feel it would apply to you and didn't want to get your hopes up."

Even though it should have been, my hope wasn't dead. I told Salanave the situation.

"I didn't even know, petit," she said thoughtfully. She had finished breakfast; the food now being consumed by greedy guests in the dining room. Now she sat for her fifteen-minute break before starting lunch, chewing on a roll at the table across from me and sipping tea. "Barnier says you would need an avocat? I'll ask around."

Two days later, she came to me with a name written on a slip of paper and a street name in Paris. I kissed her cheek and took a horse into town to find the man. I'd brought some dried meat in my satchel and perched on the ground outside the door, fully planning to wait all day if I needed to.

After about an hour, I looked up at the sound of footsteps. A man approached. He was thin and small and looked at me like it wasn't a surprise at all to see me sitting there.

"Hello," I said as I stood up, brushing off my pants. "Are you Monsieur Collet?"

"Yes, I am. Who are you?"

"My name is Louis-Benoit Zamor. I'm hoping I can speak to you about my case."

He invited me into a small room that was obviously where he

lived, disguised as an office. He walked over to a small table, which had a top that lifted on hinges. He shoved a razor and shaving supplies into the little storage area and closed it, brushing it off with his hands. A pot sat on a small stove barely large enough to hold it. He hesitated in front of the stove.

"Would you like ... café?"

His whole body had frozen in anticipation of the answer. Looking around, it was obvious it would be cruel to force him into such niceties when I doubted he even had café. For a moment I wondered how much café cost – and how little a person would have -- that one could not afford to drink it.

"No, thank you. My name is Zamor," I said. "And I want to petition for my freedom as an enslaved man." He looked at me like Barnier had, with a face full of doubt. His expression made me angry. "Everyone says that it is enough to set foot on French soil to be free, but I'm not free. How can they hold me in slavery?"

"Well, it's not a law; it's an interpretation. A very old one based on France's history and the Christian beliefs of some of the interpreters. This is politics, and none of it is cut and dry, especially not slavery. Have a seat?" He motioned me to sit on a little chair and sat opposite. "There are two institutions in the determination of every case: the Parlement of Paris and the King. They've butted heads in the past, but if the Parlement makes him too angry, he is within his rights to throw them all into the Bastille. That reality has a tempering effect, however hard they might want to push back."

"But there's precedence for enslaved people—that's what I want to know about." I told him about my situation.

"You were brought here as a slave, that's clear. What's not clear is whether you were ever registered. If not, already that's a violation, and had your owner been a normal nobleman, you might have had a case on that basis alone. But you've been bought, gifted and traded, all by the permission of the royal family. They violated their own Edict of 1716, which requires you to be reported. In 1738, Louis the Well-Beloved published another decree that declared that any slave-owner who didn't follow the Edit of 1716 would have his slave taken from him and given to the King, who would promptly send that slave to the colonies for forced labor or further enslavement."

"You mean the same king who reared me might have violated his own Edict? But what if I was owned by a normal nobleman, as you say? To be confiscated by the king and sent to the colonies—how is that punishment to the man keeping slaves?"

"It's not, save for the loss of the monetary value of the slave and, possibly, a 1000-livre deposit to the colonial authorities if the slave isn't returned within three years. The King wrote the 1738 piece after a slave successfully tried a case against his master. Where before a slave might have gone free upon winning a case, with the 1738 adjustment, a good bit of the damage of the negligent master is borne by the slave. It certainly made slaves less likely to complain, knowing they could be sent back to the colonies."

"But what changed to prompt him to update the edict?"

"Likely because in some parts of France, enslaved people didn't need to petition—the idea of freedom at the point of stepping foot on French soil was well known. The Edict of 1716 wasn't well-enforced because it wasn't an official law, and it had never been registered with Parlement. In some rural areas, no one would fight it if a slave wanted to be free, and slave owners who didn't do due diligence by registering them didn't bother to stop them leaving. But in 1738, an enslaved man named Jean Boucaux sued for his freedom and back wages because he had fallen in love with a white woman, and slaves are forbidden to marry. He cited the maxim about free soil in his case. So, the King's ministers drafted the 1738 decree. There was no new legislation until your Louis XVI's minister wrote up a new decree in 1776. Does that date mean anything to you?"

"I was kicked out of the Palace of Versailles in 1776."

"That was the same time the King's minister began drafting the *Declaration pour la police des noirs* and actually registered it this time with the Parlement of Paris in 1777. Notably, unlike the decrees in the past, it made a point of policing black people, by replacing language of slave status with language specifically related to color. All black people were required to register or be registered as nègres or noires or *gens de couleur*, and those became official designations that categorized their state of freedom—*no matter where they came from*, which encompassed all the colonies, be they in the Americas or the islands or even India. He was very specific about that. He clearly wanted to cement the notion that black people were destined to slavery."

"I'm from India," I said. "My people are of African descent, migrated to India."

"I see. He knows you personally?"

I smiled wryly. "He's like my very own brother."

That made him laugh a bit. "Well, a brother he doesn't care for, perhaps. The other thing he did was demand the cessation of black people filing petitions for freedom, putting an end to the process. Any black slave not already free would *never* become free. They'd instead be sent back to the colonies when no longer needed. And France could still claim there are no slaves on French soil."

Bile started to rise in my throat. I thought about that conversation with the Queen so long ago. She'd known, I was sure. And the King had sent her to do his dirty work. I don't know why I felt hurt. After everything I'd been through in my life, this should be no surprise. But the bitterness was strong.

"So, the King passed this decree and then sent me on my way, knowing that he'd blocked every avenue I had of filing a petition for my freedom."

"He presented it to Parlement as a decree with the goal of stopping the flow of black people to mainland France—stopping them from establishing themselves here comfortably. He suggested that the existing illegality of marriage among blacks cited in the Code Noir, along with the process of halting the stream of enslaved people coming here for freedom, would result in the eventual dilution of African blood. He wanted France to become white again. He hoped the black blood would eventually die out."

I remembered how annoyed the Queen had been with me, thinking I was having sex with noblewomen. And I thought it had only been about the mixing of the classes. It'd been about the mixing of the colors.

The avocat looked at me, pausing to give me time to digest the information. "I wonder if it was you who inspired him to write the decree. Did you, by chance, make a stink with the King for your freedom around that time? Embarrass him?"

When *wasn't* I making a stink or otherwise embarrassing them? I wanted my freedom!

"Possibly." I waved my hand. "But yes, I hoped they'd tire of me and let me go. Instead, they told me since they were taking Madame out of exile, they'd send me to live with her."

"By doing so, they made clear to anyone paying attention that you were, in fact, gifted to *her*; in effect, they handed any potential headaches created by the Well-Beloved to his mistress. Perhaps there were too many nobles asking why he got to keep his slave when they were threatened with losing their own or paying fines out of pocket for not registering theirs. Or … it could be the only reason he brought Madame out of exile was because they needed someplace to put *you*."

I looked at his face, but he wasn't laughing. "I hardly think I'm that important."

"You, probably not. But it's politics, you see. It's what you symbolize. Public perception is a powerful thing for a king. From what I know of Louis XVI, he's very concerned with what people think of him. He can't be seen as weak or a liar. If people were aware of your situation, they might have seen him as both of those things. Perhaps to his way of thinking, he gave you a reprieve; he made sure you're with someone who can afford to keep you. Otherwise, he might have sent you to the colonies to do hard labor or put you in the Bastille or in some other prison."

"For what? I didn't walk to this country on my own—they brought me here!"

"It doesn't matter. I want to make sure you understand this can only go two ways. Either way is the King's decision. It doesn't matter what Parlement suggests if he doesn't want you free. Going to them could put him in a mood not only to turn you down but to punish you as well. But if you can convince the Madame du Barry, perhaps she will speak to the King on your behalf?"

The avocat didn't know the very provocative word he used—punish—was reminding me of the horrors of what a king could do or have done to me. And now he was telling me to ask Madame to plead on my behalf. The woman who blossomed with glee every time she found a new way to turn me down was as likely to plead my case as bring the moon to the ground. "She won't."

He looked worried at that. "This puts you in a bit of a bad place. If she passes away, ownership of you will be determined by the King. Or by her will."

XV hadn't but she could free me in her will! Or...

I sat up straight. "You mean she can pass me along to someone else? There's a chance I don't even get my freedom if she dies?"

"You're considered her property, like her house and her furniture. If she doesn't specify where you go, you might be turned over to the King or her husband if she has one. And if you die first, any money or earnings you have go to her. I'm sorry."

"But if I marry..."

"Son, you can't marry. Not legally. Not without her permission."

"I mean, I know that, technically, black people can't marry, but..."

"No, it's enslaved black people who can't marry, though I know the law is rarely enforced. But with all we've spoken about today, I have to believe that, in your case, someone might enforce that law. If not the King, would Madame du Barry stop you?"

My blood ran cold. Of course, she would.

I didn't know what I'd been thinking. I knew a bit about Code Noir, but colonial life was different from here on the mainland. I'd been reading the Code Noir with compassion toward my brethren like I was removed from it all—like a man who'd made it off a sinking ship and onto an island while his shipmates struggled not to drown. I might be standing on the island watching them, but I didn't realize that a sinkhole was opening underneath me. We were all going down. Creature comforts had dulled my acceptance that I was a slave and all that really meant. I'd been a fool.

"How can a country that claims to love freedom do this to people?"

"Most people in France don't see slavery. It's been out of direct sight for centuries. And now, enslaved people are coming to the mainland at the exact time that France is at its most vulnerable and frightened. For some people, seeing one black person feels like an invasion when there's not enough food and we're plagued by droughts. Suddenly, seeing new faces—they're not so interested in freedom ... at least not for *you*. They've decided you're a danger to them and determined that if relegating you to the status of perpetual slavery gets you off the mainland, it's not so bad after all. I'm sorry for this situation. It's a stain on humanity. It's a sad thing for this country we love."

I didn't hear his last words because I was lost in my own thoughts and anger.

I went back to the Chateau in a bad mood, and when I headed to my room, stalking down the hall with my head down, I almost ran into a woman, the sight of her skirts making me skid to a stop before I could knock her down. I looked up; it was one of the women trainee servants who had most recently been lined up in front of the door, but not the interesting one. This one had a head full of blonde curls that sprouted like a riot from her head and a smug smile.

"Excuse me, Mademoiselle." I tried to step to one side, but she blocked me. Looking into her face, I saw the smile of someone who'd found a conquest. "What is it you want, Mademoiselle?"

"To work off some stress. Your face says you need it."

Ten minutes later we were in her room with her brown shift skirt around her waist and her legs straddling me as I did, indeed, try to relieve stress. We were in the thick of it when I heard the door open.

"Chloe, I—"

We both looked up and were staring into the face of the other servant girl. The interesting one. She stood there in surprise, mouth opening and closing like a fish, face flushed. "I'm so sorry to interrupt... Pardon!" She turned quickly to leave, and the door closed behind her. We heard something on the other side clatter to the ground.

"Don't mind her, she's a bit uptight, but she grows on you. Let's get back to it, shall we?"

I almost wanted to put her down, pull my pants up and leave—being caught in the act was so uncomfortable on many levels—but I was three-quarters on my way by that time. When it was over, she pulled her undergarments up and gave me a sly smile.

"I've been nice to you, Monsieur Zamor. Now's time for you to be nice to me."

Here it came.

"What do you want?" I buttoned my pants.

"It's a bargain, really. I want time with the Madame."

"You're living in her house. You can't find time?"

"Not with that hulking brute always around!" I knew who that was. "He won't let me near her, and I need to talk to her to know how she does all this. I idolize that woman. Building all this, and she coming from poor like me. I want to be her one day."

I shrugged and turned towards the door. "I'll get you a few minutes."

"And ham!"

I turned back. "What?"

"I want some ham tomorrow. That cook won't let me have any meat, and I see you take whatever you want. Tomorrow, I want some."

"Salanave runs her own kitchen. I'll bring you some, but if you tell anyone I did, you'll never get a favor from me again."

"Favor?" She patted her hair into place and smiled wickedly. "This was a fair trade, and like I said, you got a bargain. Soon, the only dick I'll entertain is noble."

Speaking of entertaining, I was in a back hallway one day and overheard Gaspard in the foyer gruffly telling someone to take her man out of the main entrance. I rounded the corner just in time to see a tall black man jerk his arm away from our new apprentice, her brow in a scowl. He opened the door to let himself out, followed by the woman. Gaspard left and when the foyer was clear, I walked over to look out the window where they seemed to be having an unpleasant conversation, if her body language was any indication.

I was used to being unseen around the Palace—nobles routinely ran into me as if the impact of our bodies crashing was their first indication that I was standing before them—so I was surprised and reminded that black people *do* see each other when the tall man suddenly glanced up at the window and looked right at me. The woman turned, too, and I stepped away. I didn't like being caught.

A few minutes later, I stood beside the window instead and was very careful to use one finger to slide the curtain just enough so I could see them, but they couldn't see me. The woman seemed to freeze at something he said, and to my eyes, the man wore a cruel smirk. She looked pained.

My mind began to race, wondering what he'd said. Seconds later, she marched away, and he yelled after her but didn't turn around, his face a mask of anger. When he climbed into his carriage and the horse took him away, I couldn't help but wonder where she'd gone to.

I walked out the front door and walked quickly around the house, only to find myself directly in front of her. She was hiding, it seemed, against the back wall and having some sort of struggle to breathe. Seeing me, her heaving gasps stopped suddenly as we stared at each other, caught once again.

And what did this man with the brilliant vocabulary say?

"Mademoiselle." I nodded and took off walking in the other direction.

33

———

I was in a spot that was little more than a hole in the wall, relaxing on a chair. After all this time, I was comfortable in Paris. The heavy, cloying atmosphere in the taverns surrounded me like a warm hug. No longer worried about hiding who I was—no one seemed to care—I lounged and shared niceties with people who recognized my face.

"More beer, page? Or cognac?" the barkeep asked. I'd drank so much beer I was sure a cloud of beer essence floated over my head. Topped off with the cognac, it would hit me all at once, I knew, but in this second, I was still lucid and looking forward to the floating feeling when I drank enough.

I looked behind him at the bottles lined up. It was hard to drink cheap wine, having grown accustomed to the best. He reached for the cognac, and my eyes fell on a dusty, lonely bottle beside it.

"What's that one?" I pointed to it.

He grimaced as he reached for it. "Made by monks who insist on dropping it off. Their little experiment of herbs and alcohol. Nobody wants to drink greens that still taste like they're growing from the ground. We like our drinks from heavily fermented and frothy grains.

I told them nobody will drink it, but they keep leaving it. I've got five more bottles back here, untouched."

"Let me taste it."

"Should have known you'd be the one taker. You're an odd one." When he opened the stopper and poured, the drink was a vivid shade of green.

"Is it a spirit?"

"It's a liqueur. Like poison, non? Could be made from the cerises du diable..."—the *devil's berries* fruit of the belladonna— "...nothing for human consumption should be that color."

"The devil's berries are dark purple, not green." I put the glass to my nose and was struck by the scent. It was like walking through the Palace's destroyed botanical gardens. Those gardens had been one thing I actually liked. As if he had a psychic link to anything that might give me pleasure, XVI had pulled up all the medicinal plants and replaced them with flowers that did nothing but sit there. I had been missing that old garden, but now I smelled it, alive in the glass.

Cautiously, I took a sip only to find it was both herbaceous and sweet. The bartender laughed at the look on my face. "I told you! Putrid!"

"Not at all. I somewhat enjoy it," I said, taking another sip. I tasted a bit of anise. Then, a bit of mint. And other things I couldn't define.

"Really? Fine, there's plenty back here. I'll keep it stocked just for you. They call it Chartreuse."

I sipped, enjoying it immensely. "Just leave the bottle," I told him, pouring myself another glass of the sweet, sweet liqueur, even though I knew liqueurs could be deceptively strong. I was still trying to forget the news from the avocat, after all.

Across the room, a man at a table of five or six—oh yes, it was hitting me now—I squinted to look at a man who had raised his voice and stood up to pound his fist on the table.

"We should do like the Americans," said a man at the bar a couple spots down from me to his drinking partner. "They fought and won their freedom. I guarantee the British will take *all* the colonies from us, exhausted as our troops are. And now all these people complaining about slave labor—it's ridiculous. Hey, you, what do you think, you?" I felt the *you* part of that hit the side of my face as my brain registered the innocuous term, *slave labor*. I looked up to find both men looking at me. What did I think? The drink had found me now and what he was saying was noise.

I twirled my finger in the air. "Blah, blah, blah."

My dismissiveness made the man raise his voice in defense instead of leaving well enough alone. "I mean, I never said it was pretty, and I know you're the same skin color, but surely you see its value? For France?"

Barnier and the avocat both said commoners didn't really know what slavery was like, but I was starting to think it was selective ignorance. Knowing was an inconvenience.

I thought of the boy who befriended me as a child on my journey to France and the little children crying in the woods. I remembered the beatings. I wondered what would have become of me had I been able to stay with the young boy. I remembered the look on his face when they took me away...

Loneliness and sadness could make you do stupid things. After speaking to the avocat, I'd gone home and had relations with Chloe just to dull my pain, but after my dalliance with the curly-headed woman, I went back to my room feeling cheap. I wished the woman with the serious face hadn't seen us. If Madame had her way, it would be cheap dalliances like that for the rest of my life, sniffing around like a dog for whatever scraps were tossed my way because she would never allow me to marry.

Now this man who sat drinking rum, likely made directly by the hands of my enslaved brethren, asked what I thought of the state of my people.

"Friend," I asked him, pointing my finger to get his attention and let him know I was specifically addressing him.

"Have you seen slavery with your own eyes? Seen what is done to enslaved people? Have you seen children ripped from their homes and beaten for asking for their mothers? Have you seen a child's handcuffs? Have you seen a person being brutalized before your eyes and there's nothing you can do because they are property? Have you seen even a fraction of the atrocities perpetrated on human beings for no reason other than financial gain for someone else? As you say, 'for France?'"

His face grew red, and his voice was indignant. "Those are lies. That's not happening; why do you spread these lies?"

I was starting to see a pattern as to what constituted a lie. Turns out a lie was simply something you didn't want to hear.

"Because I have seen it," I told him, propping my chin on my palm, my arm propped against the bar and successfully holding my head upright. "I have felt and lived it, Monsieur. Not just sat at a table and talked about it, but *experienced* it. This is my adopted country. I was ripped from *my* home as a child. Beaten for crying for *my* mother's arms. Beaten for speaking and daring to be a human being, and I never even had to go to the colonies, which I hear is much worse. I assure you I tell no lies." I took a deep swallow of my drink, which hit the back of my throat in a way I suspected might not be healthy. I hadn't planned to speak my truth, but I'd had too much of the green brew now. "They tell me the only option for me is to stay in France without my freedom or join my brethren in forced hard labor in the colonies. Or prison. Those are my options just because my skin is dark. I'm not considered a person. I overheard you over there, waxing poetic about the Americans and their revolution against tyranny. But our own tyranny you justify—and have the audacity to ask me to agree with tyranny against *myself*. Makes no sense! I say if the work of slave labor is necessary to keep people like you sitting in places like this spouting nonsense, let us all die impoverished with lips and throats dry as a bone. We deserve it." I belched a bit of sweet herb and went back to sipping.

"Well, I don't know how you got here, but look at you now in your fancy, fitted clothes." Again, with the clothes. I had no more seams to pull without leaving my clothes to lay on me in rags. "With those fine shoes on your feet, up on your high horse yet selling out your own people, I'll wager. Who paid for *your* drink?" His voice had soured with bitterness.

I'd stopped wearing silk into town, but my laced and buckled leather shoes gave me away. I wasn't willing to walk around barefoot when I had perfectly good leather shoes.

"Leave him be." A short, stocky man had quietly sat down as a buffer between us. "He doesn't need to explain himself to you."

"This isn't about you, Sebastien."

"Drop it."

I looked at the interloper and took in his scruffy chin and dark, small eyes that darted constantly, almost hidden under heavy brows, taking stock of the situation and his place in it. I'd seen him before, sometimes heading into a back room and sometimes doing like me, sitting at a bar or at a table, scoping out the room.

The troublemaker scowled but turned away and went back to his friend.

"Thank you," I said. "They call me Zamor."

"I'm called Sebastien, and I already know who you are. The black man who, for a time, came to Paris driven in a fine carriage with the shadow of the royal fleur-de-lys on its side, parked in the alley to 'disguise' itself. The black man who frays his own clothes so as not to draw attention to how fine they are, only to leave again at night in the direction of the Royal Palace." His lips quirked a little in what I realized was a smile. "You can't disappear here. We don't have a deluge of black-skinned men—without well-known titles and symbols of aristocracy—roaming the streets of Paris and frequenting taverns with no apparent inability to pay. You're readily recognizable to anyone who knows anything of the people who rule us. Until you started coming into the cafés and bars, you were only a legend."

"A legend?" I threw a glance his way that told him how ridiculous he sounded.

He nodded. "Everyone's heard the stories of the young black boy who tried repeatedly to escape Versailles, only to be dragged back by the King's men. The boy with the spirit that wouldn't let him rest even when prudence would suggest he stay still and lay low. I wondered if he'd ever escape. He would be about your age now. I suspect you are *that* Zamor. But maybe I'm wrong."

I had tried to escape two more times after the Well-Beloved passed. The guards had brought me back to an annoyed manager who told me he had no intention doing it a third time and had instructed them to just kill me dead if they had to chase me down again. But that was long ago.

This man had obviously been watching me for months, and no ill had come of it. He was a watcher and observer. Careful and smart. He was a white version of me, and I kind of liked him already. "Okay, then, you know who I am."

"Now here you sit, sipping the Chartreuse that no one else will touch—maybe for the novelty of it? —and one can only wonder, do they *let* you come now? Do you have the freedom to move about as you choose?" At my shuttered glance, he gave a grim nod. "I see. A small allowance and a leash long enough for just a taste of freedom. To keep you mollified."

I looked at him more closely and took a gamble on my instincts. "It was you, wasn't it? You're the one who left that broadside out about the slave who petitioned for freedom? Why? It's not so easy to petition, if that was your point."

He tilted his head slightly. "I know. Impossible, now. I just didn't know if you were aware of what's been happening with your people. I imagine you don't run into many where you live. Your situation is unique, but still, sometimes it helps to know what's going on."

I nodded and then answered his question. "She doesn't think there's any reason not to let me come anymore," I said honestly. "Where would I go? Can't get out of the country without proof of nationality. No one will harbor me because I still have loose ties to the Palace. I stopped trying to run long ago. Louis XV has been dead more than a decade, and I'm certain everyone thinks my desire to leave has been dead just as long."

"Ah, you've accepted your lot in life?" His small eyes looked at me with casual interest, the only thing belying his indifference his frequent darting gaze my way. I was being tested.

"One never stops wanting freedom," I said. "And I do enjoy

drinking among others, my friend. I am thoroughly enjoying this Chartreuse."

"Too much, maybe. You'll lose your guts on the ground before the night's through, drinking that like you are. There's a group of us who get together to talk. Sometimes we meet in the back room here … and other places." He gestured with his chin toward the doorway to the back room. "You should join us tonight; I'll introduce you around. With all the alcohol in you, I recommend you keep quiet and observe."

Excitement bubbled inside me. It was finally happening! But then I slowed it down. It wouldn't do for me to just be in spaces where nothing was accomplished. He needed to know that I wanted more.

"I've heard people coming out of those back rooms talking loudly and saying nothing," I said. "My time outside the Chateau is precious. If I can't use it productively, I would be happier to sit alone with my drink."

"Oh, I feel the same. I have a wife and kids and work that keeps me busy. My free time is precious. The time I spend in these places— let's just say it isn't because I wouldn't rather be spending it with my family. My wife understands there are important things happening in the world. Come meet with us once, tonight. You'll be under no oblig- ation to stay afterward. But if you enjoy being in the company of people who are doing more than just talking, you should join our club. It's invitation only." He kept his beer and stood up. "Come. Hear what's being said in the rooms of places all across this country. And then decide." He turned and headed towards the back without waiting.

He knew. He'd been watching me, probably more than I even noticed. He knew I wasn't secret police. He knew I was a desperate man, desperate for something more than survival.

I looked around the tavern, listened to the aimless chatter. The noise. Noise of nothing. Noise of a lifetime. I was done with it and done with the doubts. This was my chance to change my life.

I picked up my drink, slid off the stool and headed off to follow him through the gateway that would alter the trajectory of my life.

34

———————

E *arly 1789*

Dear Citizen,

*I was quietly respectful of my newness, listening and learning.
Sebastien and I came to trust each other—he became my connection to new groups of educated men and sources of information. Just
as the barmaid had told me months before, once I earned his trust,
Sebastien took me to other back rooms in better bars and cafes.
Once, I ran into her, and when she saw Sebastien and me heading
back, she smiled at my wink and nod—acknowledgment that I had
listened after all.*

*The men in the more reputable establishments didn't consider a
drunken rant to constitute intelligence. They were people who had a
little money and something to lose. They spoke of leadership and*

equality but did so in a measured way. They didn't ask anything of me but allowed me to listen and learn.

—Zamor

"WE'RE the Society of the Friends of the Constitution. but they call us the Jacobins," Sebastien said as we walked down a Paris street, huddled against the cold. We were headed to what he called the "headquarters" in an old monastery. I was thrilled to finally be fully accepted and barely noticed the cold, I was so anxious to get there. He went on. "We're everyone and everywhere. Writers and philosophers, shop owners, blacksmiths, fishermen, students, artists, bankers, even some nobles ...we are everyone. We just moved to the place; it's not all that far from the Tuileries Palace."

"The Palace?" It wouldn't do for me to run into a royal while I was out. I knew from experience there was no end to the number of buildings throughout France that were former palaces of some royal, but I had planned to avoid them as best I could in Paris.

"You'll have to get used to looking over your shoulder to make sure you aren't followed, if that's your worry. Valuable skill to have, *page*, just for life in general."

I wondered if once I developed that skill, my eyes would dart around like his did, always scanning and never looking settled.

"What's it cost to be in this club?" I asked, mentally counting my coins and thinking about what I would have to steal to pay my dues. "And ... do you happen to know anybody who can take some ... things ... and turn them into money for me?"

He smiled, his face seeming to crack in the cold.

"That sounds dangerously close to asking me to help you commit a crime."

"No, no ... I would never..."

"I'm just kidding you, page. Of course, I do. I know ten people who will be more than happy to help you unload your ill-gotten goods so long as you promise never to rat them out. For a small fee. And don't feel so bad about it; in these times, you'd be hard-pressed to find a common man who didn't have to do a little of something to keep food in his children's bellies. Okay, we're almost there. Membership is invitation only, and it doesn't cost much. You'll enjoy the conversation better than at the public spots where we always have to be so careful what we say, concerned about the wrong ears. No one wants to end up in the Bastille! The King might be slow to disobey his wife, but he's quick to send his secret police scouring the streets for people to throw into jail."

He talked fast and gruff and often without looking at me. He was taller than me, so I had to pay close attention to his face when he talked, or his words would go right over my head. What I was hearing from him confused me.

"Why would the King—"

"I'm going to need you to do something for me, *page*. I'm going to need you to try to forget where you live and from whose perspective you see the world and come into this place with fresh eyes. I won't have to explain when you look at life for yourself, with an open mind. Here we are! Hey!" He called to one man who was smoking outside the door. The man raised an arm in acknowledgment and kept his stream of smoky condensation going as he stamped the ground like trying to keep it into place. It was cold.

"He works along the riverfront," Sebastien explained under his breath as he pulled open one of the double doors to a large building, letting me head in first.

I was as excited as a child at Christmas, giddy with anticipation of what being allowed entry to this club would give me. The royal circle and Madame lived in an insulated world, but this was all the rest of it. This was where normal people were. This place would give me an education beyond what Barnier could teach me.

I walked into the abandoned monastery, and it was like entering the Palace for the first time, that's how breathtaking it was to me. It was a long building with a rounded ceiling that made you feel like you were walking into one end of a giant tube. On one side, there were risers for people to sit three or four levels high. On the other side there was a platform in the center with risers on either side. At the far end, steps led to a balcony where people could watch from above. The tube had one large window in the ceiling on either side to let in the sunlight. Here and there small tables were set out in the center of the room for small groups. The risers and the tables were full of people in conversation, in groups, in pairs; even solitary men talked into their mugs of beer like the suds were putting up an argument. The noise was deafening. The scene was mayhem come to life. I couldn't stop the smile spreading across my face. I'd never seen anything like it.

"You'll get used to the noise," Sebastien shouted, hitting my arm and motioning me toward to an area at the end of one of the rows under a high window. As we walked, I picked up a word here or there, all spoken in excitement. Some people looked angry, some looked excited, but all of them were caught up.

I say that and it seems so casual. But "caught up" was a serious thing. It was like a low-grade fever or the tipsiness of a few glasses of wine. It spread. It was spreading to me now. There were two men arguing right in each other's faces close enough to kiss and loud enough to drown out everything around them, and still, no one seemed to notice because they were making their own noise.

"How did these people all find each other?" I walked in a complete circle to see everything and hear everything.

"I knew you'd like it," Sebastien smiled, pointing at me. "Look at your face; you're grinning like a loon! Crazy recognizes crazy, and I suspected you were a little bit off, like me. You have to be a certain type of person to want to be here and to like this mess."

"Well, I don't know if I like it yet," I said, trying to be heard. But that was a lie—I loved the buzz. I loved the place.

We sat down, and a boy came around to plop two beers on the table. I moved to pull out my wallet to pay, and Sebastien stopped me. "Part of our dues makes sure we're kept in beer and wine. You'll be okay this time since you're with me. But now that you're one of us, we do expect you to keep up and participate in your share of the drinking here and when we go out. So, you better unload that stuff quick. Wine costs money. At midnight, this place turns into a madhouse."

"*Turns* into a madhouse?"

"It's not always this chaotic; sometimes there's order. Sometimes we let people speak about what's on their mind, you know, the changes they want to see in this kingdom. We even invite people to speak. We're in the seat of the future of this country. Do you feel it? We're sitting inside a beating heart."

I couldn't have described it better myself.

He took a long swallow of beer, the foam coming away on his mustache as he put it down. He wiped it off brusquely with his sleeve as his eyes darted all over the room. I noticed that since we'd arrived his eyes never stopped. He barely looked at me for looking at everyone else. "You can learn a lot by seeing who's huddled together. Like them over there," I followed his gaze. "The bankers who are now noblemen. They resent the fact that they had to pay for their titles."

"Pay? What do you mean?"

"Didn't you know you can buy a title? The ones living up at the Palace are likely noble-born, but plenty of others—probably a lot of the ones who visit your Madame—bought the honor. Good King XVI is handing them out like candy to whoever can afford them—anything to fund these endless wars. You'll find some newly bought titles and even a few noble-born here."

"I don't understand. I thought you said this was a place for free-thinkers and followers of the Enlightenment movement who believe in equality. Nobles love the status quo of the aristocracy, why are they here at all?"

"That's a surprising generalization coming from you, but maybe your perspective from the inside is different. Noble-born have many privileges, but they aren't allowed to work. When family money dries up, some of them would like to be allowed to earn their wealth, like commoners."

The bluest blood nobles ensconced under the King's thumb at

Versailles were well-fed and free from worry about upkeep and servants for their aging castles. I'd never thought about the others.

"And then there are the bourgeoise, the wealthiest of all us commoners. The merchants and bankers ... the educators, doctors and avocats. They're getting wealthier every day, learning how to tap into commerce and trade around the world. Yes, that includes the slave trade. If you don't mind my asking, is that why you stay with her? Are you enslaved, or is it love of the woman?"

I could see there was a lot of misinformation going around.

"Love has nothing to do with it. Is that what everyone thinks?"

He shrugged and took a drink.

"They think I'm a fool, then?" Being a fool was worse than being wronged. Being a fool was the worst thing one could think of a person. I was angry now.

"They think you like the luxury in which you live. These days that would be understandable. We all thought that until you showed up. Anyway, back to what I was saying. The wealthy bourgeoisie have none of the privileges of nobles, and they resent that when, to their way of thinking, it's their money that's driving our economy. So, some are buying titles, paying for the respect they feel they deserve."

I was eating all this up, sipping on my drink and absorbing as much as I could.

"Lastly, there's those like me, common sans-culottes. I'm a peasant, and proud to be—working with my hands building furniture like my father and his father before him. I make a decent living, but it's getting tighter every day. When people can barely afford food, they're not so worried about chairs to sit on, and that affects me and *my* family."

It was a nice brief education that led me to believe one thing.

"So, you're a reaper of the enlightened, sent out to find more?" I asked. "Why choose me, Sebastien? You just told me what you thought of me."

"Before I met you..."

"Still, why meet me at all if you thought so little of me?"

He leaned back in his chair and breathed as if contemplating what to say. His brow furrowed, deepening his eyes even more.

"When you first rolled up in Paris in that carriage, I thought, 'Will you look at this? It's the du Barry page sent by the King!' But then I couldn't stop thinking of the stories we heard about you. Those escape attempts. Gaspard and the guards dragging you back. When I saw you all grown up and walking into bars on your own steam—"

"—Been watching me that long, have you?"

"Long enough. Not much happens in Paris that I don't know about. I've never been called a 'reaper,' but I suppose I am. I come from people who've been scraping by for centuries. People who never questioned the divine right of our King. Never. Even when my grandfather was executed. Our family was Protestant once, you see. The Sun King found it necessary to purge France of Protestant pests. We converted to Catholicism, and I'm sure I don't have to explain why. And vowed to honor the Sun King even as the pieces of Grand-pere's body were being burned on the pyre. I was three. I still smell my grandfather's flesh burning."

His eyes were glazed as the past overcame him. He had to physically shake himself back into the present.

"When I saw you, I thought, maybe he lived the life he has because, like my family, he gave in to what was safe. Swallowed the bile and accepted life as he felt he had to. But maybe now he's so full up with the shit of it all he has to see if there's another way to live or he'll go mad. Maybe he should have a chance, if that's the case. And..." He pointed his glass to me on the way to his lips. "...if the King is spying on us, I'm certain he'd send someone less conspicuous. You stand out."

I had to smile at that, and he joined, his eyes crinkling as he watched me.

"Well," I said. "You're right about that. No camouflage here."

"Not yet," he said, tipping his drink back and looking at me over the rim. "But you can work on that. These clubs are sprouting up all over France," he went on. "Before the club, it was just people talking about how prices were going up and does the King know how difficult it is? Now, women are having meetings in the salons of their homes to talk about the state of the world."

"Salon parties to discuss politics?"

"They have to. There're only men here because a lot of them don't think women should be allowed in this club. I happen to think women have every right to be here, but I'm in the minority. It hasn't stopped them. Women are having their own discussions, Jacobin Club be damned. Some even use this space when the men aren't meeting. Can't say I blame them."

"Isn't anyone here worried about word getting back to the King?"

"There's an expectation of confidentiality. Coming here is as safe as speaking to a priest in a confessional. Because, in truth, we all have something to lose if we're not careful. But we take some comfort in the King isolating himself at Versailles. He hardly bothers to visit Paris—maybe he doesn't think he needs to. The only one to come here from Versailles recently is you."

It was the King's blind spot—that he couldn't see beyond the circle of his closest nobles and friends. It was the royal bubble that shielded all of us at the Palace and the Chateau from the true state of the kingdom. No one at the Palace would know how much was happening in Paris—the great King was separated from the most important of his subjects, an hour's horseback ride away.

35

____

Eventually, others noticed I was becoming a permanent fixture. One night, from across the room, I spied the blond-haired man who had tried to stop me the first time Sabastien led me into the back room at one of the cafés. Sebastien had intervened on my behalf and the man, Valentin Carne, self-professed leader of the rag-tag group, backed down. On this night, I was enjoying my drink at a table when he and I connected eyes like star-crossed lovers. Sebastien followed my gaze.

"Ah, Valentin has spotted us. Speaking of those nobles with no money..."

Valentin was on his feet and quickly jumped up on a table, clapping his hands for attention.

"Jacobins!" The din quieted a bit as they looked up at him.

"We have in our midst a new member. Sebastien has brought a guest today who knows, perhaps best of all, what it means to be in service to the royal court. You may have heard of

the royal page and supplicant upon which all other pages and supplicants are patterned?" Small smattering of laughter. "Tell us, Louis-Benoit Zamor, how do you feel about these people that keep you trapped in a gilded cage? You must love them dearly for how good they've been to you."

Muffled laughter at that annoyed me.

"You know better than to let just anyone in, Sebastian," a man with long, brown hair gathered in a tail behind his head stood and addressed us with a frown. "You endanger us all bringing him here." I took some offense to that, but being unwelcome was a common state of affairs for me. I saw Valentin suppress a smile.

"He wants the same things we want," Sebastian countered firmly, his voice booming and jaw squaring with resolve.

"And how do we know that he's not just here to spy on us for the King?" asked Valentin, arms wide and face expressive. He stood there as the red meat he'd just tossed out excited the group. Several voices behind him grumbled in agreement.

I wasn't surprised that people questioned my motives for being here, but I was surprised that they thought I would be firmly loyal to the royals.

"I could say the same about you, Monsieur Carne," I spoke up, and the room quieted. My voice quavered slightly from the attention at this, the first time I spoke, not as a page but as an individual. I quickly began to like the sound of it echoing through the room. "You wonder if I'm a spy. I wonder if you, or another of you, will turn me in for favor *from* the King. See how that works? The distrust easily goes both ways." I looked around the room at the doubtful faces. "You look at me and see an enemy, knowing that I've been enslaved since childhood. Knowing that as a black-skinned man, I'm in far more danger than any one of you and, in fact, take my life in my hands by coming here at all. I've read the philosophers and I'm told you, the intellectuals of Paris, are enlightened. But while you all have each other to lean on, I go back to where I am surrounded by people who treat me as less than a man. And you imagine I would be loyal to that?"

The faces now held me in their gaze, attentive, waiting for more.

The brown-haired man said, stepping forward to look me in the eye. "I can think of plenty of reasons you'd be loyal to that. Did you think dressing like a common man would make us forget how you live?" He looked over my outfit with derision. "Even these common clothes are more expensive than any normal sans-culottes can afford. You're used to jewelry and meat on your plate every day—*several* courses at each meal. I've been to Versailles; I've seen it. The parties with champagne overflowing. The gold on the walls and all those statues. Those animals in the menagerie eat better than the average Frenchman or woman." Once again, grumbles of agreement from others in the room.

"You must know I'm no longer living in Versailles and my—bene-factress—is no longer associated with the royal family. But yes, I admit that even as a servant, I live in luxury compared to many. Yes, meat every day if I choose. Yes, several courses at each meal. Yes, the finest wine. Yes, I had to fray these clothes because I was afraid if I didn't show some humility, I might not make it through the door. I did it because this is still worth more to me. Tell me, stranger, do you have a family? Wife? Children? Which one of them would you give up for nice clothes or a cut of meat every now and then? I was taken from everyone I loved. For two years I cried for a mother I would never see again. Forced to learn a new language and dressed up like a doll, all so I could be presented as a gift to a pampered lady who grew bored of me a week after I was delivered to her. A woman who found pleasure in allowing her friends to abuse and humiliate me. Would losing your family be worth that to you? What is your freedom worth?" I looked around the room at the enrapt faces. Their interest spurred me to continue.

"I'm named after the Well-Beloved, you know. He and his Favorite called me the child they would never have together. Then they called me the Governor of Louveciennes—a joke like the many jokes they laid on my back all my life," I said. "To this day, my requests for freedom are ignored. She smirks when she denies me freedom papers. Tells me she can't free me because who would tie her shoelaces if I'm not there? She says I'm not a slave, but if I miss a morning check-in, there's a team of guards on my tail. Even to be here took *weeks* of proving to Madame du Barry that I would never dare try to free myself. We both know if I'm not there to deliver her chocolat, she will send her security team to bring me back, and not gently, I assure you.

"And still, as pathetic as that may sound, I'm not here because I hate Madame or the royal family. My personal feelings mean little in the grand scheme of things. I come here because the prospect of creating a France where every man is *truly* equal—that means more to me than even my own freedom. My sacrifice has to be for a reason, don't you see? I can't have lost all that was important to me for nothing. You, who think I'm a spy for my captors," I looked at the man in question. "*You* sacrifice what I have, and then you can question my integrity."

The brown-haired man held my gaze a moment more, reluctant to give up his opposition, but the steam had been let out of the room. "Valentin," he said, turning to the blond man. "It's a risk we don't need to take. To have someone from the inside is asking for trouble."

"It's a valid point, and he's right to ask it," Valentin said to the group. "None of us can be too careful with someone who is a part of the very system we're trying to change."

"Do you imagine change will only come from the minds of the bourgeoisie?" I raised my voice, tired of him and needing to be heard. I wanted to be with this group of thinkers. I *needed* to be with them for my own sanity. "I understand there are nobles in this room who are closer to the crown than I ever will be. You do understand that to a poor man there's no difference between you, me, and the King— that we're all part of the 'other' that is well off while they suffer? We eat while they starve. The question is, who is this new society to be composed of?"

An errant voice grudgingly replied. "We can't change this country with only merchants, bankers, and educated commoners. We need everyone. Even the nobles and aristocrats. Even clergy. Even the poorest peasants."

"Precisely," I said. "We can't make real change without the help of everyone! And in me, you get many aspects of society in one person. I'm a bargain, you see." I smiled the smile I put on for the nobles at the Palace, and some laughter returned.

The room was silent for a long moment. One man sucked on his cigarette like it helped him to deliberate. Another man coughed. I wondered if I'd made a fool of myself, and they would immediately turn me over, like I'd been turned over as a child.

Valentin's face relaxed just enough. He looked at Sebastian and they gave quick, imperceptible nods to each other.

"Alright, blackamoor."

"Zamor. You may call me Zamor or *page*. Don't call me 'blackamoor' again. I tell you this, the day that I am free is the day that would truly mean France is a society of equal men, and the will of the people has won. I pray for that future. But today, please know if I am betrayed by anyone in this group, I revoke my allegiance to this cause. I understand my station even here and, if betrayed, I'm loyal only to myself."

He took me in for a long moment and then responded: "Only loyalty to self and the nature of man will build a stronger republic."

"I'M sure you take no offense; it was a necessary questioning," Valentin sat down with me and Sebastien, uninvited. He motioned for a drink and tossed his hair back before looking me over. "Had to test you, Friend."

"No offense taken." I didn't consider him a friend.

"We can't let just anyone in here." He kept at it like I was putting up an argument. So, I obliged.

"Jacobins can't let just anybody in? Then how did you manage?" I asked. Sebastien laughed, leaning in.

"Zamor, this man here is one of our first noble-born Jacobins, born on St. Valentine's Day and named after the saint of love," he said, nodding at the blond man. "He absolutely oozes love, don't you think? Though you'd never know he was a noble from the look of him."

"Do you need to share everyone's life story with this man, Sebastien? He's only just got here."

"I'm not talking about everyone's story, just yours. It's only fair since you not-so-gently raked him over the coals in public. I'd say he has a right to know who's questioning his commitment to the cause, Monsieur le Duc Valentin Carne."

This put a new spin on things.

"Fine," Valentin said, taking a swallow from his drink. "What do you want to know, black- ... *page*?"

I was happy he caught himself. "I assume the same complaints made about me could be made about you? And I'd rather not have some theoretical antidote. I want to know about you." I pointed at him.

"This man," Sebastien interjected, "is from one of the oldest families in France but not quite old enough to have been invited to live at the Palace."

"We didn't want to live at the Palace," Valentin said, but his eyes skirted away.

"Liar. All you nobles want to live at the Palace. It's the pinnacle of high society. Anyway, he grows up and discovers his family money is all but gone. His family home is one of those one-hundred-room mansions out in the country..."

"Forty-five rooms, thank you."

"...forty-five rooms, pardonnez-moi. Forty-five rooms, each with a ceiling about to cave in and no family fortune left. Not one livre even to pay for the serving staff. You know a noble is down on their luck when they can't afford to pay someone to wipe their asses."

Valentin responded with an obscene gesture that made Sebastien laugh.

I leaned forward eagerly, waiting for the happy wrap-up to the story, expecting to hear about how sudden poverty brought him to see the light about the importance of equality. "And what happened?"

Sebastien looked at Valentin, whose face had lost its teasing cast. He sat back in his chair.

"They came to evict us for debt. My parents and I packed up what we could and loaded it into our carriage, prepared to beg our way past the doorstep of a distant cousin. It was humiliating for them. For

people like you and Sebastien, it's just another day of being poor—
you laugh about it and joke about it and bond over it—but it's not the
same for people like us. We knew we were going to be drummed from
society, the Carne name dragged through the mud. I was only six, but
my brother was twenty, and my mother was going on about how she
would reach out to any friends she still had left to find a wealthy
elderly dowager for my brother to wed. All the wealthy noblewomen
his age in their circle were already committed."

I was familiar with the tradition of the wealthy to marry for power
rather than love.

"You already had the name. Couldn't he have looked for a wealthy
bourgeoise woman?"

"Bourgeoise," he repeated with a snort, like it was ridiculous. Ah, I
thought, even at his most desperate, still a snob. "Our reputation was
already damaged. To marry beneath us would be the death of us. No,
safer to marry a wealthy noble on her deathbed than to marry a
wealthy bourgeoise. Besides, where would we even have found one?"
He took a long swallow before continuing.

"We were packing the carriage. My brother lost his mind for a
second when they came to evict us. We'd packed everything we could
fit, but the police standing there, watching and laughing, set him off.
He ran into the kitchen and grabbed a knife, slicing the arm of one of
the officers. The sight of the blood immediately brought him back to
his senses. He dropped the knife and begged forgiveness, but it was
too late. They arrested him and threw him into the Bastille."

I waited for the part where he would explain how that turned him
into a compassionate human being. It would be a long wait.

Valentin continued. "We found an avocat willing to take his case
for free—friend of a friend. He managed to get him before the King
to plead his case and ask for mercy. We all showed up, hopeful that
the King would see our predicament and understand my brother's
lapse in judgment."

I was beginning to feel a sense of dread.

"We'd never been to the Palace, so we were as struck as everyone
by the opulence. Our lost home was nowhere near as fine. They led

us to a room where the King was sitting, a group of people, including my brother, off to the side, all there for clemency. When it was his turn, my brother stepped forward, bowed, and explained his lapse in judgment. The Well-Beloved asked my parents what they had to say, and they explained what a good man my brother was. He asked me and I told him, "I love my big brother; please let him go.' The Well-Beloved then said to me, 'That may be, but he attempted to take the life of an officer who was there to collect a lawful debt. He is a poor example of a French gentleman.' That's what that bastard said to me."

"Watch it, Valentin," Sebastien looked around to make sure no one overheard him disparage the deceased monarch. "There are eyes and ears everywhere."

Valentin rolled the glass in his hands, but he looked at me with fire in his eyes. "One by one, each person who stood before the King was denied mercy. Then, the last couple stepped forward. It was the Comte and Comtesse de Lousene. The Lousenes were one of the most well-known and connected families in France, but also broke. They, too, had panicked when they were being evicted from their home. The Comtesse Lousene ran to the study, grabbed a gun, and shot two officers dead on the spot."

"The Well-Beloved must have denied them clemency?" I prompted.

"This is the best part. Just when he started to speak, a beautiful woman stepped forward. It was almost like theatre, watching this woman interrupt, seemingly out of nowhere, to run to their defense. As the roomful of us watched, she begged the King for their lives. She got down on her knees, bowed her head, and gave him an eyeful of what was coming out of that bodice. And that horny old man was beside himself. He makes that move with his hand, that kings do, allowing her to stand, and says, 'Comte and Comtesse Lousene. The lovely Madame du Barry has saved you. Madame, I'm delighted that the first favor you ask of your King is an act of mercy!' Oh, the beautiful tears in her eyes and the applause as those two crooks smiled and hugged each other. I saw them leading my brother out of the room and ran up to her. I said, 'Madame, please ask the King for mercy for my brother. He's a good brother.' She looked down at me—I'll never forget the way she looked at me, like I was some strange thing tugging on her skirt—and she said, 'Oh, chèr, your brother committed a crime. It would be wrong to free him. He's a bad man. Our King is doing you a favor by purging him from your life.' Then she kissed me on both cheeks and walked away."

I was stunned. Not by his story, but that he'd seen a piece of the woman I knew. But I still didn't understand. "Why would she do that?"

He looked at me now, his expression fierce and angry. "Didn't you hear the story, page? The Lousenes were one of the most well-connected families in all of France. My family was purple blood, but they were brilliant blue, just one step below living at the Palace. The rest of the prisoners were barely nobles at all in relation to the King. I didn't understand as a child, but now I do. Your Madame was, even back then, planning her ascent in society. The King gave in to a common woman on noble matters. What's the value of being a noble, I ask, if a common working woman can interfere in noble matters? My brother died in the Bastille two years later of some breathing sickness. By that time, my parents and I were living with that cousin, and they didn't want to rock the boat by visiting their criminal son. They pretended I was their only son. When I came of age, I took the little left for me and bought a flat here in Paris. I have enough to keep a roof over my head and daily bread, but my family name is destroyed. I'll never marry. I'm a Jacobin because the promise of the covenant among nobles is broken. It's wrong what they did to my brother. I hated the Well-Beloved, and I hate your Jeanne du Barry to this day."

We fell silent.

"I warn you, Valentin... you'll keep your hatred to yourself," Sebastien said. "I only asked for your story; this isn't the time or place to disparage our deceased King. You know better than to say things like that out loud. They'll put you in the same cell as your brother, and you'll never get out."

"Wouldn't it be amazing if we lived in a world where we could speak the truth? Where our words weren't stifled because they might hurt a monarch's feelings? Wouldn't that be something?"

I would later learn that was a lengthy conversation for Valentin. I couldn't say I liked him much—sometimes I caught him looking at me as if I was Madame and he was imagining how he would murder her—but we had an easy truce and stayed out of each other's hair.

In the subsequent weeks, I joined them, eating up their words and growing in excitement every meeting. Sometimes we left the Club and the back rooms to enjoy less serious conversations, getting to know each other while taking drinks and coffee.

But I wasn't blind. I heard the chatter that swirled outside of the room, in the bars and the streets where regular people with tongues loosened with drink spoke without guile and expressed their anger and dissatisfaction. To my way of thinking, addressing the social ills would lessen anger toward the King. Equality would eliminate the dissatisfaction with the aristocracy, and I knew, if it was going to happen, it would be due to the Jacobin Club of Paris.

I had found my home.

36

———

It's impossible to better yourself and not feel resentment at being forced to remain the smallest representation of who you are. Being forced to serve nobles who were arrogant idiots became harder with each passing day.

But by night, while others were readying for bed, I was either engaged in lively conversations about the state of the world in downtown Paris or in my bedroom reading the work of this brilliant writer who made me yearn to define my own philosophy.

My soul was filled with hope and relief that even though he was a white man, Rousseau seemed to know just precisely what I felt in my soul. It was as if he spoke words for me.

—Zamor

I was in my room one day, tallying the value of my coins and trinkets in the personal ledger that I kept hidden in a space between the bricks in my wall when, with a quick knock, the woman with the determined face burst into my room, her arms full of folded bed sheets. I was so surprised to see her I had no time to hide my stash and even less time to tell her not to enter. She skidded to a stop, looked down at my currency and stolen loot-covered bed, and glanced back up at my face.

"Pardon, Monsieur," she said. She had a tiny lisp that was just barely noticeable. "I only came to bring you linens. The boy with the spots on his face who tends the horses told me you were in need and that you had stepped out. I'm sorry for the intrusion. Excuse me."

She left as fast as she'd come. I was still for a second and then furiously gathered my items, pushing aside the loose plank in the floor and shoving them inside. I was quick enough that by the time I opened the door, she was still in the hallway, at the end just before the kitchen.

"Mademoiselle!" I yelled to her.

She stopped and looked back, her face now a mask of trepidation. "It's none of my business. I saw nothing."

"Alright, then," I said, grudgingly satisfied. "What's your name?"

"I was never here; you have no need of my name."

She turned and walked away. Over the next week, I caught more occasional glimpses of her. Finally, one day as I was collecting the thousand necessary parts and pieces for Madame's afternoon tea on a tray, Salanave just spit it out:

"The servant girl who came with the last envoy. Her name is Véronique. You should speak to her instead of leering at her like a fool. You will make her uncomfortable, you keep doing that. No one likes to be spied on."

"*You're* foolish," I countered, caught. "I'm doing nothing of the sort." But I was a little, though not meaning to do so. Every time I saw her, that expression on her face made me wonder what she was thinking. Who was she? Where had she come from? Was she like me, a slave pretending to be a servant? Was she a real servant? Was she free? Was she alone in the world? Was she lonely?

"She seems like a nice girl. She's got a bite when she's pushed, though," Salanave went on, chopping apples for the evening tarte tatin. A bowl of sweet cream sat on the sideboard waiting to be whipped for the topping. This would follow a meal of roasted duck with potatoes and a stew of root vegetables sweetened in the sun and cooked in the oven until they were toasty with dark edges. All of this with bottles of deep red wine from the cellar, the crusty loaves of bread made every day from milled wheat flour and pots of creamy chevre.

Looking at the components of the upcoming meal laid out in the kitchen made me hungry, but I had long since lost the appetite of being by Madame's side for her dinner. I preferred to stand alone, a sentient statue in the room, to watch. If she tried to compel me, I would be so bitingly insulting as to embarrass her into leaving me be. Her guests would comment openly about how disagreeable I was, and some would ask her to send me away. I silently hoped that the pressure of a thousand unpleasant dinner embarrassments would one day convince her to give me my freedom papers since kindness and obedience had had no effect.

I much preferred to eat leftovers in the kitchen with Salanave or eat alone in my room.

The next day, after I finished visiting Barnier, I went outside to my favorite place; a particular tree behind which I could disappear and read or just sit on a peaceful day. When I rounded the tree, there she was—Véronique—standing as if waiting for me. Her dress was light brown with a white pinafore. Her hair was wrapped in white cotton. Her thin arms were crossed over her chest and her body in a stance that put me on the defense immediately as she tapped her foot in agitation.

"Why are you constantly staring at me?" she asked straightforwardly. Once again, her face held that determination. But this close I could also see the length of her eyelashes and that her color was high on her cheeks as if she was angry. She was stern and lovely.

"What? I don't. I mean, I'm not," I lied.

"Liar. You stare every chance you get. I came out here to tell you to stop it. You don't scare me, Louis-Benoit. I've heard about you and your antics... I've heard you're a thief and a scoundrel, and I've seen with my own eyes that you're both. I've heard you have a slick tongue and manage to wiggle your way out of everything, but you won't this time. I insist you stop speaking about me."

I was taken aback by the sudden attack, and my feelings were hurt, just a little. I didn't know this woman, had nothing against this woman, and here she was, attacking me.

"Mademoiselle, I hardly know who you are except for your steady determination to burst into whatever room I'm in without invitation or even the decency to knock."

"You can save the innocent act, Monsieur. I told you, I've heard all about you and your antics. I hear you've bedded half the women in the servants' quarters, some two at a time. You're a walking member of the male anatomy. I want nothing to do with you, so if you're thinking I'll join your debauched games, you have another think coming."

Hot blood rushed to my cheeks. The embarrassment of being walked in on with Chloe came back, and now, I was angry.

"What I think is that a woman of your apparent intelligence would be smarter than to listen to rumors, and yet here we are. I've said I have no untoward motive and that's what I meant. But my, my, look at you, standing there judging me, all shades of indignant. What concern is it of yours who I bed?"

"None ... but..."

"But? There's a *but*? How can there be a *but* when it's my business? It's your business that you're a prude, and I was happy to leave it that way, but since we're opening up our opinions on each other's business, I feel free to put my nose where it doesn't belong. How about I tell you I'm concerned with the sanctimonious way in which you carry yourself? And demand an explanation from you for it?"

"But that has nothing to do with you and *your* reputation. I'm not sanctimonious, I just—"

"—not sanctimonious? Mademoiselle, I'm near woozy from the cloud of judgment that floats around you; the damnation of a thousand saints exudes from your pores."

"But this is about *my reputation*. They told me…"

Her body seemed to loosen its rigid posture just a bit, but she had insulted me, and I was slightly on the offense when I continued.

"They? Who is they? Curly-haired Chloe, who laughs about you whenever you leave a room? I'll have you know, despite what she's running around telling people, she didn't even mention ham until after we'd finished our business. And then I felt obligated. I mean, at that point if I *didn't* get her the ham, I would have been an ass. Or is 'they' that other giggling one who hardly knows where she is most of the time? Or that group of miscreants who runs the servants' quarters because the housekeeper and the other three-quarters of the staff are afraid of them? You have reason to trust their word over mine? Let's put the issue to rest, shall we? I'm sorry if at odd times during the process of looking around the Chateau grounds or searching for someone or another, I may have accidentally glanced your way. I assure you I did so quite innocently. If Henri took it upon himself to throw us together, he did it on his own without any prodding from me because—as I'm sure you understand—I would not have *chosen* for you to come to my room at that precise time. But if I have glanced your way more often than others, perhaps it's unconscious on my part. I so rarely see another black person here at the Chateau, you catch my eye. I assure you, it is no more than that."

I was wrong to feel so wronged but that didn't change the fact that I did. This woman with the serious face had offended me, so I did what I did best and drove home my point while she was in a weakened state.

"But … it's not like I intruded on your private space, twice. Or like I watched you long enough to discover where you spend your quiet times and made an effort to catch you in that spot, all for the sake of telling you to leave *me* alone. One would suggest, Mademoiselle, that perhaps *you* are the scandalous one, seeking out the walking member of the male anatomy as you have."

Her lips bunched, and her cheeks had turned red. "I-I..."

"By the way, I trust you received your letter. The one I slipped under your door?" Since Salanave had confirmed her name, I could now use the information to put her off my scent and make her feel even worse. *I was the injured party here.*

"Oui..." she said, with a questioning tone.

"Good. When it arrived, I assumed you might not want the others to know that you read. It would make the other servants even more suspicious of you, as I know from experience. That would be terrible for you because they already think you're strange, and Gaspard—you don't even want him to get a whiff that you can read. He dislikes black people, as I'm sure you know. And I hear he's told the others that if anything befalls you, it's none of his concern. Even worse if the nobles find out. They take it as a personal insult if any servant, especially a black one, knows how to read. They think it makes you feel equal to them, and they don't like that."

What I was saying wasn't untrue, but still, I might have been kinder about it. If my feelings weren't ruffled.

"I didn't realize," she said, awkwardly clutching her skirt in her hands. "You gather the mail?"

"Oh, yes. There are three of us who live in this house who read: Madame, Salanave, and me, not in that order by proficiency. Believe me, you don't want to hear what Salanave will do to a sonnet. It's a crime."

"Why are you telling me this?"

"Why am I telling you?" Was she really as naïve as she sounded? *Because you hurt my feelings!* I wanted to yell. *Because I was curious and interested in you and you threw it in my face! Because you embarrassed me by catching me watching you over and over again!*

I spoke calmly. "Assuming you will want to write back to whoever sent you that letter, I recommend you slip any outgoing mail to me, and I'll make sure it gets to the post with no one being the wiser."

"Even—even after today? I'm sure you must feel I've ambushed and insulted you unfairly, and ... rightly so. I feel terrible about my behavior. How am I to be certain you aren't waiting to enact retribution for my … horrid accusations?"

Rightly so, indeed! I felt the first lick of humor in this situation. Maybe she wasn't so naïve. How was she to be certain I wouldn't want revenge?

"Oh, now, that's not so difficult to figure out. Go like this…" I took my time bringing my hands together slowly. "Put your two saintly, sanctimonious palms together like this … *and you pray*, Mademoiselle. I recommend you pray very piously. It hasn't worked for me, but I'm sure those saints that surround you in that holy cloud of goodness will be all too willing to grant your wish."

She quickly dipped and said, "Oui. Bonsoir, Monsieur," before practically running away from me.

"Bonsoir, Mademoiselle," I called after her. The thrill of retribution dissolved quickly, as revenge always does.

I decided the new apprentice was a headache I didn't need. No matter how interesting, she wasn't worth the trouble of getting to know. And I had other things on my mind.

PART III

A HERO'S BETRAYAL

37

"Might the Madame du Barry have time to join me for a meal a ... picnic?"

The man standing in the foyer was Louis Hercule Timoléon de Cosse-Brissac. A general under Louis XV, he was one of the many nobles forced to live at the Palace during the last king's rule. I hadn't seen him since the death of the Well-Beloved. He stood awkwardly holding a basket with one hand and fiddling with his coat lapel with the other.

"I will check with her, Monsieur le Duc de Cosse-Brissac ..." Most nobles liked to hear their names said out loud—the longer the name, the better. This man blushed and shook his head.

"Please, Brissac is fine; that's what everyone calls me," he said. "And you are Louis-Benoit Zamor, I know. Is that what you prefer to be called?"

I liked him already.

"Just Zamor is fine with me."

"I do realize I'm pressing my luck, showing up without an appointment. I don't want her to think me inconsiderate of her time, it's just ... when I try to plan ahead and write a note to ask, my courage flies away. I will gladly fight a battle for the King, but I'm deathly afraid of the Madame's rejection. A woman so beautiful can have any man."

Such humility among nobles was rare. He seemed almost too nice, but there was no accounting for love matches, and I certainly wasn't going to judge.

"I wouldn't worry so much," I told him. "In all my time here, I can't recall one suitor who's thought to provide a picnic. I'd say your chances are good that she will make time."

When Madame came down, he blushed and stuttered and called her lovely at least five times—would have gone for six had I not motioned him to stop, with a subtle head shake. Nobody likes a kiss ass. And then he complimented her on his memory of her intelligent, witty conversation and confessed to her it had taken him all the time since she'd come back to society to get up the nerve to approach her. Held his basket up shyly.

She was used to men telling her she was beautiful; it was his praise of her intelligence that really made her preen. The more he spoke, the more coquettish she became. I knew she was thrilled. Because while there was never a shortage of men around her, they didn't all treat her as well. And most didn't even think to court her in the same manner they would court a noble-born woman. She accepted his picnic on the back lawn, and from that moment, Brissac became an established member of the family.

When he was at the Chateau, she practically forgot about me. A quick study, he noticed how she was to me, never more apparent than after one episode where a five-minute delay of her chocolat caused her mask to slip and the shrill come out. On his own, he took to convincing her to spend time in his townhome in Paris. I thought it was just luck on my part until the time he winked at me after getting her to acquiesce. I loved him for that alone.

The freedom of these nights away from her was priceless. It was on one such evening I found my way to an old building on a small street off the main drag in the center of Paris.

The worn wooden door was ridged and dented, suggesting it might have been kicked in a time or two. I knocked, and the sturdiness of the wood told me it could take a few more kicks, if necessary, just like its owner. The door opened to Sebastien's craggy face, which brightened when he saw me.

"He's here," he called over his shoulder. "I didn't think you'd actually come."

"Why would you ask me if you didn't think I'd come? Did you not want me to come?" I asked.

"No, I wanted you to come. I just didn't think you would..." He didn't get a chance to finish his statement.

"Invite him *in*, Sebastien," called a woman's voice.

"Yes, yes, come in," he stood aside and shuffled me in.

His suspicion was justified. I almost didn't come. I'd never been anyone's guest in all my life, but I told myself it couldn't be that difficult. I'd served guests for years. I told myself I should behave as I would want a guest to treat me, that's all. But the second I stepped inside, I realized I'd come empty-handed. And now, I flushed with embarrassment, second only to Sebastien, who shuffled uncomfortably beside me like I was the first guest he'd ever invited to his home.

"Zamor, meet my wife, Elise." He gestured to a plump woman who came forward, wiping her hands on her apron. Her hair was the color of tangerines with bangs that flopped over her eyes, her face shiny as if she'd run around the block. She came at me fast and then stopped, looked at me, and made an awkward curtsy and stayed there. "Bonsoir, Monsieur Zamor."

I, just as awkwardly, tried to pull her up by her hands. "No need to curtsy for me, Madame, I'm no one special. And you will think I'm terribly rude ... as I've come empty-handed. I'm not often a guest and I ... I .... please call me Zamor."

My admission made her face relax. "We only wanted your company for the evening, Zamor, don't think anything of it. Sebastien has been telling me all about his new friend, so it is a pleasure to finally meet you. He goes out to all the seediest bars in town, and I'm always worried what he'll bring home." She was still fidgeting with the apron she wore, moving her hair off her sweaty brow with the back of one hand, oddly shy. She suddenly realized her last words might have offended me. Her whole face flushed beet red. "I-I meant..."

"Please, don't be uncomfortable with me, Madame; I fully understand what you meant. I've been in those seedy bars, and you're right to be cautious. I'm honored to make your acquaintance. Sebastien tells me stories about his intelligent, capable wife, and I'm more than anxious to speak to the smart one in the family."

The three of us laughed and the sound of it broke the spell, making us all considerably less awkward. Elise took my covering, and soon I was sitting at a table pushed between the tiny kitchen and the living area. I guess you could call it a kitchen; it was little more than a stove with burning coal heating its insides, glistening and spitting heat and steam, a basin of water and a tiny table for chopping and preparation. I crowded at the table with them and their children. The little ones—one about four and the other not much younger—looked up at me with pale round faces, the younger one with the serious brow of his father.

The apartment was small, but it had two floors with the bedrooms up above, which I understood was rare for the average sans-culotte.

"I'm pleased you were able to get away for the evening," Elise said, carrying a large pot with two cloths from the stove to the table to sit on a trivet to protect the towel that had been draped as a tablecloth. She took a large ladle and put a spoonful each into bowls in front of us. She gave me two ladles full, a half each for her children, one full one for her husband and a half for herself. She did this quickly, carrying the pot back to sit atop the stove. As soon as she turned her back, Sebastien leaned over to pour half of his soup back into her bowl. They both did this so reflexively that it must have been done a thousand times before. My heart clinched at the care they displayed for each other.

She came back to the table, wiped the steam from her brow with her apron, and sat. Then she reached for the leather wine cask on the table, and I noticed the tiny glasses on the table.

"Will you pour, Sebastien?" He did as he was told and poured a bit of red wine into the adult glasses. Putting it down, he picked up his glass. The children followed suit and raised tiny glasses of water.

"To ... family and new friends," he said. "Bon santé." *Good health*. I followed suit, feeling unexpected warmth flow through me.

"Bon santé," Elise and I repeated.

I was grateful to have Henri as a friend, but this was different. If Henri and I didn't work at the same place, we would never have been friends—would never have had an occasion to even know each other. But Sebastien and I liked each other and had things in common. His friendship was separate from anything to do with my servitude. With Sebastien, I could be my full self.

We drank and began to eat the soup. It was fatty, no doubt due to the cut of meat, and flavored lightly with onion. It was a luxury that they were able to buy meat at all.

"It's delicious, Madame," I said.

Across from me, she glanced at me a couple times as she ate, keeping her eyes low. "Nothing like what you are used to, I'm sure, but I hope you enjoy it. I'm sure nothing from my kitchen can compare with what you've tasted where you come from," she said.

Even a servant in the Palace had an elevated status in society, and even Sebastien, proponent of a new equal society, wasn't impervious to the centuries-old history that favored the nobles and those closest to them.

But for me, a private space such as this modest home was rarified air. Sebastien didn't have much, but he had this family, these rooms to call his, the freedom of all within his walls. But I couldn't say that to these people—it would seem condescending.

"You're right, Elise, I've tasted amazing food, so when I tell you this could compete with anything from the King's own kitchen, you can believe me."

Sebastien smiled broadly at the quiet pleasure on her face. "You see, amour, I'm not lying when I tell you your food is amazing. You heard it from Zamor, and I didn't even pay him to say it."

"You mean I could have gotten paid for saying that?" I asked. We laughed, and the little one interrupted.

"You know the King, Monsieur?"

Sebastien cleared his throat.

"'Does Zamor know the King,' you ask? Not only does he know the King, why he's—"

"—don't Sebastien," I couldn't help but laugh. I'd made the mistake of telling him a story or two and he took that opportunity to have his fun.

"—he's like the King's very own brother from another mother."

"Stop teasing him," Elise said. "It's not like he was lying; they were both raised by the King, sort of. Not like you, my love. Remember the lie you told my father to get him to let me see you."

"I don't tell lies, I tell exaggerated stories," Sebastien said. "All I said was that I worked for the bishop."

"He thought you were a member of the clergy, and then he caught us kissing and threatened to have you drummed out of church."

"And I said, you can try, monsieur, but the bishop would wonder why you're making him kick the man who makes his chairs out of a church he doesn't even attend."

"Papa, you lied to Grand-pere?" the older one asked, cheeks shining.

"It wasn't a lie; it was an exaggeration."

"Whatever it was, it got me married three months later," she said. "Well, that and the fact that my oldest was on his way." She leaned over and put a hand on Sebastien's. He flipped his hand and took her fingers.

"The best story I ever told because it allowed me time with your mother," he said. "Now, back to this wonderful meal. I was telling Elise how the Jacobin Club has tripled in size in the last six months. I wish you could be there with us. Tell her, Zamor, what it's like."

The interest in her eyes made me wonder if there would be women in the club soon.

"I've never seen anything like it," I said honestly. "The *excitement*. People talking about ways we can truly change this country. Crazy things like doing away with titles. And educating everyone. Every time you think of one thing, you realize how it affects something else. It feels like we're truly starting something special."

"You're caught up in the fever, too? How will that work for you, being who you are and living where you live?" she asked.

I sipped a spoonful of the fragrant, fatty soup. "Being who I am is what's pushing me to be a part of this. It's what makes me want France to be all of what it could be so I can be all of who *I* can be."

She nodded. "I'm almost afraid to believe or hope that things can change for us common people. Sebastien says you're an abolitionist. Do you really think you can do anything to stop slavery? We don't have many abolitionists here. I don't know any at all."

I hadn't even hoped to call myself that, but apparently, Sebastien saw something in me that I didn't.

"If wanting my freedom makes me an abolitionist, then I am and you are, too, if you believe that all men are equal. I don't even know where to start. But isn't that what's happening now? We're pushing the boundaries to see what's possible in ways we never dared before. And, frankly, my goals are self-serving. As long as slavery is in effect, I can be trapped in an existence I can never change. I can't leave this country at all—I'm told even the shipping ports are dangerous for someone who doesn't have some sort of proof of nationality. If I was going to fight for anything, I would fight for myself. If I don't, who will?"

"Monsieur," one of the little ones had reached over to tug on my sleeve. "Why do you wear those thin pants? Won't you get a chill in the winter? He'll get cold, won't he, Papa?"

Elise looked mortified, but Sebastien picked up where the question stopped.

"Yes, he will, son. Entirely impractical clothes he's wearing, but wealthy people have different clothes for different seasons. Besides, he's better now than when I first saw him poking around in the bars. Wore ridiculously fancy clothes; silks, satin-covered buttons, shoes with the bows and pointed toes. Lace, all in the front! He was a veritable paragon of high aristocratic fashion. The only thing missing was the powdered wig."

I thought back to my first lone trip to Paris. "I thought the wig might be a bit much," I admitted.

Elise snickered into her soup before quickly catching herself. "My apologies, Monsieur Zamor, I just can't picture you with one of those white things on your head. I like your dark curly hair just fine."

I didn't mind Sebastien poking fun at my dress. I could see his eyes and there was no hatred or animosity in them. I'd been mocked all my life and knew how it felt in my bones. This felt like something else. This felt like friendship.

38

———————

One morning, I was dusting when I looked outside and noticed the black man who had arrived the evening before. He was the driver to a nobleman who had only planned to stay for one night. The horse drawing the small carriage had been saddled, and the driver leaned against a tree outside, his hands in his pockets, to wait.

I put my rag away and walked outside, my hands in my pocket to mirror his casual stance. I walked over to him and nodded. "Monsieur."

He nodded back, "Bon Matin." *Good morning.*

"If you're waiting for them to finish breakfast, it might be a while. Madame likes to provide quite a spread."

He smiled. "A decent spread for the serving staff as well." He patted his belly. I didn't tell him I rarely ate in the servant dining area because I had a hard time digesting food in the company of people I didn't like. Most were decent, but there was a small circle of miscreants that I preferred to avoid. My breakfast was an apple and a bit of cheese out by my tree that morning.

"You've worked for the gentleman for some time?" I asked.

"About fifteen years or so. And you?"

"Me? I've been with Madame du Barry since I was a child."

"You must care for her a great deal," he said. It was a trick question. Any servant knows, rare is the person who serves out of love.

"She has kept me clothed and fed since I was young."

He nodded.

"So ..." I started. "So, are you a free man, then?"

His face closed up, and I instantly worried I'd tripped over a sensitive subject as he straightened, even though his hands remained in his pockets.

"Of course, I'm free. The man I work for may not have all the riches and wealth of your Madame—we may not have a place like this—but he's just as good a person. It doesn't take wealth to be a decent, civilized human being."

I blinked in confusion, and then it hit me. He thought because his employer had less money, I was suggesting he was less civilized than Madame. He thought the freeing of slaves was the indicator of civility. He thought I was free, and I was putting him down by suggesting he wasn't.

"I meant no disrespect, Monsieur," I said. "Of course, you are free. It's obvious from the easy way you are with each other. I see it clearly, now."

"I may not wear your fine clothes, but I have what is most important. You should take care not to look down on those who don't have as much as you. Your Madame is generous; you could afford to borrow some of her humility and perhaps take a lesson on how to treat people who don't have as much."

My skin felt hot, but my lips refused to let out the truth. To correct his error would be to expose myself. Instead, I dipped quickly. "My apologies, Monsieur. Bonjour." I turned and walked back into the house.

I didn't see the visitors leave, but the feeling of hot embarrassment stayed with me all morning and into the evening. Even though I couldn't have told anyone why I felt bad. Why was I ashamed? What had I done?

I met Madame outside her bedroom to walk her down to the dining room for dinner. As she took my arm for the descent, I began.

"The guest who left this morning, he freed the black man who was driving him years ago." She ignored me, keeping her eyes on the stairs as she descended. "So, perhaps it's time for you to free me."

"What on earth does one thing have to do with the other?"

"I thought if you realized that it was considered de rigueur" —*fashionable*— "...to free one's slaves on the mainland, you might rethink your position."

"But who would get my—"

"—any number of servants can get your chocolat, Madame--"

"—but not as well, Louis-Benoit." There was a pout in her voice now. "You carry it so well and hold my cup just so."

"I can tell you think this is funny—"

"—who would I have these fun conversations with—"

"—my life is not a joke!"

We'd reached the landing. She took her arm from mine and turned toward the

dining room, smoothing her hair into place. "I'll remind you not to take that tone with me."

I followed. "I'll remind you that I'll take whatever tone I want. Do you know what that driver called his employer? He called him 'decent.' He was insulted by the notion that a decent person would even keep a slave."

"You weren't enslaved by me. You should take this up with the people your parents sold you to. In fact, take it up with your parents. What kind of people sell their own child? I would never sell you, not for any amount of money. That's how much I love you," she said as we entered the room. Gaspard was already in position across the room.

"Stop with that nonsense. Free me. I want it and he certainly wants it." I gestured towards the man whose ears perked up to our conversation.

"And it doesn't matter what either of you want. It only matters what I want." She waited beside her chair until I finally stepped forward to pull it out for her. "How many times do I have to tell you I'm only looking out for you?"

The conversation was getting us nowhere because we'd had it a thousand times before. The dining room table was laid with crystal and gold-rimmed places. The fragrance of the fresh flowers in vases filled the room. The candles and fireplace were lit, and the room glowed with warmth. But I was icy cold with anger.

Here I was begging again for something that should have been mine long ago. Something that a good number of people on the mainland expected, even while they closed their eyes to what was happening in the colonies. It was wrong for her to keep me trapped.

"Maybe I should tell everyone that the woman they think is so gracious and kind keeps me in bondage."

Instead of taking her seat, she turned to look at me. "Fine. Tell them. Oh, poor me..." She balled her fists up to pantomime me crying like a baby, just like she did when I was set upon as a child all those years ago. Instantly, I felt just as helpless. "Poor me, I'm a slave. They make me eat oysters on the half shell and truffles and drink champagne and eat good brie. And that horrible silk is too soft against my skin! Poor you! No one will ever feel sorry for you, Zamor. I think news of me owning you might endear me to all these nobles who think you're too arrogant for your own good. They'll see it as a savvy move on my part to keep you in check. I would almost certainly have to pay a small fine, but beyond that, nothing would change *for me*, Louis, but for you—" she paused and tilted her head, putting an innocent look on her face. "How might that change your life?"

She knew. She knew how afraid I was to be pitied and humiliated. It was what I felt that morning. It was the reason I preferred to let the freed driver think I was rude rather than enslaved. Even if it wasn't a shame I should bear, it felt like it was.

If they knew my true status, it would be open season on me for the nobles. Gone would be any outward sign of respect. Gone, any decent behavior. Gone, any reference to me as "Monsieur." It would be my childhood all over again, only this time, it would never end.

And that was if I stayed. If I went public, the King could confiscate me. If Madame went around telling everyone that the Well-Beloved had bought me for her himself, and XVI found out, it could be the last of his temper. He could throw me in the Bastille or send me to the colonies, still enslaved. How would I survive in the colonies?

The sharp, feral look in her eyes told me she saw all of this on my face. The color came up on her cheeks, and I knew her little eaters were feeding, feeding, feeding...

"But it's up to you, chèr." *Dear.* The "dear" stung. "I can see you've come to your senses. Everyone knows who you are, Louis-Benoit, enslaved or not. You are mine. Like my very own son." She took my face in her hands and smiled sweetly. "I give you license to be just as mischievous as you were with my dear Well-Beloved, so you can release whatever pent-up frustration you have. I even enjoy our heated conversations and spats. I understand how difficult it is to know how unimportant you are to the world—I used to be unimportant—but you are *very* important to me. You are the Governor of Louveciennes! Where else in France will you ever be held in such high esteem? I forgive you this outburst." She kissed me on both cheeks and sat down, fluffing her skirts.

Her words sent numbness through my limbs, but it was wearing off from the heat of anger. I hated her.

Across the room, Gaspard was watching, the muscle clenching in his jaw as if he could feel the emotions, I was doing my best to keep hidden. I did what I did whenever I joined her for dinner. I stood in my spot behind her, hands clasped before me, as I willed my temper to die down to keep my hands by my side instead of wrapping around her neck.

Véronique arrived to take a spot next to a table on a third wall, close to the drinks and wine. And then, the room began to fill with guests. This dinner couldn't get any better.

All I wanted was to get through the meal and be left alone, but this wasn't going to be one of those meals. They started during the soup course. One of the guests looked at me, a sly smile on his face.

"Did your *page* help with dinner, Madame?" he asked.

Don't speak. Don't speak.

"How did you know?" I asked the guest pleasantly, stepping forward to stand beside her. "I took special care with Madame's dinner. She's always so worried about lack of flavor, so I looked around the garden and found something interesting and special. I believe it's called belladonna, a surprisingly lovely plant that reminds me so much of my dear benefactress." I said it innocently, as if I had no idea what I was saying. "I shaved lots and lots of it into her bowl in honor of my deep feeling for her." I looked down at her and smiled. "Enjoy, Madame."

I heard a few shocked gasps and stepped back, pleased with the discomfort sweeping through the room. Gaspard looked me in the eye. *I know what you're doing,* his gaze said. *You'll get it later.*

He needn't have worried, Jeanne du Barry was, as always, quick on her feet, putting up a hand to quell the quiet murmurings.

"And now, my dear guests, you have had a taste of my sweet Louis-Benoit's bracing—and often inappropriate—humor. He would no more poison me than he would poison himself. But he certainly had you in his snare, didn't he?"

Everyone relaxed at once, smiles returning. I felt my facial muscles trying to frown, but I kept it still. There were two actors in this room.

"Magnificent," one of the men said, looking me over. "Quite intelligent and such a sharp sense of humor he has."

He spoke about me like I was the pet. Just like when I was a child. Powerless. Afraid. Before I changed myself.

"And yet..." I reminded them. "She still hasn't even taken a taste." Unlike the last bluff, this one was intentional. I wanted to make her think. I wanted to make her wonder. To make her worry. To start to think maybe poking me wasn't the smartest thing to do.

The table laughed, and Madame made a point of tipping a spoonful into her mouth.

"Delicious. But ..." She hesitated and put a delicate hand to her throat. "... what is that..." coughing gently.

The room quieted. Everyone held their breath.

"Oh ... only pepper."

The room exploded with laughter, and she smiled prettily, obviously happy with the success of her teasing. The guests were now more relaxed, smiling at Madame's composure and grace.

One day it won't be! One day you'll be sorry for this. One day you'll be sorry you laughed at me!

"Darn," I said, stepping back. "I must have accidentally poisoned the cat."

They all burst into more laughter, but I hoped Madame was listening. I hoped she was paying attention to just how seriously I felt about her at that moment. I wanted her to know the thought had crossed my mind.

"I must say, Madame, your patience with the help is astounding," said one of the women, snapping her fingers at Véronique to pour more water. I watched the apprentice take the pitcher off the sideboard and make her way around the table to fill her glass. Madame opened her mouth to continue, but I jumped in on her behalf.

"But my dear lady," I said. "If not Madame, who else would have me?" Madame nodded, but her lips were pinched. Ah, she didn't like hearing her words coming from my mouth. So, I kept at it. "Why, if it weren't for the generous Comtesse du Barry, I would be starving on the street! Her little African cupid would be a little African skeleton."

Once again, it might have been a hint of brittleness in my voice that caused the laughter to die down again. I moved back into position, and Gaspard and I continued glaring at each other.

"You are so right, my dear Louis," my benefactress said, sipping from her glass of red wine. "I shall tell you the *real* reason I keep him." She turned to them, looking at each one earnestly. "It is because I would be lost without him and he without me. We are two peas in a pod. Closer than a husband and wife, we love each other like mother and son. But unfortunately, the son has grown ill-tempered and tiresome tonight and needs to be put away. You may leave, Louis," she said, pointedly looking away from me.

I turned and walked out of the room while they were talking, pacing in the hallway outside the door with the energy still in me. I was tight with frustration and anger and hurt. I was resentful and annoyed. I walked through the halls, trying to work off the tightness.

I made my way into the salon to search for something satisfying to break. I no longer did it out of anger—I wasn't a child, after all—now I broke things just because it felt good, like a back scratch or satisfying dessert.

A small dancing figurine stood on a pedestal on the far side of the parlor. It was a blond woman dancing like she didn't have a care in the world. *Yes, that was the one.* I headed across the shiny, wooden floor that shone from hand polish and the reflection of sunlight that bounced off the mirrored panels on the wall. I raised my hand to back-hand it across the room, looking forward to seeing it projectile, when suddenly there was a whirl of fabric in front of me, and there she was, Véronique, standing right in front of me. She held the piece of porcelain in her hand from where she had grabbed it.

"You will not," she said.

I was only in a moderately bad mood before; now, I felt my temper kick in.

"Mademoiselle Véronique, do you think I'm a child you can tell what to do or stop me from doing what I want? Do the Madame's things mean so much to you, or do you just want to get into her good graces so you can stay at Louveciennes for the rest of your life—no doubt the nicest place you've ever been, judging from your clothes. I won't block your naked ambition to elevate yourself, Mademoiselle, but stay out of my way. Or go run and report me if you feel so inclined; I don't care. Just do it away from me."

"And I don't care what you think of my clothes," she said, but I felt a slice of shame at the way her chin lifted slightly and wobbled a bit. "And I don't care about good graces. I care about art. You don't destroy beautiful things for no good reason."

That sounded ridiculous, and I let her see it on my face.

"Because I'm sure it's a sin," she provided by way of explanation. As if it was as simple as the sky was blue.

"Really? Because I've read the bible book. I didn't see anything about porcelain dancing ladies in Matthew or Luke. But there's plenty about false idols. It's just a piece of clay."

"Breaking it is no better than trampling a flower," she touched the figurine delicately with one finger as she spoke.

"Oh Lord, don't tell me you skip through the daisies, too, trying not to crush any," I mocked.

"You don't punish the art because you hate the people."

"Who said I hate anybody? And I respectfully disagree."

"There's nothing respectable about you."

I watched her continue to fawn over the piece, her lips moving and voice droning on about art while I lost the point of the conversation—I'm sure looking down my nose as I did.

I didn't understand this woman, but I wished I could see her face without the blue headwrap she wore today. It was plain, as was the blue cotton dress. Satin and silk were for the ladies and guests ... and me. She was only a regular servant, so no silk for her. I snapped back to focus and interrupted her.

"...Why should I care about a little piece of clay when so little care is paid to human beings by these nobles? Are you even paying attention to what is going on in the world around you? Look, if you like it so much, you should have it," I said, thinking if it was as valuable as she was treating it, perhaps I should have added it to my stash instead of trying to destroy it.

My suggestion was not taken in the spirit it was given. When she looked up at me, her eyes were flashing with anger, and she practically hissed at me. "I'm no thief, not like you, with your sticky fingers. You're not even good at it. Your thievery is the worst-kept secret in all the Chateau." She put it back on the stand, carefully.

"Pardon me. I *am* good at it, Mademoiselle. And what, exactly, makes you think my thievery is meant to be secret?" I asked.

"Why else would you hide your stash?"

I gave her a condescending look meant to tell her precisely how ridiculous she was. "I hide my stash because I don't want one of these other castle thieves to steal my stolen loot. Look," I said, growing exasperated. "You really don't know anything about me or this place at all, do you?"

"But why wouldn't you want to keep it secret?" She looked confused, still stuck. Her slightly crooked front tooth caught my eye as she continued to speak. "A normal person is ashamed to be a thief. A normal person wouldn't boast about it." She looked so confused I almost felt sorry for her.

"Where are you from?" I asked. My subject change stopped the streak of her anger.

"...Burgundy." Ah yes, it was from Burgundy that the letter was addressed.

"Are you a free woman?"

"Yes, as a matter of fact." That explained it. "As was my mother. My father was born enslaved in Saint-Domingue but was freed by the man who owned him. My mother is free, her family having been here for generations before the slave trade took over. She can trace her roots back hundreds of years. My mother is a teacher for the church, and Papa is a laborer. They met through the church. They've been happily married for thirty years."

The subject of her parents softened her, her shoulders dropping their defensive stance. She seemed to enjoy speaking of them.

Another one who was free and boasted it proudly. *Why did others deserve to be free and not me? Was it because of the type of person I was? Was freedom a reward for sanctimony? Was enslavement a punishment for people like me? Is that why I felt so ashamed of something I had no control over?*

This woman who stood before me had a charmed life if what she was saying was even moderately true. I had no ill will toward her, but why did she deserve charm and not me?

Maybe it wasn't all so wonderful, a tiny voice inside me said. It wasn't possible her life was as good as all that. I thought about the marriages I'd seen at Versailles; the couples who barely tolerated each other and cheated under each other's noses. Right here in the Chateau at that moment were three men with their mistresses instead of their wives. There was no such thing as a happily married couple that I could see. Sebastien and his wife were an aberration. Over the years, I had even wondered if my own parents had been happy or simply pretending like every other couple in the world.

"That's highly unlikely," slipped from my mouth.

"What is unlikely?"

"Loving someone like that for that long. People don't truly love like that—happily, selflessly. I'll bet your father has a woman on the side, and your mother is poisoning *his* morning cereal. It's more likely your parents are still together because it's too troublesome to be alone, and they're too lazy to go looking for other people."

Her face was still, and then, out of nowhere, I heard a sharp crack and was staring at the opposite wall before I realized she'd hit me across my face.

"Don't speak that way about my parents. You will never disrespect my family again, ever. I may be just a poor country domestique, but I pity you because you haven't an ounce of human emotion in you. Do what you want with that little piece of art. It's your conscience to worry over, not mine. I shall not waste my time teaching a grown man how to behave as one." She spared me a glare that said I was worse than horse dung and walked out, back stiff.

My conscience couldn't care less about the figurine. I watched her leave, her work shoes quiet against the floor, unlike the pretty shoes of the ladies. But her waist was tight and fit and flared with a natural fluidity of motion that told me she didn't wear hoops under her skirts to fill out her figure. The width of her hips was natural. I realized why I had such a hard time ignoring her. From the day I'd first seen her fighting against errant laundry, I was fascinated by every aspect of her. From that very first glance, she had awoken something in me that had never before seen the light of day.

39

———

"Americans are coming!" Madame's face was lit with glee as she re-folded the letter that had been delivered by courier moments earlier. The pronouncement was delivered with the pomp and circumstance of a royal decree—as if it were a sign that she was two steps away from toppling the Queen from her perch. Having watched her face transform while reading it, I knew the visitor would be important.

"Any American in particular?" I asked, watching as she delicately slid the letter back into its envelope.

"The most important one: The foreign minister, Thomas Jefferson, and his daughter. The letter is from the Marquis de LaFayette, who says Monsieur Jefferson is dying to see the view of the Marly Machine from the pavilion. They can't see it from the Palace at all. I've often said that machine would come in handy one day, didn't I? Finally, that noisy piece of nothing is bringing us something more than a headache. Hurry," she said, picking up her skirts to head towards the stairs. "Light a fire in the study and the dining room and put out the game board. And the finest crystal. Try to think of some clever writer to talk about, Louis, someone fun and undeniably French. The Austrian can't show him the best of France like I can.

What about one of those Parisian actors or musicians? What do I send you in town for if not to have something to speak to the guests about? Gaspard! Make sure all the guards are neat and in uniform. Everyone in their best, wearing white gloves, please. Tell Salanave we need something special for dinner. Louis-Benoit, come with me. You need to see the gown I'll be wearing so we can color coordinate."

"By all means, I'm sure the guests will care if we match. Heaven forbid they think I'm a grown man who can dress himself." She was too preoccupied to care about my sarcasm. Already halfway up the stairs, she was moving faster than anyone in a dress that size should be able to move.

"Hurry! They'll be here in two hours!"

Dressing me up like I was a piece of jewelry or extension of her was insulting and humiliating. I didn't like it as a child, and I definitely didn't want to do it as a grown man. Especially not in front of the Marquis de LaFayette.

I learned from my fellow Jacobins that LaFayette was a member, albeit a missing one. The sans-culottes took LaFayette's fervent support of the revolutionaries in the Americas as an indication he held the same views in his home country. Rumor on the street was that LaFayette had a fire in his blood and a sense of fairness rare in a noble. I was anxious to see him again, this nobleman who had earned the affection of the peasants.

I arrived in Madame's doorway to find her in her undergarments, a large hoop hanging from her waist and her hair tied up in ribbons to make the ringlets she liked when she wasn't wearing a wig. The room was bustling with activity as her ladies pulled out and looked over gowns. A light lavender dress was draped across the bed, and I knew that was at the top of the list. That couldn't happen.

"What a shame; I outgrew all my lavender coats," I said, turning to leave.

"Wait, wait! How about mint green? Chon, look in the closet and see if you can find that one with all the little green leaves. I know you have green, Louis, don't try to get out of it."

Merde.

"Here it is!" Chon said gleefully, flashing a malicious grin at me. I hated Chon.

"Do you see this shade?" Madame looked at me, her eyes wide and serious. "If you can't match it, find soft yellow or a darker shade of green, do you hear me?"

"You're standing right in front of me. Of course, I hear you."

"Then hurry up and get changed!" She made a gesture, shooing me out with her arms, and put a hand to her forehead. "I don't know why I put up with you. I don't know why I put up with him," she said to Chon, who fanned her with both arms, giving me a frown.

"You're giving her a headache. Out!"

In the kitchen, Salanave was instantly annoyed.

"Two hours to dinner, and they invite themselves over. Those Americans must have lost good manners in the ocean on the way to the new world. Now, I have to change the meal and worry about how it looks. Mint green?" she said thoughtfully, tapping her upper lip. "Put out the pale-yellow china with the pink roses. It will go nicely with Madame's outfit. I'll make a whitefish. Yes, whitefish will look nice. And ... a light mint sauce will be clever!" She brightened at her own brilliance. "Hurry up, and don't clash when you get dressed—I don't want my meal to look drab and unappetizing!"

I put out the china and crystal, arranging the plates in an established pattern for special guests. It was an art, arranging the plates and silver on the table. I was in the thick of it when I felt a pair of eyes on me and saw the servant girl watching me from the doorway. Well, not me so much as how I was arranging the plates. I turned back to continue my job but spoke to her.

"If it isn't Mademoiselle Véronique of Burgundy, from the East, like the rising sun," I said, my voice dripping with sarcasm. I was still annoyed and owed an apology.

"If it isn't Louis-Benoit from the deepest, deep pit of hell. Don't let me interrupt." I looked back to see her turning to leave and said, quickly: "If you're going to stare, you might as well come and help." I turned back and continued my work, and after a moment, I heard her light-footed steps. Then she was by my side.

"I don't understand what you're doing," she said, looking down at the table. "It's not like that normally."

"No, this a special, more formal setting. Etiquette demands it, dependent upon the importance of the guests." She watched the way I was laying everything out and I saw her brow furrow. I knew it just looked like a jumble of glasses, plates, and silver. I explained: "It might be hard for you to see from this vantage point with so much on the table. Here," I pulled out one of the chairs. "Step up here."

"I can't," she whispered, looking around. "That chair costs more than I could repay in a lifetime."

"I didn't tell you to break it; I told you to step on it. Go ahead. It's sturdy."

She looked around but took my outstretched hand and stood, looking down on the table. Then, her face lit up even more and it was almost painful to see how easily and totally she brightened. "I see it! It's a pattern!"

"That it is. Just like every design of every inch of the Palace. Royals love patterns: they can't tolerate anything out of place. Nothing wild or uncontrollable or natural grows at the Palace, and this place is its distant cousin."

I helped her down.

"I like patterns," she said.

"Really? But you come from the country. I would think you country women like ... wild things."

Her lips tightened, and she turned to bolt.

"Wait! Véronique, I meant nothing by it, please don't run off. I only meant that whenever I see paintings of the country, they are full of wildflowers and things that grow in abandon, that's all."

She looked at me, her gaze testing my sincerity. The tension left her shoulders.

"Well, I don't know why I like patterns; I just do and always have. But this table, you can hardly see the pattern head-on. Why do they do it if you can't tell?"

"Why wear white gloves? Why do we serve from one side? Why do we have a particular type of glass for each drink? It's all etiquette, Mademoiselle, developed by the royal court to easily sniff out who is a noble and who is not. Who is educated in the ways of the aristocracy or who thinks it's perfectly fine to eat on whatever plate is presented to them. Just another way to weed out the commoners. It's a test to see who's worthy. To see who belongs."

"The pattern is impressive, in a way. I'm used to maybe five pieces for a setting; this is all very complicated and detailed. From above it was pretty. It was like ... it all made sense."

"Like I said, it's a pattern."

"Like a dance," she said, like she was admitting to something perverse. "The symmetry is pleasing. Symmetry with artistic creativity is sublime."

I looked at her, this strange woman. She was fascinating and confusing all at once. I couldn't get a handle on her, so I let my mouth do what it does best. Run freely.

"If I didn't know you were dirt poor, I would think you were a noble putting on an act," I said.

The brightness dimmed once again. She gave me a look that said our moment was over.

"You can't be decent for even a moment, can you? Thank you, Monsieur, for your time. I'll leave you to your work."

I didn't think I'd been indecent, but she was already turning the corner. "...it's been charming..." I said to her disappearing person.

A short while later, all of us servants stood in a line out in front of the house as the carriage rolled up before us and stopped. Gaspard stepped forward to open the door, and our guests began piling out. The man dressed like a noble Frenchman came out first, taking Madame's hands to press a kiss against them affectionately.

"My dearest Madame, how kind of you to allow me to impose upon you with so little notice, but as I told Mr. Jefferson, you are kind beyond words to take us at the last minute. Please allow me to introduce my wife, Adrienne, Mr. Thomas Jefferson, and his daughter Polly."

As they greeted her, Madame's smile was serene and calm,

belying the nervousness of the past two hours. In her presence, they relaxed as if with an old friend.

I noticed another head in shadow, still sitting in the carriage. The American caught me looking.

"That's my daughter's maid," he said. "Polly wouldn't leave home without her."

The man was wigless with grayish-white hair, sparse on top and touching the top of the collar of his jacket. His French was broken badly like an eggshell underfoot, and his voice was thick with some sort of accent I'd never heard before.

Barnier had taught me the king's English but listening to the strange lilt of the man's voice as he stumbled with his French, I wondered if I would recognize the English language from his tongue. I would soon find out because Madame quickly switched to English, no doubt because her ears threatened to bleed from what he was doing to French.

"Perhaps the young ladies would like to take their lunch at a picnic on the lawn away from us old people," Madame said.

"That would be wonderful," said the American, his face flushing with relief at the change to his native tongue. I was right. The accent distorted everything. I understood him no better in English than in French.

After the guests filed inside, I stood in the doorway of the dining room for some time, waiting to see if Madame would ask me to do anything or tell me to sit at the table. But this new man was so pleased already and seemed to think everything she said was wonderful, so she barely looked my way.

"This table is stunning," the American said, gazing down at the splendor. "You French do things so beautifully. I keep telling my daughter, if just a bit of the beauty of France rubs off on us, it's worth being away from home. I know we just sent her outside, but might I ask if someone could bring my daughter in? I'd love for her to see this table."

Madame nodded to one of the younger servants, who ran off and a few minutes later the little girl showed up, blushing. I pulled a seat to the table beside her father and added another place setting.

"Everything's so beautiful, Polly. I wanted you to see it."

"You are most kind," Madame preened. "We are just a humble household, but I'm happy to accept any compliment from such an established gentleman."

A few minutes later, Madame's lover, Brissac, arrived. Madame must have sent a courier to him the second she knew we had important guests. He stepped over to me. "I fear I'm overdressed," he whispered. He was in full noble regalia, but on seeing the guest without a wig, he quickly leaned to the side to pull his own off his head. "Can you take this for me and hide it, Zamor," he said, trying desperately to push his hair with the deep V down against his fevered scalp.

"Mon chèr!" Madame called to him, standing. He entered the room and went over to her, effusively kissing her hands as always. "You are right on time, as always. Come meet our guests."

Brissac and LaFayette already knew each other, but the others were introduced. I lost track, planning just exactly how I would insert myself in the conversation when the problem was solved for me.

"It was such a surprise," said the American. "I received a letter from Washington telling me about this young man from France who left home to come fight our war. "I didn't understand why anyone would do such a thing until I met your LaFayette. Now I understand people exist who value freedom above even their own safety."

Ruddy cheeked, with a long, slim face, the man in question blushed. "I assure you, my own safety was a concern of mine."

"More a concern of mine," his wife said from beside him. "I asked my lady friends what they would do in my situation, with a husband seemingly determined to fight any war to be away from his wife."

Everyone laughed, and LaFayette reached over to pat her hand. "You know nothing could be further from the truth. Leaving you was the hardest part, and returning to you was my greatest reward. I can't explain why I had to go; I can only say I felt moved in a way I never have. To help a young country get its start—to fight for its independence ... it's an experience most people will never see in their lifetime. It's history in the making."

"Our country is an example to the world."

"But how can you have a kingdom without a king?" Madame spoke up. "Someone has to run things. Why, France exists because of hundreds of years of monarchs who've built us into what we are today. It was done with single-minded focus by one person. Why, my Louis was constantly making decisions from sunup to sundown to keep this kingdom running smoothly. Surely, his advisors and the Parlement of Paris had their roles, but the king is foundational to the success of a kingdom."

"I have to agree with the Comtesse," Brissac said. "One man has the final word—the man ordained by God to rule. That makes sense."

"Now, now, I must respectfully disagree," Jefferson said. "As all Americans do. If that man who's, as you say, ordained by God, is deficient, how can anyone follow his rule? This may not be the situation in France because you have been blessed by the intelligent monarchs from the House of Bourbon. But most of us Americans escaped the rule of an insane and cruel monarch in England."

"King George, insane?" Madame tapped her napkin to the corners of her mouth as she smiled. "He might be eccentric, but insane is going a bit far."

"I don't think it's far enough when the man believes he can use the people in his colonies to work and pour our money into his pockets and expect us to stand for it. No rights, but every right to line his coffers with our hard-earned money."

"For those who can stand for their rights, at least," LaFayette said under his breath, taking some wine.

"Now, now, we're not going into this, Gilbert..."

"I'm merely pointing out that the American colonies are reliant on slave labor, and slaves don't get to keep a cent of what they work for."

"One thing at a time," Jefferson said.

"It's 'life, liberty, and pursuit of happiness'... isn't that what you put in your new world Declaration?" LaFayette continued.

I was watching them closely. This is precisely the discussion I wanted to hear.

Brissac gave a slight smile. "Forgive Gilbert for being the consummate Frenchman. We take liberty seriously here in France, Monsieur Jefferson. You won't find slaves in France."

I looked at him and then at Madame, who shifted her gaze from me, which meant she hadn't told him.

LaFayette continued. "Just because we don't see them doesn't mean we don't have them, Brissac."

The American took a torn piece of bread and swirled it through the mint sauce on his plate, popping it into his mouth. "There are certainly many things that we need to fix in our new society, but one thing we won't have to fix is dealing with a corrupt king, and that's the most important thing. We will have a leader, but it will be one we choose, not one we're stuck with because of his bloodline. George Washington has shown himself to be a hero and patriot. Just a week ago, we began procedures to vote him in as the American colonies' first president of our new commonwealth."

LaFayette smiled broadly. "No one deserves it more. There is no kinder, more considerate, and intelligent man than George Washington. He will lead your new kingdom without a king in this experiment in freedom. I'm proud to call him a friend."

"Well," Madame said. "Your new kingdom without a king is growing larger every day, near bloated from its fill of defecting Frenchmen. Why, our own Gaspard's youngest son just left for America despite his and the boy's mother's best efforts. Isn't that right?"

Conversation stopped as we all looked over to Gaspard, whose face was mottled red. She continued.

"His oldest two are proud plantation owners in Saint Domingue, and Gaspard tried his best to keep his youngest here in France. The youngest is your pride and joy, isn't he? Left on his own in the night with nothing but a letter to his heartbroken parents. My Gaspard has been worrying all morning. I told him, 'I know he's your baby, but he's a grown man, and if he's as smart as his father, he will be perfectly fine.'"

"Better than fine," Jefferson said. "You let me know how to get in touch with him and I'll personally reach out to the boy once we go back home. America will be good to him, I promise that. Maybe someday you'll come too."

Gaspard looked loath to say anything but ground out, "Never. France is my home. My boy will come to his senses and return."

As if she couldn't see how uncomfortable he was, Madame continued. I was enjoying every moment of this.

"It's particularly hard on him because his youngest is the closest to him. His mother raised the oldest two but was woefully neglectful of the youngest once she moved on with that lover of hers, isn't that right?"

The red moved up his face slowly like a geyser rising.

"It wasn't a loss at all. That woman did nothing but complain about how much he worked. I explained to him, 'Women come and go, but that youngest child of yours—who hasn't had a chance to be polluted by her lies—he loves and depends on you much more than the others. That's the one you should pour your love onto. That's the one that hasn't been ruined by his mother's lies about you.' What kind of mother castigates her children's father for working? My goodness, in my world, a working man is considered a good thing."

"But better if he's wealthy enough not to have to work for money, correct?" said LaFayette. They all laughed.

"Well, France only has one king at a time, and the Well-Beloved was the only man who could afford me."

"Though I try to come a close second," Brissac said, smiling.

Gaspard had gone quiet, his eyes avoiding everyone. I learned more about the man in five minutes than I'd known my whole life.

The conversation moved on to more mundane things, and I excused myself. I was on my way to the kitchen to tell Salanave what I heard when a sight out the window caught my eye. A young black woman was sitting on a blanket outside. I remembered the head in the carriage.

"Is that the girl's maid?" I asked Salanave.

"It is. I think they forgot she was here. The man called his daughter back inside near an hour ago."

I was plagued with curiosity, and though it was fall, the day was warm enough to give me the excuse I needed.

"I'll take her some lemon water," I said, pouring a glass.

The sun was high, but there was a nice breeze in the air. I took in the details of her, from her age of about fifteen to her chaste, simple dress and her pretty smile as I walked toward her.

"Mademoiselle, I thought you might own a bit of thirst." My English must have been rough because she smiled.

"Thank you, Sir ... I'm sorry, I don't know your name."

After she took the glass, I bowed a bit. "Zamor, Louis-Benoit Zamor." She blushed at me bowing, and her age struck me again.

"You don't need to bow for me, sir. I'm just the maid, Sally."

"I shall, indeed, bow for you, Mademoiselle, because you are our most esteemed and honored guest. If you don't mind my asking, where in the Americas do you abide?"

She frowned, trying to figure out what I was saying. "We're from Virginia, if that's what you mean," she said, taking a drink as if very thirsty. She had a peculiar way of speaking, with a lot of "uhs" in the middle of words. Like the man. I wondered if this was unique to Virginia, or if all Americans spoke like this.

"And are you of the population of black people forced to labor?" She looked at me peculiarly. "Do you like it here in France better than the new colonies? Would you live here if you could?"

"I like it here a lot but ... what is it to you, Mister Zamor?"

"I beg apologies. I do not mean to appear rude. I am studying on the situation of the black people of the American colonies, notwithstanding." I was sweating now, fearful of what I was saying to this woman and hoping it made sense. "What are the circumstances of your existence? The people who hold you in their grasp, do they abusive to you? Will the man free you so you can stay?"

The man at the dinner table seemed reasonable. Maybe he would free her legally in their country and she could live in France if she liked it?

"Uhn uhn, I can't stay here," she said.

"Why not? If I were you, I'd convince that man to free me," I said, like a hypocrite. "Don't you want to be free?" Yes, that's what I said.

Her back stiffened and her face took on a wistful sadness.

I was normally good at reading people and knowing when I offend them—whether or not that's my intent—but I didn't know I'd offended her immediately, I was so caught in my struggling English. Her face flushed. "You think I'm stupid. We stupid American darkies don't know how to take freedom when it's right in front of us. I can see on your face that's what you think of me, Mr. Zamor. Well, you can take your thoughts and leave, I ain't got time for your foolishness."

"No, no, I didn't mean to insult you," I said on a plea, switching to French. "It's only ... it's not easy for some of us, but you ... there wouldn't be a group of armed men coming after you if you left, would there? I only meant, once you're home, if you can convince him, you could come back to France and try your hand on your own."

I must have sounded ridiculous to her, pleading her own cause to her. Maybe it was the fact that I was jabbering on in French. By now her young face had shut down, and her back was even stiffer if that was possible.

"I'd like to be left to enjoy my lemon water, sir," she said.

"But..." her quivering lip stopped me, as did her skin going pale and the way she wiped a hand across her brow, awash in sweat. "Are you alright?

"Oui," she sighed, grown tired of me.

I fidgeted, but she didn't seem inclined to speak further. "D'accord, Mademoiselle." *Okay*, I said softly, bowing quickly and walking away. By the time I reached the kitchen, Véronique was putting little tea sandwiches on a plate.

"What did you say to her? She's upset."

"Not from anything I said," I said, half sincere. I didn't know what I said that upset her so much.

"Mhmm," Véronique's lips were pursed as she headed to the door.

"She doesn't speak much French," I warned her. I didn't tell her the girl spoke better French than I spoke English.

"Food may help," Véronique said. "We don't need to talk much. Poor petite fille,"—*little girl*— "alone in another country and the very important Monsieur Jefferson can't be bothered. Why bring her at all, I ask?"

Véronique stalked across the lawn, her demeanor brightening when she reached the young girl, who looked up at her with a smile, eyes on the plate of food. In two seconds, I could see Véronique alternately speaking and then gesturing with her hands. I might have imagined it, but I could have sworn I saw her pantomime a character that seemed similar to the way I moved. Soon they were smiling and chatting, Véronique sitting down on the blanket beside her, eating with her, smoothing out the wrinkles and tossing back her head to laugh like they were old friends.

"She's good with people, that Véronique," Salanave said, coming up beside me.

"I think she's mocking me."

"Yes, probably, you provide so much good material. Ah, look at how they smile."

We both watched out the window, standing next to each other, speculatively, each with our arms crossed over our chests.

"Véronique is an exceptionally nice young lady," Salanave said. I snorted and she continued. "Unless provoked. Just naturally a sweet girl. I hear people from other parts of the country are nice. In the provinces. But we don't have much use for niceness in Paris or at Versailles."

"Or Louveciennes," I agreed.

"I don't know about that. When I go into town, they seem very nice. It's here where people aren't nice at all. Here and the Palace. And Paris."

"You mean here and the places where we go? Do you think maybe we're just not nice people, Salanave?"

She crooked an eyebrow at me. "You think?" The sarcasm on her face made us both dissolve in laughter. Could be that was why we liked each other so much.

I stood watching Véronique talk to the girl long after Salanave had gone about her business. I was disappointed I made such an ill impression on the girl. It made me worry. How would I ever manage if I were to travel outside of France after I was free?

40

———

M arch 1789

Dear Citizen,

I was becoming a known regular in Paris. It was thrilling to be in the middle of the action! At the Palace, I was relegated to what I could overhear in the tunnels, information I could ferret from other servants, the comings and goings I saw with my own eyes, and my own deductions. But being in Paris helped me pull all the pieces together.

I knew the King was concerned about finances because his Minister of Finance, Necker, was in and out of the Palace with increasing frequency. What I didn't know until I heard the news in Paris was that he had called an Estates General. I didn't even know what an Estates General was. I had to ask the Jacobins to explain it to me like a child. They were only too happy to oblige, taking great sport at spelling out each word, and exaggerating their explanations with hand gestures and shadow puppets against the wall of the club in the candlelight. The show took longer than it needed, as they were drunk and constantly interrupting their own stories with hysterical laughter at my ignorance. "What rock have you been living under, page?" one gentleman asked, and not that politely.

France was comprised of three estates representing all its people (I was aware of that!). The First Estate was the clergy. The Second Estate, the nobles, including the King. And the Third (largest) Estate was all the rest: the common sans-culottes, poor peasants, and newly wealthy bourgeois.

An Estates General was the calling together of all the chosen repre-sentatives of the three estates to convene meetings to discuss the state of the country. It only happened under dire circumstances, so the fact that XVI called one said a lot. He also sent out a request to all the outlying provinces for their cahiers de doléances—lists of grievances—for his review.

It was a shockingly progressive action on the King's part as the Estates General hadn't been convened in over 200 years.

—Zamor

THREE NIGHTS after the Jefferson visit, I hurried into the Jacobin Club late. As I passed the sans-culottes who congregated at the door, one of them announced me with a flourish.

"Presenting ... the du Barry blackamoor!" Several waves of his arm in a poor attempt at a royal flourish. "Better known as ... *the page.* You might miss him if you arrive in Paris after midnight when he has to scurry away because his wife—I mean the Comtesse—is waiting up for him!"

Laughter followed me into the club. If it weren't for the derisive term, I might have taken their joshing as a sign of affection. It didn't matter—my focus was on the evening's speaker. I pulled my satchel, the handle of which was looped across my neck and body, off in preparation of pulling out paper to make notes.

"There you are," Sebastien's voice sounded from where he'd come up beside me. "After all the strings I had to pull to get Jacques Brissot here, I would have killed you if you'd missed him. He brought a friend."

I tried to hold onto Sebastien's voice in the din, following him to where a small crowd surrounded the man in question. Sebastien had to speak directly into my ear to be heard.

"He just finished speaking. He says he submitted a grievance to the King himself, complaining about slavery. And he spoke to Necker on his opposition to the slave trade."

It was an interesting move to come at the problem from a financial perspective, but I wasn't sure it was the way to go. Slavery was bringing in too much money for anyone to consider it anything but a benefit. If it was an issue of finances, they'd do better to convince the King to force taxes on his favored nobles and the Second Estate. Express to him how much stronger the country could be if they were paying their fair share.

"Monsieur Jacques Brissot, this is Louis-Benoit Zamor," Sebastien said as I stepped forward to shake the speaker's hand. He had a serious face with dark hair that poked from under his wig and dark eyes that looked too sensitive.

"Good to meet you, Monsieur Brissot," I said. "I've been long wanting to speak to someone in this group about the slave trade. I work as a page for Madame Comtesse Jeanne du Barry." I didn't like saying it, but I wanted to be upfront from the start.

The man's face relaxed into something of a smile, and he took my hand. "Jacques is fine. Good to meet you Monsieur Zamor. Are you, by chance, here on behalf of the Comtesse?"

"Just Zamor is fine, and no—I'm here for myself and myself alone. The Madame is devoutly loyal to the crown and the status quo."

"Well, that's disappointing, but it's good to see a black man in this club, Zamor, especially with all that's going on."

"My apologies for missing what must have been an excellent presentation. Sebastien tells me you've spoken with Necker?" Necker had an expressionless face with lips that were constantly pursed, even more so when stressed. Lately, he'd been coming and going from the King's offices with lips so tight it was a miracle they didn't fold in on themselves.

"Yes, he speaks prettily but has yet to do anything in relation to abolition. As I told the group, Necker's commitment only extends as far as is convenient. He likes the money that slavery brings, and until he can find a way to make up for it, he won't fight hard to undo it. But the King's recent call for grievances was just the opportunity I needed. Anticipating my meeting with Necker wouldn't produce any results, I listed my opposition to the slave trade as a grievance against humanity. Perhaps the King will look at the issue differently when it's reflected to him on paper. I encouraged everyone in our society to do the same."

"Society?"

He then explained his role with the Society of the Friends of the Blacks, an organization of nobles against slavery. I was excited that this man cared enough about the slave trade to list it as a grievance and that there were others who felt the same. Excited there was such a society!

"We're not as effective yet as the abolitionists in England. I spent a good bit of time traveling to England and the Americas to get some ideas of how our own group should proceed. The truth is we are stymied—many of our society are not as willing to push back as they would if they didn't have much to lose, if you understand what I mean. The membership dues are prohibitive and, not knowing your financial situation, I wouldn't dare take your money for an organization that still hasn't figured out a course of action. Right now, all I manage is to be a nuisance to the King, and I can do that for free."

I felt quick disappointment. I knew he meant well, but for his group—unless it personally affected them, the members of his society were unwilling to put their necks out too far.

"Believe me," he said, seeing the expression on my face. "There's more passion in this room."

"Passion? I've seen no passion at all for abolition; that's why I was so looking forward to meeting you."

"They're passionate for *change*, which is where it starts. And there is strength in the diversity of the Jacobins. Our society is only for nobles, but every estate is represented in this club. Even though none of these people are directly impacted, they're closer to understanding you than a society of nobles ever will be. Forgive me for asking a sensitive question, but does this situation personally impact you? And does the King know you're a Jacobin?"

I didn't want to admit it. Again, my feelings were more complex than I could explain even to myself. "Yes, I am personally impacted, and, no, the King doesn't pay much attention to servants." Though XVI was almost friendly, in passing, seeing his face had taken on new meaning since I found about the Police des Noir. Now, when XVI smiled at me in the halls of Versailles, I saw his duplicitous grandfather reborn. "Still, I see no wisdom in flaunting my new activities."

"Of course. But if you have ideas I can help with, I will support you, Zamor. I think it's a mortal sin for one man to enslave another, and this country will be judged for it later. If you find a way to move the hearts of the people of this club, it would truly be a credit to the new republic. New blood like you might be the key. In the meantime, I know other black men who you might do well to know. Let's set up a time for you to meet—"

His voice was suddenly drowned out by a crowd that moved towards us with a vibrant, amicable, familiar voice. I looked up to see General LaFayette in the center of the adoring crowd. He came over and clapped a hand on Brissot's back as if they were long friends, spotting me at the same time. I hesitated while his face creased in confusion, trying to place me.

"General," I started. "Such a treat and an honor to have you here. I'm the page at the Chateau de Louveciennes."

"Ah, Madame du Barry! Yes, now I remember, I was there just a few nights ago," he explained to Brissot. "I brought Monsieur Jefferson and his daughter."

"And the young woman he's enslaved," I reminded him. "His daughter's maid, Sally."

"Gentlemen, you'll excuse me," Brissot said, stepping away to take up a conversation across the room.

LaFayette gave a brief nod at Brissot's departure, but his eyes didn't leave my face. "Despicable practice, slavery, but we are working to end it. Even Jefferson. He is adamant it should be ended."

"I did hear the conversation at the dinner table."

"Ah, yes, I didn't see you there. Then you know, he believes in equality just like me."

"If that's the case, he might start with himself—if he were so inclined—by freeing the people he calls his own. Like Sally."

He nodded, his eyes sharp. "I see now how it must look to you as a black man, but he's a good family man, and he's good to his slaves. Change can't happen in a day, and one man can't do it alone. But he sees the light, and that's something ... compared to the others. I feel like I've also seen you at the Palace, oui?"

I nodded. Yes, I'd been there when he and his wife had come, greeted warmly by the Queen. I'd only been on the periphery, standing in doorways and passing in hallways and dusting rooms where he always seemed to be the center of attention. Now, as I watched his face, it seemed it was all rushing to him at once ... the many, many times I was there, but he hadn't really looked.

Discomfort held me still for a moment as I worried I'd said too much.

"Oh, don't worry, Monsieur," he said soberly. "I can see you are uncomfortable now. It can be awkward coming here as a friend of the Court, non? I feel the same sometimes, but I don't find the House of Bourbon and the ideals of the Jacobin Club to be diametrically opposed. We're all concerned with the future of France. I happen to feel the common people deserve a little more respect, that's all. No one will hear from me that I've seen you here."

That was all I needed to know. I proceeded. "Monsieur Brissot was telling me that the King is preoccupied with the country's finances. This is strange, considering I heard we have been, and continue to, fund the Americans in their never-ending battle against England. Is it true you helped the Americans spend French funds? I do hope they're truly worth it."

He smiled. "You hear a lot, but I'm pretty good at reading between the lines. You want to know how we can afford to help America when we are relying so heavily on slave labor? I can see you are a single-minded man and any cause other than freeing your brethren is insignificant. But helping the new country is a long-term investment. Their success will prove to the King that a system of government that also gives voice to the people can be a healthy thing." His face tightened. "I must admit, I went to America only mildly against slavery. Once I saw it in person ... my opinion changed. It's wrong. I feel every day it continues, it will be that much more difficult to unravel, but it must be unraveled. Once America has fully separated itself from England and our alliance is secured, I'm sure both countries would be willing to sit down and consider how to dissolve the slave trade."

"I heard that some of the enslaved can escape to the north?" I asked, remembering what Barnier had said.

"One thing I didn't truly understand when I went over there was the scale of the place. The land is vast. You can ride on horseback for weeks, months even, and not span the length or depth. Some areas that push further into the west are so dry and dusty you can easily die in the elements. Wolves and bears in the forests. Natives all around ready to kill the settlers. Harsh seasons and cold so strong it can freeze a man solid overnight in the winter. Snow deep enough to be buried in. I imagine a few people may manage to escape north to the area of New France—or what used to be New France—but compared to the numbers enslaved, they are few. With what they would have to survive to get north to New France, it is madness to try."

"Surely they are safe once they get there?"

"New France is wild also. Anyone who arrives there is only as safe as the hands into which they fall." He sighed. "I'm sorry my news is grim, but you must understand the Americas function on slave labor. Without it, there aren't enough people to build the towns or till the soil. And they all use it, even at the highest levels of power."

"So much so that even the American foreign minister to France feels comfortable bringing a woman he's enslaved to France, where, by rights, she should be free. Without worry of repercussion," I mumbled.

"Yes, even President Washington. It's normal, you see. Even poor people sometimes have slaves to do their work in the Americas. But there *are* people who want to see it end. I've heard from reliable sources that the enslaved people themselves sometimes form clandestine groups to meet and try to have an inner revolution of sorts. They work together to try to free and protect each other. And white people help, sometimes. All hope is not lost."

My lips wiggled with the need to contradict and correct him, but now was not the time. We weren't friends, just yet. I pulled back to take another tack.

"They've written a declaration, correct?" I asked as if I didn't know. "I've only been able to find some passages of it, not the whole thing..."

"Yes, the Declaration of Independence. Brilliant document, and Jefferson was one of its authors. The country has only just begun, and they are making strides from the old ways of us Europeans."

"Would you be open to sitting down over coffee to chat about it?"

41

———

Back at the Chateau, an invitation to stay to very old money, blue-blooded guests had been accepted. Madame was thrilled these people from a higher echelon of society were coming, and I was supposed to be on my best behavior.

When the carriage arrived three hours early, the head house-keeper, Gaspard, and one of the three most recent servant trainees went out to greet them. I knew Chloe, the curly-headed blond, and Véronique of the East. I didn't know this third one with the long dark hair, though I heard her giggling often enough and saw the way she would stop whatever she was doing whenever Madame walked into a room, her eyes big like she was gazing on God himself. Pauline, that was her name!

The family of three was led inside to the foyer, and I decided to make myself scarce, stepping into a doorway. The couple came in first, followed by a boy who looked about sixteen. Gaspard closed the door behind him and asked them to wait while he fetched Madame. The second he stepped out of the room, the boy started.

"I don't want to stay. I want to go home!" he whined.

"May I take your coats?" Pauline stepped forward, and the couple shed their outerwear. The boy walked around the foyer, looking at the art on the wall, an expression of disdain on his face.

"May I take your coat, Monsieur?" Pauline asked, chasing after him. Her arms were already full, but the boy had yet to give up his. Instead, he was taking great joy walking leisurely through the foyer in an 8-pattern, stopping, asking himself, "Do I want you to take my coat?" And then when she caught up with him, he'd start walking, only to do the same thing again.

I watched from the doorway as Pauline chased after him for a good three circuits around the room before I lost patience and stepped forward.

"Mon Dieu, boy, do you want to give your coat or not?"

The parents, who had seemed blissfully unaware of everything, snapped to attention, noticing me.

"They didn't tell us there'd be blackamoors here," the woman said.

"We've come all this *way*," whined the man, letting me know where his son got his petulance. "I'm not traveling again until I get a good night's sleep. I'm told Madame's table is almost as good as the King's."

"It had better be," said the woman. "Or I will be sure to let everyone know how disappointed I am."

The boy stared at me pointedly, took off his coat and dropped it on top of the others in Pauline's arms, almost causing her to drop everything. She turned and walked by inches to the coatroom while Gaspard entered, informing them that though Madame was indisposed, the housekeeper would show them upstairs to their rooms.

"No greeting, I see," the woman said under her breath. "Bad manners, I'd say."

They took the stairs, one by one. On his way up the stairs, the boy's face hardened as he looked around, no doubt for Pauline.

I knew people like him. Sometimes, the young ones keenly understood their station in life and began honing their cruelty towards peasants early on. Like animals in the wild teach their young to hunt—although such animals have the excuse of needing to eat—

these people allowed their son, who had clearly chosen Pauline as his prey, his freedom in pursuit.

He continued preying on her later at dinner. I stood in a doorway; there was no way Madame would invite me to sit beside her with these people so open about their discomfort at my presence. I didn't mind. Why would I wish to break bread with such as these? Standing in the doorway meant I could be the first out as soon as she seemed not to need me. My plan was to stay quiet and keep to myself.

The housekeeper must have been short-staffed because Pauline and Véronique were serving and clearing. By the time the diners were onto the main meat dish, the ladies had gone back and forth to the kitchen three times, staying in the room in case anything was needed. Véronique stood at the far end, and Pauline was on the other wall closest to the fireplace, leaning over to stoke the fire every few minutes.

Satiated and arrogant, the boy leaned back in his seat insolently, his eyes stuck on Pauline every time I looked at him. I could almost feel his gaze withering her confidence as she kept her eyes down in deference. Then, while his parents were making small talk with Madame, he picked up a fork and threw it across the room at Pauline. The ping of delicate silver hitting the stone fireplace surprised us all for a moment. I looked at Madame, whose lips pinched just a slight bit. I waited for someone to rebuke him, but the parents went back to talking as soon as the utensil landed at the woman's feet.

It was going to be one of those nights.

I couldn't have said what made him want to single out Pauline when the mother was sneaking glances at me and Véronique—two black people in one space was almost too much for her to fathom— but it was likely Pauline's fear that appealed to him. People like him preferred to torment the most vulnerable and to savor the effects of their cruelty.

Seconds later, it was the salad fork. This time they didn't even look up.

To her credit, Pauline didn't make a lot of noise about it, but her eyes were wide as she dodged that one.

A muscle twitched in my jaw.

By the time he pitched his spoon, I couldn't take it.

"Monsieur, you seem to be having difficulty keeping your silver. Have your parents forgotten to teach you or do you need me to come show you how to hold it in your hand like a big boy?" I snapped.

The mother's head swiveled quickly to me. Deaf to the sound of her son chucking silver across the room, she suddenly regained her hearing ability when it came to me. "Don't you speak to my son, blackamoor! Madame, I beg you to keep control over your servants. If we must tolerate them, surely you can see how inappropriate it is to have them speak to us."

"I'd suggest you focus on your delinquent son and not worry about me," I said.

"How dare you!" the man stood up, indignant.

"Madame!" the woman whined. So, the boy got it from both of them.

"Now, now," Madame said. "Let's calm down. Louis-Benoit is a member of this household; he speaks as freely as you or I. Please sit down, Monsieur; we're all friends here. He's just a child, Louis-Benoit, and he's bored. He's having a bit of fun. Pauline doesn't mind, do you, chère?"

It was a ridiculous question, and Madame knew it was. I felt a lick of anger as she turned to the man. "But I do implore you to remind your son he's a guest in someone's home. Will you sit down, Monsieur? You are so tall and imposing you cast a shadow on the room."

The man shook his jacket lapels, preening under her subtle appeal to his manhood, sitting back down even as his wife looked at Madame with newly sharp eyes.

The mollified husband asked about the wine and proceeded to go on about the taste and smell of it. He was still going on about it when the boy picked up his water glass, drained it, and threw it across the room at the fireplace right beside Pauline's face. She screamed and turned towards the wall.

"Pauline!" Véronique cried on her way across the room.

I moved quickly to the girl.

"My crystal!" Madame screamed.

I stepped forward, and when Pauline partially turned, staggering a bit, I saw red and realized the glass had shattered and a piece had bounced back into her face.

Reaching her first, I saw the sliver of broken glass embedded in her cheek, just below her eye. She was reaching a shaky hand up. I stopped her hand with mine to prevent her accidentally pushing it in further. With my other hand, I took my handkerchief from my pocket. Her whole body began to shake.

"It's alright," I said. Up close, her eyes were large and fevered. "You've got a small piece of glass in your face. I don't know if it's a clean piece, and I don't want to do damage removing it. We should wait for a doctor."

"It will take an hour or so," Véronique said. "That's how long it took the last time we called him when that boy broke his arm."

"I can't wait that long," Pauline was going into shock. "Get it out."

"But—"

"Get it out! Get it out!" Her lips shivered as she said it, desperate.

It looked like only one piece, the rest having fallen to the floor. I looked at Véronique, who nodded.

"Okay, I'm going to take it out really quickly, okay?' She gave a jerk for a nod, and I grabbed the shard and pulled it slowly. It came out followed by a stream of blood. I laid the square of cloth on her face. Almost immediately, it was saturated with blood.

Behind me I could hear Madame speaking to the guests. "That crystal was a gift to me; it's irreplaceable." Véronique was walking Pauline out of the room when Madame's words made her stop. Sometimes in life you can tell the exact moment when someone's opinion of someone else changes. Véronique was now seeing Madame's *other* side. She'd never be able to un-see that ugliness.

"Take her to Salanave; she'll know what to do," I whispered.

Véronique nodded and helped Pauline from the room, looking back before disappearing into the hallway.

"Louis-Benoit, is it fixable?" Madame asked. "My glass. Can you fix it?"

I looked down at the shattered bits of glass and the splatter of blood on top. "No, it's not fixable."

"It was an accident," the father was going on. "As you said, he's a boy with a lot of energy! Surely you can understand. Apologize to Madame du Barry right now."

The boy didn't apologize, and he hadn't shifted from his position on the chair since lobbing the glass. His face was just as impassive as if nothing had happened.

I left the room, and on my way down the hallway I heard the sound of more shattering glass and then: "That's it! Pack your bags; you're leaving this house tonight!"

I DIDN'T SEE the girl for days and then she wandered through the house, quiet as a ghost. Without the sound of her signature giggling, she was barely noticeable. And then finally, about two weeks later, Madame told me Pauline was going home that day.

"Was the injury that bad?" I asked.

"Well, it's healing," Madame said, sipping chocolat between bites of butter-slathered bread taken in her suite. "It's just that the scar is so ugly, she takes away everyone's appetite the second she enters a room. She was no beauty before, but at least she had perfect skin. That's gone now."

"The scar will fade in time."

"Surely, but it will be on *her* time, not mine."

"Does she want to go home?"

"You, always asking what people *want*. It doesn't *matter* what she wants; this is my home. I'll not have people saying I have ugly servants. This is a working home. This is the most splendid and well-regarded home in all of France, second only to the Palace, and we all have a role. In this house, part of the servant's role is to be a beautiful thing to look at, like my art and the paintings on the wall. And if they can be useful, besides, then all the better. But the housekeeper says the girl isn't even all that useful. She knew this was a temporary apprenticeship."

"But are you allowing the others to stay?"

"Have you seen Chloe and Véronique? You have to ask me why they're allowed to stay after what I just told you?"

"Will you give the girl money to help out?"

"Help out? Why would I help out? She's been living here free."

"Working."

"*Learning.* She signed up for this knowing what it was. Look, you are uncharacteristically concerned about someone other than yourself, and it's charming, but I'm doing her a kindness. She needs to go where she's loved, with people who care about her. I have myself and my reputation to worry about; the last thing I need is the Queen finding out I keep scarred girls around the house—she'll make me a laughingstock. People will stop coming."

"Why *do* they come, anyway? It's not as though we're running a business that we need a constant flow of guests."

"They come to be treated like royalty without having to put up with the disgrace that is our Queen. I'm welcoming our visitors to a taste of what it feels like to be pampered. It's a public service."

Later, I looked out of the parlor window and saw Pauline standing outside with her bags. Gaspard was aggressively gesturing Véronique and Chloe back inside. They obviously wanted to stay to see her off, but the asshole was living up to his name. He picked up Pauline's bag and threw it inside the empty carriage and then proceeded to yell at her, causing her to flinch. Gaspard could have allowed Chloe and Véronique to see the girl off, as scared as she was. Something about seeing her in the rain, alone, and being yelled at caused me to hurry outside.

I went out the front door and jogged quickly up to her.

"Mademoiselle Pauline, please allow me," I said, holding out my hand to her.

She turned to me, her face pale. The scar had been stitched up by the doctor. Now she was left with a gash that started below her eye and ended on the apple of her cheek. Her bloodless skin made her look like a doll that had been patched up, only the wound still red. Dead eyes looked at my hand like she didn't know what to do with it.

"Mind your business, page," Gaspard said. "Treating the trash like she's something won't make her life any easier. With that face, she needs to get used to being treated like the pathetic thing she is." He leaned down toward her in a whisper, but I heard what he said. "I bet you're sorry now you weren't nicer to me when you had the chance."

She winced like the words were a weapon against her and looked down at the ground as if she didn't have the right to look up. I knew that feeling. It was wrong.

"I'll take it from here, thank you, Manager."

Gaspard hesitated, annoyed he had no real reason to stay longer to torture the girl.

"I don't take orders from you, *page*."

"Will Madame's orders do? She asked me to make sure the girl gets off successfully, and that won't happen as long as you're standing here berating her, so..." *Leave me alone to get it done.*

He hesitated. I felt his desire to stay and do more harm as keenly as if he were on his knees begging for it.

"Mademoiselle," I said quietly, trying to cut through Gaspard's bluster to reach her. When she looked back up, her eyes were haunted. I knew those eyes. I knew she was trying to escape—trying not to see or feel or know what was before her in her future. But here, in this moment, I was before her. Sometimes all it took was the slightest bit of kindness. Just an ounce of humanity.

"Are you ready, Mademoiselle? This is a big thing, leaving a place you've been in for so long, isn't it? A little bit difficult, I'm sure."

She focused on me, finally.

"Now, you're awake?" Gaspard sneered at her, annoyed with her and. But I felt him move away and then heard his steps carry him back into the house.

"Please allow me."

She looked at my hand again and then, finally, slid her hand into mine. I helped her step up into the carriage. I didn't know the woman and had barely said two words to her, but when she huddled on the seat, seeming to sink into it, I was sad for her. It would be very difficult for a poor woman without even her looks. I could see fear all over her. But if she could remember that the whole world wasn't cruel, maybe she could take one day at a time and find her way.

"Do you have bread to eat on the ride?"

She nodded shyly.

"Good. Once you're home, I know your family will hold you close. And very soon you'll feel better and brighter than you did today. Your friends here will miss you terribly; let their love and memories of friendship keep you warm. Don't despair, Mademoiselle Pauline, if you can survive the manager and this place, you can survive *anything*. Always keep your head up, and when people look at you, they will see your pride and dignity before all. Why, look at me. People barely notice I'm not an attractive man since I behave as though I'm the handsomest man in all of France. You'll get the hang of it in no time."

She hung on my words like they were gospel, her eyes gripping and greedy, trying to scope out some courage from me, of all people. Then, she said softly: "Thank you, Monsieur Zamor. Thank you for your words and your kindness. I shall never forget it."

The sound of the driver tsk-ing the horse made me step away, and I walked with them a little as she put her hand up to the glass in the window and looked at me. I gave her a little, genuine smile, and her face relaxed. She kept watching me like I was a hero. I was nothing of the sort, but in that moment, I was happy I could pretend to be one.

I stepped back as the driver took her away.

42

———————

I wasn't a hero, but I knew a real one. I finally had that meeting with LaFayette, at the Café Procope, to continue our discussion over cups of hot, steaming coffee. Finishing with the niceties, I moved those cups to the side and pulled the copy of the Declaration of Independence I had begged and borrowed to get from my satchel.

Lafayette looked surprised as I unfolded it. "I was going to apologize for not having a copy readily available, but I see you are more than equipped," he said.

I was already in the zone, reading out loud: "Listen to this...

'...We hold these truths to be self-evident, that all men are created equal, that they are endowed by their Creator with certain unalienable Rights, that among these are Life, Liberty and the pursuit of Happiness.--That to secure these rights, Governments are instituted among Men, deriving their just powers from the consent of the governed, --That whenever any Form of Government becomes destructive of these ends, it is the Right of the People to alter or to abolish it, and to institute new Government, laying its foundation on such principles and organizing its powers in such form, as to them shall seem most likely to effect their Safety and Happiness.'

...and then this part...

> '...But when a long train of abuses and usurpations, pursuing invariably
> the same Object evinces a design to reduce them under absolute Despotism,
> it is their right, it is their duty, to throw off such Government, and to
> provide new Guards for their future security.'"

I LOOKED AT HIM. "Isn't that what we're trying to do? This sounds like the words of an Enlightenment philosopher."

LaFayette nodded, looking at the passages. "Yes, Jefferson said he read the works of John Locke."

"He might have been writing the words of Rousseau."

"You've read Rousseau?"

"Of course. Just as the United States has, France must recognize these rights in a document that is as clear."

"What, a declaration of our own?"

"I don't see why not. We're having these discussions about how to be a better society. Isn't that what the Enlightenment was about? We don't have to be a new country to have new ideas. To think in a different way."

"I thought you just wanted to discuss abolition," he said.

"*Just* abolition? Don't you see, abolition of slavery is *everything*. If the least powerful man is equal to the most powerful, isn't that the very definition of equality? And a statement that says so would fall in line with those ideals."

"But these are two separate issues," he said, rolling up his sleeves and gesturing with both hands toward the paper. "One is about national identity, and the other is about a condition that we both agree must end, but..."

"Ah," I wagged a finger at him. "Respectfully, we disagree. You see this condition as an issue separate from identity. I feel provisions against this condition—provisions that ensure that the institution of slavery is condemned and outlawed—are the same that apply to the oppression of every man. If we expect equality to truly be a part of our national identity, we must tackle that of those with the least power first, then everything else will fall into place. What better way than to create a document that outlines exactly how we think of ourselves and our people? A path to follow, in writing. The American declaration is a discussion of their separation from England. We have no need to be free of a sovereign on foreign soil. But we do need all our people to feel free within our own kingdom. How about the Declaration of the Rights of Man."

"Man? Or citizen?"

"Why not both? For that matter, all men want to be citizens, correct? I would like to be a citizen, but my skin color doesn't allow it. At least white sans-culottes can become landowners if they have enough money to move into the bourgeois class, but black men never can and, thus, can never be citizens. We can never vote. Did you know that only men who acknowledge and practice the Catholic sacraments are even considered legal? What about the Protestants and the Jews? How is it possible that even people born on the mainland can never reap the benefits of this land? Yet all the poor pay taxes to the King. If black men are counted fully as men and citizens, *first*, all those other issues go away. I'll wager most sans-culottes would gladly pay taxes if it came with inclusion into this society and a guarantee of equality. To have that put down on paper — that all men in France are truly equal—that would send a message to the world!"

I knew my words were coming fast and hot, my voice tight with excitement, but I couldn't contain myself now. I began digging in my bag again and pulled out a sheet of paper on which I'd jotted some ideas. I smoothed it out atop the other paper.

"As I said, much of the American declaration reads like a list of complaints against the King of England. I see no need to antagonize our King. We *want* the cooperation and support of King Louis XVI— we need to be clear about that. He's convening the Estates General now, I and I heard through the grapevine that he's growing frustrated with the size of the list of grievances he asked for. Let's frame it differently. We won't talk about what we hate. Let's talk about what we want."

"You're saying to list our desires instead of our grievances?"

"*Yes!* No dilly-dallying around, wasting time complaining. That's the thing about these kings, the more they're reminded of what they're doing wrong, the more resentful they are toward the people pointing it out. And you know that applies to XVI, especially. He denied you permission to even go to the Americas. You did it, anyway, and by returning a hero, you make the whole of France look good. Now, he pretends like he was for it all along. We have to appeal to his ego. We make our document clear and succinct. Look, I've started something. See what you think." I had jotted down one and two-word thoughts. He leaned over to look, reading aloud.

"... resist oppression' ... 'all black persons granted equal rights as those of white persons in the kingdom that owns no slaves'..."

He looked at me with a wry smile and a head shake. "These are radical changes, Zamor."

"Yes, and without these radical changes, the document loses its teeth. Without them, it's just a weak copy of the American version. We must do something to make it *ours*. Unique to France. A document people will never forget."

Lafayette began reading aloud the points on the paper.

"...all men equal regardless of skin color or religion ... the right to own property ... the right to worship whatever religion they choose, freely ..."

He gave another small, wry smile and a head shake. "I'm at a disadvantage, Monsieur. I believed this would be a casual conversation about ideas with an easy-going freethinker. Now I find myself in the presence of a radical Jacobin abolitionist who came prepared to make a case. I can't help but wonder if you're making it to the wrong person? Thomas Jefferson helped draft America's document; I'd be happy to set you up to meet with him if you'd like?"

"No, I wouldn't." He looked up quickly at my abruptness. I softened my tone. "My apologies. You're right, I did come here under false pretenses, with an agenda. I know the Declaration of Independence well, and I came here to speak to you because of the importance of your position as both a well-respected nobleman and friend to the King. I'm sorry for misrepresenting this as a casual conversation, but I'm not sorry for taking this opportunity."

He motioned for more coffee, his face settling into a frown. "To lead an effort to draft a document like this is important. I can think of other men who would be better. Brissot or … Thomas Jefferson."

"I believe Brissot would be open to the idea, but even with his society, he's made little progress with the King. And I don't mean to sound impertinent, but I don't understand your obsession with Jefferson. He doesn't seem to be someone whose interests align with the abolition of slavery. His feet barely touch the ground from the cloud of hypocrisy he floats on. And frankly, I doubt the Declaration of Independence would even exist had he not borrowed the ideals of European Enlightenment philosophers. We have our own excellent philosophers whose words are the basis for this re-inspection of our government. *You* would need to be at the helm."

"I'm a general, a fighter, and a nobleman. I'm not a writer. What about you?"

"I'd be happy to write all day and night on something like this, but I'm a black man and a servant. I'm the *page*. No one is going to take my words seriously. Not yet. Even at the Jacobin Club, some still refer to me with derision. But you're a national hero. You're loved by sans-culottes *and* Royalists, French *and* Americans. You've made yourself a bridge between worlds and classes, Monsieur. It's a difficult thing to be loved by all and hated by none. No one can bring together all the pieces of the puzzle like you. You could make them listen, and if people listen, so will our King. I can guarantee he will listen to nothing of substance from me."

He looked like he had a headache, rubbing his forehead. "I can't commit to anything, you understand?"

I nodded, feeling a small surge of hope. "I only ask that you consider it."

He didn't agree, but as he quietly finished his coffee, I was sure I recognized the fire in his eyes.

43

———

I was brushing Lightning in the stables pen gently because she had been ridden hard that morning by the guards who had no care for the health or condition of horses. The sun filtered through the high windows and the hay crunched under my feet as I spoke soft words to her. I bent over to dip my brush in the bucket, and the sight of skirts caught the corner of my eye. It was the servant girl, Véronique, in the doorway, standing as if she didn't know whether she should stay or go. Again.

"Are you here to help me?" I asked.

"I'm not coming closer. I saw that horse kick two people last week, Monsieur."

"Yes, well, she doesn't like most people."

"And she likes you?"

"Yes, because she's my horse. Given to me as a parting gift by the Queen."

I saw her put her fingers to hide a quick smile. "Ah, that explains it. So, the Queen got rid of two ill-tempered creatures at the same time, did she?"

"That was a little mean of you, Véronique of the East." And, uncharacteristically spicy. It had been a few days since Pauline left and it seemed she had changed in that time. The previous look of scared determination was gone. These days she walked with some sort of inner strength that had been missing before. But in this moment, she was fidgeting.

"What shall I call you?" she asked me.

"You mean instead of demon from hell?"

She smiled outright at that and stepped forward a bit. It was a surprise, her smile. I thought she hated me. "You can call me Zamor, or page, like most people do. That's what my friends in town call me. Come, don't be afraid of Lightning. Have you been around horses before?"

"All my life. I'm from the country, remember? Wild and free?" She took another step closer. "But our horses were always well-mannered. I suppose you can't train a horse to be what you don't know how to be yourself."

"Ouch, you keep wounding me, Mademoiselle. It's good I have thick skin." At that point Lightning rolled her big head straight into Véronique. One minute the woman was standing there on the other side of the horse; the next, she had disappeared.

I dropped my brush and rushed to the other side where I found Véronique on the ground, laughing soundlessly, having not yet caught her breath.

"Are you alright?" I asked, coming to help her off the ground. Her large brown eyes looked up, and for a second it was as if she didn't know if she could trust me. Her eyes so big and vulnerable, for a split second, made me catch my breath. "Take my hand."

I reached down and she clasped my hand, let me pull her up. "I'm sorry about that. Lightning is protective of me."

"Against me?" she asked.

"Against everyone," I explained. I took Lightning's big head in my hands and rubbed behind her ears, speaking to her softly, reaching out for Véronique's hand again. She hesitated a moment and then allowed me to take it. I placed it on Lightning's nose along with mine.

"Véronique of the East is a friend. No more knocking her down."

"It's okay," Véronique said. "I think she was just sizing me up, weren't you, girl? And maybe she was right to be on guard. It's almost as if she knows what I did."

"If this is your way of apologizing, there's no need," I said.

She waited a long moment, and when next she spoke, I heard shame in her voice. "There is, most certainly, need. I am sorry for hitting you. I do apologize. I've been missing my parents terribly and they are the only good thing I know in this world, so I was overly sensitive. It's no excuse, but it is an explanation for my behavior. They would be ashamed of my actions, just as I am, no matter how I felt in the moment."

I snuck a few sideways glances at her, waiting for the 'but' to come: *but* you were asking for it … *but* you deserved it … *but* you're a horrible person. But … nothing came. It seemed like she really meant it. I'd never been apologized to before. I softened.

"Well, I spoke disrespectfully, that's true. You shouldn't let what people say hurt you if it is not true; it gives them power over you."

"I don't understand you, Monsieur. You behave terribly one minute and then you do something unexpected. You delivered my mail before even knowing me. And I saw you with Pauline; you were very kind to help her both the day she was injured and when she left. Gaspard wouldn't allow us to stay to see her off. It cost him nothing to let us say goodbye, but he forced us to leave out of spite."

"If Gaspard doesn't want me to do something, you can guarantee I'll take great pleasure in doing it. Besides, I get tired of this place chewing up servants and spitting us out, like we're barely human. The girl didn't deserve what happened to her just for having the bad judgment to come here."

"Why do you stay? Sometimes it seems like you hate it. Many people would be happy to be the page to Madame du Barry."

"Spoken with all the wisdom of a peasant from the country," I quipped before I could stop myself. I was sharp because I didn't want her to know just how twisted my situation was or how tethered I was to this place. But my sarcasm was, once again, taken badly. When next she spoke, it was obvious she inferred the worst possible reasons for my presence here.

"Maybe you just like being the most famous. I've heard noble ladies throughout the countryside have taken black pages. You are all the rage. Willing to do anything and everything to put on a show. The people tell me they aspire to be just like you..." she then put her hands up and down in supplication. "...Oh, great Governor of Louveciennes."

My skin prickled with embarrassment. I wasn't sensitive about much except this, and I'd had enough from her. My temper flared. "You mock and insult me."

My face must have told her she'd gone too far. "I-I'm only trying to understand."

I dropped the brush in the bucket. "You think I want little black children to be stolen away from their mothers and given to selfish, wealthy nobles as party favors like I was? That I would want anything to do with that, much less set the example? Governor of Louveciennes?" My face twisted. "The nasty joke of a powerful man who thought nothing of toying with a child with little hope and no one to save him. It kept many people laughing in their cups and, apparently, still does. Even servant women who have plenty of compassion for inanimate objects but none for people like me."

"I apologize if I offend," she said softly. Too late.

"There is no part of me or what I am that I have ever wanted anyone to emulate. The fact that you think I do is the worst thing you could say to me. It is the *cruelest* thing you could say, worse than a slap across the face. Bien, Mademoiselle ... now you can go on your way and leave me to my horse."

I had unloaded on her, and perhaps she didn't deserve it all, but she humiliated me.

She straightened but didn't leave.

"Monsieur, you shouldn't let what I say hurt you if it is not true," she threw my words back at me softly. "Someone recently told me that."

"Oh, but it's all true, Mademoiselle. I am a degenerate supplicant. I am the court jester. I am proud to be unpleasant and unpalatable because it gets people to leave me alone. I wear my bad humor fondly. I hate everyone and if it is the truth and I admit it then you have no power over me, do you, Mademoiselle?"

I sounded petulant, even to my own ears, but couldn't stop feeling what I felt. I rubbed the brushes against each other in the water, but when I didn't hear her leave, I looked up. She stood watching me with her large brown eyes.

"Is that your truth, then? You despise everyone and that's it?" The way she said it so simply made me feel small and—worse—pathetic. Her dark eyes were searching my face and her brow furrowed as if studying for the answer. I felt vulnerable in a way I didn't like, even though I longed to continue speaking with her. I wanted to lean into the small strand of genuine conversation and connection that I sensed existed. But I'd also been alone and on the defensive for so long that genuine feelings were dangerous. I worried this serious woman could do me in.

I looked back down at the brushes. "And why on earth should I explain my truth to you? Who are you to deserve it?" I bit my tongue from saying more, though it was difficult; biting words came so easy to me. After a pause, I heard her feet carrying her away. I didn't give her the benefit of watching her leave.

Later, I calmed down. Only then could I be honest with myself.

I liked her. I liked the way she spoke and how determined she was. I liked the way she thought about everything she said. I liked that she was intelligent and proud to show it. I liked that she had a bit of a sense of humor, and she wasn't intimidated by me or this place. Plus, I was physically attracted to her, with her serious face and hidden attributes. Even in plain servant's dress, she couldn't hide her comeliness.

I had never approached a woman I admired. I had been with servant women and noblewomen to satisfy my needs, being no more to them than they were to me—even knowing some who did it on a dare—just to ease the loneliness. But I'd never been in a relationship. I was confident of my mind, but my body—with my short stature, broken bones healed badly, slightly hunched from what I believed was a spinal injury—I was not what most women would desire. Initiating something real with a woman would open me to the ridicule I detested.

I avoided her as best I could. And then one night, I was in bed reading when I heard the envelope scrape against the wood of the floor and heard the steps quickly walking away. I put the book down and swung the covers back, walking across the room to take the letter that had been slid under the door ...

Dear Monsieur Zamor,

It must beg your pardon. After all our miscommunications I so enjoyed speaking with you that I spoke too freely. You cut such a stern figure I would be surprised that anything I might say could truly wound you, but your reaction to our last conversation and your pointed effort to avoid me tells me otherwise. I can't apologize enough for my error and miscalculation.

Though I must admit, I am grateful for having seen the wound because in doing so I see your heart and know you are not the man I originally thought you were. Perhaps, you are the man who was so good to Pauline that day. Perhaps you are a good man, albeit blunt and slightly uncouth.

You have every reason to be angry with me, but I hope time will dull your anger. I would be dishonest if I did not admit how much I enjoy speaking with you—when we are not misunderstanding one another—and how much I look forward to speaking again, if you are open to it.

Sincerely,

Mademoiselle Véronique

The paper crinkled in my hand as I stared down at it, waiting for it to change. She wrote words of kindness and forgiveness and conciliation, down in ink on paper. A letter to me and to me alone! I ran my finger over the salutation: Dear Monsieur Zamor. She addressed me as if I was a man. A gentleman, even. Like she respected me.

My previous anger melted away. Her words offered me something I never expected and didn't know how much I wanted until that moment.

I walked over to my small table and pulled out a sheet of paper from my bag, sitting down. I opened a bottle of ink and pulled out my quill and got to writing in the candlelight, quickly, before I could change my mind.

Dear Mademoiselle Véronique...

I started and stopped just as quickly, fidgeting with the pen. Worrying over what to say, suddenly nervous. It was silly of me, really, to try to hold a conversation with this woman who was as different from me as night from day. And yet...

I started again.

It was good of you to write to me. Perhaps, like me, you are much clearer in the written word.

Before we go further, I must make a confession that has been weighing on me. You were correct that in the beginning I was watching you, but I assure you for only the best reasons. You carry yourself with such dignity and self-respect I could not help but observe. When you brought it to light, I lied and told you it was your imagination. That was wrong of me. I lie occasionally when I am caught. It's a well-established flaw in my character I don't know if I'll get rid of any time soon.

Our latest interaction left me wanting to speak with you further. I will admit, I have thought about writing to you before but was worried a letter from me would find a home in the fire before being read. I feared I was too late and that you had already formed a solid opinion of me. I'm happy I was wrong.

I would like to meet again so that maybe I can find the words that are in my head—and not only the words of insolence, impatience and indifference that quickly spring to my lips—so we might be friends? Your apology is received and eagerly accepted. I, too, must apologize for my part in our interactions thus far! Not only the most recent but all interactions from the moment you arrived. I realized after I said it that I may have given the impression that delivering your mail to you would come at a cost. Sincerely, I never meant it that way. I was only hurt because I felt I had done you a favor while you were thinking the worst of me. I would never hide your mail and would always do my best to get it out, whether I was angry with you or not.

I sincerely appreciate your note and this opportunity to set things straight. I'm much more clear-minded when I write, unlike when I speak to you. It seems when I speak all sense leaves me, and I don't want to reawaken your original opinion of me as an evil man nor leave you to think me a fool.

With truest sincerity,

Monsieur Zamor

At the end of it my fingers shook like I had palsy. In the middle of the night, I stepped out of my room in my dressing cloak and slippers, making my way as quietly as I could down the hallway of the servants' quarters. I prayed silently to myself that she wouldn't suddenly open the door and find me there. I slid the envelope under her door. The sound was loud in the night. Then I turned and walked away as quickly as I could.

The next day I was passing by the back door where lines were suspended to hold damp linens. It was a particularly windy day. The sky a sharp blue as if painted by watercolor dabbled with water and I saw Véronique struggling to hold down the ends of a bed linen. No sooner had she straightened it and turned away then it flew up to drape her like a lover's arms. She straightened it again, and I stepped into her view. As she saw me, it fluttered up again and she fought the gentle billows.

Laughter escaped me as her face, caught surprised, wore a lovely soft look of confused innocence. She caught my gaze briefly and then laughed herself as the linen attacked once again. This time, I heard her laughter, and between flapping sheets her smile was sweet.

"If you're going to stand there, at least be of use, Governor." The look in her eyes took the sting away from her use of my title. I helped hold down the fabric while she secured it. She did so with determination and soon had them in line. I watched her as she worked, once again, in silence. It was easy to be in silence around her. It seemed fitting with only the sound of the buttressing wind and the sky so blue.

I looked at her sneakily because I didn't want her to see me staring. The gray dress was ugly at best, but against it, her skin was a lovely, living warm chestnut. She looked at me, and I looked away quickly.

"You have control of the attacking linens, Mademoiselle?"

"Ah, Monsieur, control is not normally something I have to fight for."

I couldn't stop the quick laugh that escaped me.

It occurred to me that it was something, this connection of mine to the woman from the east. What, I didn't know. But it was something. For the first time in all my days I felt something that wasn't as lofty as friendship or as base as lust. It was something. I couldn't say what.

It was something.

44

———————

M *ay, 1789*

WHEN APPLAUSE BROKE OUT, I knew Gilbert LaFayette had arrived at the Club. Valentin went over to him, his normally sallow cheeks bright. He clapped the Marquis on the back and jumped up onto the nearest table.

"To those of you who haven't heard, our own Jacobin friend, the Marquis de LaFayette, spoke up for the Third Estate at the latest meeting of the Estates-General, insisting that the Third Estate have more votes. And even though he was shouted down..." laughter at that. "... because this esteemed nobleman stood with the common people and bourgeois, for once the Third Estate will have a meeting with the King directly!"

The slim-faced hero smiled humbly. "We're calling ourselves the National Assembly. Mostly Third Estate representatives but with some of us from the First and Second Estates who believe fair is fair.

And, yes, we will get to speak with the King on issues important to the common people."

Applause broke out in earnest again. The room was floating with buoyant spirits, optimism, and love for this rarest of men, LaFayette. He had earned our love by doing more than just pretend to care about the people. By standing for them, he showed himself to be a true friend.

"This is spectacular," Sebastien said, guzzling a beer, his eyes shining. "The Third Estate with their own audience with the King? Finally! That's all we ever wanted. If things continue like this, we might have our improved republic in a year. Six months, maybe."

I returned his smile because I felt his excitement even as a small pinch of doubt worked my nerves. I didn't have the heart to tell him the King was a sneaky snake. I suspected the King was either avoiding making a decision or leading everyone to think they had a hand in the country's fate when he had already destroyed things beyond repair. He was that type of person.

But perhaps I was too jaded—perhaps I'd be proven wrong. It was possible I was looking at XVI through the same glasses as his grandfather, the lying Well-Beloved.

After the meeting, LaFayette made his way over to me. Finally!

"Have you decided?" I asked.

"I thought about what you said, and there's never been a leader who wasn't afraid of what he was going to undertake. I was afraid when I went to America, but I knew I must. I never even imagined drafting an important document, but once you brought it to me, it seems wrong not to proceed. This republic is moving forward, and I believe I can help. So, yes, friend, I'm writing it. I thought you were crazy, but now I'm as excited as you."

I smiled and clapped him on the back. I knew he was the right person to approach. "There's no better voice."

"I must tell you something. I know you don't like him, but I asked Thomas Jefferson to look over my draft. As a political leader, I feel he can give me guidance." My face showed my feelings. "I know you think he's a hypocrite, but he's just a good man stuck between a rock and a hard place. He's kind to his slaves, to the point of being considered a pushover by other slave owners. But he knows if *he* doesn't give them safe harbor they could end up in much worse hands. That has to mean something."

It meant something to *him*, apparently. But I couldn't look a gift horse in the mouth. Maybe by drafting something for France, the innocent Mr. Jefferson would re-think his own complicity in the slave trade.

"I'll rely on your good judgment," I said. "I look forward to seeing the final work and know France will be the better for it. So, when is this meeting with the new National Assembly and the King?"

45

———————

Dear Citizen,

Sometimes, being invisible had its advantages.

On Saturday, June 17th, 1789, I made an excuse to spend the day at the Palace so I could see the delegates of the Third Estate gather to meet with the King. I wouldn't know it at the time, but that day would become a day known for many years to come.

—Zamor

After parking Lightning in the stables, I walked the grounds of the Palace to the area that held the administrative outbuildings. When I reached the meeting hall, a group of men were standing outside the front door. Checking the miniature clock I kept in my breast pocket, I noticed it was past time for the meeting to begin. My plan had been to plant myself near the doors to listen and, if anyone should ask, pretend to be working the grounds and checking the shrubs. But with hundreds of people lingering outside of the doors and talking amongst themselves, nobody noticed me.

Working my way through the crowd, I finally got to where I could see, between the bodies, a chain looped through the handles of the doors just behind two armed royal guards.

I knew it! *Sneaky, sneaky bastard!* I thought. I knew the King wouldn't be happy about this group of commoners and nobles and clergy defected from the other Estates, but I had hoped he wouldn't stand in the way of this meeting. Instead, he proved my cynicism was correct all along.

"Maybe they didn't know we would need the space," someone said. The faces on those closest to me told me *they* knew it was no accident; no one forgot. There was no need for guards if no one was expected at the venue. No, they had been expected and were being rejected.

"This is shameful," came a voice. "They won't hear us in the Estates General, and now he makes it clear he won't allow us to even discuss amongst ourselves. He thinks nothing of the Third Estate. Ninety-nine percent of the country, and he doesn't care to hear what they have to say."

"Well, we're the National Assembly now. Not only the Third Estate, but brave men from the other two who know it isn't right how we're treated. Perhaps the fact that we were bold enough to come together on our own was too much for him to bear."

I could tell from the faces that went red which of the men were nobles, because they weren't used to being snubbed. I couldn't see LaFayette, but was sure he was there somewhere, red-faced and embarrassed. The only ones that didn't look surprised were those in the long pants and drab sans-culotte clothing. They were familiar with the feeling. So was I.

"Do we wait and try again in the next meeting?"

"Try to be ignored again? That shouldn't be too hard."

"Well, why don't we just meet now, without him?"

"Where? They've chained the doors."

Good sense told me to keep my mouth shut. As the crowd mumbled amongst themselves, I could feel the heat rising off the man next to me and took a look at him. He shuffled with discomfort, his long pants barely covering the shabby, worn shoes on his feet. He wore an outer shirt over his rough shift, an attempt to dress up for this formal occasion. His face wore a combination of confusion and overwhelm. He was one of the sans-culottes studded throughout the crowd of wealthy bourgeoise and even wealthier nobles.

Aside from the air of resignation and disappointment, you could tell the sans-culottes from their silence. The others were jabbering to each other, used to having their voices heard. But the commoners—even being on the Palace grounds must have been frightening.

I knew that feeling. And I knew, just as I'd stepped out of my bubble to discover a new world in Paris, the peasants in the crowd were doing something just as frightening and just as significant. They came because they hoped for change, just like me.

I cleared my throat and those closest to me looked my way. One of the men in silk looked me over.

"I've seen you at the Palace, haven't I? Do you work here?"

"So to speak. Did I hear correctly? Are you all looking for space to meet?"

I had their attention now, but I didn't want the attention of the guards who might recognize me, so I made quick work of motioning those closest to me to follow. At first it was just a couple, but soon, I had several hundred following me a short way down the road like I was the Pied Piper of Versailles. We reached a large building I knew was normally unlocked. Once there, I pulled the door, which opened without resistance, and a couple of them stepped inside, looking around at the large space with high, tall windows allowing the filtered light inside.

"But there aren't any chairs," someone complained.

"My apologies, Monsieur," I responded. "I thought you wanted to have a discussion, not a nap." My comment brought laughter, and a few more people stepped forward to look inside. A man stepped up to me.

"What is this place?"

"It's the indoor salle du jeu de paume." *The room for the palm game.* It was a game that harkened back to medieval France where the goal was to smack a ball against the walls with the palm of one's hands. Now, they used rackets instead of their hands. In England they now called it *tennis*. "The nets are down, so it's just an empty space for now, but there's a table over in the far corner and a few chairs for those who need them. Seems large enough for this group."

"This will do well," he said. "Thank you, Monsieur...?"

"Not at all. I'm only the *page*. It is a page's job to serve, after all. But I wonder if I could sit in. I know I'm not a voting member of the Third Estate and I won't understand *anything* you important people are doing, but I am interested in learning. If the group doesn't mind?" False modesty but whatever it took...

"I don't see why not."

I stayed on the sidelines and watched as the group filtered in. I know some of my fellow Jacobins were there, but there were too many bodies to find anyone. I sat down and listened as the minutes turned into hours and the discussion changed from broad, general terms to something much different. I watched as they began to talk about drafting a constitution—something in writing to use to govern our country.

For the very same reason I prompted LaFayette to write down a declaration, I was equally happy these men wanted to write the laws that would govern. My mouth watered from desire to contribute, but I wasn't a chosen representative of anybody yet. I reminded myself that this was just the first step to what I hoped would be complex and lasting change. Once LaFayette finished his document, it would be much easier for me because that work would lay the groundwork for what I hoped to do. If his declaration served its purpose, maybe I would be a free man soon!

Gone all day, I finally slipped out when a glance outside the door signaled nightfall. There was a man on the periphery, like me, who had taken a large pad out of his bag and was sketching the scene. With so many people in the room, it seemed an impossible task, but he sketched like a madman. I left as they began lighting torches to put into the wall sconces, walking back to the stables to get Lightning for a breathless ride back under dark of night.

That next evening, some of the Jacobin delegates who had been in the room relayed the evening's events to the rest. One of them stood in the center of the room, reading off a piece of paper on which he'd copied the words they'd agreed on in that tennis court after I left.

"The National Assembly, considering that it has been summoned to establish the constitution of the kingdom, to effect the regeneration of public order, and to maintain the true principles of monarchy; that nothing can prevent it from continuing its deliberations in whatever place it may be forced to establish itself; and, finally, that wheresoever its members are assembled, there is the National Assembly... It decrees that all members of this Assembly shall immediately take a solemn oath not to separate, and to reassemble wherever circumstances require, until the constitution of the kingdom is established and consolidated upon firm foundations; and that, the said oath taken, all members and each one individually shall ratify this steadfast resolution by signature."

"And then everyone lined up to sign the oath. There were hundreds of signatures on that document," the man said, smiling. "I've never been so proud of my countrymen in all my life."

The feeling spread through the room and several rounds of beer left us boisterous and giddy with excitement. But I soon heard through the grapevine, the King was pissed. Though I spent the following days close to the Chateau—Madame grew ill-tempered in direct proportion to the amount of time that I spent away from her—I heard from Henri that he'd heard from a Palace stable hand that the King had pitched a fit to rival all fits, demanding the members of the new National Assembly rejoin the Estates-General to finish the meetings.

"They refused!" a nobleman informed Madame over dinner a couple of nights later. He chewed on a piece of delicate lamb with appreciation. He was one of three guests at the house and the only one without a spouse or partner. He showered Madame with attention like a man who was trying to woo his next partner. "The King was very patient with them, but imagine, refusing our King."

Madame was no stranger to being hit on, but the man was below any station she was interested in. Still, she knew how to charm even those she was rejecting.

"You are always so knowledgeable about what's happening in the world. It's a pleasure to have someone here so well-informed about what's happening at court. Though I was never one particularly interested in politics. Our dear King preferred to spend our time together without the ugly details of politics. Our home was a place of gentle, loving conversations on amiable subjects like art and music."

And drunken parties. Orgies. Debauchery.

"I can understand that, Madame," the man simpered. "If I were fortunate enough to have been in the Well-Beloved's shoes, politics would be the last thing on my mind."

The table laughed, but then another man picked up the string.

"But if the Third Estate won't join the meetings, what is the King going to do? We need those meetings to straighten out our finances, correct?"

"I don't know," said the nobleman, sipping cabernet. "But they don't call themselves the Third Estate anymore, it seems. They've taken to calling themselves the National Assembly, or the National Convention because it seems they've been joined by several noblemen and religious leaders from the other estates. It's almost like another version of that filthy Jacobin Club, only this one has misguided nobles with the power to hold up our country's proceedings."

"How presumptuous," said one of the women, "thinking they can create their own national organization. I'm part of the nation, and I refuse to recognize them. Poof." She made a gesture with her fingertips as if to disappear them from existence, laughing at her own cleverness.

"What I don't understand is, why would anyone from the higher estates join the peasants and encourage this bad behavior?" Madame said.

"The King is trying to save our country, and they're being difficult," the noblewoman declared. "We never should have allowed poor people to have an estate in the first place. What do they know about the responsibilities of a government?"

I felt Madame's eyes on me. "What do you think, Louis-Benoit?" She cut into her lamb and ate a small piece. "You've been spending time in Paris making new friends. Have you heard anything about this disobedience?"

All of a sudden, all eyes were on me. I didn't think Madame knew anything about what I was doing, but her innocent question was one I'd rather not have to answer at all.

"Me? I haven't heard anything," I lied.

"Oh, but really, all that time you spend in the city, and you've heard nothing? Don't pretend; I know you're paying attention. Louis-Benoit is a fan of Rousseau. Carries that *Social Contract* book around all the time ... thinks I don't notice," she told the table, earning me sour looks and a couple of once-overs.

The nobleman speared some lamb and gave me a dirty look. "Your servant can read?"

"He's the page of the Favorite of the King of France, of course he can read. Better than even some nobles. Louis-Benoit knows three languages, he's a self-taught violinist, and he's an avid student of the world."

Under their speculative looks, I added, "*And* I can walk and talk and think and speak, too. Oh, and I can hear, so feel free to address any questions pertaining to me directly to me," I said.

"You see," Madame said. "He speaks his mind freely, though that could use some reining in. I'm just too soft-hearted when it comes to him. He came to me as a tiny child, you see, it's almost like he's my very own son. So, I ask you, again, Louis-Benoit, what have you heard?"

But the nobleman interrupted. "I'm sorry, before you answer that, can someone tell me who this Rousseau fellow is?"

Thank God. I was able to go into an explanation of Rousseau though I tamped down my interest in him. I described him as a man who liked to pick flowers. A nature-loving fool. I didn't want anyone thinking I was as much of a fan as I was. And Madame didn't ask me any more about what I knew, convinced my interest in the writer was more about how his love of nature reminded me of my homeland of Africa. Of course, I'd never lived in Africa, but I stopped trying to convince her of that years ago.

The King tried hard to undo the National Assembly, but legally, there could be no Estates-General without all three Estates. He made promises to stop taxing poor people so much and to take on no new loans. He even made a laundry list of concessions based on the list of grievances from the provinces, but the damage had already been done. The National Assembly had power, and it was difficult to put things back when the King had bungled things so badly already.

Desperate, XVI then doubled down on bad decisions and increased the number of royal army guards throughout Paris, perhaps to intimidate the people of Paris into falling in line. He succeeded in causing fear to spread through the streets, permeating everything, including the Jacobin Club. Sans-culottes members of the new National Assembly—or National Convention, as they were now known—were afraid they would be rounded up and jailed for creating the body. Everyone was afraid of retribution from the King, and rightly so. Just a generation previously, protest was enough to get a person executed. Now, royal guards were walking through Paris like they just wanted *any* reason to stop someone and haul them away to the secret prisons. Everyone was on edge, and I was afraid we would lose the momentum of this brand-new committee along with any progress made so far.

To my way of thinking, XVI was losing public support fast, yet that support was precisely what the new republic would need to build change. Why shouldn't we use his weakness against him?

Sebastien and I decided, with the increased guard presences stationed at the Jacobin Club, we'd go to the back room of a local tavern to unwind. The darkened room was swarming with bodies. I saw Valentin across the room and figured if he was far enough away, it would be harder for him to shut me down. I stood up as Sebastien looked up from his beer in surprise. I clapped my hands, and the ruckus quieted down.

"Is this how we build our new republic?" I asked loudly to get attention. The din quieted as the drinking stopped, and they looked my way. "We gather here in bars and complain and gossip and hope and wring our hands, wishing that somehow, someway, we can earn the King's respect? He showed us what he thinks of us by locking our delegates out of the meeting room. How long will it take for us to see that he'll never respect us? The King has his nobles and his guards and police, but we have the sans-culottes. We *are* the sans-culottes. Ninety-eight percent of this country is in the Third Estate, yet all of us together have one vote in the Estates-General, while the clergy and the nobles have one as well. Since when does ninety-eight percent constitute an equal vote to one percent? And then, the clergy and nobles join to outvote the Third Estate entirely. How is that fair when that two percent has the backing of the King himself? No wonder we've never been heard. No wonder we're the only ones paying taxes. No wonder we're the beggars while they enjoy being begged from. And then the commoner has to fear being arrested for expressing dissatisfaction." I pointed to the door.

"I can't go out in the main room and say this. Police roam the streets waiting to arrest anyone who speaks like this, so we have to hide in the back, in the dark, like rats. The King *told* us he wanted to hear our grievances. He agreed to meet with the Third Estate, and all they wanted was to be heard. Instead, he reneged on the sincere request to speak to him directly, like human beings. It's almost like they used the opportunity to see who would take the bait. Like a bit of cheese in the trap he set for us. God-willing the Tennis Court Oath never gets into the hand of our monarch, or his police will pick off each and every man, one at a time! He doesn't care what pains the common people. *We* have to care. In order to have a strong republic, this movement of ours has to move outside of back rooms of taverns and clandestine meeting places, and even beyond the Jacobin Club."

"What do you suggest?" Valentin asked, having worked his way around the room to show up as the thorn in my side. "You want us to go door to door to drum up membership? I guess you want us to announce our plans in the streets and then hold out our wrists for the police to shackle them?"

"Thank you for always having such insightful questions, Valentin. No, it serves no one for us to be picked off one by one. But we've been thinking about it all wrong, behaving as if we're some clandestine group of miscreants trying to get people to join our club of wayward, misguided fools. What we are is the voice of ninety-eight percent. We're the voice of the country. We need to speak to the sans-culottes with that one voice. Not in words of dissent, but in words of aspiration. Right now, the Jacobins are as far removed from the circumstances of the common man as the King. We need to show them we stand for the masses in a way they understand and appreciate.

"How?" Valentin said, rolling his eyes. "You're talking but saying nothing, page. Enlighten us or pipe down and let me enjoy my beer."

Valentin always knew how to get a laugh, and this time was no exception. I ignored his smirking face and spoke around him to a lot of unfamiliar faces.

"The King is unsure of making drastic change, but he's comfortable with his power," I said. "A symptom of being maintained and sheltered within Palace walls, he takes his power for granted because it's never been challenged. Let's shake that comfort. The other night I was with a friend in Paris and watched the secret police come and drag a man away. I'm told the man might not get trial, that he's more likely to rot in the Bastille without ever even having a chance to defend himself. I'm told there's not a sans-culotte in Paris who doesn't know someone who's been dragged to that particular prison, correct? What if that's where we make our stand?"

"But that's pointless," a dark-haired man with serious eyes declared. "There's hardly anyone there right now—and none who could rouse enough people or interest to care. It's practically empty."

"What is your name?" I asked the dark-haired man.

"Camille."

"Camille, don't you see?" I implored him, the idea bringing a small smile to my lips. "Aren't there weapons at the Bastille? The prison is sitting right here in the middle of Paris, away from the King, away from the royal guards, empty and poorly guarded with only the Marquis de Sade there to give the guards much grief, which I am sure he enjoys if his reputation is to be believed." That earned laughter and more attention. "Few people means less chance of anyone being harmed, and by taking it we can send a strong message to the people that they are heard. Maybe by taking the prison playground of the King we'll send the message that if he will not give us the simple respect and dignity of hearing our concerns, we will force him to notice us by going to the people."

Understanding slowly gathered in the eyes of this stranger, who nodded. "What is *your* name?"

"They call me *the page*."

I learned later Camille Desmoulins was a member of the new National Assembly and close friend to two men who were well-known among the burgeoning group: Georges Danton and Maximilien Robespierre.

46

———————

I was still riding on the high of my brief spot in the limelight the next day at the Chateau when my daydreaming was interrupted.

"You fool!" cried the visiting noblewoman.

I was sitting beside Madame with two of her maids, she on the bench and us a blanket on the ground around her. We'd been listening to her read when a commotion and the sound of a clatter across the green lawn drew our attention. The visiting guest was standing and making a fuss over a tray of teacups that appeared to have been dropped by Véronique.

We heard Véronique's plea. "My apologies, Madame. I will get another tray immediately."

"Oh no," Madame put the book down and stood, moving quickly over the grass to comfort her guest who was making a bigger scene with each passing second. I followed. At the scene of the crime, from all her gesturing, I noticed the small droplet of tea on the visitor's dress that was causing Véronique to flush with worry.

The guest brushed at the tiny spot as though a full pot had landed on her. It was what I hated about nobles, how they took pleasure into making a mountain out of a molehill, knowing full well how much trouble they could cause the person serving them. Not today. I would deflect.

I said: "My, what a fuss over a small thing. It's hardly as if it makes the dress any more unattractive than it already is."

The visitor's maids gasped.

"Louis-Benoit!" Madame said, as if it was the first time she'd ever heard my sarcasm. I saw the briefest quirk of a smile on her face before she masked it.

"Madame, how can you allow your servant to speak to me like that? It's simply not done."

According to the gossip columns and tabloids, talking to Madame like that was the least I was doing so the woman's shock was an act. Now that I had access to the pamphlets in Paris, I could read for myself all of the debauchery I was supposed to be up to at the Chateau and it sometimes even made *me* blush.

In truth, while I usually played the respectful servant, Madame and I had devolved to commonly sniping at one another. I would let loose, and she would threaten to be rid of me, and some noble would mutter about how much we sounded like husband and wife. And then I would hear through the grapevine of another gossip rag talking about how we'd secretly married, and I was the Count of Louveciennes. Speculating about our relationship was what these guests to the Chateau did best.

The only time we got along was when I was too bored to speak or when we had a common enemy—then we would combine our spite to take the enemy down before going back to separate camps.

As for Véronique, she and I had a healthy, respectful appreciation for each other. Today, Véronique looked at me like I wasn't doing her any favors but, alas, my tongue was loosed, and it was always difficult to reel it in once started.

"Have I said anything untrue? You wear a dress covered in brown spots; it's hardly going to change the pattern if one more brown spot lands on it. Am I not correct, Madame?" I turned to my benefactress whose lips were pinched because I was doing exactly what I had done since I was a child—the dirty work of Madame who likely didn't want this particular woman at her home, anyway. I was doing her a favor. The enemy of my enemy, and all that...

She passed on the opportunity to reprimand me. Her long silence told the tale better than words could.

"They told me not to come here," the woman said, her lips thinning with anger. "But I wanted to give the estimable Madame du Barry an opportunity to prove that she was not the classless *putain*" —*whore*— "I always thought her to be. It appears my first impression was correct."

This guest had been a friend of the Queen that Madame was hoping to win to her side, but it was obvious, with the quickness with which she turned, that the woman came with ill intentions. No doubt, she would run back to the Palace to gossip about how badly this house was run.

The visitor lifted her skirts and headed toward the house. "Please. Stop." Madame followed, weakly asking forgiveness and complaining that she didn't know what had gotten into me, followed by five snickering maids in total. She turned and winked at her ladies, sending them into fits of laughter. I knew she would keep up her protestations until the guest had packed up her things and left. Madame knew how to make someone feel unwanted if it suited her.

But Véronique had hurried away in the other direction with her empty cups wobbling on the tray, so I followed. I was certain she heard me as she dropped off the items in the kitchen. I said nothing as I watched her face, reddish brown and tight. Salanave didn't say a word. Véronique continued out the back door and walked to the side of the Chateau. When I reached her, she jumped right in as if we were already in a conversation.

"The skinny one pushed me. I have never spilled on anyone, ever. Ever!"

"D'Accord, I believe you."

She quickly wiped a tear away and stalked around in a little circle, hands on her hips, trying to stop her face from crumpling. I was surprised. She was a strong woman.

"Véronique of the East, why do you take it so deeply to heart? You take me to task easily, and I'm no slouch. But these people bring you to tears over one slip."

"You don't understand. It's an honor to have been taken under Noblewomen Martin's wing, my benefactress back home. She sent me here to learn how to serve royalty. I've been serving since I was young, but this could give me credibility that could sustain my future. Security. Without this, things could go back to being..."

She stopped and though everything in me wanted to know what she was so afraid of things going back to, some latent sensibility in me didn't push for answers.

"I understand. It's important for you to do well. But fear will assure you do horribly. In order to be the best servant you can, you have to care the least. Then, you'll do excellent work."

She looked at me like I was crazy but smiled a little, swiping away the tear on her cheek. "Page, that's the most ridiculous thing I've ever heard."

And you are the most beautiful woman I have ever seen.

The thought popping into my mind almost made me lose track of my thoughts, but I got them back quickly, shrugging. "Maybe so. But when I stopped giving a shit, I stopped making nervous, stupid mistakes. And when I did make mistakes, I no longer cared. I began to sleep well at night. And I no longer cried."

"You cried? Why do I feel like that's not true?"

"I cried. Many, many tears." I laughed a bit. "Many years ago! I will tell you, Véronique of the East, I have been around these people almost all my life. They have all the money, all the opportunities, and you would think with all that they could at least be decent to the people who help them every day. But they are so bereft of human decency they will take from you and grind you underfoot without losing a moment of sleep. You want to serve royalty, do so with that reality guiding your way and don't let their words hurt your soul."

She sighed but her shoulders lost their tenseness. "My soul isn't hurt, Zamor, I'm just afraid of what it means if I fail. If I stay and learn, I make more money."

"For...?"

She started to speak and then hesitated, that little frown between her eyebrows. "It will sound silly to you."

"Probably. Tell me, anyway."

She smiled at my obnoxiousness, and I was happy to see it.

"When I was a little girl, my parents and I took a trip out to the country, not too far from here. There was a house close to the river at Croissy-Sur-Seine, where the jagged edges meet? It's been empty for two years. I knew a man who found the owner is ready and eager to sell. It's like it's waiting for me."

"You want a house? What for?"

"To live a quiet, peaceful life in, Zamor. To bake and cook. In the morning I'll sip my tea. And I'll grow flowers outside my front door. And all day long I'll sew dresses—I like to sew, by the way—that I'll sell to noblewomen to pay for food and heating oil. I'll have one of those wooden figures made for my very own that I can lay and hang my designs on while I work, like a real tailor, but in my own home. And at night I'll sit beside the fire and read my books, or sketch new dresses, or just warm my toes. And the last thing I will do before I go to bed at night will be to stand at my back door and look out at the Seine under the moonlight."

Her face was shining and soft, already standing in the home of her imagination, in the midst of her dream. But I was still there on the cold, hard ground.

"But you're a woman," I said. "Women can't own property." I could almost see her transport away from her fantasy and back to the hard ground with me. Her face lost its softness.

"I haven't figured everything out yet."

"Is there a husband in that dream of yours, because that's the only way you'll get that house, you know. And is that really it? That's what you want? That's your dream? All of it?"

"Two hundred livres. Every penny I can spare goes to save for it. When I go back to live with Madame Martin, I can run her household as nicely as if it was a royal place, like here. And in five years ... or ten ... I'll have my house."

"Five or ten years? Someone might have bought it by then. Surely the price will go up or it will have fallen into disrepair."

"Maybe not. It's called hope, Zamor. It's enough to keep the best of us going. What about you? What do you want, if a house is too pedestrian of a dream for you?"

"But if you have your freedom and a little money you could go anywhere, a beautiful woman like you. Buy an apartment in Paris, something nice in the center of all the activity and the Seine runs right through downtown Paris. Go to the opera or the theatre. Enjoy parties and social engagements."

"You've lived among aristocrats too long. Only noblewomen can live lives of entertainment and parties, Zamor. I could never afford that. I will work. Besides, it doesn't appeal to me. I want the peace of just being able to take care of myself. I don't have to be at the parties so long as my dresses are." She snuck a look at me. "Though I do love music. Occasionally, back home, Noblewoman Martin would invite musicians to play in our salon. When Madame has them here, I sneak and listen, it's so lovely. Aside from the art, there's not much I envy about nobles. What about you? What will you do with that wealth of stash that is the worst-kept secret in the house? It seems enough to get you a start in Paris? I keep wondering why you are still here, and wanting to ask you, but I don't want to get on your bad side when we're on speaking terms now. The only thing that makes sense to me is that, maybe, you're not a free man? Is that why you were so upset with me, before?"

She'd found me out. The sun was hot in the sky, but it was safer to look at than her eyes when I answered.

"She doesn't like to admit it out loud, but she won't give me my freedom," I admitted. "When I'm gone for longer than a day the guards come and find me. I have to be here every morning to bring her chocolat, after all. I stopped running away when I was a teenager. Seemed no point when I realized everyone was going to bring me right back."

I braced myself to lose her friendship. Because if she said

anything that sounded close to pity, I would cut her off then and there.

"Then I understand why you're always so angry. That's your dream, isn't it? Not the opera or the parties or all that you just said. You dream for me the life you want for yourself. Above all, you want to be free."

I looked at her. There was no pity in her voice or on her face, but it was jarring how perceptive she was. She cut too quickly to the truth to be comfortable. I didn't respond.

She nodded. "How would you live? The country is going through very difficult times. Back home, it was always tight but now I see how good me and my family—and our town—had it when compared to some of the poverty I see here close to the wealthiest. Sometimes I feel guilty knowing that my life is so much better simply because I was born on the mainland and not in the Americas ... feeling like I don't deserve this life when so many of our brethren are suffering. It's so difficult for the slaves in the islands and the Americas—if you heard the stories my father told me you'd be horrified—compared to that maybe it's not so bad here...?"

I winced. Just that quickly, our moment was over. Blood rushed through my face as her words pricked at the guilt just below the surface, my guilt at knowing what befell the other children in the camp. That caravan of hell-bound slavers with children on an endless trek, cursed to continue traveling the forests in those rickety carts until someone could be convinced to buy them and deliver them to even more misery.

I could almost hear those children's voices now, like I was still sitting around that campfire. I could hear the little boy who was my protector as if he whispered directly into my ear: *You complain about not having freedom, you still have your limbs! You complain about getting chocolat every morning? You're not getting whipped for serving it too hot or cold or slowly! You want to complain about not being free? You can get on a horse and ride, you have friends you can laugh with, you can read without punishment, you can worship and sing and make love, freely. You're not working your fingers to the bone day and night, out in the hot sun with your skin baking and your feet blistering, being sliced with a whip every time you take a moment to try to stretch a knot out of your cramping muscles. Little food and water, only to get too little sleep to do it all over again tomorrow. You complain? Remember us. Remember me!*

Or the little girl who helped teach me French, happy to come to the mainland because it might possibly lead to her sister, even though she had no idea where in France that sister might be. Likely not privy to a schoolteacher with a map to show her just how large this kingdom was. Like me, thinking France was the size of a village rather than its actual size of a village times one thousand. That sweet, kind soul rewarded with...

THE THREE OF us rode away from the schoolhouse in the woods to an equally remote spot at a little clearing in the center of a fork in the road. Two other wagons were parked, each on a different fork.

"Get out," our teacher ordered us as he climbed down from the front and walked over to the man from one of the wagons. We climbed out of the back bed and watched as the one stranger handed our teacher a little pouch, and then came over to the girl.

"I'm here from your new master. He's registered you already, so I'll be driving you straight to his home. Go ahead and get in the back."

She looked at me, squeezed my hand quickly, and then gave a small nod. Then, she walked over to climb into the back of the new wagon, her eyes conveying strength even though I'd felt a little tremble in her hand when she held mine. But once she was inside, he reached down into the floor bed and pulled out some strange iron contraption that he pulled open. Then, he reached over and clamped it around her neck, fastening it with another piece of iron that screwed in and screwed it closed, moving that portion to the back of her so the cold, unforgiving iron lay against her skin.

The whole time it was happening, she was still and quiet as if stunned, but I could feel the fear growing like a cloud even in her silence. Her eyes grew wide, and she began to whimper as she realized it was a collar. Even at the camp they'd only used rope to secure us. I'd never seen such a thing—never on a person.

"Take it off," I called to him. "Take it off, it's scaring her."

And maybe it was the sound of the panic in my voice that spoke to hers because her whimper grew into full-blown screaming. Screaming and pulling at the thing around her neck; Trying to unscrew the bolt with fumbling fingers. Screaming and crying. Panicked and desperate.

I ran toward her. "Put it on me, I'll go instead!" I would rather have that thing on me than to see it on such a kind, gentle soul. I managed to grab her hand, briefly, as her eyes swung my way, unfocused in panic and face awash in tears. She was still screaming in bursts while we held onto each other for a moment until her driver ripped her arm away and then delivered a blow to her head with a closed fist that stopped her screaming. The top part of her body fell like a sack back into the bed of the wagon and she didn't move. The man pushed on her and took out another iron thing from the bed, and I could hear another clamp fasten, but couldn't see her anymore. A set of hands jerked me away as the girl's new driver stomped over to me.

"Now you've made me hit her. They use those irons all the time in the new Americas, keeps them calm and in line," he yelled into my face, wiping the spittle from his mouth with the back of his hands, his eyes skittish and red. "She was fine until you started her up. I wouldn't have had to do it if you hadn't started her up! She needs to know what won't be tolerated. We don't have time for that nonsense out in the country."

Out in the country? How would she ever find her sister? What did they need her for out in the country? What was going to happen to her?

"Take me, instead, kind Monsieur," I tried my new language skills to flatter him. "I'll work harder than her. She's soft, take me, instead."

"We asked for a female one. Back up, now."

"Just take that thing off her neck, then," I asked. That was all I wanted. That was all she needed, not to feel like she was trapped like an animal. Not to feel like she wasn't a person. But his eyes showed he was unmoved—like he wasn't a person.

Water sprung from my eyes. "Take it off, take it off, take it off...!"

Maybe I'd gone into my own panic, hiccupping and breathing too hard *to keep up with it right, feeling like I was being suffocated by that thing around her neck. I began crying, screaming, waving my arms, and struggling against several sets of arms trying to get to her...*

But then, a blow came from behind and the world twisted as I fell backwards onto the ground and into darkness. I lost hours or days, dreaming of her being carried away on the floor of that rickety wagon as if she was a hog or a goat. I dreamed of her working hard at a home in the country with no hope for help or relief, and no sister in sight ... that iron thing around her neck. I dreamed of telling her I was sorry for starting her up and scaring her. I should have kept my mouth shut like he said, and he wouldn't have hit her. I dreamed of thanking her for her kindness and helping me learn when she didn't have to. I dreamed of her waking up and feeling the hard road underneath the wheels of that horse-drawn carriage, realizing that the hope that had kept her going since she'd been taken was for naught. I dreamt all these things until the moment my eyes opened, and I was lying on rose-colored velvet seats in a fancy carriage, traveling to the world's most stunning palace where I would eat caviar, drink wine, and sit by the side of the greatest thing that ever lived.

I'D MANAGED to bury that memory deep down until this moment, thinking of the little girl and the many before me who had it so much worse, without the luxury to stand around the grounds of a beautiful home dreaming of what they wanted to do with their lives. Dreaming only of how to survive hell one more day. A day that never ended.

And here was Véronique, putting light to my shame like my conscience come to life. It was just like someone like her, to consider the condition of others before thinking of herself. Shining light on who I *wasn't*.

"Well, you're not in my shoes so don't presume to tell me what to do or feel or what someone else is suffering. Do you think I don't know that people much better people than me are in chains? They all deserve freedom before me, *I know that*. But even the devil himself walks free, so why not me? Why never me?" My hissed response came out of me quickly and harshly.

After a moment of silence, I looked at her face, and the consternation on her features.

"That's not what I was saying, at all, Zamor. The only people who deserve to be in shackles are the people who think they have the right to put them on others. No human being deserves what they're doing to our people. How could you think I would mean such a thing?"

Because she said that compared to them, I should be happy, that's why! But I reminded myself it was Véronique, not an enemy. Reminded myself she knew nothing about my past and had no reason to try to make me feel guilty. I could do that on my own. I softened my tone.

"I'm sorry. I just feel like people don't understand what it's like. Comfort without freedom isn't enough. Knowing that someone can own me, do what they want with me, is stifling. I live what I've been dealt, not what I prefer. I know you meant no harm." *But don't ever say that to me again.*

"No, it's my fault," she said, eyes looking chastened. "For being so clumsy and insensitive. It's just that I've never met an enslaved person like you. Can you leave if you use the money from your stolen loot to find a place to live? I hear how easily you and Madame speak with each other and how she even asks your advice sometimes about guests and such. Maybe if she understood how much you wanted your freedom...?"

The air was still but for the sound of birds chirping, the occasional sound of the sway of trees, and distance conversations of people strolling the grounds. Louder than all that was Véronique's misunderstanding of my relationship with my benefactress. Her innocence, brighter than the brilliant sun in the sky.

I didn't want to go into all the ways I was blocked. Legally, every penny I made belonged to Madame. I couldn't so much as rent a room without freedom papers—I'd already asked around in Paris. Nothing mattered without my freedom. I didn't want to taint Véronique with that truth.

"Don't you worry, I'll figure something out. Every fox has to survive its own hunt, and all that."

She nodded, soberly. "Then that is what I want for you, before all else. Once you're free, will you spend your nights at the opera and theater and parties, like you said?"

"Well, yes to Paris. But not so many parties for me, I don't think. Parties are better left to beautiful people. I'd spend my time writing. And reading, that's all," I shrugged. "I want to be a regular free black Frenchman, free to write by candlelight and get paid for it, like Rousseau. And after I marry and have children I'll teach them to read and write and they will be free to share their thoughts, as well."

"Ah, that explains the mystery of that satchel I see you carrying sometimes, I knew it was more than books. It's your own writing. The other servants think you're rubbing your education in their faces because they can't read."

"Ah, well, I'm sorry for them."

"You don't sound sorry."

"That's because I'm not. I should apologize because I received an education? Do those noble brats apologize?" I was ready to be indignant but when I glanced over, the way she looked away from me and the little frown that sprouted up between her brows told me this had nothing to do with me. *She* was fighting some inner struggle.

"It's not all that much of a benefit," she mumbled, picking at her skirt. "Some people would say it's a hindrance. That it's a useless skill, especially for a woman. Plenty suitors told my father it made me a less valuable prospect."

"Now, who's the one making light of their present circumstances? Maybe it's not a benefit at this Chateau in your current state but it is a benefit. Enslaved people know the value. From what Barnier tells me, black people in the Americas want to read and write so badly the government forbids it. At least here on the mainland reading and writing isn't illegal. Literacy is just like the table setting; it's a door through which most people can never enter. It's a bridge across classes; a window into the minds of the people who run this world. It has nothing at all to do with intelligence and *everything* to do with privilege. If there wasn't value to it these wealthy people wouldn't be working so hard to keep it for themselves. Take me, I was only taught to help make the royal court forget that the Favorite was a commoner. 'Read to her, Zamor ... and let her read to you,' the Well-Beloved used to tell me. I covered up for her when she stumbled over the largest words, so no one noticed how hard she worked to get it right. She still reads very slowly so she doesn't stumble. But when she does, I cause a diversion to get the attention off of her. I don't even realize I'm doing it, anymore, I'm so well-trained to save her. And you best believe, I incur the wrath of nobles who hate the fact that I'm literate. My education wasn't a free gift to me, Véronique. I've paid for it with every beating and burning, and I won't apologize for it. Anyone thinks I'm rubbing their face in it? I want them to bend over so I can rub even harder."

I stopped to take a breath, dismayed to see the look on her face. "Don't you dare look sad for me, Véronique of the East, I'm still standing. And I'll tell you right now, I like you a great deal, but I won't tolerate your pity. That look on your face is getting dangerously close to it."

"I don't pity you, Zamor. Whatever I feel, it's not pity."

I nodded. "Good," I said, grudgingly sharing a smile with her. "These people who think there's no value in reading or writing can't see the forest for the trees. Enlightenment writers have spurred a movement. It will serve you someday, I'm sure. And any suitor who would think you aren't valuable, for any reason, is a man who doesn't know or deserve *you*. You are splendid with or without words."

It wasn't until later that evening, going over our conversation, that I picked out the bits of it that had been glossed over. I wrote her a letter.

Dear Véronique,

If a little house on the banks of a river is your dream, then you should have it. If anyone can manage it, you can. Don't give up, no matter what people like me might say. I'm a known skeptic and cynic but the world is run by people like you.

A few years ago, I watched as a balloon was lifted to the air from the grounds of the Palace. Until that moment I never had an idea that it might ever be possible for a human being to fly through the sky. But seeing that balloon lift—even though the basket was full of animals and not humans—suddenly the possibility of human flight seemed reasonable and inevitable.

This is all to say, if men can create a way to carry us to the sky than surely, as brilliant as you are, you will find a way to get that house of yours by the river. I have faith in you, Mademoiselle.

Your friend,

Zamor

P.S. I'm sorry I was so abrasive. I'm not angry at you. I could never be angry at you.

47

Dear Citizen,

What is a pattern but a plan? Putting the pieces of a plan together, like weaving or sewing. I never considered how much of any plan was a pattern until I met the woman who liked to sew and loved patterns. To me, uniformity was an evil thing, but through the eyes of Véronique, I would soon see the beauty of patterns. The beauty of how something that could potentially be stifling and soulless could become something beautiful and free.

—Zamor

I was with Madame in the parlor with a noblewoman from the southeast who was sitting beside her on the little sofa chatting about the weather, when Véronique came into the room with a tray of coffee, small china cups, and a small plate of sablé butter cookies. I was leaning against a wall by a window as far away from Madame as I could get, reading a book.

At Véronique's entrance, the conversation stopped, and I looked up. She was leaning down to fill the cups with coffee and I noticed her average gray work dress was adorned with a colorful bodice. The splash of color brought out the jewel of her skin tone and caught the attention of the noblewoman, who stopped the conversation.

"Madame du Barry, you do always find the most fashionable clothes, even for your staff."

Madame looked up at Véronique. "Except on rare occasions, my staff dress themselves, chère," Madame said. Under heavy scrutiny, the color in Véronique's cheeks rose. "Where did you get that dress, Véronique?"

"I made it, Madame."

"No, not the café, the dress."

"Yes, Madame, I made the dress."

"Yourself?" Madame asked.

"Yes, Madame." Véronique continued pouring the hot liquid as the ladies looked over her outfit. It was a work dress, for sure, but the tightness of the seams and the fit of it over Véronique's curves was a masterpiece. No wonder she always looked so good, I thought; her clothes were made for her very own body. Not simple, ill-fitting shifts, but work tailored like gowns.

"And the bodice—where did you get that material? I've never seen that pattern before."

"The bodice is not a print, Madame, it's embroidered. I did that myself, as well. It's something I like to do in my spare time."

"Making dresses and intricate embroidery in your spare time?" the guest asked. "Do you make fine gowns, too? I can think of many a noblewoman who would pay well for work like that. It's quite impressive. Your staff is multitalented, Madame."

"It appears so. I wish I could claim her for ours, but Véronique is a guest of sorts, though I had been meaning to speak with her about staying with us, permanently. Her benefactress sent her here for training. Had she mentioned Véronique's skill with a needle, I might have hired her on the spot. Perhaps, Véronique, you can train some of us. I was never very good at embroidery but always wanted to learn, properly."

"And perhaps you could take on a little work for me?" the other woman said, eyes still on the dress. "If you have time and it's alright with you, Madame du Barry?"

"Of course. Véronique doesn't work for me all twenty-four hours of the day. Véronique, I see no reason why an enterprising woman such as yourself shouldn't put your skills to use. I might ask you to do a little work for me, also. We would all pay, of course."

"Certainly, Madame."

Véronique blushed and I could feel the smile she tried to hide in the press of her lips. She gave a small nod and, turning, spotted me there on the other side of the room, nodded imperceptibly. I returned the gesture.

VÉRONIQUE of the East was always such a bright spot in any day I happened to glimpse her, even in passing, that I forgot that it wasn't all sunshine and roses for her, either.

One day I was passing by the doorway to the storage pantry and overheard scuffling coming from inside. I walked to the door, pushing it open to see Gaspard's back and then, as he shifted, I noticed Véronique on the far side of the room. Both were panting, but my eyes were drawn to the glint of the small knife she held in her hand. Her face was drawn and tight but with a look that said she was in the middle of a battle.

So, this was it, I thought. Today was the day I was going to die because I instantly felt like attacking a man double my size. But a lifetime of learned behavior in precarious situations kicked in and before I knew it, I was speaking.

"Is everything alright here?" I asked, as calmly as if I'd walked in on them picking daisies. Gaspard whirled, saw me, and straightened, eyes like a caught animal. I knew the look on his face was less about being caught and more about being caught by *me* doing something even more repugnant than usual.

"Mind your business, blackamoor."

"Well, I can't do that, Manager," I said, eyeing the shelves like I was looking for something. "I've been sent here to get supplies and you know me, thorough to a fault. Shame, you'll have to do your assaulting of this young woman somewhere else because I can't find anything on these shelves."

"Idiot. Forget the both of you. And you, girl, pull a knife on me again and you'll be sorry you were born."

She didn't respond, nor did she retreat, though the second he turned away, the hand holding the knife quivered with the tension of her firm grip. I saw in her eyes she fully intended to use it if necessary.

"Move!" He shoved me on his way out the door. Closing it behind him, I turned back to her.

"Are you alright, Véronique?"

"Yes, of course," she said, but her eyes were still on the door where he'd left.

"You'll need to find a new hiding place for that in case he tries to disarm you the next time he gets you alone," I told her. At that moment she seemed to realize she still held the knife out in front of her in the ready-to-jab position, and straightened, and then looked worried.

"I don't know where else to put it that I can get to easily."

I pointed up and she cocked her head at me.

"Up there," I said. "In your headwrap. It's a natural hiding place. Just have to be careful not to cut off your hair. I've never seen it, but I'm sure it's lovely." That last part came out more wistfully than I intended. Fortunately, she was preoccupied.

"Ah, good idea." She carefully pushed it up under the fabric. At my questioning glance she said, "It's good to be prepared. Especially in unfamiliar places. You never know who will come for you. Usually, I'm more careful."

"It's not your fault—it's not like you get a warning when someone's about to trap you in a closet. Did he hurt you? I'll make him sorry if he did. I know I don't look like much, but I have my ways. He has no right to touch you."

"They never do, but that doesn't seem to stop them from trying."

She smoothed her skirt down. "I don't want you doing anything for my sake. Don't worry, I can take care of myself."

"You shouldn't have to." She gave me a mirthless smile that told me what she thought of shouldn'ts. I tried a different tack. "I'll speak to Madame. Gaspard is a son of a bitch, but I never knew him to attack women like that, though he gets worse every year."

"Please don't; I'm fine. I don't want to lose my place here and if I make a fuss, I'm certain to be the one to go, just like Pauline. And that will leave me out in the cold."

Her shaky voice told me how much that decision took from her, and I felt for her.

"You could never be out in the cold. You're Véronique of the East. The sun shines wherever you are." It was true, but she gave me another look as though tiring of my teasing and stepped around me to pass into the hall. But I wasn't teasing.

"Véronique," I called. She stopped and turned back. "Exactly how many dresses do you need to sew for these spoiled noblewomen to get you to that house where the jagged edges meet at Croissy-sur-Seine? Away from people like Gaspard?"

She smiled slightly, thinking of her dreams and not the man who'd just left.

"I don't know, but I'm happy to do it. I'm already working for two ladies. My plan is finally working." She blushed like a girl in love for the first time. *Oh, to have her look at me like that.* She picked up her skirts and moved past me, on about her day.

Memory of the sight of her standing in that room with a knife raised to protect herself stayed with me. It wasn't right that a person like her should have to protect themselves like that and, apparently, not for the first time. People like me—I expected to be set upon at any time—but I was just one step short of pure evil myself. *Evil is as evil does*, they said. But Véronique was a decent person with morals and values. The way she held that knife, the determination on her face, despite the fear in her eyes, stuck with me.

Whenever Véronique was around I found it hard to keep my eyes from straying to her. When she wasn't around, I found it hard to stop thinking of her. Even her dreams fascinated me. Women weren't legally allowed to be tailors or dressmakers, not on their own. They could apprentice, but there were no women store owners or unions. And yet she was trying to do it anyway. She was determined to get it, just like she was determined to get that house. I wondered in what condition it was in and planned to look for it the next time I was out on a ride.

Why should she spend her time doing a thousand little jobs for many women when she could do a few jobs for one woman and get all the money she needed? And I could get further into her good graces, and maybe closer to her.

I started in on Madame, leaving suggestions both subtle and outright. I told her that her dresses were looking old and dated. I mentioned that perhaps the church would appreciate one of her old gowns to cut up and use for cleaning rags. And then, I hammered the final hint home.

We were sitting in the parlor reading, she on one settee and me on another, when I said, casually: "Everyone looks the same these days, don't they, Madame?"

"What?" She looked up and followed my gaze as a group of ladies passed by the window. "Well, yes. People look the same because they all have good taste and like similar things."

"But good taste doesn't always mean the same. In any given circle, there's one person who leads and the others who follow. Look at the Queen. Who would have dared put the size of headdresses on their heads as is currently fashionable if she hadn't done it first?"

"It's not so fashionable anymore," she groused.

"But no one will stop as long as the Queen is still doing it. Unless they have a reason."

Regarding her looks, there wasn't much Madame Jeanne du Barry was insecure about. Even though she was aging, some said maturity made her even more beautiful. The thing she was most sensitive to was fashion because, even with her handsome wealth, she didn't have a king funding her wardrobe anymore. She didn't have designers clamoring for her attention like they did for the Queen's.

"It's not about money, really," I continued, pressing my point. "It's more about the courage to be bold, don't you think? And French women are *bold*."

Her face was impassive, but I could see the clicking behind her eyes as she plotted the next step in her never-ending war against her nemesis.

She didn't speak on it after that and I stopped my campaign—you had to know when to stop with the pressure—and one day Salanave told me Madame had sought out Véronique in the laundry and informed her she was having several bolts of French silk delivered in a vibrant cerulean blue of the same shade she'd seen in Véronique's embroidered bodice and could she do her the honor of creating a dress for her?

And my work was done.

48

———

My lungs burned from sucking in the little bit of air that Fabien allowed me to breathe as he put all his body weight on top of me. The dirty tiles of the butchering room floor smashed against my cheek until I felt like it would pop.

"Tap out, friend, before I accidentally break your face!" Fabien yelled. I could hear the smile in his voice over the sound of our grunting and struggling.

It occurred to me at that moment that perhaps I shouldn't have made the trip to Versailles today. But I had been heaving so much laundry, helping to chop wood, helping to carry baggage for visitors —I'd felt particularly strong this morning. And yet here I was again, face down on the ground with a stronger, larger white man on top of me, his beefy forearm around my neck. It wasn't a good look for me, and my body was a mass of pain.

I grunted and heaved, pushing my hips up, and felt the burden on my upper chest and shoulder, and then rolled a bit. He exhaled loudly as his shoulder and chin took the brunt of that shifted weight. I got a foot under me and used my arms to keep him in place. Then I moved both of us so we were more sideways than him on top. Suddenly, there was a trickle more of oxygen in my airway. I took it and used it to fuel me. I dipped my chin a bit, so he had less real estate on my windpipe. I wound up my free arm and delivered an elbow deep into his gut. The sound of his sucking in air coincided with the rush as his grip on me loosened just a tiny bit. That was enough.

I flipped my whole body and was suddenly on top of him, one arm a bar in front of his neck, the other around the backside to secure it. The surprise in his eyes and the spittle from his lips made the moment sweet.

We sat like that for a long moment as he tried to loosen my arms, tried to get leverage to pummel my chest and abdomen, but without enough space. Like one strange amoeba struggling to split. His face whitened in slow motion and his mouth hissed with the effort to breathe. And then, suddenly, he reached his left hand out and slapped the ground.

I heard the sound but was so stunned I did nothing. His eyes bugged, and he slapped several times, louder, before I quickly released him, sitting up to look in amazement at my own arms.

Fabien coughed and sucked in air, pushing me off.

"I beat you," I said. "I beat you. Fabien, the fighter, I beat *you*!"

"You want a medal, son," he said with a craggy voice as we both got to our feet. But when he looked at me sideways, I saw pride on his face and a grudging, pained smile. "I told you. See what you can do when the pain doesn't hold you back? If you ever tell anyone this happened, I will murder you with my bare hands. I have a reputation to uphold."

"No worries, friend," I said. "It is good enough that you and I know who the better man is." He swiped at me with a fake punch, which I easily deflected. Pride flushed through me with every pump of blood. It hadn't been a wasted trip after all.

We parted with his promise and warning that the next time he would put the world right again and beat me. Then I went outside to the gardens and strolled, looking for other servants who were prone to share bits of gossip with me. At one point, the servant I was speaking with stopped suddenly and straightened. I knew that look.

I straightened myself and turned around, the two of us bowed courteously to the approaching contingent. Marie Antoinette and four ladies came upon us, each one's skirts taking up more of the walkway. When the Queen was in front of me, I bowed.

"Zamor," she said.

"Your Majesty," I straightened.

She wore her signature deep red lips and black dot on her lower cheek. The diamonds that circled her neck glinted in the sun. The silk of her gown made a soft swish every time she shifted. She wasn't beautiful, but she was striking.

"It is always good to see you here at Versailles," she said. She only spoke to me to pass information or insults on to Madame. Today was no different. After a short, discreet beat, she made today's insult. "I trust your Madame du Barry is well and healthy. Silly me, I know she's healthy if the size of her cheeks is any indication. Beauty is so fleeting. Please do send my condolences on the death of the Duc de Richelieu. I know how close and dear a customer—I mean, friend— he was to the Madame before she was presented to this court. I am certain the training of Richelieu and the many, many others like him went a long way towards earning her the favor of our dear deceased innocent King, the Well-Beloved."

The four ladies dissolved into laughter though the Queen's face remained stoic.

"I will pass along the sad news and your condolences, Your Majesty."

"Please do. I would pass it along myself, but a Queen must be prudent where she is seen and, as she knows, it is forbidden for her to come here. The church simply will not allow further desecration of this hallowed ground. What can I say? We don't want to displease God. But *you* are always welcome, Zamor. It occurs to me that the death of the Duc might hold meaning to you, also, as he was the one who chose you to be gifted to the Madame all those years ago. Do you remember him? Thin man in the most colorful clothing?"

My mind worked furiously and found a memory of a man approaching the inner circle of a fire with a group of enslaved children and the slavers who abused them. The man with the bag of coins. The man who looked like a painted whore. And that camp with me and the other stolen children—children who would go on to be sent to hell. A hell I managed to escape through no doing of my own. I felt a familiar flash of pain and guilt.

"No, I have no memory of him," I lied. Her sharp gaze flicked to my lips that had hardened a bit. I'm sure she read the lie.

"I always say, Zamor, it is not the doing of something, it is the making the best of what has already been done. Richelieu helped to take you from your family, and that must have hurt. But look at where you are. You are welcome to walk among the gods, young man. You are welcome where others are not."

I didn't respond because I couldn't say out loud that I did not agree. That would be treason. I said nothing.

"Enjoy this lovely day, Zamor. And please, help yourself to croissants in the kitchen. Take plenty back to Louveciennes, like I know you like to do. Tell the Madame that pastries from the Queen's kitchen are a gift—may they provide solace in this difficult time. Or may she choke on them. Either way is fine." She picked up her skirts.

"Yes, Your Majesty."

She was on the move again, and her maids followed. The servant girl and I waited until they were well past, traded the little gossip we had, and parted. I had no doubt in fifteen minutes anyone who had not known already that Richelieu was a former client of Madame's would know now.

My victory over Fabien soured. All that was left was to get my pastries and leave.

I was in the kitchen, in the middle of shoving croissants wrapped in paper into my bag, when I felt something tug on my top jacket behind me. I turned and, seeing nothing, looked toward my hem to find a little black boy of about five years standing there looking up at me. He wore a satin yellow coat over a lace cravat and purple breeches. His chubby legs were stocking'd in white and his feet encased in leather shoes with a buckle on each foot. The sight of him was so unexpected—and jarringly familiar—that I just stared for a long time.

"Are you Monsieur Zamor?" he asked.

"Yes, I am. Who are you?"

"Jean," he said.

"That tells me nothing," I snapped. "Who are you, Jean? Where do you come from? Why are you here? What do you want?"

"I live here. The Queen is my maman."

"What are you talking about?" I asked, my heart leaping at the possibility I'd uncovered some scandal my sources had been slow to tell me about. But no, the child before me didn't seem to be mixed race. "When did you come here?"

"I don't know," he said, his face growing in confusion.

"How did you get here?"

"The man, the man brought me. They said the Queen is my maman. She is nice. She gave me papers that she says makes me free. I don't know what that means."

My mind was busy translating, trying to make sense of this. "Where were you before you came here? Where did you live?"

"The wagon."

My mind worked. This child was barely five. I remembered my trip from Bengal, the years in transport. They must have pulled this little boy from his mother's breast for him to be here so young.

"Did anyone tell you that you are a gift?"

"Yes, Monsieur. They said I was special for the Queen. And then that she was my maman. She told me a black man comes sometimes and 'roots around in the kitchen.' She says 'Zamor takes our pastries and thinks we don't know but we do.' It's lonely here. The other kids call me names. Will you be my friend?"

"What? No, I won't be your friend. I don't need or want any friends. Go away."

But he continued looking up at me with something like happiness. Like he hadn't heard what I said. I turned around to shove the last of the croissants in my bag, save one. I sighed at my own weakness, turned around and handed it to the child. I'm certain he had free rein to take as many croissants from the kitchen as he wanted, but the giving of it to him meant something special. His face lit up and he bit into it immediately, the flaky soft center pulled from the roll by his baby teeth.

"There, there," I said, brusquely. "Go on your way, now." I turned to leave.

"I come with you," he started to follow.

"No, you don't. You have a maman, remember? You stay here with them."

"Zamor is family, too. Maman says so. 'Like the King's own brother!' she says."

I smiled wryly at that. These royals, always with a sense of humor. "Yes, well, you don't know how these people treat their family." I gave him one last look and turned around and left. He watched me until I was no longer in sight.

It was never my intent to cross paths with the child again, but it soon seemed every time I was at Versailles, usually when I was in the kitchen, he showed up. He would watch me take pastries, ask me to be his friend, and when I said no, I would give him the last croissant, and he would smile like sunshine.

49

———

After succeeding in handing her her dream on a platter, I knew one day Véronique would find me to thank me. Indeed, Véronique caught me outside one day, but instead of gratitude on her face, I saw annoyance.

"You've been after Madame to notice my work. She said you've been at her nonstop."

I smiled, very smugly. "There's no need to thank me…"

"Thank you? I didn't ask you to do it.

I was starting to feel she was less than appreciative. "You didn't have to ask. You needed something. I could help you, so I did."

"I never asked a favor of you, Page."

Uh oh, now I was *Page* and not Zamor. Not a good sign.

It was a hot day and the brightness of the sun hurt my eyes as I squinted into it, looking up at her. I stood and dusted off the back of my pants with one hand, still clutching my book with the other. Without the light blinding me, I noticed the tired, doubtful look on her face as she, alternately, glanced at me and then averted her face from me in a manner I couldn't decipher.

"If you think putting in a word for me will earn you a spot in my bed you're sorely mistaken. I was gaining attention on my own without any help from you. Is that what you thought would happen?"

My smile died. I hadn't put a lot of thought into it, but it was true that I liked her face, her energy, and the flare of her hips. Maybe, on a subconscious level, part of me had determined that if I smoothed her path, in gratitude she would allow me a taste of those hips and a warm spot in her bed. Was that so wrong?

I wondered what had happened since last we met to have her questioning my motives but then I remembered where we lived. It could have been anything, Lying wasn't a difficult thing for me but, for some reason, lying *to her* took work. My throat was slack where it should have been firm and my hesitation to test it affirmed her suspicion.

"If I want anything from you, I'll ask it," she said. "I didn't ask. I only engaged in conversation."

"I didn't do it for that reason," I lied. It was a weak attempt as my voice couldn't work up the conviction to make it believable. I immediately tried another tact. "But even if I did, that's the way things work. People exchange favors; it's the way it's done."

"Not everywhere, it's not."

"Everywhere I've been."

"Not everywhere. Not with the people I know, it's not. Intimacy as a transaction, it isn't normal. I feel sorry for you if that's how you get women."

"Like I said, everyone around here does it."

"I thought you were different but you're no better than Gaspard."

Her soft words, along with her with eyes spearing me with a bruised look, sent a rush of heated pain through me that almost made me stumble on the green grass.

"I-I might be an opportunist but I'm no rapist, Mademoiselle. And I'm sorry, but in this place, it is acceptable to satisfy one's needs by engaging in consensual fair trade..."

"Fair trade, that's what you call it?"

"...it's not such a big thing. People have needs, that's all. It's natural, and all that. We're all here stuck in this house with nothing to do. No theatre, music only occasionally. Relations are free and we'd go crazy if we didn't have some sort of release."

"Then I feel sorry for all these people, too. It's a sorry state of affairs when that is normal."

"If it repulses you so much perhaps you shouldn't have chosen to work in the home of the world's most well-known prostitute. Don't come to this place, willingly, and then complain that you're surrounded by sinners. Are you so pure you can't tolerate that other people enjoy relations?"

"It's not relations that's the problem. It's not even the trading of it, it's the *expectation* of it. What kind of life is it when people can't just be decent to one another for the sake of it? I don't care what everyone around here is doing. You can't buy me, not for any reason. I will go to Madame myself and tell her that I never asked for your help rather than be indebted to you or anyone."

"Don't."

"Don't what?"

"Don't lose this opportunity and don't put me in the awkward position of explaining myself to Madame, it's none of her business who I-I...." I fell off, losing steam from her threat. "You've made your point and sufficiently chastened me for committing the mortal sin of wanting you. You said no; that is all that needs to be said. You owe me nothing. D'Accord?"

"I don't mind the help for help's sake. But not for something ugly."

"I said, d'accord. The only one making something ugly out of it is you, Mademoiselle."

She had already turned away, walking briskly over the lawn towards the chateau. I bridled with embarrassment, telling myself over the next week to ignore the woman. But when Chloe sidled into my room one night, coming at me with hands and lips, the words she whispered into my ear stopped me.

"I need twenty minutes with Madame. It's your lucky night Governor."

I had been with her for fun before. Chloe and I had relations sometimes just out of boredom. But there was always the question of who owed what hanging over every encounter.

This night, it felt different. I felt I couldn't perform properly with thoughts laying heavy on me. "Not tonight, Chloe."

She started to push up my dressing gown when I stopped her hands.

"What's wrong, are you sick?" she asked.

"Look, I'll get you your time with Madame, but you... you need to leave."

"You'll get me my time for free? If you think you're going to hold it over my head indefinitely—"

"_No, I'll just get it for you, Chloe, it's not that big a deal."

She looked at me, scrutinizing my face. "This has something to do with *her*, doesn't it? The black cleaning woman masquerading as Mother Mary, doesn't it? I see the way your eyes follow her around like a sick cow. She's made you ashamed to do what's perfectly natural. She's not like you and me, you know that? We're sharp and tough because we need to be. People like her make people like us weak. She'll ruin you."

"It's got nothing to do with her," I mumbled.

"Liar."

"I've got no problem with you Chloe. This has been fun, it truly has, but it's run its course for me. I'll get you your time but it's the last so make it count."

She studied my face with quizzical amusement, then gave me a wry smile. "D'Accord, Governor. You'll never get what I can give you from the ice princess. Your loss."

I was certain Chloe was right. I didn't expect to ever have *anything* from the ice princess, as she'd called her. But one thing I did have was a new curiosity about things I'd always just taken for granted. What was it the Queen said? That I'd grown into being the worst of the royal court? It was the way it was done, but maybe it didn't have to be.

As for Mademoiselle Véronique, I didn't see much of her for a while, as we were both, likely, avoiding each other. I was a good bit angry at her for, once again, shaming me. And while I wanted to believe she was thinking about me, whenever I did manage to catch a glimpse of her, she was flushed and hurried, with eyes shining of fire. Whatever she thought of me it was, obviously, second to her true passion.

The clothes she was making for Madame would be beautiful.

50

Dear Citizen,

I imagine you're thinking my life at the Chateau and my focus on the lovely servant woman was taking all my attention, but that's not true. I learned how to consciously switch my mindset. At the Chateau, I was du Barry's Page. In Paris, I was the bright, new voice and promise of the new republic.

--Zamor

"Here's the copy I presented today to the National Convention," LaFayette said, pulling me aside at the Club one night. Sebastien gave me an encouraging look because he knew how anxious I was to speak with LaFayette. I'd been trying not to hound him, but I was chomping at the bit.

"You presented it? I didn't even realize it was finished." I said, my greedy eyes watching him as he passed the page to me, taking it with fumbling fingers.

"Yes, it's done. I was hoping to speak with you first, but in light of the King firing Necker this morning, it felt like the right time to present it to the Convention." His voice had an odd tone of hesitance.

I didn't care why; I was just excited it was done!

As I read, the smile left my face. By the time I reached the end, even the memory of the smile was gone. I looked at LaFayette. He had the grace to appear mildly ashamed.

"There's nothing on this page about abolition or slavery," I said. "There's nothing here that even mentions black people. It was the first thing in my notes. You read my notes, it was the first thing. I explained to you that it was important."

"I know. Look, Thomas and I discussed it at length. We decided it was prudent to keep the language to something the country could get behind. And truly, equality among all men, naturally, suggests even slaves."

"No, it doesn't, naturally, suggest anything. What would have, *naturally*, suggested slavery would have been the words 'slavery.' Or 'black people' or 'freedom for enslaved people.' Any of those would have suggested it, but none of that is here."

"I know you're disappointed, but it had to be something the Convention would support—"

"—completely misses the point—"

"—general enough that it wouldn't be controversial—"

"—not a word. There's not a word about the slaves toiling away right now—"

"—you're taking this as a personal affront—"

"—Yes, Gilbert, yes! This is a *personal* affront to me. You read my notes! What part of anything I wrote suggested this was a small issue to me?" I realized my voice had risen from the quiet around me. When conversations began again, he spoke.

"Zamor, it made sense to ensure this was something they would support, and they do. Nothing else matters if we don't have the Convention behind us on the initial step. They might have rejected it out of hand, otherwise. We can work to change things in the future using this document as a foundation. Friend ... they gave a rousing round of applause and a standing ovation. It received resounding support, Zamor."

"I'm sure it did," I nodded, wanting to cry. I handed him back his paper.

I had been naïve to expect him to do as I'd asked. He'd written a brilliant document, no doubt, but it wouldn't help me or my situation. At my quiet, he continued to try to convince me.

"I firmly believe we can use this to create the change we both want. Our society can't keep people enslaved when all people are considered equal, don't you see?"

"Certainly, it can. Ask your friend, Mr. Jefferson. He's an expert on saying one thing and doing another. Ask the people in the colonies. Or simply ask me. I'll tell you all about how our society can say one thing and do another."

"Zamor…"

"I would have had more respect if you'd just laughed in my face. If you're not going to do something, just say you're not going to do it. Don't make me think you care and then show me your ass. Maybe it's your noble blood. You're more like the King than I thought."

His face grew sober, but I was no longer in a mood to hear anything he had to say. Sebastien called out to me as I walked out of the building.

Lafayette's *Declaration of the Rights of Man and Citizen* was truly a beautifully written—incomplete—piece of political poetry. I could see the words in my mind's eye as I left the building and walked out into the sunshine. It would make him famous, that love letter to the French Republic. It was everything that any white man who thought he believed in equality and fraternity could ever ask for. But to me, it was frosting without the cake, all fluff and no substance. It was the first piece of literature adopted by the brand-new republic and it didn't say a word about the condition of black people or slavery. At all.

Not a word about me or my freedom.

It broke my heart.

~

I DROWNED myself in wine that night, went through my satchel and tore up pages of my written words to bits, feeding balls of it to my little fireplace. My reward was a splitting headache the next morning and a fifteen-minute delay in the delivery of Madame's chocolat. I woke up, checked my little clock, and rushed to pull on my shoes, still in yesterday's clothes, running, grabbing it from Salanave, and moving as fast as I could through the house to deliver it. She sat in bed reading, her eyes never leaving her paper, as I set it on the table beside her bed, her lips pinched and annoyed as I gave a brief apology. She would be a beast to me for that, I knew.

I left the room and waited for Gaspard to show up and deliver a blow to my ribs. Anticipation tightened my muscles as I expected him around every corner, as I knew he loved to catch me by surprise with a punch. It was in that mood that I entered the kitchen a bit later. Salanave pushed a wooden box covered with an embroidered cloth against my chest forcing me to put my arms up to grab it. "Here, take these gifts from Madame to the Queen."

"Why are we giving gifts to the Queen?"

"Hush and listen." She pointed to the air.

"Salanave, have you gone mad?"

"The noise! The noise you don't hear?"

The ever-present grinding of the Marly Machine was absent. "They came up here a little while ago. Seems some poor man got himself caught in the wheels. They had to stop the machine to get what was left of him out. Almost an hour and no noise. I don't miss it, but the Palace will be wanting to know what's happened—you know how much the King loves showing off with those fountains. Go. Go!" She turned to leave, then, "And take Véronique with you. She's never been to the Palace and it's time she has. Go load this into the coach and I'll send her out."

Just what I needed.

Before leaving, Madame summoned me, spending a quarter-hour complaining, having worked herself into a lather. *The chocolat wasn't hot enough*, she said. *You get slower the older you get!* was how she started off. *Where did you get that color jacket; how am I supposed to match you?! Why are you always underfoot? Why are you never around when I need you? Why do I keep you here?*

I lost my temper and reminded her if she wanted it hot, she could go to the kitchen and sip it directly from the pot on its fire. And that if she was tired of me, the solution was simple. She told me to leave and come back when I found my-expletive- manners. I told her no amount of manners would allow me to ignore the massive amount of merde that spewed from her lips. She called me an ugly, ungrateful gutter urchin. I called her a classless leech. She kicked me out of her room and I, finally, found Gaspard's fist waiting for my stomach when I closed her door behind me, doubling me over. As I was coughing, trying not to lose the entire bottle of wine from the night before, I called to his retreating back. "Is that all you've got? What happened to the strength in that hand; you're weak as a child?!" Blame it on the fact that I was still half-drunk. He turned around, his face a storm cloud. It wasn't even that bad an insult, but it made him ridiculously angry. He looked about to come back but caught himself, turned and left.

That was my morning.

By the time Véronique climbed onto the seat next to me I was in a foul mood. I could feel her eyes on me and knew she sensed my inner fury. We didn't make much conversation on the ride, but halfway there she broke the silence.

"Is everything alright?"

"No," I said. At her expression I relaxed my voice and glanced at her from under my lids. She was composed, didn't look flustered in the least. "I'm sorry, it's not you."

"Oh, I know that," she said. We hadn't spoken since she'd dressed me down for trying to help her. Though my wounded pride had healed a bit, I hadn't made an effort to speak to her. I was still a little indignant at the way she'd thrown my desire back in my face.

"Well, I wouldn't know what you know," I said. "I would have thought an intelligent person such as yourself would know when a person was trying to help you out, but my efforts somehow got twisted around and I became a villain. So, pardon me for thinking you would take my ill mood and turn yourself into the victim of it."

"Trying to help *yourself* out is more accurate, but no matter. You are pardoned, Monsieur."

I pinched my lips to keep from responding, the effort almost turning my lips inside out.

We talked very little for most of the ride until our approach to the Palace caused her to go rigid beside me. When we pulled into the stables, she seemed to hold her breath. I handed the reins to the stable hand. By the time I reached her side, she was already on the ground, having gotten there on her own. She couldn't even allow me that. That she would think I wasn't going to help her made me even more cranky. I was a gentleman, after all. Sort of.

I pulled the crate out of the carriage and told her: "This way."

Fairly stomping out of the stables into the bright light, we began the long walk to the front gates. Somewhere along the way I lost the sound of her feet. Stopping, I turned to see her standing still, eyes wide, moving everywhere, like she couldn't possibly take it all in.

I remembered the first time I'd seen it so long ago. I could almost feel it in her as the amazement was reflected in her eyes. I stood there a moment longer, trying to give her time to soak it all up. The longer I watched her, the more her reaction softened me, but I wasn't ready to give up my bad mood.

I turned toward the Palace and called back, "Come on, Mademoiselle Clair, we don't have all day."

She kept up with me easily and soon enough the Palace Manager found me—as he always did to when I roamed the main building. It was the same one who'd laughed at me all those years ago. He'd aged badly.

"Madame du Barry begs our sincerest apologies for our proximity to the faulty Marly Machine. It is on its way to being right as rain." I tried to hand him the box to pass along, but his arms didn't move.

"She'll want you to deliver any gifts to her directly. Follow me."

He turned and began walking down the hall.

"I'll wait here," Véronique said.

"No, you're coming with me. Don't you want to meet the Queen?"

"I couldn't! I wouldn't know what to do."

"Just wait inside the door. It shouldn't take long."

She looked reluctant, her face a mask of fear, but we followed the Manager and then both entered the parlor where the Queen was sitting. It wasn't uncommon for her to receive guests, so she normally accommodated. I was rarely a guest in this fashion. Véronique followed my lead as I bowed, then she stayed back just inside the doorway. The Manager stepped forward, bowed, and spoke softly into her ear, stepping away. When the Queen gestured for me to come closer, I came forward, bowed, and waited. She gestured with her finger for me to place the crate on the floor beside her.

"Louis-Benoit, you are looking well. Bringing gifts from Madame, I hear. What a nice surprise. To what do I owe this pleasure?"

"Madame du Barry begs our sincerest apologies for our proximity to the faulty Marly Machine. It is on its way to being right as rain," I repeated.

"I hope whoever caused the malfunction in the machine has been properly punished for inconveniencing the court. Why, it makes the nobles positively morose when they walk by a fountain that isn't spewing water. What's a fountain without water?"

"Yes, Your Majesty, I'm certain the offender will be properly punished once they can get all the bits of him out of the machinery."

"Zamor, always with the sense of humor and way with words. And who is that young woman at the door who came with you?"

Véronique looked like a deer caught in headlights. She didn't know what to do so she dipped quickly, head down.

"That is Véronique. Her benefactress sent her to the Chateau de Louveciennes to learn the ways of running a royal household."

"What?" She tipped her head back in laughter, her maids joining her in the mirth. "Poor girl. Young lady, I regret your benefactress will be disappointed. You can't run a royal household if you are not a royal, nor can you teach it. But if you should want a true lesson, I will arrange for you to spend a day here at Versailles. Maybe you can learn something that you could take back to teach Madame du Barry. All the years she lived in this house and still never learned the first rule of etiquette which is not to behave like a drunken gutter rat when among royalty. Please, do come back anytime."

"Uhm ... thank you, Your Majesty." Véronique said, quickly curtseying. I should have warned her about how they hated each other.

"Now, let's take a look at this gift, shall we?" Her maids converged on the crate and seemed to be describing everything in the box to her, whispering it in her ear. The Queen did a double-take and then sat back straight again.

"Have you had a chance to look at the contents of this box, page?"

Warning bells went off in my head at the seemingly innocuous question. Nothing was innocuous with Marie Antoinette. And a question wasn't a question when it came from Marie Antoinette.

"I regret I did not have the opportunity, Your Majesty."

"Well, I'm happy to know that you were only ignorant and not willfully disobedient. I have pastries—as if we don't already have the best—and flowers—as though I don't have access to the most beautiful and bountiful blossoms—and ..." she actually leaned over to pull out a large earthen pot, tipped it, and proceeded to dump it over onto the floor as her maids laughed and gasped at the growing pool of thick white liquid. "... a pot of that putrid cauliflower velouté." She shook it so all of it was on the floor in a pool of murky white. "I do believe your Madame is trying to get you hanged, Zamor." She handed the empty pot to a servant and wiped her hands against each other as if wiping off filth. "If I weren't so fond of you, you would be twirling in the gallows right now. My advice: The next time you bring something to me, check to see what the Madame du Barry is asking you to deliver to your Queen and use your own judgment or I will take the insult as a slight from you both. I'm surprised to have to tell you this; you know how she is, better than anyone. You know you can't trust that woman. Now leave me."

"Yes, Your Majesty." I seethed as I bowed and walked backwards out until I reached the door. Véronique followed me out, curtsying before leaving.

Madame had set me up. Bitch.

"Let's go to the kitchen before we leave," I told Véronique. She kept up as I stalked through the Palace, outside, and on into the massive building that housed the kitchen.

"This is amazing," she murmured, taking in the two giant wood-burning ovens built into the wall and all the little ovens, chopping tables, hundreds of pots and pans, and all the people who moved in and around, including one of the cooks who always avoided me—and did so today. I opened the burlap bag that I'd slung over my shoulder on the way out of the wagon and made a beeline to the counter where the pastries were laid out on the table.

"What are you doing?" she asked.

"I'm taking breads and pastries, what does it look like I'm doing?" I began wrapping buttery rolls in bakery paper and shoving them into my bag. Soon enough I felt a small tug on my coat. Down at my side was the boy.

"Hello," he said. His face was soft and lit up from inside with that blasted inner glow he always had.

"How is it you're always around?" I asked him. "Don't you have some place to be? Aren't they giving you schooling? Where is Barnier?"

"You were gone a long time, Monsieur Zamor," the child said, as if I had to answer to him for my absence. I looked at Véronique, who wore a quizzical smile on her face. I grudgingly gestured towards him.

"This is Jean. He was adopted by the Queen. This is Véronique Clair."

"Hello, Jean," she smiled at him.

"Hello, Mademoiselle Clair."

"He was taken like me," I continued, memories making me bitter. "Though he's free. There's *that*, at least. But look at him. Too young to remember his own mother."

"My maman said you would be back and here you are."

"She's not your mother. Stop calling her that!" I snapped at the child. His lips wiggled, dangerously, his brown eyes welling up. "And be happy that she isn't, boy. These people are not even kind to their families and you ... you will never be considered her child. It is best you know that now instead of fooling yourself for years thinking that they care one bit about you. You were bought, child. No matter how you feel, you will forever be only a plaything to them." I started to leave, stopped, handed him a croissant, and then continued. "Come, Véronique."

"Don't speak to me like that," she said, spearing me with a look that told me to go to hell. Then she bent and whispered to him, "There, there..."

I didn't hear the rest because I strode away. Soon enough she caught up with me and we walked outside to the stables. By the time we reached the wagon and climbed in for the return ride, we were both in a foul mood. Lightning, sensing my impending temper, rolled her head around to give me a look from the one eye I could see, warning me I'd better not strike her with that whip. I tsk-ed her instead, and we were off. After a few quiet minutes, my passenger gave in, her mind back at the Palace.

"That was unnecessary," Véronique said. "The child obviously looks up to you."

"I never asked him to."

"Don't take away his hope. He has to believe in someone until he's old enough to understand what's happened to him. And old enough to find his faith in God," she said.

"Faith in God? What's God got to do with it?"

"Forgive him, Father..." she said to the sky, quickly crossing her chest as I rolled my eyes. "I told him not to pay any mind, Zamor is just having a bad day. But to talk to God when he's lonely and God will help him feel better because God never has any bad days."

I couldn't help but smirk at that. I didn't have a good grasp on God making folks feel better. I'd gotten brief respite for that one moment in church years ago, but God had been silent since then. And I didn't know if I trusted a god who would put me where I was in the first place. Maybe I deserved it, but that little child in the Palace ... he didn't. It was a bigger conversation than I wanted to have in a wagon riding over bumpy road. But I did feel a little bad about snapping at the boy.

"Anyone you ask around here would suggest God had a very bad day when he made me," I said, fine with self-recrimination if it would prevent her thinking I was a monster.

"Today, I would agree with them."

"But I'll have you know my mother used to call me the greatest thing God put on this earth." The memory had come to me fast and unbidden. "The greatest thing He ever made. So, if one were to believe in God, that would suggest that even at his worst, He is pretty incredible because here I sit, a miracle beside you."

"Ah, mothers and their glowing opinions of their children," she said. "I can only imagine what a handful little Louis-Benoit might have been."

"Louis-Benoit isn't my real name. It's the name they gave me. I don't remember my real name, but I can tell you I was just as brilliant a child as I am now. When I was very young my mother was always patient and gentle with me." *Until she saw the evil inside me, stopped loving me, and sold me away.*

"What was she like?"

The question was difficult, it had been so long.

"When I was very little, she hugged me a lot and thought I was precocious instead of annoying. Sometimes I sing this little tune that she made for me, as a lullaby, I think. I've forgotten her face and mannerisms, but I don't want to forget her song."

She was looked at me, expectantly.

"No, absolutely not."

"Hum just a little of it for me. You owe me for how miserable you've made my first trip to the Palace. And just for being yourself, in general." I glanced over at the little smile on her lips. Damn, she made a good point.

I looked left and right to ensure that we were alone on the road with only trees and nature animals to hear. I began to hum quietly and then more forcefully as the nerves fell away. She joined me once she caught the melody, and we went through it, laughingly, several times before satisfied. I felt better by the time we finished in laughter and even more so when she put a hand on mine, briefly. I looked at it, brown and small. A hard-working hand. It felt good.

"It's a lovely gift from your mother," she said, looking back at the road. "She must have loved you a great deal."

But she sold me, said the little voice in me. I moved on.

"What about your childhood?" I asked.

"Me, oh I was a wild little thing."

"You? You're such a composed woman," I said. That made her laugh.

"Well, if composed women hang upside down in trees and run around with the boys and pull worms out of the ground, I was a composed, then. Me and my friend Guy were as rowdy as two kids can be. The only halfway proper thing I do is embroidery and even that, I don't do like the other ladies. My father and his people in Saint-Domingue love color, and so I grew up loving it, as well. My embroidery-work is not so much what you find with the noblewomen —they like color but most tend to stick to pastels—but I love the bright bursts of color."

"This Guy, is he still your play friend or has he graduated to a suitor? Is he the man who came for you that day at the chateau?" She grew quiet and sadness spread over her smooth brown face. "I'm sorry, did I say something wrong?"

"No, that was Hubert who visited me. Hubert was my intended, who I rejected. Guy was my friend who took his own life before I came."

"Why? What could have caused him to do such a thing to his family? To you?"

"Don't say that about him. He was a good man!"

I'd done it again. I'd insulted her somehow. "I'm sorry. I didn't mean anything by it. I'm sorry for your friend, truly. And you."

Her eyes had a sheen of moisture. "No, I'm sorry. I'm sensitive about Guy. He took his own life rather than be tried and convicted for a bad incident with a nobleman. He did it protecting me. But by protecting me, he lost his job and his good name ... everything! And then he lost all hope. So, when you ask what could have caused him to do such a thing, ultimately, it was me. I caused it."

"No." I looked at her face, lips pressed together to keep herself from crying. "Véronique, it wasn't your fault. You can't think that. He stood up for you because he loved you—and didn't need to be asked to do it. But after ... sometimes, a person can be struck in just the wrong way and nothing anyone can say can stop them from doing something they wouldn't, if in their right mind. Maybe your friend simply wasn't in his right mind. Maybe on any other day he would have been able to move through his grief. You can't blame yourself."

"Our parents were like family and afterwards they couldn't even look at me. I had to leave. My home, my town—it was choking me to death with guilt and regret and I feel bad even for that. My parents love me and tried to make a match for me—that's who you saw that day—but I couldn't stay, and I couldn't marry that man. So, that's that."

I reached over to place my hand on hers, this time. She glanced at it but didn't pull her hand away.

"But you say I can't blame myself," she continued. "But I should be telling you the same thing," she said.

"What do you mean?"

"Little Jean. I'm ashamed of what I said to you that day, suggesting you wanted to be the most famous page. Watching you with that little boy makes me think of how young and innocent you must have been when they brought you. You hate that innocence, don't you? You feel that if you were less naïve, what happened to you might not have been so traumatic or happened at all. But that's the thing, Zamor. We're all human. No amount of hardening him up can ever protect him if he's set upon by predators, like you were."

Damn Salanave.

"Respectfully, you're wrong. And a hypocrite."

"What do you mean?"

"Why do you carry that knife? You carry it in anticipation of protecting yourself from a predator, correct? That child can't defend himself with a knife, but he needs to know there are predators. He needs to see people as the evil they can be. *That's* his protection. If my harshness causes him to be less trusting of strangers then it's worth it," I said. "I don't care if he hates me. Cruelty is more persuasive than kindness, and I know how to be cruel."

"Do you think trusting others caused what happened to you? Or was it evil people who were going to do what they were going to do, no matter if you trusted them or not?"

I huffed in annoyance. She was twisting my words.

"I don't think you're cruel," she continued. "But you're wrong. Children *should* be trusting and innocent. That's the very definition of childhood. They should expect good in the world. Eternal optimism is a far better protection for them than fear ever will be. Without hope, nothing else matters."

I disagreed. Maybe life for her in the east was such that she could encourage softness in children. I knew a different childhood. Still, this woman had a way of pulling things out of me that I had no desire to explore.

We rode for a few minutes in silence and then...

"I'm staying here, you know."

"What?" My heart leapt a little in my chest.

"Madame told me I can stay on as a real servant. She will pay me a small bit, even, plus room and board. I think she wants to see what all I can sew for her. Chloe, too. Though I have no idea why she's keeping Chloe on, the girl doesn't work. Do we have time for another stop before heading back to the Chateau?"

I took her direction as she led us past the Chateau and to a small church in the town of Louveciennes.

"There's a Notre Dame Cathedrale at the Palace, I could have taken you there."

"The church for royals and nobles?" she shook her head. "I feel more comfortable in this one with regular common people. Salanave brought me here and I've come to really like it. Come in with me? I find church helps me to be a much calmer person."

"Should I be a calmer person?" I asked. "Will calm serve me, do you think? I kind of feel like I get more done when I'm roused."

"You know, when my father was a little boy at Saint-Domingue the overseer would whip anyone who tried to go to church. He told me his family and friends had to worship in their own way. They didn't have a bible and couldn't read it if they did. What they had was a soul-deep belief in a higher being. They knew to their core that people—even powerful slave owners—had a moral obligation to someone or something. You said literacy is special, which is why they keep us from it. Why do you think they kept my father and his people away from church? Could it be the same? Because I read the Bible and it doesn't put any man or woman above me because of the color of their skin. Knowing that is powerful, don't you think?"

We had reached the spot and as soon as I stopped the buggy, she was already climbing down. She grabbed her bag from the seat and headed toward the small building.

"It's up to you, page, but as an outside observer, you being roused for attack isn't particularly attractive. It was painful watching you berate a little boy who, even though he wanted to cry, told me it was alright because you are his friend."

I winced.

"I just think, if you have a question about what mood God was in when he put you on this earth, this might be the place to ask."

I watched her walk the short way to the door. I was willing to sit there in the carriage and wait for her to come out. But maybe…

I climbed down, looped Lightning's reins around the closest tree, and followed her inside to see what the place had to offer someone like me.

51

Dear Citizen,

I would have been happy to have never seen LaFayette again, since it was he who ushered in one of the greatest betrayals I had experienced in my life, but he would soon become the messenger of my greatest success.

—Zamor

"**I**s the Duc du Brissac here?" LaFayette came through the front door of the Chateau, his face just short of panic. He looked at me with unfocused eyes that told me he had other things on his mind than whether anyone caught on that we knew each other.

I sent another servant up to get du Brissac, but just when LaFayette turned to speak with me, the Duc's feet sounded on the stairs and we both looked up to see him trotting down.

"There's been an attack on the armory," LaFayette said without preamble once Brissac laid eyes on him. A darling of both the new republic and the royal court, General LaFayette had taken a role of greater prominence after the release of his document, resulting in him working with the highest echelon of security. But he wasn't in the thick of all the discussions among sans-culottes. The shock on his face was real. "Last night a group of men overtook the guards at the prison. They released the prisoners and took the weapons."

"The weapons..." Brissac's expanded forehead crinkled with worry, his head moving from side-to-side with his thought process, mouth open in the universal expression of fear combined with surprise. LaFayette was stiff and brittle with the stress that had taken hold of his spinal column and drained the blood from his face. Gaspard enter the foyer with a couple of guards, on alert like hounds at a hunt. Madame came down the steps from the second floor, her face reflecting the atmosphere. Everyone came out of the woodwork when a general showed up on the doorstep talking of an emergency.

And me, I was listening, but my body felt like it was melting; LaFayette's words registering with my nervous system before my brain.

They'd taken the armory. LaFayette was confirming what I never imagined would ever happen: The leaders of the new republic had listened and done what I said. My conversation with Camille Desmoulins had taken flight! They'd taken the armory!

It was the oddest sensation, as if the top of my head had opened and a cool breeze flowed from the openness down through my body, infusing my limbs with a flood of euphoria. Even my facial muscles relaxed with completeness as if something pure and new sprouted from the core of me.

"What does this mean, chèr?" Madame asked Brissac. "Surely, they can find the prisoners and round them up before any real damage is done, can't they?"

"It's not prisoners we're worried about, Madame..." LaFayette explained, his face looking pained.

"...it's the weapons," Brissac finished, his voice deep and gravelly. "It's the weapons that we're worried about."

"But who was it? The Prussians?" Her face tightened. "Was it the Queen's people?"

"Madame, it wasn't an attack from outsiders. It was Frenchmen," LaFayette told her. "It was sans-culottes. A group of Parisiens."

They continued to talk but I only partially heard them, my head floating on a cloud of amazement.

In all my life, I had never been taken seriously. In all my life, my opinion meant nothing. But this changed everything. I already had a voice; all I ever needed was someone willing to hear it. Willing to listen.

I was on a cloud until I noticed the foyer was quiet. Brissac and LaFayette were leaving through the front door, followed by Gaspard and the house guards. Then, it was just me and Madame in the foyer, Madame staring at the closed front door. Quiet as a church.

What was she thinking? I wondered. Would she turn around and see my involvement written on my face—the truth of it was emitting like an odor through my pores? Would she turn and feel it in the way I was standing, the way I was holding my arms, the way I was suddenly ten feet tall in my own mind?

It was quiet like the air before a storm. Quiet like the dead of night. Quiet like the world had vastly changed and we were on the dawn of a new existence.

She turned around and her furrowed brow smoothed itself out as she looked at me. "Louis ..."

I waited for it. I waited for that sharpness in her eyes to cut through my persona to see the real me. I didn't want to be found out, but I didn't see how I wouldn't be with the shock of this event quaking me in my shoes.

"Louis..." she said, her brow smoothing. "My chocolat will be cold now. Go get my bowl and warm it, s'il vous plait."—*If you please*— "And you can take the Duc's bowl away. I don't think he'll be back today."

The air left me in a quiet sigh as she turned and headed back up the stairs.

I did as I was told and after delivering her newly warmed chocolat, I ran into Henri in the hallway outside the kitchen, his cheeks ruddy and eyes shining.

"Did you hear? They took the armory. They're calling it the storming of the Bastille, Zamor," he whispered, loudly, with fever in his eyes. "The people stormed the Bastille! I heard it myself this morning in town. They fired the King's weapons on his own army. They said no one has ever thought of doing anything so brazen." He hesitated and then stared at me hard, his normal soft gaze, focused on me. "Was it you?"

Things had been strange for Henri and me lately. He was still my friend and we talked when we could, but the more time I spent in Paris the less we seemed to have to talk about.

My face was on fire from wanting to tell him, yes, yes, yes! But Henri wasn't a man to tell a secret to. When he was excited, he could barely keep it off his face and his voice rose in proportion to his excitement. Even now, his hand tapped like his fingers were anxious to tell the secret, and I couldn't afford to be found out yet.

"Of course not," I lied. "I don't know what you mean."

Hurt flashed in his eyes. I could see he knew I was lying, but I couldn't allow his disappointment to blunt my joy.

Lying in bed that night, I was a different man. *Enslaved, treated like an animal, short, misshapen, spat upon, and mocked, Zamor,* I thought. *I'm something new, now.* I was on my way to being a free man. I could feel it in my blood!

I imagined myself in the basket of that balloon sent up into the sky from the grounds of Versailles all those years ago. I felt myself escaping not to the cold, cold Labyrinth, but to the beautiful blue sky. On my way to a new, free world.

～

Dear Citizen,

I thought I hated patterns but never considered the ones I was making. Patterns in my regular visits to Paris. Patterns set by conditioning my benefactress to allow me to leave, trusting I'd return.

Patterns in getting new, important people in Paris familiar with my face.

I truly I hadn't consciously come up with a plan for my freedom but after the storming of the Bastille, I realized a lot of plans happened like that. Processes were put in motion by people with no idea of where those steps might lead. All along, I took those steps, decidedly, consistently waiting—hoping—for some direction along the way.

I tell you, good citizen, that night when I closed my eyes, I could almost feel myself sitting atop Lightning's back that very first time, the wind from the night breeze cooling my face as we rode through the darkness. I now felt the wind of breaking out of the status quo.

I was no longer a rose tamed into submission. I had become one of the errant, wild things more suited for pruning. Or, more appropriately, I had become the belladonna sprouting among order, primed to disrupt the garden. The belladonna: a flower determined to survive and take out anything in its path, if necessary.

If you had asked me, I'd have told you I was simply a man with a stroke of dumb luck. I wasn't truly dangerous ... yet. I didn't know danger was rising within me, waiting for its time. I told myself I was a common sans-culotte servant, too powerless to be dangerous. What harm could a black man with no power possibly have?

I was only the page, after all.

—-Zamor

Book One

~Fin~

· · ·

Did you enjoy this book?

Your feedback helps me provide the best quality stories and helps other readers like you discover great books.

It would mean the world to me if you took 2 minutes to share your thoughts about this book as a review on the retailer of your choice. Thanks!

With the Storming of the Bastille, the French Revolution has begun, and the story of the Page from Chittagong continues...

Just as the Ancien Régime refused to loosen its reliance on slave trade, the new republic seems equally resistant to include slaves among those deserving of equality. But with the words of Enlightenment philosophers behind him, Louis Benoit-Zamor is determined to prove to these new leaders that freedom from slavery is precisely what the new republic should champion. As a Jacobin of Paris, Zamor will soon meet more political and military titans—Danton, Bologne, Dumas, and Robespierre—in his quest to create a republic that will recognize him as a free man of France. And he will lend his talent with words to the rising voices of the movement.

King Louis XVI's rule is jeopardized as the country falls further into ruin. Printing presses and publishing houses will sprout up around Paris faster than the King and his censors can stop them, giving voice to the common man. And despite all the King's failures, it is his wife, Queen Marie Antoinette, who will become the easiest target of the country's wrath.

During this shining era, Zamor will have his time in the sun, developing friendships and seeing his words in print. He will become braver, feel more hopeful, and love a free black woman from Burgundy named Véronique Clair like he's never dared. After years of smallness, the burgeoning revolution will unearth the greatness within him, putting everything he's ever wanted within his grasp.

But, he's still a slave.

Madame Jeanne du Barry's claim to love Zamor like a son grows thinner every day. He wonders at the value of becoming a rising voice among the Jacobins if he can't free himself—*a fox has to survive its own hunt,* after all.

And while he's focused on France's transformation from a kingdom into a republic, discontent takes root and blossoms at the Chateau. Like the beautiful devil's berries of the belladonna flower, buds of jealousy and envy will grow in abandon at the former royal hunting lodge. This discontent will culminate in an act of betrayal so heinous it will forever change the relationship between "mother and son". As France is busy becoming something new, Louis Benoit-Zamor will learn just how evil the most beautiful can be.

Vive la Revolution. *Long live the Revolution.*

Next to come...

THE DEVIL'S BERRIES
(LES CERISES DU DIABLE)
The Last Favorite's Page: Book Two

If you enjoyed this book, get on the list at:
https://www.gildedorangebooks.com

ACKNOWLEDGMENTS

I want to acknowledge thanks and appreciation to the people who provided assistance on my quest to understand this amazing time in France's history.

Dr. Susan Peabody who did her best to explain to me the laws regarding slavery on mainland France during the late 18th century. Any misrepresentations of the law should not be attributed to her, but to my lay-person understanding of her material.

Dr. Pierre Boulle who, graciously, shared his notes on Louis-Benoit Zamor, with me.

The National Library of France whose researchers helped to corroborate the little bit of information on Zamor that I could find.

Thank you to Joyce and Teresa for being the best sisters I could ask for and putting up with me going on and on about this story and my minor obsession with France.

Lastly, this story was inspired by the life of Louis-Benoit Zamor.

The challenge of creating a story about a real person of whom very little information exists is that you try to be as accurate as possible, but end up absorbing a bit of everything. I tapped into journals and articles, Wikipedia, and explored internet chatter to help build a snapshot of Zamor. I attempted to hone in on common threads, creating the story that seemed most plausible. I freely admit, I took creative license in what I focused on and what I ignored, as the story demanded.

I do understand there will be those who disagree with my interpretation of the life of Louis-Benoit Zamor. His is a French story, after all. While I've not been able to find a fictionalized biography of him in English, I know of at least two novels written in French, though I've not read them. Perhaps, those who have read those novels will let me know if any similarities exist.

I ask that this story be taken in the spirit in which it is written – to balance the scales a bit so that this man who has been called a villain for so long can be seen as a real human being who managed to live through a complex and amazing time. My hope is that this three-book series will generate interest and prompt someone, somewhere, to reveal more information on the life story of this man, almost lost to time.

Keep reading!

9 798986 060057